House of Cards

Tech Billionaires book 1

A Novel

by:
Ainsley St Claire

Copyright 2020 Ainsley St Claire

All rights reserved. No part of this publication may be reproduced, distributed or transmitted in any form or by any means, including photocopying, recording or other electronic or mechanical methods, without the prior written permission of the author, except in the case of brief quotations embodied in critical reviews and certain other noncommercial uses permitted by copyright law.

This is a work of fiction. Names, characters, places and incidents are a production of the author's imagination. Locations and public names are sometimes used for atmospheric purposes. Any resemblance to actual people, living or dead, or to businesses, companies, events, institutions or locations is completely coincidental.

Tech Billionaires: House of Cards/Ainsley St Claire—1st edition

Dedication & Thank you

*For my amazing husband who supports me and loves me.
Our love is my inspiration.*

Thank you to my editor, Jessica Royer Ocken who tore this book apart and helped me put it back together again.

Thank you to my typo hunter team, each of you are so important to making this as close to perfect as we can get: Anne, Courtnay, Linda, Lynda, and Nancy.

Chapter 1

Jonathan

I'm nervous. As I move through my casino, I stop to breathe into my hand and take a quick smell.

It doesn't smell like anything other than my clean hand. Does this really work to tell if your breath is bad? I don't know. But I need to figure it out before Maggie gets here.

I've been in love with Maggie Reinhardt since we were teenagers, and she called out of the blue to tell me she's flying in and wants to see me.

She was here a few months ago during the pre-opening for the Shangri-la, my casino resort on the Las Vegas strip, when her brother's venture capital firm held a corporate meeting here, and he and his fiancée eloped. We reconnected, fell into bed, and it was amazing. It was everything I've ever dreamed of. We've traded emails and texts and phone calls since then, and I've been asking her to come back. But she's busy with work, and then her dad passed away last month. I went home to Minneapolis for the funeral, but the family was surrounded, and I was buried in the Shangri-la's official opening back here, so I didn't stay long, and Maggie and I didn't really connect.

Her father was an icon. He inherited a high-end department store called Reinhardt Hudson when Maggie and her brother were young, and over time he added what became the second-largest discount retailer, Bullseye, and a mid-level department store called Murphy's to the company fold. He was a real pioneer in the retail world. But as I understand it, neither of his sons wants to take over as chairman of the board now that he's gone.

One of those sons, Maggie's brother Christopher, is my best friend. He's held that title since we were in diapers. He told me a while back that when their father was gone, they'd find someone to run the day-to-day operations at the company, so he or Stevie would probably just chair the board in name only. Maggie manages the Reinhardt Foundation, but I'm hoping she won't be tied to living in Minneapolis forever.

When she gets here, I'm going to make my move. I'm going to ask her to move to Vegas, and we'll start making plans to get married. That's all there is to it.

I've loved her for most of my life, and I created the Shangri-la for her.

This is a good plan, I tell myself as I move through the casino. I love the musical sound the slot machines make. I even have a section of my hotel with old-time slots that actually use coins. They say they aren't as profitable as today's machines, but everyone loves the musical beat of coins hitting the tray as the machine spits out winnings.

My hotel is not yet a year old, and already we're

working in the black. I love this town.

Anyway, I never take time off, but while Maggie is here, it will be essential. Shortly after I arrive at the staff meeting this morning, which is held over breakfast, I drop the bomb.

"Listen," I tell them. "I'm thinking of taking a few days off this week."

My team consists of my head of marketing, head of sales, the head of the casino, the head of guest relations, the head of guest rooms, the head of security, the head of housekeeping, and the head of maintenance. These people are essential to my operation and have been with me since I started with my concept. They all stop mid-bite and look at me. I'm expecting some push back.

"It's your hotel," says Gillian Reece, my head of guest relations and right-hand woman. "You don't have to run anything by us."

I nod, a bit surprised. "Good. I have a friend coming into town, and I want to spend some time with her."

"Uh-oh..." my head of casino teases. "It's a her? May your dry spell be broken."

I smile. I'm not going to dignify that with a response.

Maggie and I haven't said we're exclusive, and when you own a large resort that's the newest shiny object for tourists to visit, you don't have a lot of time to date. If I have an occasion that requires someone on my arm, it's only a friend.

Our staff discussion quickly dissolves into lots of ribbing and teasing. I don't mind. I like that we're close.

When our meeting breaks up, Gillian approaches me. "We'll make sure her stay is perfect."

I know what she's after. She will spoil Maggie to death, but that's *my* job. "I'm not telling you her name so you don't pester her in any way."

"*Moi*? Pester her?" Her smile stretches like the Hoover Dam. "I would never think of doing that."

I shake my head to make sure she knows. "Really, it's not a big deal. This is a friend I grew up with, and she's my best friend's baby sister. It's been three years since I've had a day off. *Just a couple days,*" I stress. "I want to hang out with someone who remembers what I looked like as a pimple-faced, awkward teenager."

She harrumphs. "Somehow I doubt you were ever an awkward teenager."

I was, but I'm not going to debate that with her. To ensure the Shangri-la's success, I expel a lot of energy and stress at the gym, so I'm in pretty decent shape.

As I head off down the hall, I begin to remember how perfect Maggie was beneath me, on top of me, and in front of me, and how delicious she tasted. No, I have every intention of enjoying every second and ordering room service for however long her stay might be.

I'm meeting her in less than an hour. She didn't give me much notice, but I was able to sneak in a quick trip to my favorite esthetician for a facial, and I don't want to be too vain, but I also did some primping with a fresh haircut and a manzilian wax. It hurt like a motherfucker, but it's clean and tidy and makes me super sensitive. I'm ready for a lot of up-close-and-personal time. I want Maggie to know I'm going to spend the rest of my life making her happy.

I'm used to walking the property multiple times a day, so I decide to do a quick pass through as I return to my apartment to meet Maggie. I live onsite and made sure the home I set up faced the mountains—away from the strip—and my offices were in a tower across the property, so I'd have to wander through to get to work. I try not to be too predictable and walk through at the same time or take the same path, so I see everything going on at my resort.

As I stroll along today, the employees I encounter have looks of pure terror on their faces. If they had cartoon bubbles above their heads, they'd read, *Don't talk to me.* I don't know why they're nervous. I never call anyone out specifically. I make a mental note to bring it up with my team and have them address it, if it's worth it.

"Hello, Mr. Best."

Ah! *Here's one willing to speak to me.* I discreetly glance at her name tag. "Hello, Janice. How are the tables running?"

"Very well, sir. We've had a table of frat boys that's run hot and cold all night. It may break up now that it's daylight."

I chuckle. "That's very good news." I staff beautiful cocktail waitresses, and my pit boss probably put one of our most stunning dealers—who happens to be married to him—on the table to keep the boys in place and spending money.

My casino manager approaches me. "Hey, boss."

"Hi. Sounds like it was a good night last night?"

"Yes, it was. Spring break will do that."

New York City tells the world it's a town that never sleeps, but here in Vegas that's not just a saying, it's our reality. There's something going on here twenty-four hours a day, seven days a week. There really isn't a slow period. During the summer, when Las Vegas is miserably hot, the conventions are buzzing. At Thanksgiving, the Canadians come down in full force because of the deals and because they've already celebrated Thanksgiving. And while it's a little quieter, all the non-Christians come in full force over Christmas. Maybe it's because I grew up in Minneapolis and hate the snow, but I love the desert. I love the heat. And I'm finding out I love the casino resort business.

I exit out the far side of the casino floor and head across the property to my apartment. I hardly slept last night. I worked late clearing as much off of my plate as I could so I could take a few days off, and then I was just too excited. Maggie and I have been flirting for months now, and I've spent my life getting ready for this moment.

When I reach my apartment, I settle in at my desk and watch her flight arrive from my computer. A little while later I can see her walk onto our property via the security camera feeds. My heart picks up, and my cock is immediately hard.

Her blond hair flows with just the right amount of curl. She's breathtaking. I watch men and women notice her, but she doesn't see it. That's one of her many amazing qualities.

At first glance, no one would know she's an heiress to a major department store. I thumb the engagement ring I bought at Cartier months ago. I saw it and knew I wanted to buy it for her. I think she'll like it. It's not too ostentatious, but it's a beautiful eight-karat center stone with the eternity band covered in half-karat diamonds, all set in platinum. I tuck it away in my safe and shut the computer off.

Moments later, there's a knock at my apartment door. I open it, and her face lights up.

"Jonnie!" She's the only person on this planet who can call me that. She steps in for a hug and holds on a few seconds.

I'm ready for this every day for the rest of my life. "Mag-pie. You look stunning."

"I left the Twin Cities before dawn this morning. I'm tired, grumpy, and I'm sure my makeup is running."

She looks perfect.

"You're fabulous. Come in." I usher her into my apartment, toward the view of the mountains and the golden hues of the desert.

I feel jittery. Maybe if I take her right to the bedroom and fuck her senseless, we can get it out of the way and then talk about our future.

"I was really excited to get your message," I tell her.

She smiles, and I want to kiss her like crazy.

"It's been hectic since Dad's death. The reading of his will had some...surprises for all of us." She looks away for a moment. "But Christopher and Stevie have been great," she continues. "My mom, though... She is surprisingly upset."

She sits on the couch, and I sit next to her. I reach for her hand, and the chemistry is electric. My cock is so hard right now, and I need to taste her. I lean in for a kiss, but she places her hands on my shoulders.

I can see the line she gets between her eyes when she's worried about something.

"Your mom may be a little cold at times, but I'm sure she's grieving in her own way."

She looks at me with a tight smile.

"What is it?"

"Jonnie, I didn't want to tell you this over the phone, but..."

My stomach drops.

"...Alex and I are getting married."

Chapter 2

Maggie

It physically hurts to tell Jonnie we can't be involved anymore. I can barely believe I had the guts to say it, since everything in me wants it not to be true. I've had a crush on Johnathan Best since I was in middle school. I spent the better part of my youth dreaming about him, and over the past few months he's shown me how fun and fantastic a relationship can be. And believe me, that was a welcome change since my life at home revolves almost entirely around work and my family's standing in the community.

But none of that matters, because I don't have a choice.

I've always known that our company is first and foremost a family affair. That's been drilled into me since I was a child. Most children learn to identify cars, or maybe planes. I could identify retail chains and read a profit-and-loss statement before I was ten. At my grandfather's knee, we learned the importance of growing the family business and never taking it public to be at the mercy of stockholders. We were taught business first and family second. We celebrated when other families gave up their businesses to non-family members, went public, or closed their doors. All the better for us. When my grandfather died, my father assumed his role in the company and pushed the same agenda.

It has to be a Reinhardt son at the helm. And once my father was gone, we all knew the duty would fall to one of his sons—otherwise the company would have to be dissolved. The problem is, neither of my brothers is particularly available for the job. Christopher emancipated himself from my parents at age sixteen, and though he's still part of my life, he will never run the company. And my brother Stevie is not only not interested, he's not particularly qualified since he's spent most of the past several years surfing and smoking pot in Hawaii. (I, on the other hand, went to business school and have been growing the foundation portion of the company for several years now. But, you know, I'm a girl, so it doesn't officially matter—insert eye roll.)

When my father got sick, Christopher and I devised a plan to hire someone to run the day-to-day operations of the company, which would leave me free to continue my work with the Reinhardt Foundation, and Christopher agreed to take the title of board chair. This probably wasn't exactly what my grandfather envisioned—especially since Christopher isn't legally an heir anymore—but it seemed workable to us and would allow the company to continue meeting the terms of the will as a family business.

However, after my father passed and we gathered for the reading of his will, we realized he had changed one of the provisions my grandfather originally established. Rather than being run by a Reinhardt son, my father had made the chairman of the board position open to any Reinhardt heir, throwing me into the running as well. But the real kicker? He *left* my grandfather's archaic provision that says the head of the company must be married.

After my brothers had gone home, my mother turned her sights on me. She rejected Christopher's compromise proposal out of hand, and said it was clearly up to me to carry the company forward, as a *real* heir. And I'd have to get married to do so.

Whatever Jonnie and I have, we're nowhere near ready for marriage, and I haven't opened that relationship to my mother's scrutiny anyway. It would never survive.

But Mother had a solution all ready for me—so ready that I now realize she'd likely been working on it for months. The Walker family, owners of Elite Electronics, are close family friends of ours, and their son, Alex, has been my best friend since we were little. Our parents have joked for years that someday Alex and I would marry, but now I've learned my mother isn't kidding.

Not only does marrying Alex Walker fulfill the will requirements, it also brings Elite Electronics into the Reinhardt Hudson fold, creating a merger and keeping the family company firmly in hand all at the same time. Mother gets giddy whenever she talks about it, and she's set out to plan the wedding of the century.

In my mother's eyes I have no prospects of a good man, so why on earth wouldn't this be perfect? I've tried a few times to explain my position, but if she's going to insist on a strict interpretation of the will, I've begun to see that this is the only way to keep what my family has built for generations intact. And so I'm stuck.

My announcement that I'm getting married is still hanging in the air, Jonnie's face blank, when his phone rings.

What terrible timing—or maybe it's the best timing ever, since I'm not certain hashing this out face to face with Jonnie is a task my resolve is up for. He draws me in like a magnet, and I already want to just cave, forget about everything, and let him take me to bed.

But I owe it to him to explain why I'm marrying Alex, even though my heart wants to be here with him and leave my scheming mother behind to manipulate someone else.

Jonnie listens on his phone for a few moments, an urgent look in his eyes and signaling to me with one finger — a plea asking me to wait. I know he wants to tell me what I already know: I'm making a mistake. In many ways it feels like a mistake to me, too. But it's an unavoidable one, and I worry he'll never understand.

"Okay. I'll be right there," he says. "Tell Queen Diva to hold on." He disconnects his call and throws his hands up, exasperated. "I'm sorry. I really want to have this conversation." He reaches for both my hands, and I look at him. "I really, really do. I just have a crisis I have to attend to."

I nod. Waiting a little bit won't change my mind, and if I say too much now, I'll start to cry.

He squeezes my hands. "I need to have this conversation with you. I want to understand." He searches my eyes. "This is not what I was expecting when you said you wanted to meet with me. We've got to discuss this. Please give me the chance to talk to you."

With a deep sigh, I nod. "I have two hours, and then I have to leave for my return flight. I'll wait as long as I can."

"You're leaving so soon?"

I nod. "I'm sorry. I need to be back for a Reinhardt board meeting tomorrow."

He leans in and gives me a kiss on the forehead before running toward the door. He looks over his shoulder. "I promise, I'll be back as soon as I can."

The door closes behind him, and I know he won't be back in time. Queen Diva is exactly as described: a high-maintenance performer who has more talent in her little finger than I have in my entire body. She's his in-house talent, and he's shared with me before that she gets herself worked up about things and it's difficult, but she's worth all the hassle.

She packs the house five shows a week—over a hundred and forty shows a year. The Shangri-la keeps fifty percent of each ticket sold, and her theater seats just under three thousand people. Which means she earns more than forty million dollars a year—and before costs, so does the Shangri-la. That's not chump change.

I walk back and forth in front of the full-length windows and look out over the desert. The hues of orange and purple are stunning and so different from anything I grew up with. Minnesota's state motto is the Land of 10,000 Lakes. Granted, we also say the mosquitoes are the size of small birds because of all the water. It's the opposite here, and I like the dryness and heat.

I continue to pace in front of the window, one minute willing Jonnie to return so he can talk me out of this decision and the next praying Queen Diva keeps him so we don't have to have this wretched conversation in person. I'll never convince him. I'm not sure I'm convinced. I just am out of other options.

Time inches by. I check my watch every fifteen seconds and my email every five. Waiting. Wishing. Hoping. Dreading. The silence is deafening, and I jump each time I hear a subtle bump or flicker—probably the air vents or nothing at all. No Jonnie.

Finally I can't take it anymore, and it's time to return to the airport. I need to leave. Taking a piece of paper from my purse, I write a note: *I'm sorry. Magpie*

As I walk out of his apartment and through the hotel to my waiting car, I secretly want him to see me. I want him to find me one last time. Marrying Alex means I'm preserving the company, but I'm losing an incredible lover and a great friend.

On my flight home, I can't stop crying.

"Is everything okay?" the flight attendant asks.

I wipe my eyes, knowing my mascara is probably all over my face. "Just a bad break up," I explain.

She nods sympathetically and after a moment places a glass of amber liquid in front of me. "A double scotch. It may burn going down, but it'll help numb the pain."

I try to crack a smile. "Thank you." I take a small pull from the glass and marvel at how I've changed the course of my life. After a few minutes, the drink does as she's promised, and my tears dry as the numbing begins.

When I arrive in Minneapolis, Richard, our family driver, is waiting to meet me. He takes one look at me and brings me into his arms. Once again I begin to cry. He and Hazel always know how to make me feel better.

Richard Patterson and his wife, Hazel, our housekeeper, have been surrogate parents to my brothers and me. I adore them. They never had children but essentially raised us as their own. They attended everything we did and made life bearable. They were supportive when my oldest brother, Christopher, emancipated himself in high school and worked his way through college and into the profession of his choice. They guided him to the U—as they call the University of Minnesota—and then to the University of North Carolina for medical school, instead of Carlton and business school like Father wanted. When my younger brother, Stevie, announced he wanted nothing to do with Reinhardt's and moved to Hawaii and opened a surf shack on Kauai instead of going to college, Hazel and Richard were the ones who visited him and eventually talked him into coming home. I was the child who always did as my parents asked and when they asked. I'm the dutiful daughter, and my mother never fails to capitalize on that.

"How was your trip?" Richard asks.

He knows the pressure I'm under.

"It was okay. But can we take the long way home? I'm not ready to face my mother."

We drive the scenic route from the airport toward our family home, Reinhardt House, in the upscale St. Louis Park neighborhood of downtown Minneapolis. I suppose it's a little strange that I still live there at age thirty-one, but that's just how it's done in our family—or it would be if either of my brothers played by the rules. I have my own space, and for a long time it helped me feel a part of the Reinhardt tradition. Only lately has it begun to seem suffocating.

I can see signs of spring trying to burst forth in the scenery outside my window, but as we drive, my thoughts inevitably return to Jonnie. He was the coolest guy on our high school campus. He had this level of confidence most boys don't find until later. His swagger had all the girls swooning; his blue eyes melted even some of the teachers' panties, and he had a mop of hair that always looked perfect. I learned quickly that girls wanted to hang out with me to get access to my brothers and Jonnie, which made me cautious about other women—a trait I've kept to this day. But I never got to hang out with any of their friends. The three of them wouldn't let any other boys near me. I blame them for my desperate high school love life, which seemed to follow me to college.

Even better than Jonnie in high school, though, is the Jonnie I reconnected with last fall at Christopher and Bella's surprise wedding. He showed me around the Shangri-la—almost as if he wanted my approval. His excitement and enthusiasm were contagious, and it doesn't hurt that he's even more handsome than he was in school. His hard, muscular body has filled out and his eyes are still a mesmerizing blue that make my panties wet. I was glued to his side the whole weekend, and after the wedding, we landed in bed, which fulfilled a lifetime of fantasies for me—and more. I was innocent in so many ways, and he was kind and gentle. I couldn't have asked for a more kind and patient lover.

And since then, I've talked to him via text or phone every single day. Until now. That's likely over, and I'm heartbroken that my duty as a Reinhardt daughter has officially eclipsed my ability to manage my personal life.

I one-hundred-percent hate this, though I do adore Alex Walker. He's been my best friend since we were in kindergarten, and I've known since second grade that he likes boys—just like I do. I love him regardless, but I don't want to marry him. I don't want a loveless marriage that's nothing more than a business transaction.

I fucking hate my mother.

I hate the situation she and Alex's father have created for us.

When Richard pulls up in front of the house, I remain in the car. I'm still not quite ready to get out and face my future. After a moment, Richard comes around and patiently holds the door open. I finally check my makeup, and as predicted, it's a mess. I take a moment to fix it, as I don't need additional criticism from my mother. She has a comment about everything I do—what I wear, my makeup, my hair, how I spend my free time, and the color of my nail polish.

Eventually I exit the car, stand next to Richard, and take a deep breath.

"You can do this," he says, just loud enough for me to hear.

I adore this man. I reach for his hand, and he gives me a comforting squeeze.

When I reach the door, I enter to find my mother standing in the foyer in her navy blue St. John knit suit, which is impeccably tailored to her petite frame. She's also wearing stockings and Ferragamo ballet flats, and predictably, every hair in her bob is perfect, despite the humidity. There's nothing out of place behind her false smile.

She looks at me with one eyebrow up.

"I'm home," I tell her.

She smiles. "Good. I have some wedding details to go over with you. We have the photographers coming. We need to make the official announcement in the society papers so no one thinks we're rushing this and you're pregnant."

I snicker. Alex once told me a vagina looked like a closet with the curtains poking out and smelled like a fish market. There's no way we'll ever consummate our marriage.

"—and the right people must be able to plan and save the date," my mother prattles on. "This is going to be the society event not only here in Minneapolis, but across the country."

"Yes, Mother." There is so much I'd rather say to her, but my heart aches, and I don't have the energy to fight with her right now. Since my father's death, she has become more and more difficult, and I've realized how much my father tempered her.

"I have a few things to manage for the Foundation, but I'll circle back with you this evening."

Before she can comment further, I go to my room, shut the door, and crawl into my bed. I hug my pillow and cry until I fall asleep.

Chapter 3

Jonathan

I can feel myself tapping my toe, though I'm trying not to be obvious about how irritated I am that I have to be part of this meeting between Queen Diva and her decorator. Apparently she won't go on stage until we solve this problem—which isn't actually a problem as far as I'm concerned.

We opened the Shangri-la less than six months ago, and she picked all of her colors and fabrics for the interior design of her space at the time. Unfortunately, she's now figured out what works and what doesn't when you have the same dressing room day-in and day-out.

Rather than just have her decorator put together a proposal and then together we determine who is going to pay for what, she's decided to hold me hostage—like she does—

until I agree to pay for it out of my budget and on her time frame. I should get major points for not freaking out immediately. I'm trying to sit and listen as her designer walks us through.

I'm not a designer, but I've just built a three-thousand room hotel, and I know what things cost. This is easily a half-million-dollar redecoration of her dressing room. Good grief.

Queen Diva brings in more than enough money, but I still need to keep the creditors from snapping at our heels.

When the designer starts in on fabrics and the color palette, I suddenly, painfully realize I don't care about silk and damask and subtle shades of gray and silver.

I can't focus on this right now. Maggie is in my apartment, and I need to figure out why she's getting married—to Alex of all people. He doesn't even like women.

"Queen Diva consistently performs to a sold-out crowd, and her shows are sold out through the end of the year. She needs an oasis, a place where she can take a soothing break from the stressors of being a high-caliber performer," the designer continues.

"Whatever she wants," I snap. "Just tell me what it's going to cost, and we'll figure it out. We'll do our best to make it happen." I manage to leave it at that, though I want to yell, *My life is falling apart while I'm listening to a decorator ramble about something that is not urgent!*

I'm finally able to extricate myself after two fucking hours of this crap. My bodyguard Caden is close behind, but with every step I take toward my apartment, something else comes up. I jog through the casino as several employees try to catch my attention.

"I'll be back," I yell. "I have something I have to tend to."

Why does every single one of my area managers need something from me? I know these guys handle more in a day than I ever could, but really? Why now?

"The new washing machines have blown the circuits,

so not only are we sitting in the dark, but we don't have any way to run the machines. The electricians are working on it, but they have to ship a part in from Los Angeles. What should we do?"

I need a vacation—that's all there is to it. I need a break, physically separate from this place. That's the only way.

"We have a highly intoxicated person who we're sure is staying here at the hotel, but we can't tell what room. He passed out in the casino. We've moved him to the infirmary and are watching his vitals. Should we let him sleep it off or call an ambulance?"

I dart around crowds, rushing to get to Maggie.

"Roulette table four seems to be triggering black thirty-seven one out of ten times. It's also running black 80 percent of the time. All the tables are full, but should we close it down and have maintenance check it? It's just on the border of the Nevada Gaming Commission radar for non-compliance."

I shake my head and don't slow down. When I'm finally free of the questions and mini emergencies, I race the rest of the way to my apartment. This is the one time I really wish it wasn't so secluded.

I know in my heart of hearts that Maggie has left by now, but I still want to try to see her. I still hope she wants to stay and talk to me. I have to talk her out of this sham marriage. It must be a sham. We connected when we were together last fall. The sex was magnetic. I shut my eyes and pray that she waited for me to return.

The elevator hardly opens before I squeeze out, leaving Caden behind, and run my hand over the touchpad to open the door to my place. I can smell her faint floral perfume, but when I look around, the apartment is too quiet. She's gone.

My heart sinks. Why would she do this? I see a note and rush over to read it, but it doesn't do anything other than apologize. She's sorry for what? For breaking my heart? For leaving without talking to me? For marrying someone who could never love her as much as I do?

I crumple the paper in my hand and throw it across the room. "Dammit!" Pulling the phone from my pocket, I call her, but it goes directly to her voice mail.

I know the person who runs the airport. I'm half tempted to figure out which plane she's on, stop it on the tarmac, and make them bring it back to the terminal. That would allow me to talk to her, but possibly not with the results I want.

There must be a reason she's had to do this…

I blow out a big breath of air and send her a text.

Me: I'm so sorry I missed you. I tried to get back before you left. Please call me. Please talk to me. Tell me what's going on. I'm worried about you and I care for you.

After a primal scream to release some frustration, I pour myself three fingers of bourbon and try to figure out how I can fix this. It's the only thing I can do.

Chapter 4

Jonathan

I'm staring out at Las Vegas from my office. Hordes of people crowd the sidewalks, exploring everything the Strip has to offer, despite the incredible heat—even in April. Maggie is not returning my calls or texts, so I haven't talked to her in three days. After talking every day for months, that feels like three years.

For all I know she's blocked me. But why? Did I miss some serious signals? I don't think so, but I don't have any way to get an outside perspective on this. No one knows what happened between Maggie and me at the wedding. I think Christopher might kill me if he knew. *Jesus.* How did I get into this mess?

I need to go to her. I need to talk to her and understand why. I will do what ever it takes.

My admin rings me from her desk outside my office door. "Mr. Best?"

"Yes, Lola?"

"Our favorite friend is having a problem and needs you."

I roll my eyes. *Queen Diva strikes again.* I'll get to Maggie as soon as I can…right after this, it seems. "Let her know I'm on my way."

"Yes, sir. Will do."

As I exit my office, Lola asks in a low voice, "Is she really worth all this trouble?"

"You've seen our P&L statement."

The answer is an unequivocal yes. She sells out five shows a week. There's also a spike in casino revenues before and after each of her shows. She's difficult on a good day, but even then, she's worth it.

Caden follows me down to the Diva Lounge. As I round the corner to her dressing room, she's screaming profanity, and I hear a glass shatter. I'm tempted to turn around and hide, but she'll only track me down. I tried that once, and it was worse when she found me.

"—that motherfucker. Who do they think they are?"

Even Caden flinches. He remains at the door and gives me a sympathetic smile. I walk in to find her manager/loser husband, Frankie, (who I think is taking her for every penny) only half paying attention to her tirade. He tried to negotiate a free room for his little trysts when we first set up the contract, but I was smarter than that. What happens between the two of them is their business, but I'm not going to involve the resort in their mess.

"You can't be talking about me?" I say lightly.

"I need the security footage of all activity back here," she demands

"Why? What happened?" I ask, the hair on my neck

standing straight up.

"Do you see that?" She points to her costume rack. Each outfit is hand-sewn and fit for her and cost me between ten and fifty grand. She wears them each evening during her show, making eight costume changes a night. She also has two spares in case she changes her mind, so what I see is a bundle of sparkling chaos on a rack. "It's missing."

I'm not sure what she's talking about. "What's missing?"

"The turquoise one."

She's all worked up—waving her arms and pacing.

Her assistant, Renee, comes in with a towel and water. She pulls a fan from her pocket and starts waving it at her. "Queenie, be careful. We don't want you to do anything to your voice. That is your instrument and getting upset is only going to put you on course for straining it."

I nod. Turning to her husband, I find him on his phone, mostly oblivious to the drama.

"Frankie, what's going on?" I ask.

"Her backup dress for the third change is missing."

"Could one of the fitters have taken it for repair or anything?" I ask.

"Absolutely not," Queen Diva interrupts. "These costumes are my uniforms. They aren't to leave my dressing room without my permission, and everyone knows that."

I'm taking everything in. This is Las Vegas, and of course, everything is captured on security cameras and saved to a cloud drive—minus what happens *in* her dressing room.

"I'll have security pull the footage of who has come and gone from your dressing room for the last week."

"What about inside?" her assistant asks in a disgusted tone.

"Well, for privacy reasons, we don't record what happens in private dressing rooms. Queen Diva made sure it was added to her contract," I remind them, "despite my assuring you we only record public areas."

Queen Diva throws her hands up in frustration. "That dress was my third favorite. I can't believe someone stole it."

I take a deep breath. I need to ask the next question, but I dread the answer. "Is there anything else missing? You are *the* Queen Diva, and something as simple as a hairbrush could be worth a fortune on a fan site or internet auction house—let alone your beautiful and expensive costume. Is anything else missing?"

Her assistant fans her, and her husband texts away on his phone.

"Well...I don't think so. I was planning on wearing it tonight, so I was looking for it when I got here," she says in a meek voice.

This is a good sign. She's calmed down and now we can get somewhere.

Frankie stands. "Okay, I just alerted *Inquiring Minds* and *News America*, and they will cover the missing dress."

I can feel my blood pressure going through the roof. "Why did you do that?"

Who thinks broadcasting a break-in is a good idea? That will put a lot of pressure on my security team.

He ignores my question in favor of bickering with his wife.

I lean in and kiss her cheek as I interrupt. "Queen, you're going to have a fantastic night. We'll get you that footage and another dress as fast as they can make one. Don't let this affect you and your show. Try to get some rest."

"Will you come tonight?" she begs.

I definitely don't want to. I want to sit in my boxers on my couch and watch the Minnesota Wild hockey game. Or figure out what I'm going to do about Maggie. But I paint a smile on my face. "Of course. I'll be in my box so you can't miss me."

I have no idea who's planning to be in my box in the theater tonight, so now I'll have to make nice with whomever sales has put there.

"Thank you," Queen and her assistant say at the same time.

I gesture between Queen and Frankie. "Don't stress about this."

Queen nods. Frankie's back to looking at his phone.

I walk out, exhausted, and Caden falls into step behind me. The makeup sex must be amazing; otherwise I can't understand why she keeps him around.

I walk into the Network Operations Center or NOC and Travis Deck, the head of hotel security, joins me. I hired him away from Clear Security last year. He's from Vegas and has a good relationship with my buddy Jim Adelson, CEO of Clear, so we came up with a deal. Jim's guys are here to back us up, particularly with visiting VIPs—both famous and just filthy rich—and to fill in gaps when needed. But now Travis is my in-house man all the time.

"Hey, Travis."

"I saw you go back to Queen's dressing room. I also noticed her assistant fussing with water and a towel. Is everything okay?"

"Not really."

I explain what's missing and ask him to review the tapes. I also ask him to pay close attention to Frankie, since he's making this into a publicity stunt.

"Let's make sure he didn't take the dress without her knowing to drum up attention for her and her shows."

Travis nods. "We did run one guy off last week. Those rabid fans and vulture paparazzi are always circling."

"Thanks. Anything else I should know about?" I ask.

"Same old, same old. Gillian got a new whale from The Gate resort next door, so we've got some extra security wandering around."

I like the sound of that. "Keep me posted." I look at my watch. If I'm going to finish my work and be on time for Queen's show, I need to get back to my office and accomplish something. "I'll be in the box in the Diva Lounge tonight."

"Lucky you." He looks at a clipboard. "Looks like a few folks from Banner Post will be there, too."

Well, maybe my time won't be wasted after all. With representatives from one of tech's biggest companies, maybe I'll land okay.

I arrive in the box shortly before the show starts and make small talk with the Banner Post folks. They're excited about the show, and I can't blame them. I wish I felt more excited, but I had hoped to be with Maggie tonight — here or in my room — and my mind can't stop thinking over all the plans I had that now seem unlikely to come true anytime soon.

The orchestra begins with Tchaikovsky's 1812 Overture. It plays softly in the background for the full seventeen minutes. Only those who have seen Queen Diva's show here before know that this is the precursor. The lights slowly dim as the song approaches its climax, and then it's totally dark. I can feel the anticipation as the audience waits for her arrival.

Just as the big booms of the drums signal the high point of the song, bright lights flare behind Queen Diva's drummer, and we see her backlit, the fractured light reflecting off from the sequins on her dress.

The crowd is on their feet, clapping and screaming her name. And she begins one of her biggest hits.

Her show is highly choreographed. Not only does she have back-up singers and dancers, but the light effects are brilliant. And, she changes her outfits without anyone realizing she's stepped away. She never misses a mark or a note.

It's pure entertainment for two hours. Everyone gets their money's worth with a Queen Diva show.

After the performance, I lead the Banner Post team

backstage and introduce them to Queen. These are seasoned professionals, but they're still over-the-moon excited. The diva is gracious and poses for pictures and signs autographs. As Gillian leads them away, I kiss Queen's cheek and whisper in her ear, "You were amazing."

She gives me a shy smile. "Thank you for coming. It means a lot to me that you keep your word."

With that I fade into the shadows, and within ten minutes, I'm back home sitting in my boxer shorts as I watch the Montreal Canadians beat up my Minnesota Wild. With a beer in hand, on my own damn couch, I can be as loud as I want. I'm moving toward serious relaxation, despite watching a losing game. I missed the beginning, but Queen's show was outstanding, and I'm glad I went. It actually took my mind off Maggie a bit. Then my phone rings.

There's only one person who would dare call me in the middle of the game, and that's because he's watching it, too.

"Yeah?" I mutter into the phone.

"Can you believe they suck this bad tonight?" demands Christopher Reinhardt.

My heart hurts as I think, once again, of his sister, Maggie. I wonder what she's doing right now.

"I mean, did they leave the team at home and bring the Eden Prairie High School team instead?" he asks.

"No, shit," I agree. "They're sucking wind. And I was worried when I missed the first period."

"You didn't miss much. I have to turn this off or Bella's going to make me sleep in the guest room tonight. She's working on her dissertation, and I'm being too loud."

"Other than getting in trouble with your bride, what else is going on in the life of a fancy venture capitalist?"

Sullivan Healy Newhouse, Christopher's firm, has been amazingly successful.

"Not much. We've been busy at SHN with some new investments, and we have an offer on the table for Bella's company, which would make her CEO of a huge corporation—as long as she can finish her Ph.D."

"Is that good news or bad?" I ask.

"Could go either way. How's your love life?"

I've never told him about my feelings for Maggie. That would break the cardinal rule of dating your best friend's sister. Because after you break her heart, you can't be friends. Of course in my case, she broke mine.

"I don't have time to date," I tell him.

"No way, man. I don't believe that. Every time I open the gossip columns, you have some stunning woman on your arm."

I scoff. "Those pictures are staged. Don't pay attention to them."

This Maggie thing is killing me. I need to tell someone about it. Telling Christopher will be tough, but he is my best friend... Maybe if I don't tell him who the girl is.

"Actually, I really like this one woman," I tell him. "She doesn't live here."

"Do I know her?" he teases.

Yes, but I'm not going to spend the night explaining that to you. "Nope. Anyway, I was just getting ready to convince her to move to Vegas so we could settle down—"

"You're going to settle down? That's surprising. I've never thought of you as a family man."

I bristle. "I never said *family*. I just thought having this *one* woman with me would be a good thing."

In truth, if Maggie wanted kids, I would happily have them with her.

"What happened?"

"Before I could say anything, she told me she was marrying someone else."

"Did she know you were heading in that direction?"

Evidently not. "I felt like we needed to at least live in the same zip code before we plotted every detail of our future."

"You don't love her," he assures me. "If you loved her, you'd move heaven and earth for her."

How little he knows. I *literally* moved all sorts of the earth for her to build this complex. I even called it the Magpie while it was in process.

"I was ready to give it a try." I sigh. I need to change the subject. "I was hanging out with one of your buddies at the Queen Diva show tonight."

"Who?"

"Nate Lancaster and his wife, Cecelia."

"Cool. What were they doing in Vegas?"

"Looking for another high-end card game. He wants me to put together a group of players like I did at your wedding."

"Nice. Count me in. That was a great game. Nothing like playing poker with a bunch of math geniuses. They don't care about bluffs; they just figure out the cards."

"No shit. I was thinking twelve players including you and maybe Mason Sullivan from your office. Plus, Nate mentioned Jackson Graham and Landon Walsh."

"That's five people so far—or will you play and make it six?"

"You all are too good for me. I'll just make sure you don't make a mess of my hotel."

"You know who was doing well that weekend is Mia Couture. She's a badass poker player."

"I also think Viviana Prentis would be good."

"I love it. That'll get your mind off that other woman."

"Sure. I'll put it together. Watch for the invite."

"No problem. Hey, did you hear Maggie and Alex are getting married?"

"I thought Alex was gay."

"So did I." He takes a big breath. "Our parents have talked about the two of them marrying since they were little. I guess the pressure finally got to them. Who knows what Maggie is doing."

"It's not like she *has* to marry the guy."

"Something hinky is going on, but I'm not sure what.

Mother makes everyone cower, and I'm sure she's bullied her way into the middle of this. The way she operates it'll probably be the society event of the year. Make sure you're there, and maybe you can bring this mysterious woman you're all hot and bothered about."

Unlikely. "Sure. It's now four-nothing with three minutes left. I'm going to bed. I have to be up at five tomorrow."

"Got it. Catch ya later." Christopher hangs up.

Lying in bed a little while later, I keep thinking about what he said—that her mom put pressure on them to marry. I need to get to the bottom of this.

Chapter 5

Maggie

It's morning, but I don't want to get out of bed. I can see the sun shining through a crack in the curtains. To hell with this beautiful day.

My phone vibrates on the side table. I don't want to know who's calling. They can leave a message.

A great sigh rushes from me. Today I have a long laundry list of things to accomplish, plus quite a few things my mother wants me to do—#1 being get excited about getting married. Ugh.

If I have any hope of standing upright today, I should focus on the Foundation. That's work I can be proud of, and I need to remember that without Reinhardt Corporation, there's no Reinhardt Foundation. So I'm making the right choice. The

Foundation recently adopted a nonprofit in San Francisco, and I'm working with their director to expand one of their student programs across the nation. I have a teleconference meeting in two hours.

But that's a while from now. I'll get ready later. I turn the television on and stare at it. *Boring.*

I don't want to go downstairs. My mother is likely lurking nearby, as she always is when she wants something from me. Right now she wants an obedient daughter — someone who will go along with her plans and not complain. Well, I'm not there.

So thankfully I have everything I need in my bedroom. It's bigger than most apartments with a sitting room/office, plus a mini fridge and a stash of snacks. I don't have to see anyone for a while.

There's a subtle knock at my door. I'm sure it's my mother, though she's not usually subtle. She wants to meet with dressmakers next week, and she wants me to go to the gym and primp for a photoshoot. She wants to meet the caterer and walk through the wedding venue with the planner. I want to curl up and hide in my bed.

The knock becomes more insistent. I'm surprised she hasn't barged right in. When I hear it a third time, I'm over it.

"Come in," I bark.

"Sorry about this," Alex says as he opens the door.

"Oh, hey. I thought you were my mother."

"I don't look that good in a bob," he teases.

I can't help but smile. "Or a St. John knit suit."

"You're right. I don't have the bust or the hips."

I grin. "What brings you here?"

"Wedding planning." He lies down on the bed next to me. "I'm sorry you've been dragged into this."

I gaze at him. Alex and I have been best friends since elementary school. "You were dragged into this, too."

"Well, that's true," he agrees.

"It's going to be such an 'advantageous marriage',

though." I use air quotes since this is what our parents keep telling us.

"You know, it won't be that bad," Alex tells me. "At least we like each other and enjoy hanging out together."

"I know. I just wasn't prepared to completely sacrifice my personal life for the family business."

"It's not like this is the first arranged marriage for either of our families. Maybe it's because I know my father would blow a gasket if I married a man, but I kind of like the idea of being married to my best friend."

"But that's just it," I tell him. "You're not supposed to be married to your friend for business reasons. It's supposed to be a kind of love you and I are never going to have."

He shrugs. "At least you're not pregnant."

My stomach turns. I will never have a family. "We have to figure this out." I sit up in bed and mute the television. "What do you see for our married life?"

"I guess I just thought we'd have a marriage on paper, separate bedrooms, and our own lives."

The fact that he seems even remotely okay with this makes me more depressed than I already am.

"We can refuse, if we do it together," I reason. "There has to be a way to get my mother to be more flexible about the will requirements."

Alex looks down for a moment, and when he looks back up at me, his face has changed. "You have to help me, Maggie. I have no other options. I know your mother wants this, but my father wants it too. If I don't marry you, I will lose my inheritance and financial support. I have absolutely no skills. I'm an expert at going to spas and being pampered. I'm great at giving a blow job, but I can't legally be paid for that."

I open my mouth, but he doesn't let me respond.

"Please..." He reaches for me and pulls me into a hug, "Do this for me *and* for you—for your family business. It'll be in name only. What you do on your own is up to you."

I look at him, and the weight of all this feels even

heavier. Now it's not just the future of the Reinhardt family business, but my best friend's livelihood as well? How did we get to the point that this marriage is the only possible choice?

I pull him in tight. "I fucking hate our parents; I hate their snobby attitudes, and I hate that we're in the middle of their ridiculous focus on merging the businesses. I could care less about their wishes, but to liquidate everything my great-grandfather, grandfather, and father built isn't how I was raised."

"I agree," he says, muffled into my shoulder. "And you're the best hope for Elite, too. As I mentioned, I certainly have no skills."

My maternal great-grandfather was the founder of Hudson's department stores. My paternal great-grandfather founded Reinhardt's. Both stores were started as five and dime stores after the Depression. They were intense rivals. Over time, both my grandfathers grew their businesses into high-end department stores and focused their growth in opposite parts of the United States. Reinhardt's was the leading department store in the west, and Hudson's was well-known in the east. Finally, once they got older, they came up with the idea of the future merger of their companies, and they arranged the marriage of my parents. For a while, my father had a thriving law practice, but when my grandfather died, to meet the terms of the will, he had to take over the family business.

My father knew swings in the economy affected the business, so he diversified the stores, creating the current crown jewel in our fortune. Going back to the roots of the five and dime, we opened a discount retail store called Bullseye. The long hours and push for perfection meant my father was rarely home, and my mother spent a lot of her time involved in the community. We knew he'd grown close to his long-time secretary, Nancy, and rumors swirled about an affair. Then when I was in middle school, my dad launched a mid-level department store he called Murphy's—also the name of his secretary's son, and he acknowledged that my siblings and I had a half brother.

Around the same time, Alex's grandfather started Elite, an electronics store in downtown Minneapolis. It became the place where everyone bought anything that plugged in. When Alex's father took over the business, he got advice from my dad and grew his own business into one of the largest high-end electronics stores around.

I ease myself out of bed and check the clothes in my closet. "Would you care if I wore sweatpants today?"

"No, but your mother might."

I roll my eyes. Instead of sweats, I pull out a beautiful designer outfit made just for our stores and put it on.

"You look lovely," Alex says. "Your mother will be very pleased."

Once I'm dressed, we walk together downstairs to the kitchen. Hazel, our housekeeper, has made a beautiful breakfast, and my mother is there reading the newspaper. She glances at us as we enter. "I knew Alex could get you out of bed."

I give her a plastic smile as I walk over to Hazel and give her a tight embrace. "Thanks for making my favorite breakfast. You're the absolute best."

She nods.

I don't want my mother to go too crazy over my affection toward the housekeeper, so I point her toward the chocolate crepes with whipped cream and strawberries.

"You do have a wedding dress to wear soon," my mother notes. "Hazel, we're going to need to put her on a diet."

"I'll go with an empire waist and no one will know."

"They'll think you're pregnant." She looks over at Hazel to make her point. "No more than a thousand calories a day." Picking up her phone, she types out a message. When she's done, she looks up at me. "I just confirmed Rachel to meet you each morning for a long workout and a run."

"Is that really necessary?" Alex asks. "Curves look good on Maggie."

She gives him her laser death stare, and he sits back.

"Mom, you can force us to do this, but it doesn't mean I'll do it happily."

"Yes, it does." She gets up and leaves the room.

I groan. "I hate the way she leaves the room so you either have to follow her out to reply or she gets the last word."

Hazel pats me on the back and fills my cup with strong coffee. "Don't worry, sweetheart."

"Thanks," I mumble.

After my teleconference for the Foundation—which feels rushed because I know Mother is counting the moments until I'm done—Alex and I spend the afternoon with her, meeting with the wedding planner and going through all her plans. Mother and the planner, Veronique, have decided my bridesmaids will wear lavender silk dresses. They've also decided who will be in the wedding party. I hardly know one of the attendants, but when I protest, Mother gives me the ice stare that tells me to get in, buckle up, and shut up; this is their ride, not mine.

The day evaporates, and before I know it, we're home for dinner.

"I'm eating in my room," I announce.

"That's fine," Mother says. "I had Hazel clear out your snack drawer."

I roll my eyes. "I don't care. I just need to recharge and be alone."

I hate this more than I can say. Opening the door to my room, I spot my cell phone, which I accidentally left behind all day. There are sixteen messages. My so-called friends are getting excited, but it's not like they don't know Alex is gay and this is a sham, so I'm not sure how seriously to take their support. They're all just people Mother has put in my life anyway. Then I see the text message. My heart stops and crumbles all over again.

Jonnie: I miss you.

Tears pool in my eyes. I'm tired, hungry, and miserable. I never knew it was possible to fight within myself so much. This is what has to be done, so why does it feel so awful? And poor Jonnie. I thought telling him I was getting married would be the end of it—who wants to bother with that? But he genuinely seems to want to understand, which means I have to find the strength to talk it through with him. Strength I'm not sure I have.

My brothers have left me to fend for myself, and until I had Jonnie, I didn't feel like there was anyone in my life I could truly share this sort of thing with. I miss him. Over those few months before my father's death, he'd become the best thing in my life. And right now he's the one genuine person I can think of. I've always called Alex my best friend, but I think that's just because I didn't know what was possible. He was never interested in the business side of my life and now he's acting weird about all this wedding stuff.

I pour myself a glass of wine, and after a little while I respond.

Me: I miss you, too.

Jonnie: Can we talk?

Me: I've been wedding planning all day. I'm exhausted.

Jonnie: How's that going?

Me: I have no control over anything. I learned today who my attendants are and the color they'll be wearing, the flowers they'll be holding, and what my bouquet will look

like.

Jonnie: This just doesn't make any sense to me. I need you to tell me what's going on.

Me: Simply put, it's about my father's will and what it requires for the future of the company. Alex and I have to do this. I know that sounds crazy, but it's the truth. I don't expect you to understand.

Jonnie: I want to understand. I want to talk it through with you so we can find another way.

I need to change the subject or it will only further depress me.

Me: Could we talk about something else right now? I could use a distraction. How are things at the Shangri-la?

Jonnie: Good, but not the same if I'm not doing it all for you.

I snort. *All for me?* I don't think so.

Me: You're successful at whatever you put your mind to.

Jonnie: Particularly when I have motivation.

Me: We need to find you some strong motivation then. Chocolate? Coffee? Bourbon?

Jonnie: You

Me: Cookies, trips, clothes, jewelry?

Jonnie: I'm serious.

Me: I know. It just can't happen.

Jonnie: That's not acceptable.

Me: I should go. My mother has me on a diet, and I need to eat something before I start eating this phone.

Jonnie: You're perfect just the way you are. You don't need to change a thing.

I would love to share that with my mother, but I'll never let her know he's in my life — in any capacity.

Me: Goodnight.

Chapter 6

Jonathan

Maggie has avoided any decent conversation with me for almost a month. She sounds wrecked and damn near despondent when I do manage to reach her, so I never want to make things worse or more stressful for her. But that's getting me nowhere, except closer and closer to this ridiculous wedding she seems committed to. Today I'm determined I'm going to talk to her—a real conversation, even if I have to fly home to do it. This is impossible.

I take another look over the list of players we've invited to the high-stakes poker game Nate Lancaster asked me to put together. I crafted the invitation carefully, making sure everyone who received it understood that Nate had asked for the game.

Now I just need to sit down with Travis, my head of security, and Gillian in guest relations, to make sure we can cover everything from the security and casino perspective.

Right on time, they appear in my office, and I hand them copies of the list.

"These guys are billionaires?" Travis asks.

I nod. "On paper at least—as far as the SEC knows."

Gillian shakes her head. "Nate Lancaster is more than a billionaire on paper."

"I suppose they all are," I relent.

"Well, I think the game should be Texas Hold'em, and the buy-in at least three million," Gillian says. "A million for them is like a thousand dollars to a normal person. It should hurt at least a little bit."

"Nate suggested a five million buy-in." I shrug. "All they can do is say no."

"Exactly. What else should we offer?" Gillian asks.

"Box seats to Queen Diva?" I offer.

"Nate just did that," Gillian reminds us.

"Sure, but no one else did," Travis adds.

She shrugs. "We can comp a suite. These guys will order tons of food and room service, so that will become a moneymaker."

I nod. "What else would make it enticing?"

Gillian sits up straight in her chair. "Will most of them be bringing someone? We can set up a tour of the stores along The Boardwalk."

I like that idea. The Boardwalk is fifty A-plus stores housed on the property—all the high-end retailers in the world. They're mostly Italian, but there are also a few French ones, and we recently introduced a Japanese designer.

"That might work. I'm not sure who Viviana and Mia will bring, but we can offer a high-end bourbon tasting at The Derby restaurant. They'd enjoy that," I suggest.

"Plus, if they get drunk enough, they could all lose,"

Travis adds.

I snort. "That would probably bankrupt us if it got out, but I still think they'd enjoy the tasting."

"What about a cooking lesson from Tammy Flint?" Gillian suggests. "She's the new hit on the Food Channel, and her restaurant on The Boardwalk is doing really well."

"If you can talk Tammy into coming, we can cover her costs, but don't let her negotiate a rent discount on her restaurant. I want to pay her for her time," I say.

"Shopping, a show, liquor, food, and gambling — what else could they want?" Gillian shrugs as she steps out for a moment to confirm with Tammy. When she returns, she has a big smile. "She loves the idea and says she won't take any money for it."

"We'll do something for her," I muse.

Now that we've hashed out some details, I put the finishing touches on an email to Nate to update him on the perks we can offer. My phone rings within seconds. I answer as Gillian and Travis leave.

"This is exactly what I was hoping for." I recognize Nate's voice instantly. "Thanks for putting it together."

"I'm happy to help."

"Cecelia is going to love the shopping thing and will drool all over Tammy Flint. Who did you end up inviting?"

I rattle off the list of mostly tech billionaires. They all carry a level of fame, but between their security and the Shangri-la's security, we'll be fine.

As we talk, I write a few things down in my notebook to prepare for their arrival once they confirm.

"Perfect," Nate says. "I'll send them personal emails to follow up and convince them to come with all these perks."

"Is the buy-in too much? I thought that was what you said, but we weren't sure about your friend Walker Clifton, since he's a U.S. Attorney."

Nate snorts. "You don't need to worry about Walker. His family found gold in San Francisco generations ago, and they've turned that into many things, including eighteen apartment buildings down in the Marina."

I sit back and smile. This is going to be good. "Outstanding. Should I email you as the remaining players commit? We've tentatively reserved suites for all the players and their entourages."

"Sounds great," Nate says.

"The first night we'll have two tables with the five million buy-in, and the second night can be the top players with a ten million buy-in. Done." I sit back, trying not to laugh out loud. I grew up with people who had money, but not like these guys.

"Perfect," Nate says. "We're all set. I'll talk to you again soon."

I've just hung up the phone when Lola is at my door. "Queen Diva again."

I sigh. "Tell Travis to meet me at her dressing room with the video we discussed."

"Will do. I'll let her know you're on the way."

On my way across the hotel I'm stopped by my pit boss. "How's it going this afternoon?" I ask him.

"Not bad, sir. The blonde at table eight has maxed out her credit card and seems to be out of luck. She keeps asking if the house will extend her credit."

I shake my head. I feel for people who think if they play just one more hand, their luck will change. "Call Gillian and have her come down and sit with the woman. See what's going on. If she needs a job, we can try to move her into a cocktail waitress gig, or if she'd prefer, we can recommend her to one of the restaurants or stores on The Boardwalk."

"Thank you, sir. I'll make the call."

I make money when people lose, but for some, walking away is really tough. I want my guests to have fun, not look for a high building and jump.

When Caden and I arrive at Queen Diva's dressing room, Travis is waiting for me. "You didn't go in?"

He shakes his head. "No way. She's mad as a hornet."

We turn, bracing ourselves for the impending barrage. Caden stays at the door. *Pussy*. This is going to be ugly.

"Do you know why she's upset?" I say in a low voice.

"Nope. I just heard her ranting and raving, and her assistant ran down the hall, muttering to herself."

"Don't worry too much about the assistant. She's paid about what you are."

He lifts an eyebrow.

"I insisted on that in the contract. It comes out of Queen's profits, but she's on our payroll."

"I'm not sure that's enough," Travis says.

"All right, let's put our big boy pants on." I take a deep breath and open the door. "Hello, Queen. What can I do for you today?"

Her husband gives me a grateful look, probably glad I'm moving into the hot seat now.

"The dress from my first act is now missing."

I notice Travis fingering a jump drive. "When was the last time you saw the dress?" I ask her.

"When I took it off during my costume change at last night's show."

I prepare for the verbal assault, and as it begins, I hold up my hand. "We have a duplicate already made. This isn't catastrophic. And let's not notify the media. This gets out and people will be climbing the walls to get at your costumes."

She looks horrified and turns to her husband. "You caused this mess. You were the one that thought letting the media know what happened would prevent it from happening again, and now another dress is missing. We may have multiple thieves, you clueless son of a bitch."

He's a broken man, but that *was* my concern when he decided to alert the tabloids.

"Well, there's nothing we can do to change that now," I tell Queen. "But let's not add any more fuel to the fire, okay?"

She nods, and turns her ire back to me. "What are you

doing to protect *our* investment?"

Travis steps forward. "We've watched the video from the camera outside your room for the past few weeks. We've noted the people coming and going and even followed a few through the hotel to see if the dress can be seen, but we're not having any luck." He hands her the jump drive. "Everything is on here. You're welcome to see if something looks suspicious to you. My team was looking for the dress, but you may find someone who wasn't supposed to be in your dressing room that we don't know."

She takes the drive and hands it to her husband. "*You* can watch this."

He nods.

"Make sure everyone entering and exiting your room was allowed to be there so we can be more precise in our search. And just to confirm, the dress you wear in your first act is the same one on all the promotion materials and billboards, correct?" Travis asks.

She nods. "Yes, that's the dress." She reaches for a picture. "Here is a complete view. It's my heaviest dress — weighs over fifteen pounds. It would be difficult to stuff it under your arm and not be noticed."

Travis nods. "I agree. That's very helpful. Anything else you can think of?"

"Yes, I want one of your security guards in the room when I'm not here."

I blanch at the thought. Paying someone to be here constantly would be a colossal waste of time, talent, and money.

"I may have another solution," Travis says. "But I'll have Kian from my team come down until we can iron out the details."

She seems happy, and that will make a difference. I'm equally frustrated that the dresses are missing, but I think it's an inside job, and I'm not about to do marriage counseling.

After we leave, Travis says, "Kian can sit there, but

rather than leaving her costumes on the rack in her room, we should have one of her costumers come to a specific location where they're locked away and covered. With a security escort, they can be moved—at least until we discover why her husband is stealing the gowns."

I nod. "That's who I think it is, too. Can you prove it?"

"Nope. But he's pretty shifty, if you ask me."

"Agreed. Keep me posted."

After an eighteen-hour day, I fall into bed and realize I never reached out to Maggie. I can't wait another day.

Me: I miss you. If you don't talk to me, I'm going to show up at your house and make Hazel let me in.

Maggie: I'm here. I'm sorry.

Me: I'm calling. Please answer the phone.

I send my text and immediately call.

Maggie picks up the phone but doesn't say anything.

"Are you there?" I ask.

"Yes." I hear her sigh. "I miss you, too. I don't have a lot of friends, you know."

"Then why aren't you talking to me?"

"Because I already know what you're going to say."

"Take me through it. I want to understand everything."

"You know my family's expectations—business first, family second. My grandfather's will lays it out. I've always known that. I just never realized it was going to affect me so personally." She runs me through the details of her father's will and the bombs that dropped at the reading.

"It's ridiculous that you have to be married, but

especially to Alex. He doesn't even like women. Why does your mother care who it is?"

"My mother and Alex's father want an Elite Electronics in every Bullseye. It's an extra bonus for the future of both companies."

"This makes no fucking sense. You're a human being." I'm holding the phone so tight my hand hurts.

She's silent a moment.

"You know you can put Elite in the stores without marrying Alex."

"Maybe, but my *mother* is requiring the marriage, and I have no doubt she'll challenge things with the executor if I don't do what she wants. I have to be married before I take charge, or we have to dissolve the company. It's a smart business decision."

"You have two brothers," I point out. She sounds like she's been brainwashed.

"I do, but Christopher is emancipated, and Stevie is uninterested and unqualified. I'm the only one left to fight for my family legacy—the only one who cares that Reinhardt Hudson's and Bullseye continue to exist, because they're what fund the Foundation that I love, and they represent generations of work that I'm not willing to walk away from. You don't get it. I can't walk away." Her voice begins to crack. "If we dissolve the company, that means over five hundred thousand people don't have jobs, can't feed themselves, and can't pay their bills. What choice do I have?"

My heart hurts. "That's a lot of pressure on you," I say gently. Do Christopher and Stevie even understand?"

"Christopher has tried to help, but he bailed a long time ago, so of course he thinks the wedding is my idea. We didn't think she would enforce the provision immediately."

I sigh. "Yes, he's known for a long time that your mother is a psycho."

She laughs, and at least I can sense a crack in her determination. "Okay, well. There *is* that."

"Christopher told me once that you were just going to hire someone to run the company after your father died." There have to be other options.

"Yeah, that was our plan, and we hired George Dayton to run the company even before my father was gone. One of us was going to be board chair, and he's president of the company. Unfortunately, my mother and the family lawyer have decided our plan doesn't meet the will's requirements, and if challenged, they believe we'd have to dissolve."

"Who would challenge it?"

"Well, like I said, my mother to start with. But I don't know — maybe a competitor? We just can't take the chance of losing the company."

"But Alex? I mean, there's no secret he's gay. That doesn't even make sense. You won't be fooling anyone. That doesn't meet the will's requirements either, if you ask me."

"No, he's pretty out." She sighs again. "But it seems Herbert Walker feels the only way the merger can be completed is if Alex heads part of the company."

I lie back in my bed and stare out into the Nevada desert. I need to approach this from another angle.

"But what about us?" I ask softly.

How can her brothers do this to her? Don't they get it? How can they just leave this for her to manage on her own?

"We'll always be friends... I hope," she says.

"What if I want to be more than friends?" I challenge.

She snorts. "It not like people in my family don't have affairs."

"But what if you married me instead of Alex?" I put it out there and hold my breath.

"You are terribly sweet to offer, but your life is in Las Vegas, and mine is here. That's not a real marriage either."

I want to show her we can fight this, but I don't think she's listening anymore. What she says next confirms it.

"It's late, and I have a full day of work tomorrow, so I need to get some rest," she tells me. "I promise to not be so difficult to reach."

"Maggie, I want to figure this out. Don't give up. I'm here for you."

"Good night, Jonnie."

Chapter 7

Jonathan

I'm slogging my way through a pile of paperwork at my desk the next afternoon, when my phone buzzes to life on my desk.

Christopher: Dude!

Me: How old are you?

Christopher: 33 and you?

Me: Same. I think I'm more than dude.

Christopher: Ah, yes. Excuse me, Mr. Shangri-la CEO

and owner.

Me: What do you want?

Christopher: I'm downstairs.

Me: Are you fucking with me?

Christopher: Nope. I'm in line to check in. Bella sent me away for the weekend so I thought I'd come hang with you.

Me: Get out of line. You're staying at my place.

Christopher: Only if you aren't going to sit around in your boxers on the couch all weekend.

Gawd, he knows me well.

Me: Get your ass up here. Tell Connie at the concierge desk you're looking for the executive offices. And if she's worried you're some hoodlum, she can call me.

Christopher: How old are you again? Now you're sounding like you're 90.

Me: Each minute you wait is a drink you'll have to buy me, and my tastes are expensive these days.

Christopher: Hold on, she just gave me directions. I'm on my way.

I can't believe he's here. It's like the universe is conspiring to help me figure out this Maggie situation—and hang out with my best friend in the process, though I'm still pissed at him for the position he's left Maggie in. Not that we can talk about that... Aaaggh. This is going to be complicated.

I call to my assistant in the other room. "Lola, there's a gangly looking guy on his way up. Just point him in here."

"Hello?" Christopher bellows as he enters the outer office.

"I think he's here," Lola says.

"I apologize for his thoughtlessness already."

A moment later she appears holding a bouquet of flowers. "He's already forgiven."

"You're such a kiss ass," I tell him.

"Hey, she tolerates you, and I'm stealing you away for a few days, so she's stuck with extra work to cover your ass." Christopher lumbers in and dumps his bag inside the door.

"You're still a kiss ass," I mutter.

I walk over to give him a hug with a lot of backslapping. "Why didn't you tell me you were coming?"

"After talking to you the other night, I felt like you could use a break. Plus, Bella is super stressed right now and needs some space. I could go home to Minneapolis, but I haven't wanted to deal with my family since I was in high school."

My heart cracks a little, but I manage to nod and smile. "Lola, can you reschedule the rest of my day?"

"Of course. Already done. I moved your afternoon meeting to Monday. It's after three on Friday, and I told your trainer you'd make it up to him. And I scheduled time on the golf course tomorrow for you."

I eye Christopher, and he shrugs. "I brought my clubs. Left them out there."

"He owes you more than flowers," I tell Lola.

"I'm only doing my job." She waves goodbye as she turns to leave.

Christopher plops down in the guest chair, leans back, and puts his feet up. "So, what's there to do in this town?"

"Not that much," I tell him. "Anything specific you have in mind?"

"Watch the Wild game on Sunday."

"The Twins play Sunday, too."

"Oh yeah, another team from the hometown. Got any decent-sized televisions around here?"

"I guess if the seventy-five inch is too small, we can hit the sportsbook."

"Now we're talking. I need to get some practice in if I'm going to ante up five mill for a poker game in a few weeks. Bella's going to have my balls for that."

"Why? She knows five million is pocket change for you, doesn't she?"

"Yes, but she's very conservative about how we spend. I think she worries it's going to go away."

"She knows that will never happen, though, right?"

He shrugs. "She grew up where money was tight. I love that she wants to be frugal. She has a healthy chunk of change since her startup was funded, but she didn't grow up like that."

"You're a lucky man."

"In more ways than you know."

I arrange to have his suitcase and clubs delivered to my apartment, and we head down to the VIP bar. We navigate our way through the hotel with Caden in close proximity.

"I want to show you this," I tell him.

We take a seat at the bar, and he looks around at what always reminds me of an old-time club—dark paneled walls, the smell of cigars, and Peter, the bartender, dressed in a bow tie, black vest, and pants.

Said bartender nods at me. "What can I get for you?"

"Peter, I'd like the bottle of Michter's Celebration Sour Mash Whiskey." I turn to Christopher. "It has an amazing brawny spice and leather flavor, with a bit of oak."

"Sounds like you memorized the marketing materials."

We study the bottle when it arrives. "Michter's distillery was the first in the United States, but it was forced to close during Prohibition in 1919. They resurrected the brand in the 1990s."

"How do you know all this?"

"The owner stays here at the hotel, and I bought a case. It was expensive, but right up the alley of people who come into the VIP lounge."

"Do we drink it over ice?"

"According to the owner, yes — one large chunk." I give Peter a nod, and he places a clear square of ice in the tumbler in front of each of us and pours two fingers.

We take a sip. "This is incredible," Christopher marvels.

It burns for a second but goes down like butter. "I love this stuff. I was told that after the barrel blending, the mixture is hand-bottled and finished with this eighteen-karat-gold lettered label. You should see the special boxes it came in."

"I need to order some of this," Christopher says, taking another sip. "In fact, I need some partner gifts — maybe this is my answer."

I listen to him talk about his work and realize he's the only true friend I have. I have work friends, but no one that I can totally be myself with. He's known me most of my life, and despite my warts, he still shows up when he knows I'm struggling. I want to tell him all about what's going on with Maggie — get his perspective on the whole thing — but if I did that, I'd have to come clean about my feelings for her.

He made me promise when I was fifteen that I'd leave her alone. He made it very clear that if I crossed that line, he'd beat me to a pulp, and I'd never have children. I don't know if he still means that, but I'm not sure I'm brave enough to risk it at the moment. I'm losing her. I can't afford to lose him, too.

"So tell me about this woman," he prods, as if he can read my thoughts.

"I'm not ready to talk about it."

"Makes sense. You've just sipped some expensive stuff. We need to find you the cheap crap. Maybe some Mad Dog?" he teases.

"That shit tastes like cough syrup."

"But you'll get drunk, and then you can open up and tell me."

"I'll tell you at some point." Or not.

We move to the sportsbook but hardly pay attention to the college football game playing. Our alma mater plays in the Big Ten, but they tend to run from the middle of the pack to the bottom, and they don't get a ton of press coverage outside the Midwest.

Christopher gives me a funny look. "Everything here uses the software you built in grad school, doesn't it?"

I nod. "We're close to being able to market it to other hotels."

"What exactly does it do?"

"Are you asking as my friend or as a potential broker for my business?"

"I do work with some of the foremost developers in the country. If you need help there, I've got you covered, but my usual area is pharma. I'm interested as your friend."

"Okay." I glance up at the ceiling. The software is my baby. I have two developers who work from offices here on property on a secure server, and we're building this together. "The competitors in this space aren't quite as advanced as we are. They use large cash registers, and the systems don't talk well to one another without someone pushing buttons behind the scenes." I take a deep pull on my drink. "After you check in at the hotel, you have the ability to enter your room by fingerprint."

"I hope it's more accurate than my phone, or everyone will be locked out."

I smile. "It is. We store the prints but don't upload them where law enforcement could get to them. Once you're a guest of the Shangri-la, we track everything to maximize your experience. We know if you spend two hundred dollars at the blackjack table and move to the nickel slots, which shows you see, which restaurants or stores on The Broadway you visit. Your information runs in real time from one spot to the other."

"That's so Big Brother."

"We're trying really hard to not make it that way. We don't use facial recognition, and our systems don't register you until you check in. Plus, as soon as you check out, your information is dumped from our system. If you're a frequent guest and member of our loyalty program, we maintain some of the bigger-picture information in a different system. But this level of detail helps housekeeping with bed linens and towel counts for their cart. If we know you like to drink Michter's whiskey and like to play mah-jongg, the internal systems will move a bottle around so you have it at your table without a thirty-minute wait. No one has to send a guy to go find it at the VIP lounge. The software is designed to give you a feeling of first-class accommodation without having to add a ton of staff."

"Do you think there's a use outside of a place like this?"

"Absolutely. We think our software's perfect for all-inclusive resorts or even your basic three-star hotel looking to step up their customer service."

"How are you going to market this?"

"I've been pretty focused on making it work well here, so I haven't figured that out."

"We should have a conversation with Mason and Cameron from my firm—"

"Not sure I want to give up any piece of the pie to investors."

Christopher grins wide. "That's the beauty of venture capital. I think they could put you with someone who would take the load off your plate. Yes, you're giving up some control and a piece of the pie, but they can catapult you to the next level, and you can be as involved or as uninvolved as you'd like. You have an amazing piece of technology, and the software is being tried and tested in a private resort with over three thousand rooms and fifty thousand guests using the casino each day."

"I'm happy to listen, but I'm not promising anything." I do know that at some point I'm going to have to focus on the either the software or the hotel. It can't be both.

"Perfect. Are you drunk enough yet to talk about this woman?"

He's going to keep harassing me. He's like a dog with a bone sometimes. Staring into the amber liquid in my glass, I open up. "I've known her for a long time. I realized early that she was my 'it' girl."

"Why are you just telling me now? I mean, I watched you screw your way through half a sorority in college."

"Well, I knew, but she scared the shit out of me. I wasn't ready yet."

"Okay, I felt that way for a minute when I met Bella," Christopher quips.

"Fuck you. Never mind."

"I'm sorry. Don't stop."

"Every time she said she liked something, I stored it in a file in the back of my mind. I knew I wanted to build this for her someday. I hated the winter in Minnesota, and I love the vibrant colors of the desert. So, while in grad school, I developed this software with this place in mind. I built the Shangri-la for her."

"But you never told her?"

"We talked on occasion. But I wanted it to be a surprise. I wanted it to be a grand gesture."

He looks around. "This is definitely a grand gesture. What happened?"

I shrug. "She flew out. I was going to ask her to move here. I had a ring, and I was going to propose."

"You bought a ring? Didn't you skip the dating part?"

"I bought her a ring. It wasn't like we would get married tomorrow, but I wanted her to feel like moving here came with a commitment from me. I was ready to show her everything and give her everything. But before I could even start, she told me she was marrying someone else."

He makes a face. "Are you sure you'd been reading her feelings the right way?"

I nod. "I know she cares about me."

"Then why didn't you talk her out of it?"

"I'm trying, but she's convinced herself it's the right thing to do."

"Then why aren't you on a plane to her right now?"

I scrub my hands through my hair. This is the part I can't figure out how to handle. "She mostly shuts me down when I try to bring it up. I'm not sure what would happen if I showed up in person. I don't want to make things worse—she's already under a lot of stress—and I also have quite a few things happening here."

He nods thoughtfully. "That sucks. I still think you're going to have to go there. And I don't get why you never told me. I could have been priming the pump for you."

I laugh. He would cut my balls off if he knew.

Christopher put his arm around my shoulders. "You are an amazing brother-from-another-mother and friend. I know there's a fantastic woman out there for you—when the time is right."

Chapter 8

Maggie

The man sits down at his desk. "You have such a great body. Why hide it under that sweater?"

I blush. "Thank you."

He leans forward and scrutinizes me like he's about to make a business deal. "I'm just going to come out and ask, princess. What are you doing here? What is it you want? What do you think is going to happen?"

The room feels warmer...and it's becoming harder to breathe.

All I can muster is, "I have this fantasy..."

"Go on." He sits forward with his hands clasped in front of him. His eyebrows rise, and his glare gives me the impression he has x-ray vision.

I cross my arms and legs, but that still doesn't hide me from his gaze.

"What's your fantasy?" he asks.

My face starts to flush and my breathing grows heavier. "I want you to fuck me." My eyes bug, not believing the words that just came out of my mouth.

In contrast, he keeps his eyes on me, his poker face not revealing what he's thinking at all.

"What do you mean by that, princess?" he says. "How do you want to be used?"

I look at the ground. "I want to be stripped and —"

"Stop right there," he demands. "You want to be stripped naked? How do I know this isn't some joke? How about you strip right now? If you can't do it here in my office, what's your plan?"

I'm stunned like a deer in the headlights. I glance around. The door is closed, but people are walking by his office. It's not that private. What if we get caught? Everyone has a cell phone today. What if someone records us and posts it on some porn site? I want this, but do I want it this bad?

"You may as well just leave if you can't."

I stand, trembling, and his face falls in disappointment. But a grin forms as he watches me grip the bottom of my shirt and pull it up over my head.

"What a slutty little bra you have there for such an innocent-looking girl," he growls.

I almost forgot I wasn't wearing my normal underwear. I blush, knowing my nipples are straining behind the satin lace demi cups.

"Come on, princess, don't waste my time. Continue," he cajoles.

I unbutton my pants and without thinking, I pull them down—nearly pulling my thong down too, which I stop and fix. *Stupid.* I'm about to be completely naked, so why does that matter? I'm just prolonging the inevitable.

I turn around and undo my bra, holding it over my

breasts as I turn back around to face him. He's holding his hand out. I close my eyes, take in a deep breath, and hand it to him. When I open my eyes, he's breathing in my scent.

"Mmmmm…so innocent. Smells like fresh flowers."

I look down and start to remove my thong, shaking.

"Look at me while you do that," he says sternly.

I stare at his stunning azure eyes, realizing he's controlling me as I slowly let them drop to the ground. Again, he holds out his hand. I pick them up and hand them to him. He smiles, and I glance outside the office, trying to ignore the heat in my face. No one seems to notice what we're doing. My pulse drops from an adagio beat to an andante.

He licks the crotch and moans as if he's just tasted the most delicious thing. "I guess not so innocent, being this wet," he comments.

I'm embarrassed, knowing he's right.

"Let's continue," he says.

I stand there shaking as he stares at me. "Turn around," he demands.

I quickly twirl.

"Slower, and try to be sexy."

I turn more slowly, and when my back is to him, he says, "Stop, bend over, grab your ass cheeks, and spread them wide."

I do as he says.

"Now stand and finish your sexy turn." I turn around and stare at him, biting my bottom lip.

"What do you want?" When I don't answer he prompts me. "Use your words."

"I want you," I rasp.

He grins like he just won the lottery. "Prove it to me."

He clears his desk and pats the spot in front of him. "Take a seat right here."

I step around to sit on it, knees at my chest and feet on the desk.

For the first time he touches me, his hands so close to

my pussy, but holding my ankles as he removes each sandal. The hair on the back of his hands brushes against me, and I nearly gasp, feeling sensitive all over.

"Spread your legs and show me how wet you are."

I adjust my legs and reach down to spread the lips of my pussy. Wetness drips down to my asshole. He leans forward, so close I can feel his breath, and softly blows on my clit. My nipples pebble, and I shudder in excitement.

"Do you play with this beautiful pussy?"

All I can do is nod.

"Remember, use your words. Do you or don't you, princess?" He stares at me sternly.

"Yes..."

"Yes what, princess?"

"I play with myself a lot, sir," I rush out.

Why did I say a lot? And why did I call him sir?

"Show me how, or this conversation is over."

With my legs still spread, I massage my breasts with one hand and reach down with the other to rub my clit. I close my eyes, trying to imagine he's the one doing this rather than watching.

"Open your eyes!" he demands.

My lids shoot open.

"So you want to be stripped, and what do you want me to do to you?"

I moan. "I want to feel you inside me."

His eyes become hooded, which distracts me.

"Don't stop what you're doing," he demands. "I want to watch you make yourself come."

I dip my fingers deep inside my wetness and circle my hard nub as I pull and twist my nipple.

He reaches for my wet hand and puts it in his mouth, licking my taste off of me. "Don't stop. Do you like a thick, fat cock buried deep inside you?"

"Yes...please..." He releases my hand, and my fingers return to tweaking my nipples and rubbing my clit like they have a mind of their own, pleasuring me for his sake, not mine.

He unbuckles his belt, and his pants fall to the floor. His black boxer briefs hug his bulbous cock. He's excited about this as well.

"Mmmmmm..." I writhe on his desk, biting my lip and losing control.

I close my eyes, and his hands touch me all over, moving from my neck to my tits. I'm not sure where he is, but his hands learn every inch of my body — my stomach, around to my hips, my back, the sides of my legs, and down to my ankles. Knowing people could be watching further excites me now.

My strength is going, and I lie back on the desk, legs still spread as he moves between them. I hold my ankles, hoping I don't fall off. All I can picture is this man, his head between my legs and his tongue circling the lips of my pussy — finding my clit, touching every inch of me like a blind man. Every time he hits my clit, electricity shoots through my body and I fight the urge to moan. Then another shock hits me when his tongue licks my asshole.

I'm so close. I'm almost there. He rubs his cock up and down my slit and pushes inside me.

My phone starts to ring, and I sit straight up. Only I'm not on a desk, I'm in my bed — and I'm no longer having the most delicious dream. I'm all wet and horny. Ever since I was with Jonnie last fall, I've had these naughty dreams. The scenario varies, but they're always hot and sexy.

"Hullo?" I groan into the phone.

"Are you still in bed?" my mother demands.

"Yes. Why do you care? It's Saturday morning, Mother. Can't I sleep in?"

"No! You were supposed to work out with Rachel at five and be meeting with the wedding planner in a half hour downtown."

I find the clock. I don't want to go. It'll be tight, and I'd rather stay here and continue my sexy dream. His face is never quite clear, but it's Jonnie's voice and eyes, so I'm always sure it's him.

"I'll be there. I'm just trying to psych myself up."

"Do what you have to do, and be on time," she says.

I roll my eyes as I hang up the phone. I adjust my cami, which has my boobs hanging out—and not in any appealing way. I truly don't want to meet the wedding planner. Alex is going as my buffer, but it's a waste of time. This marriage isn't real, and the wedding planner and my mother have already made all the decisions. I just need to know the day, time, and location.

There's a knock at my bedroom door.

"Come in," I mumble.

"Hello, my darling." Alex sweeps into the room, his hips swaying like he's dancing.

"What has you so chipper?"

"I hung out with Charles last night." He wiggles his eyebrows.

When I don't respond, he waves his hand at me. "Why aren't you ready? Trying to piss Mother off, are we?"

"No. I just was up half the night thinking about the mess we're in." I rub my eyes. "You adore your mother."

"Yes, but she mostly lives in Florida—far away from me and my father."

"That doesn't bother you?"

His face contorts. "No, why would it. They have a marriage in name only. They have their own lives and, when needed, they show up together. The only difference between their marriage and ours is that we'll always be friends."

Alex is my friend, but that honestly sounds terrible to me. I can't understand why it's remotely appealing to him.

∞

The rose smell in the air overwhelms me as I walk into the bridal boutique.

"You're late," Veronique, the planner, announces.

"Sorry," I mumble.

"Well, at least you're here. I've never had a bride less excited to get married."

"I guess you've never organized an arranged marriage?" I give her my best stink eye.

"Pish, pish." She rolls her eyes and swings at an imaginary fly. She takes in Alex, who is six-foot-two and has blond hair with a bit of curl on top, broad shoulders, and gorgeous blue eyes. "He's stunning, and you make a gorgeous couple. Love will come later."

Alex gives her a strained smile.

Rather than argue, I charge ahead. "What's on today's list?"

She smiles and leads us to a table with six bouquets of white roses. With her best Vanna White impression, she waves to the bouquets. "Which do you prefer?"

Is this some kind of joke? I examine them and don't notice any real differences. "They all look the same."

You would have thought I climbed on the table and shook my ta-tas in her face. Her lips purse like I squirted lemon juice from them into her mouth.

With a big sigh and a slap to her hips, she begins. "This first bouquet is a White Chocolate rose. The stems are captured with a blue satin ribbon. The second bouquet is a Polar Star rose, and the stems are bound with burlap and pearled pins. The third bouquet is the Tibet rose, and the stems are bound with white satin ribbon and a fine blue ribbon."

I couldn't care less. "You showed me the bouquet my mother wants. Why have we changed our minds?"

She yammers on, explaining the differences between the six bouquets. I'm only half listening.

"Why the light blue ribbon? Is that for 'something

blue'?"

A guttural growl emerges from Veronique. "No. It's the color your bridesmaids are wearing."

"I thought they were wearing lavender?"

"That was last week. I sent you an email on the change."

I stare down at my shoe and toe the design in the handwoven carpet, praying for strength.

"Which bouquet?"

I point to one.

"Oh, I love the Mondial rose," she says. "It's so beautiful, and the dark green satin ribbon makes it look like you're just holding stems." She turns to Alex. "Isn't she going to be beautiful?"

Alex puts his arms around me. "She's always beautiful."

Somehow it takes four hours to get through all the decisions Veronique and my mother have already made.

As we prepare to leave, Veronique hands me a list. "Here's the list of guests your families have provided for the wedding. Please let me know if you're adding anyone else."

I take the stack of paper, which is over an inch thick. I thumb through the pages of names. I'm puzzled.

"They're listed in alphabetical order, according to whose list they came from," Veronique explains. "Once we receive their affirmative response, we'll begin planning the tables. We're expecting twelve hundred guests."

I told my mother this was to be no more than two hundred people—that was *plenty big*, I stressed to her. Did she listen? No. My blood pressure skyrockets. I'm over this. I'm going along with this charade; the least she could do is the one simple thing I've asked.

Tucking the list in my bag, I throw it over my shoulder. Alex has been reading something on his phone and stands. He thanks Veronique, and we leave the store.

"Can you believe they've invited over twelve hundred

people?"

"That is a lot." He stops and gives me a hug. "Look, I left something at Charles' last night. I need to run. Can you grab a rideshare home?"

Fantastic. This is the life I'm getting. "Sure," I say, fighting back tears.

∞

When I walk in the door at home, the house is quiet. I'm not sure where Hazel is, but something smells delicious in the kitchen.

I walk down to the wine cellar, find myself an expensive bottle of pinot gris, and head to my room before I even put my bag down.

I open my phone and read back through months of texts between me and Jonnie. I hate this so much. I find a glass of what I hope is water, dump it down my bathroom sink, and open the bottle, refilling the glass.

The cool wine sits in my mouth for mere seconds, and I hardly taste it. The second swig I savor a minute before swallowing.

I've always been a rule follower. Christopher was so upset with my parents when we were growing up that he emancipated himself, and before that he split his time between Jonnie's and his bedroom here. Hazel would sneak him in and out before my mother came home.

Stevie, my younger brother, was no better. I think he was high for most of high school. According to my dad, he spent his inheritance before he was twenty on booze, drugs, and women. But he did get to live in Hawaii for a few years.

I remember the strain my brothers' behavior caused, so I wanted to be good, not a troublemaker. I've always done what my parents told me. And look where that got me. Now I'm thinking that may not have been the best plan.

The bottle is well over half gone. My head is no longer hurting, and I feel a bit tipsy and ready for dinner with my mother. It's only the two of us tonight. My least favorite.

I walk downstairs and hear her laughing. The ice queen never laughs. We must be having dinner with someone. Hmm.... I can't quite place the voice until I round the corner and see Alex and his father, Herbert.

I'm in sweatpants with *Juicy* plastered on my ass. They're from about six seasons ago, but I love how comfortable they are. And I'm not wearing a bra, so the girls are on high beams. My thought was they'd be a nice *fuck you* to my mother, but now I'm feeling a bit underdressed.

"I didn't realize we were expecting guests," I say.

My mother looks at me with disdain. "I told you last week and again this morning."

"I'll run upstairs and change," I offer.

"You look beautiful just the way you are." Alex steps in and kisses me on the cheek. "And you're ahead on the drinks," he whispers.

"Yes, that's right. You look beautiful," Herbert says, staring at my tits.

Alex's father has had multiple liaisons and makes the gossip columns regularly. Yuck!

We sit at the table, and Hazel pours me a glass of water. She must know I got the bottle of wine.

Alex sits next to me, and our parents sit next to each other across the table from us. "So, tell us, how did it go with Veronique today?" my mother prompts.

I nod. "I finalized the roses for my bouquet, and she did another round of measurements."

My mother grins. "I told her you were on a diet so she should check."

I feel my face heat.

"She's perfect just the way she is." Alex's father gives me a lecherous grin as he stares at my tits again.

I don't know what to say to that. I squirm in my seat.

Hazel reappears and sets down a pear and Gorgonzola salad with my favorite candied pecans. I'm starved.

"Is that on her diet?" my mother asks.

"Yes, ma'am. She's fine." Hazel winks at me, and I dig in.

Dinner is a parade of snarky comments, and Herbert continues to stare at my tits. I swear he even licks his lips while we go through their plans. My mother giggles like a schoolgirl with Alex's dad, and I'm grossed out.

When dinner is over, Alex and I excuse ourselves to my room.

"I hope you wear a condom," his father calls.

"Oh, she's on birth control," my mother assures him.

Alex turns a shade of green.

"We can run away," I tell him as I flop down on my bed.

"If only it was that easy," he says.

"Do you really want to go through with this?" I ask.

"It's not like we have a choice."

Chapter 9

Jonathan

After a busy couple of weeks, a high-stakes Texas Hold'em poker tournament is exactly what I need to distract me. It's Saturday, and the players are scheduled to arrive today for the weekend. I'm most excited to hang out with Christopher again. Maybe I'll find a way to bring up Maggie in conversation and get his take on her situation without tipping my hand.

I'm also just looking forward to watching them play. When money isn't the object, winning comes from outthinking some of the most strategic minds of our time, and it's inspiring. Plus, I figure they'll be bragging about their investments, and I'll be taking notes. Geniuses—all of them.

They should be here any time now, and we've got the poker room all set up. It's private and easy for security to keep would-be onlookers out.

I spot Gillian getting everything organized. "Are we all set?"

"Yep. I have Frannie at table one and Laura at table two. The players can figure out who they want to sit with on their own. Donna is at the bar, and Michael and Wendy are here to make sure anything they need or want is within reach."

"Perfect. Last time they did this, I watched a player take the majority share of an up-and-coming startup and end up making millions."

Finn was thankfully only an investor and laughed it off when he lost.

"I remember," Gillian says with a laugh. "Like Nate Lancaster needed any more money."

A little while later, I begin greeting everyone as they arrive, and we all drink expensive Scotch and enjoy catching up. It's easy to understand why they relish times like this to get together. This is a rare opportunity for them to catch up without the swarming chatter of fans surrounding them. Many have brought spouses or significant others, and a few already hang out together, like Christopher's wife, Bella, and Nate's wife, Cecelia. But others are more just ornaments—like Jackson's girlfriend. She's obviously spent a lot of time with a plastic surgeon. I'm not sure she can close her lips with all the collagen. And her tits are big and don't point down.

I walk over to Bella and kiss her cheek. "So glad to have you back."

"Where's *my* love?" Cecelia teases.

"Right here." I open my arms wide, and she walks in for a hug and a kiss on both cheeks.

"Someone's trying to snake your wife out from under you," Jackson Graham calls to Nate. Jackson has a progressive environmental startup that seems to be making money faster than they can print it, as my father would say.

Gillian helps everyone get settled and makes sure their needs are being met. These are her whales, and by the end of the tournament she'll probably clear six figures in tips — which she'll graciously share with her team.

As the players sit down, there's an empty spot.

"Jonathan, we're short a player until Landon arrives," Walker Clifton says. "You can use his money. Care to join us?"

I laugh. "Are you sure? I don't want to be responsible for bankrupting him."

Walker slaps the seat next to him. "Park it here. Go ahead. Go all in on a shitty hand and he'll learn not to take a business call. Or you could pony up yourself. I wouldn't mind owning this beautiful resort."

I laugh, but that will never happen. I've worked too hard to lose everything in a poker game. "You wouldn't want the headache and lack of social life that comes with it," I assure him.

The room erupts in laughter, and I allow myself to ease into the game. The flop saves me on the first hand, and I actually win.

"Looks like the house may be rigging it," Mia Couture teases. She owns a lucrative data mining company that's often on the wrong side of federal regulators. But I don't think it's her fault that people put everything on the internet.

"Pure luck," I tell her.

We play two more hands, and I lose everything I'd won. Landon returns and seems content to watch me play, but I don't want the stress of losing someone else's money. I get up and show him to his chair.

"Thank you for sitting in for me," he says. "I appreciate the help."

I nod. "You're even. I won once and lost the last two."

He clasps his hands together and cracks his knuckles. "Ladies and gentlemen, I just agreed to the sale of my prize company, and I'm now six billion dollars richer. I'm in this game to win it."

The room crackles with energy. Christopher grins at me and shakes his head. We both know that for several at the table, the game just got a heck of a lot more expensive. But a few million dollars isn't much to these high rollers.

This is a different world than mine. Christopher is easily a billionaire, and while he inherited his starter money from his grandfather, he's worked hard for what he has—which is a booming venture capital company—and he uses his fortune as he pleases for the most part. The rest of his family is fiercely protective of their wealth. They view money as something that brings a level of privilege and entry into the right circles, and there's an unwritten rule that requires their money to move from generation to generation. They have no patience for people they see as "new money." This is a huge part of Maggie's disaster right now.

People like Nate Lancaster who've earned their fortune themselves and seem focused on giving much of it away are "new money," as far as the Reinhardts are concerned, and not to be taken seriously. Nate and Cecelia have a foundation that gives money to schools all over the world to level the playing field in technology. His company also provides dynamic prostheses to landmine survivors, and they're working in third world countries to eradicate polio. The Lancasters earned their wealth through calculated risks and view it as a gift that needs to be shared. Very different. Maggie's right that she's the only one who cares about keeping the Reinhardt Foundation in operation.

Over the next six hours, Nate loses his private plane and Landon Walsh loses a beautiful piece of property in Aspen. He inherited his billions and plays around with several companies in the tech field. They slowly whittle down to one table of six players, but they're still going strong.

Christopher bowed out relatively early. He still lost five million dollars, but he assured me his most recent bonus was much larger than that. He said Bella wasn't crazy about the spend, but she'd told him it was his money.

"Let's go hang out," he urges. Watching people — even these people — play poker is not that thrilling after a while.

I nod and lead him to the VIP lounge. There are some gaming tables there, and a few people play twenty-one at two hundred dollars a hand.

Christopher pulls me into a corner to catch up.

"We're trying hard to have a baby," he announces. "Don't get me wrong, I love all the practice, but it's becoming stressful."

I crack a smile as I nod. "I don't feel bad about the practice, but I *am* sorry it's not happening as quickly as you'd like."

"We may see a fertility specialist. We joke that if we were twenty and drug addicts, we'd have no problem getting pregnant."

I shake my head. "Can you remember sex ed in high school? They made getting pregnant sound so easy."

"It probably was in those days." He snorts.

"I remember wearing two raincoats whenever I had sex. I wasn't taking any chances."

He laughs. "Remember when you didn't realize you'd lost one of those raincoats and Tiffany found it later?"

The thought gives me a chill. "Oh, God. That was a mess. She was so stressed she'd end up pregnant, she started to plan our wedding."

"That's right! I forgot about the wedding. That thing was huge. Well, at least she made me best man."

"You'd still be my best man," I assure him.

There's a lull in our conversation as I mentally sort through the crazy girls from high school, and Christopher probably does the same.

"So, tell me what's going on," he says after a few minutes.

"Not much, really. I'm just trying to take it one day at a

time. The Shangri-la is doing fantastic, probably thanks to you. I couldn't have planned a bigger public relations splash than to have half of Silicon Valley here—along with U2—for your corporate meeting before we were even officially open."

"I seem to remember you recently said you created this place for a woman."

I shrink back in my seat. I didn't mean to let that out of the bag—particularly to him. No one else knows the truth behind the Shangri-la. On the other hand, the thought of Maggie trapped with Alex makes me nauseous. Nothing I say is working, but maybe together, Christopher and I could find a way to get her out of it.

"I did tell you that." I take a deep breath. "I mean...you know..." He stares at me patiently, and I finally give in. "I've loved her from afar for a very long time. She didn't know, apparently. I'm not the best communicator. But I made design decisions for this place based on what I thought she'd like."

Christopher grins like a Cheshire cat. "I don't think a woman has ever had so much power over you. Isn't it awesome to be in love?"

A real sense of relief washes over me, because it's taken me a long time to realize that is what I feel for Maggie. "I've known for a while she's the one for me."

"Great. How are you doing convincing her of that? Did you ever go see her?"

I look down. "No."

Christopher sits up straight. "What? How is that even possible? You've got to be kidding. I know you, man. When you want something, you go after it. What's holding you back?" He looks around the lounge. "I mean, show her this place. Shower her with flowers and fight for her. If you love this woman half as much as you say you do, don't give up. Bella tried to run from me, and I fought for her."

"I'll think about it."

He slaps me on the back. "Good. But you've been thinking a while now. Might be good to move on to something else. Now, what do you want to do?"

I glance at my watch. "I think your loser college team is playing in the sportsbook."

"My Tarheels are going to win it all again this year."

Our conversation then switches to men's college basketball, and I'm saved before I start babbling that it's his *sister* I did all this for.

We walk over to the sportsbook and spend the evening enjoying some drinks and college ball. The Tarheels are slaughtering their opponent. I stop drinking as the second half starts and instead knock back a few waters. When the game ends, it's after eleven, and I have a morning meeting for breakfast.

"I'm going to head up to my apartment," I tell Christopher.

"Thanks, man. I'm done myself. Bella texted me she's back at the room. I should go too." He takes the last pull of his drink and stands to walk with me.

As we weave our way through the casino and lobby to his room and my apartment, I'm stopped twice by people who recognize me. In both cases, they're drunk gamblers who want pictures with me. Christopher is a great sport and takes photos that aren't too bad. But when a drunk woman asks me to sign her chest, I politely decline.

"I didn't realize I knew a rock star," Christopher teases.

I laugh. In a different crowd, I'd be invisible. It's mostly just drunk people who get excited to see me. "I have an early meeting, and then we have a tee time at nine," I tell him. "Lola must have figured you'd lose the first round, and we'd have a late night."

"Oh man! That hurts. See if I bring her flowers again." He chuckles. "She knows us too well."

"We can meet down here about eight-thirty, and the second round of the tournament starts in the late afternoon. You going to watch how it all shakes out?"

"Ab-so-fucking-lutely," he says. "I'm pulling for

Viviana to take it all."

I nod as I turn and I walk away. "Text me in the morning when you get going."

"Sure. I think Bella wants some quality time with me by the pool sometime tomorrow. I can do that in the afternoon before the tournament."

"She's seen you naked, right?"

His eyebrow rises.

"Man, you don't tan," I explain. "You turn a nice lobster red."

A grin bursts out, and he pushes my shoulder. "Get out of here. My wife in a bikini is a sight to behold—and you need to stay away. Fuck off."

I flip him the bird. "See you tomorrow."

I send Christopher off to his elevator and his wife and decide I should check in at the private poker room before heading to my apartment.

Gillian is there setting up for tomorrow with Vincent, the pit boss.

"How did it end up?" I ask.

"I think everyone is happy. No significantly bruised egos...yet," she says.

"I've got to be honest, boss. These guys throw in some serious shit," Vincent adds. "I left after the plane and Aspen property changed hands."

"How bad did it get?" I ask. "I'm always worried they'll throw in wives, girlfriends, or children. That would get my gaming license pulled if it were to get out."

"There was talk about nights with women," Gillian says, shaking her head.

My stomach turns.

"But a nasty look from Nate shut that down."

"That's good. That can't be happening."

"The bets are getting aggressive, though," Vincent says. "I suspect we'll see some pieces of companies exchange hands. A two-hundred-acre ranch in Montana was up for grabs tonight."

I shake my head in disbelief. Too much money with too little consequence.

"They're all trying to show who has the bigger dick," Gillian snarks.

A whiteboard on the wall lists all the players and where they're sitting money wise. Mia's ended up after the last hand—she's at the top of the board and two pieces of property richer, plus the controlling share of a successful electronics company.

"Looks to me like tonight's winner doesn't have a dick," I note.

"I watched her in the last hand. She had some decent cards, but I don't think she had the best ones. She's the biggest risk-taker of them all." Gillian grins. "I aspire to be that woman."

"Let's see how it ends up tomorrow," Vincent warns.

When I finally get to my apartment, it's after midnight. In the quiet, I can hear Christopher's advice echoing in my head. I need to make a move. No standing back. If I want Maggie in my life, I need to make that clear and fight for her. It's late, but after I change into more comfortable clothes, I text her anyway.

Me: Hay.

Maggie: Isn't hay for horses?

I grin. Not only is she up but she's calling me on my typo. My cock twitches in my boxers. God, I wish she was here. I want to ask her so many questions.

But she's not here, and based on recent experience, I

need to ease into this and somehow gain her trust or she'll shut down the conversation completely. Maybe instead of arguing, I'll try to remind her of how I know she feels about me.

Me: I wish you were here.

Maggie: Me, too.

All these delicious thoughts run through my head. I'd love to see her bright blue eyes widen as I push into her.

Me: What are you wearing?

Maggie: Clothes.

I snort. She isn't going to make this easy. But I'm going to convince her she belongs with me.

Me: You're making this very hard, you know.

Maggie: We had fun when you were hard... ;) And I am never easy.

There we go..

Me: Have you ever been easy?

Maggie: Are we playing Have You Ever?

This could get interesting. My cock twitches again. Yes, very interesting.

Me: I wasn't but I am now.

Me: Well?

I force myself to wait for her answer. I don't want to go too hard at it. I need to go slow.

Maggie: Only with you.

Maggie: My turn. Have you ever had sex in a car?

She's younger than Christopher and me, but I'm sure she heard stories when we were in school.

Me: In high school.

Maggie: I was only checking the rumor. Have you ever had sex with any of my friends?

This could go the wrong way. I need to ask *her* questions.

Me: In high school. My turn. Have you kissed any of my friends?

Maggie: Nope. We all know your only friend is my brother. Eww.

I like that she's funny.

Me: I have friends other than Christopher, but the idea of you kissing him does skeeve me out. Didn't you kiss Tommy Rogers?

She was all hot for Tommy when we were in school. Christopher heard her telling one of her friends she was planning on losing her virginity to him. We put a stop to that.

Maggie: He flirted with me, and you and Christopher

beat the crap out of him. No other guy would look twice at me after that. You are personally responsible for my lack of experience with boys in high school.

That makes me feel a little proud.

Me: I'll happily take that. How old were you when you lost your virginity?

Maggie: Doesn't matter. We all know when you did. All the girls used to talk about you and Christopher. I think they did it to make sure I knew.

Me: Most of them were lying. I'll keep asking until you tell me.

Maggie: When was the first time you had sex with two girls?

This was a huge lie when we were in high school.

Me: I did not have sex with Christy Hansen and Jennifer Duval together.

Maggie: Okay.

Again, I need to shift this back to her.

Me: Do you masturbate?

Maggie: Of course. Masturbation's very natural you know.

I think back to her luscious body and my hands running all over it. My cock is hard in my gym shorts.

Me: Have you ever performed for someone?

Maggie: Don't you remember? I'm pretty shy. No performing.

She was a little shy, but so beautiful. She should be proud of her body.

Me: You've got a beautiful body.

Maggie: That's not what my mother tells me.

Her mother is a critical bitch, and I hate what she does to Maggie.

Me: Forget your mother. You've got great curves and amazing soft white tits with sweet little pink nipples. You're stunning naked and with clothes. I'm getting hard just thinking about when we were together.

Maggie: Have you ever considered body piercings?

Me: Who says I don't have one?

Maggie: I must have missed your Prince Albert.

The image alone makes my cock hurt, and the idea of getting the head of it pierced makes me shrink. Is that what she wants? She didn't strike me as kinky, but I could like kink.

Me: Would it turn you on to have a piece of metal rubbing up and down your g-spot while fucking me?

Maggie: xyaigh

Me: What does that mean?

Me: Answer the question.

Maggie: I'm busy.

It takes her a minute to respond. There's a two-hour time difference, so it's quite late where she is.

Me: Are you alone?

Maggie: Hold

Me: ???

It takes a few minutes. Did I get her in trouble with her mother?

Maggie: I got so excited I had to take care of myself.

Me: Are you fucking with me?

Maggie: No, but I wish.

My cock aches, and I want to put it inside her so badly right now.

Me: When can I see you?

Nothing.

Me: Will you come back to Vegas and visit me?

Maggie: I can't. It wouldn't be a good idea. I'm getting married.

Me: What can I do to stop this?

Maggie: You can't.

I can't take it anymore, so I call her. It rings four times before she answers. I begin to wonder if she isn't alone.

"Hello?"

"Let's sit down with Christopher and Stevie. We can fix this. Please. I beg you. Don't marry Alex."

She's quiet for a few moments. "I'm sorry," she whispers, and the phone line goes dead.

In the morning, it suddenly comes to me during my meeting. Christopher is right. I need to go to Maggie. I need to get to Minneapolis to see Maggie and have a conversation. It's important that she understands how I feel and that I need her in my life. Maybe that will give her the strength to fight this situation.

Suddenly I'm more assured and determined than I've ever been. Now I need to figure out when I can get out of here.

When the meeting concludes, I zip back to my office before meeting Christopher for golf, and log in to check the manifest for the hotel's private jet—it's in the clear starting tomorrow. We usually use it when we need to bring in whales, but the next two we're expecting are flying in on their own private jets. I don't have to worry about preventing money from entering the hotel if I borrow the plane.

I grab the phone and dial Gillian. "Hey, I'd like to go home for a few days. The plane looks free tomorrow. Does it have anything going I don't know about?"

"No, but if you fly out, I may be able to talk someone I've been working on into coming back with you for a few days. Is everything okay with your parents?"

"Yes, I just need to take care of something, and it's better to do it in person."

"No problem," she assures me. "Will we see you today?"

"Of course. I'll stop by later before the tournament starts again. I'm playing golf this morning with Christopher."

"No problem. Be sure to hit them long and straight."

Chapter 10

Maggie

On Sunday, after a reasonably leisurely morning, I sit in a café, in the back, drinking a nice cool glass of pinot grigio and waiting for Alex. I keep thinking about my conversation with Jonnie. It killed me to hang up on him, and talking to him just reminds me what I'm never going to have. I cried myself to sleep last night. My eyes are dry, and my throat is sore today.

Alex enters the café and heads my direction. He kisses me on the cheek with a grin that reaches from ear to ear.

"Hello, my lovely. I just left Charles." He sits down and leans in. "He was amazing last night."

I force a smile and take a deep pull on my wine.

Normally these comments don't bother me—Alex is who he is—but right now they sting. This doesn't seem nearly as hard on him as it is on me.

He looks at me with a wrinkle in his brow. "What's wrong?"

I look away. I'm not sure hashing this out with him is going to make me feel any better. I just don't think he gets it. No one does.

"We've been best friends forever," he prods. "Don't start holding out on me now."

I fight the tears I can feel behind my eyes. "As much as I care about you, the thought of marrying you makes me sad," I tell him. "And I don't feel like our upcoming wedding is upsetting to you in the same way it is me. That makes me feel really alone."

He sighs, and when I look over at him, his expression is unreadable.

"I understand you and Charles are tight, and that's certainly fine," I tell him. "But if I marry you, I don't think I'm ever going to have something like that in my life."

He shrugs, picking at a packet of sugar on the table. "I've told you you'll be free to live your life as you see fit. This is a business arrangement. We both know that. But it just has to happen. I'll help you any way I can." He sighs again. "We can move into my family home. My mother is essentially living down in Boca, and once the business moves over to us, my dad may join her."

"What about Charles?" I ask.

"What we do in our house is up to us." He says it so simply, as if it actually were true. "Our parents lead separate lives. I guess I expect us to do the same, but at least be friends."

I sigh. "I want more than friendship. I want intimacy. A family unit. Love." The tears build again, and I'm not sure I can stop them if they start.

He shrugs. "It may not be perfect, but I won't be

stopping you from getting as close to that as you can. I love you. We're going to get through this and put on a happy face for our families, high society, and all the vultures who are looking to pull us apart. This will all work out fine. I promise."

He squeezes me tight, and the waitress puts down another glass and a bottle of pinot grigio.

"It looked like you needed this." She winks at me, and I force a smile.

"Thank you. You read my mind."

"If you want, you can even move Richard and Hazel into our house," he says with a wave of his hand. "I know you love them. Your mother will hate the idea, but she'll get over it. Once the business transitions, she'll probably want to move south anyway. She'll never miss them. Stevie and his girlfriend can move into your family home and hire their own staff."

At times like these, Alex drives me crazy. He can be so cavalier when it comes to these huge decisions—like these things have never occurred to him as important before.

He also definitely underestimates my mother. I have no doubt she plans on sticking around and micromanaging me and any and all decisions I make

"This wedding is stressing you out," he says, shaking his head. "Leave it to your mother and the pros. Go out. Have some fun. Go get laid, for God's sake. It'll do your icky mood some good."

I give him the go-fuck-yourself-and-die look. He *so* does not understand anything I'm trying to explain.

"Jesus. Okay, don't go get laid and stay in your mood." He throws up his hands. "We're best friends. We love spending time together, so that isn't an issue. I was telling Charles the other day how much fun we have." He bats his eyelashes at me. "We'll attend all the social events together, hold hands, play kissy face, and do our thing."

He acts like everything is going to be so simple. How

can this be enough for him?

"How does Charles feel about not being able to express his feelings towards you in public?"

"He understands that our marriage is arranged and we don't have anything to say about it—the entire charade is for legal and business reasons. He's clear that he and I will be monogamous. He also understands that our marriage needs to look authentic, so he can't be hanging all over me in public." Alex scans the room and makes sure no one is eavesdropping. "Mags, it's not like we were ever popular enough that anybody would care."

I take a breath. It's hard to muster the energy to fight this. He's obviously not going to fight it with me—or even understand why I would want to.

"What we do behind closed doors is between us," he reminds me again. "I'm giving you carte blanche to have affairs."

I rest my head in my hands for a moment. Right now Alex actually sounds like my mother. She recently told me marrying for love would be a colossal waste—and she was kind enough to point out that I wasn't likely to have any prospects anyway. She believes my place in the family is to be married to the right person, who has the proper pedigree, and offers something to the success of the family business. Evidently that's what Alex thinks too.

No part of me wants to do this, but after this conversation, I'm not about to tell Alex about my situation with Jonnie. He seems all in on our marriage, which means he might go running to my mother. And nothing good could come from my mother knowing about Jonnie. She destroys everything in her path.

After lunch, Alex drives me back to my house. My

mother is waiting for us in the foyer. I drop my purse on the table and kiss her on the cheek. She lights up when she sees Alex.

"Alex, so wonderful to see you," she says, sounding just as fake as she does when she *doesn't* mean what she says.

They air kiss each other's cheeks. Alex squeezes my hand and winks at me.

"Darling, how was your lunch?" she asks.

"It was fine. I drank too much wine, so Alex drove me home."

I love that her face becomes hard. She doesn't enjoy anything in life, so excess is a completely foreign concept. I take great pride in the way she purses her lips because it will cause wrinkles.

Alex takes this as his cue and quickly escapes.

"What were you two up to at lunch that had you drinking so much?" Her face contorts as if she's taken a bite of lemon. "You realize alcohol is bad for your skin and isn't on your diet."

I take a deep breath and decide I can be just as bitchy as she is. It's only proof that I got some Hudson genes from her. "We're working out the rules of our impending nuptials."

She stands straight and her left eyebrow arches. "Rules? You're married. You find a way to live as a couple. Your father and I did it, as do Alex's parents, Jacqueline and Herbert. You'll have babies, and the businesses will combine."

"Mom, you realize Alex and I have zero interest in consummating this relationship. He's gay. It could mean I never have children," I taunt.

She snorts. "Nonsense. That's just silly. He'll change his mind."

"Mom, he's not going to change his mind, and I don't want to be stuck like you were in a loveless marriage."

She gets all stiff and hoity-toity. "Our relationship wasn't loveless. Your father and I had great respect and admiration for one another. This is how we do things and how we protect the family legacy."

I have just enough liquid courage to be brutally honest with her. "Mom, there has to be another way. I don't want to do this."

"You don't have a choice."

"I'm over eighteen. You bet your ass I have a choice. And while Alex may be resigned to this sham of a wedding, I'm not."

She takes a big breath, and I'm ready to be verbally bludgeoned. I watch her figure out how to make me do something I don't want to do.

"You love Alex, and this is essential for the future of Reinhardt's," she tells me.

"I do love him, but not as a husband. I love him like I love Christopher and Stevie. The business will go on without a family member chairing the board for the time being, and without Elite. We could fight that marriage clause in the will, and then I'd be happy to do the job." I take a deep breath. "You need to cancel the wedding unless you plan on being embarrassed in front of all your society friends. I won't be showing up."

I turn and walk upstairs to my room. I lie on my bed with a bottle of water from the mini fridge. I wish I could be this honest with her all the time. It's quite a strange feeling, actually. She makes it so hard to tolerate her. Now I need to prepare for the fallout.

∞

When I wake Monday morning, I find a manila envelope under my door. My mother's passive-aggressive way to confirm my participation in this wedding is inside the envelope, and it turns my stomach.

"Bitch," I say out loud, but only the spiders hiding in the corners of my room hear.

I make myself a coffee and sit down to read through the documents.

The largest stack is my father's will. It was read to us when he died, so there are no surprises. The fact that he gave a quarter of his estate to his secretary, Nancy, and a quarter to each of his children was a bit shocking originally, but I've since realized Nancy was my father's soul mate and love of his life. She wasn't just an affair. It makes me wish I'd gotten to know their son, Murphy, better. But he died a few years ago—or at least we were told he did.

My mother has taken the liberty of highlighting the portions of the will that stipulate that the company must be managed by a married heir to my father. Otherwise, the company must be liquidated, including the Reinhardt Foundation.

Next is a promissory note that indicates a significant loan from the Foundation to Herbert Walker, Alex's dad, which is completely illegal and could send me to jail. The document has my signature, but anyone can tell it's a forgery. At least I hope they can. *Really, Mother?* This is the most troubling item so far.

Underneath this is a second stack of promissory notes, each signed by Alex for withdrawals against his inheritance. He's mentioned his financial troubles before, but I didn't think it was anything like this. Thumbing through the stack, it seems the totals are well over a million dollars. What is he doing with all this money? I flip through again, and the signatures look authentic. Mine was forged, though, so who knows. *Is this really your signature, Alex?* I can't imagine a conversation with him about this will go well. And I guess this is supposed to make me feel guilty about leaving him financially destitute if we don't marry. But I'm not sure it's having that effect.

I don't know what to think right now.

I read everything again, stuff it back in the envelope, and feel even angrier about this situation. I fucking hate my mother. And I'm pissed at my dad, who could have taken out the marriage provision before he died, but he didn't. He knew my passion was running the Foundation. Why doesn't anyone ever consider Stevie to run the company? Okay, actually I know why. He skipped college in favor of spending his inheritance, and he was high for probably the entire time he lived in Hawaii. Not great qualifications for running a corporation. I scream out my frustration to no one in particular.

Then I take a deep breath, and prepare to start my day, dutiful daughter that I am. Honestly, the Foundation is probably my one rebellion. I get in the shower and try to wash away my anger. It doesn't work. Instead I dream of running off and hiding from every last bit of this. Let them try to find me.

When I'm still raging as I dry off, I conclude that I'm not going to be much good at working today. Alex told me he was spending the day at the Lakes Spa… Maybe he was on to something.

Chapter 11

Jonathan

On Monday morning, I arrive at the office shortly after Lola does.

"How was the tournament?" she asks.

"Excellent. Mia Couture won the whole thing. It was fantastic to see. I've decided to run home to Minneapolis today. Can you clear my schedule for a day or two?"

She pulls up my calendar and pokes around on her computer for a moment. "I can, except you have a meeting with the Nevada Gaming Commission. They won't wait. Should I have Daniel Peters in gaming cover that?"

"Yes, and if Gillian can be there, that would be ideal. That way gaming and guest relations are represented."

She agrees, and after we touch base about a few other things, I head into my office. Confident things will be under control for a few days, I focus on the task at hand. I could hardly sleep last night—I'm so keyed up about seeing Maggie. Face to face, surely I can convince her to change her plans and give us a chance.

I arrange a car for my arrival and a place to stay. Less than an hour after that, my bodyguard Caden and I board my jet for the flight from McCarran to Minneapolis.

"Would you like a drink or a snack, Mr. Best?" the flight attendant asks.

I give her my order, and she brings me Johnnie Walker Blue neat with a warmed bowl of mixed nuts. "Thank you, Nicole."

I have plenty of work to do, but instead I think what's about to happen. If Maggie doesn't want to marry me right away—or ever—I'll understand. But I convinced the bank to loan me almost a billion dollars to build my hotel. I convinced my team we'd create something different and original, and clearly we did. Maggie still seems to have feelings for me, so I just need to talk her into fighting this ridiculous wedding.

My ride is waiting when we arrive in Minneapolis, and once I settle in the backseat, with Caden up front, I text Maggie.

Me: Hey, what are you up to this afternoon?

Maggie: I'm taking a me day at the Lakes Spa.

That would be a nice place to surprise her...

Me: What are you doing at Lakes?

Maggie: I'm getting a massage and maybe a Brazilian.

I almost choke.

Me: Really? Any chance I might get to see it?

Maggie: Only if you're going to be local.

I smile. *Oh, there's a sliver of light at the door. I'm going to kick it down.*

Me: I might be able to make a trip for that.

Maggie: It's not nice to tease me.

Rather than respond, I give the driver directions to the Lakes Spa. It's not far from where we grew up. I sent my spa manager from the Shangri-la here and to a few of the other top spas in the country when we were looking for what we wanted in our spa.

The car drops me off. I leave Caden behind and enter the building. Immediately scented candles and soft music wash over me, and I feel right at home, despite being in dress pants and a pressed shirt with the sleeves rolled up.

"Welcome to the Lakes Spa," a woman whose name tag reads Heather says.

"Hello. I have a friend enjoying the spa that I'd like to surprise. May I go back?"

"Do you have an appointment?"

I give her my best smile, which usually works on women. "I don't, but—"

"I'm sorry, sir," she interrupts. "Without an appointment, I can't allow you back."

I hadn't thought about that, and we'd do the same at the Shangri-la. I try to gloss over the fact that she called me *sir*. I'm not that much older than she is.

"Okay, that makes sense. Do you have any treatments available that would give me access to the spa?"

She sets an appointment for me. I can always blow it off

if I can talk Maggie into stepping away with me. It'll be worth it to see her and the look of surprise on her face.

I follow a man in white yoga pants to the dressing room, where he shows me my locker and the sauna. I quickly change into a robe and go in search of my surprise, slipping my cell phone into my pocket.

I walk into the large central area. Soft water trickling plays over the loudspeakers, and the two grand fireplaces are crackling. I scan the room, which is dotted with people drinking water and wine, leafing through magazines, and reading books. I finally spot her. She's sitting with Alex, and my stomach drops. *Fuck!*

Before I can decide how to play this, she sees me. Her eyes go wide, and her face lights up. I can't very well back out now.

She stands up and we meet in the middle of the room. "What are you doing here?" She hugs me, pressing the softness of her breasts against me, and it takes all my self-control to not pull her out of here and take her to my hotel immediately.

"You said I should come see you," I murmur.

"I'm glad you're here." She turns and says, "You remember Alex from school, don't you?"

"Nice to see you again, Alex."

"Jonathan, the *big* casino owner in Vegas." He doesn't seem very happy I'm here. He'd probably be less happy if he knew my plan.

"Well, we call it a resort."

He nods, and the only thing we haven't done is pull our dicks out and measure them. This is a mistake, and I need to leave. I shouldn't be here. I want to fight for Maggie, but I don't want to put her on the spot with her fake fiancé sitting next to her.

"My, don't you look handsome," Alex says. "How are things going at that *resort* of yours? I would love to see it sometime." His eyes roam up and down and settle on my cock, hidden behind the robe. He's definitely talking about more than my resort.

I paint a smile on my face. "You're welcome anytime. Let me know and I'm happy to set up the VIP treatment for you."

Maggie's name is called over the intercom.

"Will you be here when I get done?" she asks.

I nod. "I plan to be. If for some reason you don't see me, it's because I'm in my own appointment, but we can meet back here."

She flashes me a brilliant smile. "Great. Have a glass of wine, relax, and enjoy yourself. I'll be back."

Alex's name is called next. "See you in ninety minutes." He waves as he walks away.

I'm relieved I don't have to sit here and make conversation with him. My name is called next, and a woman takes me to a pedicure chair. I feel silly, but it was the only thing available that would get me beyond the check-in desk.

"What color would you like?" the nail tech asks.

I give her my choice and sit in the vibrating chair, not sure if my nuts are going to go numb. My feet are extra sensitive, so I jump about ten feet when she rubs them with a pumice stone. It tickles. This is why I usually avoid pedicures like the plague.

This is not relaxing at all. How do people do this all the time?

When I'm done, I walk carefully back out to the waiting area and grab a copy of the *Star Tribune* sports section. I love the hometown news on my favorite teams. The Twins are already in the middle of the pack, and they've only been playing a week or so this season. I can't remember if they're home this week; that could be fun, if I can talk Maggie into joining me. I understand sporting events are good dates.

Alex joins me after a few minutes. "Gawd, I love a deep massage."

I nod. "I sent the head of my spa here to check out the

amenities when we were getting started. I think when you come to the Shangri-la, you'll enjoy our spa, too."

"That sounds wonderful. Maggie and I should make plans to come soon. She's been bouncing back and forth to San Francisco working on something for Bullseye or the Foundation or something."

"Yep. She's headed there in a few weeks to deal with the expansion. Can you believe all the locations they have this year?"

"How was your massage?" he asks, changing the subject.

"Didn't have one. I was a walk-in, and the only service they had was a pedicure."

"Oh, I love pedicures."

"Not me. My feet are crazy sensitive. It was pure torture."

"What color did you pick?"

I spot Maggie walking toward us, carrying a giant glass of water with cucumber slices. Her hair is a golden mess, and she has the dazed look of just having had the orgasm of her life. Since I know that look firsthand, my cock wakes up.

"I'm sorry?" I ask, realizing I can't remember the question.

Alex spots Maggie. "She saw Janice today, and she has magic hands."

Maggie takes a gulp of water. "My massage was incredible. All the stress is gone from my shoulders." She rolls her shoulders.

"Did she give you a happily ever after?" Alex teases.

She swats her hand at him. "No. Of course not! She just knows what she's doing."

"Jonathan was just telling me about his pedicure," Alex says.

"Oh? What color did you choose?"

"Just clear," I tell them.

Alex slips his foot out of his sandal and shows us his

blue toes. "I don't know," he says, waggling his brows. "Colored toes are kind of sexy." He winks at Maggie, and she rolls her eyes.

He strikes me as a little too saucy for someone who has a major life change approaching. He can't possibly have Maggie's best interest at heart. *Whatever.* We sit and make small talk about a couple of people we know in common from high school. But we ran in different circles, so we quickly run out of conversation because we don't have a lot of the same friends.

"I have some plans tonight, so I'm going to head out." Alex leans down and kisses Maggie on the cheek. "You two have fun." I could swear he winked at her.

We watch Alex depart. Maggie hasn't asked why I'm here.

I lean in close. "I thought you were getting something else done."

"I was waxed *before* the massage."

"Why do you do it?"

"I like how it feels afterward."

I'm excited by that thought. "It must hurt."

"Uh, yeah. Having hot wax put on your bits and pieces? Trust me, not a fun feeling. But it's nice afterward for a few weeks." Maggie giggles, and I love the sound.

"What?" I ask.

"They do a manzilian. It's the man's version of a Brazilian. Alex gets it all the time."

"Do you prefer your men with no chest hair?" My heart beats faster. With only a few scraps of thin terrycloth robe between us, my cock is alert, and I'm not hiding it from her. She looks incredibly sexy.

"I like hair on a man—something to run my fingers through." She takes another sip of her water. "Do you prefer a woman without hair?"

"It doesn't bother me either way," I lean in again. "But you did promise me a peek, and I very much want to examine the precision of your Brazilian."

She turns the most beautiful shade of scarlet and doesn't answer. I stare at her and imagine her showing me her beautiful pink lips.

"What brings you to Minneapolis?" she asks.

"You." The scarlet across her cheeks spreads down her chest, and I'm sure she just shuddered. She bites her bottom lip, and I want to pull her into a massage room, crush her up against me, and make love to her until she comes all over my face, fingers, and dick. But I need her to get over this farce that she's marrying Alex first.

"There's a lot going on here," she explains.

I nod. "I understand you're still planning a wedding?"

"Yes."

"Alex seems to know we were together." I lay it out there.

"We haven't discussed it specifically," she whispers. "But he thinks getting laid solves all life's problems. He'd like me to be in a better mood."

"I don't see how your mood can improve until you're back in control of your personal life," I tell her, though that may have been a bit too frank.

She sits back hard in her chair, and her hands tremble. "The future of the company requires this." Tears shine in her eyes. "And Alex has to do this or he's left destitute."

"I understand the pressure you feel about preserving the company, but it isn't your job to make sure Alex keeps his money," I tell her, trying to keep my anger in check.

"No, but his father is making the Elite merger contingent upon Alex running at least some portion of the company, and that can only be done if he's family."

"This is not how normal businesses—normal families, normal *people*—operate. There are so many reasons this doesn't make sense," I tell her. *Why doesn't she realize this is crazy?*

She just shrugs.

"Okay, hear me out." My mind races as I try to pull something together that will reach her. "You don't need Elite in all the Bullseye stores. You already have an electronics section. Why title it Elite?"

"It's not just having the name. We want their *stores*, which means we want their inventory and their employees. And like us, they own all their real estate, and we want that too."

"Okay, but at what cost to you? Why does it have to be *you*?" I'm becoming desperate. I know her parents had a fucked-up relationship, but I can't imagine them requiring this. How could any woman think this is remotely acceptable? An arranged marriage in our culture and at this time? This is preposterous.

The look on my face must reflect my feelings, because she tries again to make me understand.

"I'm sorry. I don't know how to explain it. I feel like I don't have a choice. I can't walk away from something my family has spent generations building, and Mother doesn't care anything about the Foundation. If I don't see it through, no one will. And I'm helping my friend in the process."

But what about you? I want to scream. I have to take a different approach. Preserving the family business is one thing, but this can't be the only way. She needs to understand that her mother is talking her into something unnecessary. "Stevie told me he's planning to marry Genevieve."

She seems surprised. I reach for her, but she doesn't reach back. "Mag-pie, you don't have to marry *Alex* to run the company. And you can't make this merger your responsibility. You should make your own choice too. Please, I have money. I'm begging you."

"I'm sorry." Tears form in her eyes. "It's so complicated. I have to think of Alex too..." She wraps her arms around herself and won't look at me.

I want to throw the vase of flowers on the table into the fireplace. She's not making sense.

"What can I do to change your mind?" I lower my voice. "I happily did that last fall. Maybe you need me to do it again?"

She turns a delightful shade of red, and I remember her soft pink nipples. I want to suckle them.

"I...don't...want to...lead you on," she tells me.

"You aren't leading me on if you'll at least consider what I'm offering. Come with me to Las Vegas. Please. Let's find a way out of this. We can be happy. I know it."

"I..." The pause seems interminable. "Can't." She straightens up. "If you came here for me, I'm sorry. But I'm marrying Alex."

I rub my hands over my face, completely and utterly overwhelmed. If I don't leave, I might say something I regret. "I have to go. I'm going to see my parents. They're celebrating their fortieth wedding anniversary next year and still adore one another," I add out of spite. "You have my number if you change your mind."

Disappointment and hurt are evident on her face, but still she says nothing.

I shake my head. "You've given up, and that's heartbreaking. I understand your devotion to your family business, but I don't understand how I can want more for you than you want for yourself."

I leave her sitting there and return to the men's changing room. Once I'm dressed, I walk out to my waiting car and direct the driver to my parents'.

Chapter 12

Maggie

I hadn't been expecting Jonnie at the Lakes Spa, and the look on his face when I told him again that I had to marry Alex just destroyed me. I know I'm ruining the only possibility for happiness I'll ever have, but I have no idea what else to do. I've tried to explain it to him, but he doesn't understand. My family demands this. My friend's future is dependent on it. I can't see my way out. After he left, I went into the sauna and cried and sweated every tear out of my body.

I get dressed as slowly as possible. My heart is broken into a thousand pieces. I should never have flirted with Jonnie. I have to let him go. Even if I'm free to have affairs once I get married, Jonnie wants more from me, and I want to give him more—he deserves better.

Shit, I never should have slept with him all those months ago. If I hadn't done that, I wouldn't know what amazing sex is.

That thought accompanies me all the way home, and when I arrive, my mother is waiting for me in the foyer. "You're late," she says in the caustic tone she has when she's upset.

"I don't have any plans this evening, so I wasn't in any hurry," I tell her. "I'm sorry. Did I miss something?"

"I heard Jonathan Best flew in to see you this afternoon. How did he know you were at the Lakes Spa?"

"He texted and asked what I was doing. I certainly didn't invite him. I thought he was in Las Vegas. But he showed up about five minutes after I told him."

"What did he want?"

"I don't think he flew in just to see me, Mother."

"He showed up at the Lakes Spa without an appointment and talked to you and Alex. Are you planning on eloping in Las Vegas? Are you going to destroy all the work I've done to position you in our community?"

I'm relieved to realize she believes Jonnie wants me to have the wedding at his hotel. It hasn't occurred to her that he would be pursuing me. *Of course it hasn't.*

I shake my head. "No, I've told you a big wedding isn't what I want. And an elopement isn't even what I want. I've made it pretty clear that I don't want any of this, but you've made it clear you don't care. So I guess we're all planned for next month. You and the wedding planner have done everything. All I have to do is show up and shut up."

I try to walk past her to the kitchen and find myself some sort of dinner, but she steps in front of me. "I don't like it when you talk that way."

"What do you want from me, Mother? Neither Alex or I want this wedding. You and Herbert have just made it impossible to do anything else."

I give up trying to get to the kitchen and instead head up the grand staircase to go to my room.

"You will go through this. Do you understand me?"

When I turn back to look at her, she's seething. It's like she's sprouted devil horns. Her face is beet red. "We'll lose everything if you start thinking with your..." She points at my waist. "Your vagina and not your head."

I want to laugh. I've never heard my mother utter the word *vagina* before. She's over the edge, and I can't help but push her a little more.

"No, I don't understand at all," I tell her. "I don't understand why I have to give up my personal life for a business. Stevie is planning to marry Genevieve. Why not make him do this? Or better yet, why not find another way? No one should have to do this!"

I storm up the stairs, and she yells after me. "Stevie is not going to marry Genevieve. I promise you that. She's white trash, and I will not allow that in our family. I don't care who you sleep with on the side, but you will marry Alex."

"Are you drunk?" I scream at the top of my lungs. "Genevieve is beautiful and kind. Not ugly like you!"

"Mark my words, he will marry Mary Elizabeth Fairchild."

"I hate you!" I yell, slamming the door to my bedroom. I'm almost thirty-one years old, and I'm behaving like a child, but that woman makes me so angry.

I dump my purse and bag on my bed and kick my shoes off into the corner. I'll pick those up later. I fall face first onto my bed.

My cell phone rings. I glance at the caller ID and am perversely disappointed it isn't Jonnie. Instead it's Alex calling.

"Hello?"

"Hey. My father confronted me about Jonathan being at the Lakes. Does your mom know?"

"Yes. She was at the door waiting for me when I

walked in. She wanted to make sure we weren't going to elope in Vegas like Christopher. If she knew the real reason he came to see me, she'd blow a gasket."

"Did you at least have sex with him?"

"No!"

Alex is quiet. Too quiet.

"Alex, what did your dad say?"

He expels a big breath, and when he speaks again, his voice is shaky. "He knows about Charles and told me I'm not allowed to see him. He told me after we marry, I can sleep with other women, but I can't sleep with any men."

"I'm sorry." This could ruin Alex's personal life as well, it seems. Maybe now he'll see my perspective and be willing to scrap the whole thing. "Maybe we need a different plan — one that allows you to see Charles and keep your inheritance. Maybe we don't get married. It's a risk, but honestly, what can they do? They're not about to just let the companies go, right?"

He sighs. "I hate this," he finally says. "But you know that won't work. You're my best friend in the whole world, and I know you deserve better than being married to me. You deserve somebody who wants that stinky smelly fish."

I laugh halfheartedly because I know he's trying to cheer me up, but I'm still not sure he's taking my perspective seriously.

"If I had any other option, I'd take it," he says with a sigh. "But you know I don't."

He sounds resigned, but now that we're getting down to the wire, I'm not sure what they can do to make us. I can't see my mother with a shotgun...

"We could both refuse to do this. We could sit down with an attorney and work through how the company would be structured after the merger to make them more comfortable with us not marrying."

I hear glasses clink and liquid splashing. Alex is going to get drunk and go on a bender. That will really improve things.

"Please don't drink," I say softly.

"The love of my life is going to move on to another guy, and I'm going to be screwed," he whines.

I could say the same thing, but despite what Alex says, he's too focused on Charles and his financial situation to care about me.

I blow out a breath. "Alex, you know I love you right?"

"And I love you, too." He sniffles.

"We're going to figure this out," I tell him.

We talk a short time longer, and when we hang up, I know I need to talk to Jonnie about what happened today and apologize. I want to help him understand my situation. After what happened today, though, I'm not sure that's still an option. I text him.

Me: I'm sorry.

No rotating bubbles.
No phone call.
No response.

Chapter 13

Jonathan

After my confrontation with Maggie at the spa, I am shaking with anger. But more than that, despair washes over me. I know she cares about me — I can see it in her eyes — but if she's not willing to fight for us, what can I do?

I know it will ground me to be around people who want me around, so I'm glad to be on the way to my parents' house. I grew up with everything I could have wanted and then some. My father has retired now, but he was the chief legal officer for a large national bank headquartered here in Minneapolis. He worked hard and made good money for many years.

My mother stayed at home. She was in the Junior League, ran the PTA at my school, and came to every sports game and fundraiser I had. My younger sister has Down syndrome and is the center of my parents' universe, even though she lives independently in a group home now. But I'm the apple of their eye.

As we pull up to my childhood home, I know I don't get back here often enough. I make a point of talking to my family on Friday evenings, and we see each other once a quarter—that is, when they're not exploring the globe. Last year they visited India and enjoyed the Taj Mahal and saw the Northern Lights from Iceland. This year they're heading south to a Costa Rican sloth sanctuary and will jet over to New Zealand for wine tasting.

I have a key, though I didn't bring it. But when I try the front door, it opens easily. "Hello? Is anybody home?" I call.

My mother steps out from the kitchen, looking like 1955 in a dress with an apron. She must have been doing dishes because she begins to dry her hands.

"Oh, my goodness. Is that you? What brings you home?"

"Unfortunately, I'm not here for very long, Mom, but I thought I'd stop and say hello. I wasn't sure if my schedule was going to give me time to come by, so I thought it would be better to surprise you than have to cancel if I couldn't make it."

She pulls me into a warm embrace, and I can feel my anger and frustration ebbing away—at least for the moment. My mother is the best. She was the first woman I loved, and I know she loves me regardless of anything I could ever do wrong.

"Jim! Jim, look who's here," she calls. "Come quick!"

The squeak of the footrest folding into the recliner sounds from the TV room, and my father appears. Mom still hasn't let me go.

"Well, look who's decided to come on home," my father says.

My mom holds my hand as he steps in and hugs me.

"Great to see you, son."

We move as a group to the living room, and I take a seat with my mother next to me, still holding my hand tightly, as if I'm going to evaporate.

My father sits across from the dark marble coffee table with a goofy grin. "What have you been up to?"

"Shangri-la stuff mostly. We've managed to get rid of the big kinks, but a few small ones remain. I think we have you down to come check it out yourself next month?"

He nods enthusiastically. "We're looking forward to it. Can't wait." He claps his hands and rubs them together. "I have a feeling I'm going to be lucky on this trip."

I smile. "I bet you are, Dad. I think we set up a couple of shows, and of course, we'll give you some time to play cards. You looking to play Texas Hold'em or blackjack?"

"Seven-card stud. I've been practicing on an app on my iPad."

I chuckle, he's an odds guy, and I'll bet he does well. "Can't wait to see that."

My mother rolls her eyes. "I'm taking the bank cards with *me* when I go shopping. At least if I go crazy, we'll have some nice things to show for it."

"I'm not going to go too crazy," he grumbles good-naturedly. "I'm looking forward to taking you to the cleaners, though, son."

I laugh.

"I would love a big windfall." My mom giggles, making eyes at my father. "If anybody deserves it, you do."

I love that after more than thirty-nine years of marriage, they're still in love.

"What brought you home?" Mom asks.

"I had a little bit of business here. Just a quick trip."

"Can I fix you a snack? Make you some dinner?"

I glance at my watch... It's early evening. The flight home is just over two hours, so I can head home tonight.

"I can give you a couple of hours. We can do dinner.

I'm fine with eating here, or I'm happy to take you out. I have a car out front if you'd like to go somewhere."

She waves at me as if she always has enough dinner made in case I come by. "No," she says. "I want to spend this time looking at my beautiful son. God, you're more and more handsome each time I see you. What's going on with you and all the girls?" She wiggles her eyebrows, and I roll my eyes.

"No girls in my life to speak of," I assure her.

I can't bring myself to tell my parents about Maggie.

My parents went through hell when Christopher essentially moved in with us during high school and his emancipation. Maggie's mother made sure my parents were miserable. She had Child Protective Services accusing them of not taking good enough care of my sister. They tried to get my father fired from the bank and accused him of malfeasance in the press. She also did a real number on my mom with their friends.

My parents knew Christopher's parents would be upset by his actions, but I think if they'd known everything that was coming, they would have done things differently. I can't open that can of worms again. Maggie and I need to keep our parents out of this. They'd understand why I'm not telling them.

My dad chuckles. "You always were a ladies man."

There's no getting anything past my dad. I remember in ninth grade I snuck Jenny Malone into the basement, where we watched television and made out for hours. I didn't hear my dad come home, but he walked down to tell me dinner was ready and stood there to walk Jenny out. He didn't say anything to me or my mother about it.

"Even in preschool, you would complain that the girls wanted to kiss you all the time," my mother brags.

"Yes, and I remember I got engaged to three girls when I was in kindergarten," I reminisce.

"Oh gosh, yes. You explained you'd have to have three jobs to support them, and your dad and I both agreed, but we weren't sure even three jobs would cover expenses for the girls you were planning to marry."

We laugh together, and they tell me what's going on with their friends and catch me up on all the local gossip.

Over a spaghetti dinner, Mom asks, "How is Christopher doing?"

"He's busy. I think he and Bella are trying really hard to have a baby."

"The practice part is fun," my father muses and winks at my mom.

I'm a little grossed out, but I smile.

"They better not get too stressed about it, or it might get harder," he adds.

"They're busy with work in San Francisco," I continue. "Though I got to see them for a poker tournament earlier this week. I wish I could talk them into coming to Las Vegas more often."

"They're newlyweds. I would hope they're spending lots of time together," my mother says.

"I think they make their relationship a priority, but Bella has her own company and is completing her dissertation this spring. Christopher is still investing, and he's interested in my software. He wants to connect me with his partners."

"Is that what you want?" my dad asks.

I shrug. "I'm not sure. But eventually, my focus will need to be on the software *or* the resort."

My mom pats my hand. "You'll know what you need to do when the time is right."

I tell them all about the buy-in at the big poker tournament Christopher participated in and how he lost during the first round.

"I imagine you were quite the player, since you own the casino and all." My dad winks.

I shake my head, chasing the last of my sauce with some bread. "That game was too rich for my blood. I know better than to gamble with a group that's way smarter than me and spends their whole lives strategizing."

"You could have knocked their socks off," my father insists.

As we clean up the kitchen, I think again about Maggie and how lucky I am to have such a loving and supportive family.

I miss them so much, but I need to go.

I begin gathering my things. "I guess I should get going. I have the hotel's plane, and they're going to need it back."

We say our goodbyes. "See you in a few weeks." My mother gives me several hugs, and as I walk out the door, she whispers in my ear, "Don't worry, sweetheart, the right woman is out there for you. You're too good of a catch for one not to find you."

My mom must have figured out that I came because of a woman. She's so smart. I smile. "Thanks, Mom. That's exactly what I needed to hear."

On the flight back, I start going through my email, though I struggle to pay attention. There's so much going on back in Vegas. I have a very capable management team, but some things still seem to fall to me since I don't have an assistant manager yet.

As soon as we hit the tarmac, and I turn my phone on, and it rings.

"Hello?"

"Welcome home, Mr. Best," Kian greets me.

"Thank you. It's late, so I'll just be heading back to my apartment."

"Yes, sir. When we arrive, I'll let the night manager on duty know you're back on property."

"Thank you."

The hotel limo is sitting at the base of the stairs as Caden and I exit the plane, and I'm back in the hotel less than twenty minutes after wheels down. Not bad. I'm feeling pretty proud of myself. I have a decent bottle of bourbon waiting for me in my apartment that I'm sure is calling my name.

As I walk through the hotel lobby, a woman approaches me. Her hair is a mess, and she looks like she's been crying. "Excuse me, aren't you Mr. Best?"

My bodyguard, Caden, moves between us.

She steps back. "I'm sorry. I just need some help."

I step around the bodyguard. "What can I do for you?"

"My room was ransacked, and my boyfriend is missing." She begins to cry.

"Please call Travis in security," I tell Caden.

He nods and steps away.

"I went to the Cirque show with my mother," the woman explains. "My boyfriend wasn't interested and wanted to play some blackjack. When I returned to my room after the show, it had been turned upside down, and my jewelry pouch on the nightstand was missing. I called his cellphone, but it rang in the room. I don't know what to do." Tears stream down her face.

Travis and another member of the security team arrive to take over the conversation. I'll let them figure out if we need to call the police, so after a few more minutes, I extricate myself. It's already midnight. I hear them tell her they'll accompany her to her room to check out what's going on and that the police are on their way.

Chances are, her boyfriend decided to go gambling and fell on what he saw as a hot streak — or cold streak that he's sure is going to become a hot streak — and he's been gambling all night. God forbid he took her jewelry pouch and sold the contents for cash. That does happen, though. It's one of the ugly sides of gambling.

When I arrive at my apartment, I'm ready to crash. I've been up since five this morning. I left here thinking I might spend time with Maggie for a few days, and now I'm alone again. I kick myself for thinking it was going to be at all easy to change her mind. I need a new strategy.

I pour myself a drink and sit in the dark, looking out over the desert. The blackness is a backdrop to the city lights.

My mind jockeys, moving through each thing I did wrong—not telling her how I felt years ago, not telling her how I felt last fall when we were together, getting upset with *her* and not her situation, and leaving without resolving anything.

My phone chirps, breaking me out of the spinning in my head. It's the head of my maintenance department. "Sorry to bother you, sir."

Is the moon full? What has my phone ringing all night long? "What can I do for you, Michael?"

"We have a problem. There was a leak in a bathroom on the eighth floor of the East Tower, and it has affected the three bathrooms below it."

"Do we know what happened?"

"From what we've pieced together, on the way to dinner and the Cirque show tonight, someone threw a leather jacket over the side of the bathtub and it was heavy enough that it started the water—not rushing, of course, but a steady stream—and part of the jacket blocked the drain. After running for what we estimate was about six hours, it overflowed and leaked down the interior walls. The three rooms below will require major repairs."

I sit up and with my elbows on my knees rub my hand over my face, feeling the two-day-old beard. *You've got to be shitting me.*

I take a few deep breaths to calm myself. The occupant of the room will be liable, but chances are they can't afford what sounds like a fifty-thousand-dollar renovation.

"Okay, what's your plan?"

"Well, sir, we're sold out, but we need to vacate those rooms."

"Do we know who's in them? Are they whales or guests at an event or conference? Any type of VIP?"

"Not that we know of."

"Check with Gillian. Make sure none of the guests are hers. We have a few of the big suites available for VIP walk-ins, if we need those. I'd rather find them a room here than with a competitor."

"We'll move the guests to the hotel next door only if we have to, " he confirms.

We certainly would never want to turn someone away without a back-up plan—we make the least amount of money on our rooms. It's the shows, restaurants, and gambling that bring in the most, and if people stay at other hotels, they spend their money there.

"Okay. Talk to Gillian to see if she can work out use of the suites to accommodate us." As my brain spins with how to manage four rooms, I add, "Let's make sure we compensate those who have to move, particularly if they have to stay across the street. I want them to get VIP tickets to Queen's show, and comp dinners at any restaurant in the hotel. Make sure we apologize profusely, and see if you can't get them set up for another stay."

"No problem. I'll work with Gillian to get that taken care of. Sorry to disturb you."

I sigh. I can't go to sleep now. I'm past the point of exhaustion. I've been up for more than twenty hours, and my brain is beyond the point of rest. *Who needs sleep anyway?*

I pour myself another bourbon and turn the TV on. My mind now runs a circuit from Maggie, to the woman who stopped me when I got back, to all the people we're displacing, to the long list of things I need to get done. I can't even follow the movie I picked.

I move to my bedroom and lie down. I don't close the drapes so I can look out across the desert. I wonder what Maggie's doing. Probably like everyone else, she's sleeping. I can't sleep.

As I debate coffee or a shower, my phone chirps again. It's Lilly, the head of HR. What's she doing calling me at three-thirty in the morning? She only calls when something isn't good.

I walk over to my espresso machine and answer the call. "What's up, Lilly?"

"The police are down here with me and security in the sportsbook—"

"Is this the issue about the missing jewelry pouch and the boyfriend?" I interject.

"Nooo, but it sounds like you're having an interesting night," she says.

"You have no idea."

"We had a drunk patron fondle one of our cocktail waitresses," she tells me.

I look to the stars. The moon must be full.

"Anyway, she's really upset," Lilly continues. "He tweaked her nipple pretty hard."

The hair on the back of my neck stands up. *Who does this ass think he is?*

"I can be right down." I start looking for my pants. It wouldn't do for me to show up in my boxer shorts.

"Hold on. I don't think that's necessary. She didn't take too kindly to being touched, so she clocked him."

Good for her. I'm impressed.

"He claims she chipped his tooth," Lilly adds. "There's blood everywhere, and he probably has a broken nose."

I roll my eyes. Rather than own it, he's blaming her.

"He's talking about pressing charges."

Are you fucking kidding me? I shake my head in disbelief.

"They've called an ambulance."

"What are the police saying?"

"Officially, they may have to arrest her. Unofficially, he got what he deserved."

"If it went down as you say, we'll have it on video, and we'll cover her legal fees. See if you can grab Gillian. She's around, dealing with an issue where four guest rooms have been damaged. Ask her if she can get this figured out, too. She's good with this kind of thing. If we can avoid our employee getting arrested, let's give her the rest of her shift off with pay. Apologize to her, and let's have security get the footage of the event over to the police tonight."

"Great. I'll work on that. Sorry to bother you. You sound exhausted."

"I am. But I'll rally."

My espresso is ready, and I take my first sip. The caffeine hits my blood, and I feel more ready to charge on.

"You should get some sleep, and I'll have a report for you by the time you wake up."

"Thanks, Lilly."

Sleep? That would be nice. Maybe if I worked out, the exhaustion would help me sleep. I walk into my home gym to run on the treadmill and lift a few weights, yet my brain bounces from one thing to another.

I decide I'd better get into the shower before my phone rings again. When the warm water hits me, the tension in my shoulders relaxes, and my eyelids become heavy. Maybe I will finally be able to sleep.

Drying off, I move to my bedroom, but as I hit the black-out blinds, my phone chirps. It's six o'clock in the morning, and it's Queen Diva this time. Almost anyone else I'd let roll to voice mail, but this I need to answer.

"Hello, Miss Queen. How was the show last night?"

"You were out of the hotel last night." It's not a question but a statement. "Do you know how I know?"

I chuckle. "I went to Minneapolis to see my parents. How did you know?"

"You know that saying 'When the cat's away, the mice will play?' I swear to God, this place is not as tight a ship when you're not here."

"I'm not sure if that's a compliment or not. How was your show? Did everything go okay?"

"Last night went well, if you don't mind that my forty-two-carat amethyst ring is missing."

"You've got to be joking? How is that possible?" I sit up straight and try to make sure all my synapses are connecting properly. "When was the last time you saw it?"

"I wore it with the second dress, and when I changed, I left it in the box on my dressing table, as I do every night. When I went to put it on with the fourth dress, it was missing. We've checked the dressing room from top to bottom. It's gone."

"Have you notified Travis in security?"

"Yes, and the police will be by later today after I get some sleep."

Sleep. I crave sleep.

"I'll try to be there."

"Jonathan, you've got to talk to Travis in security. If his team can't catch the thief, we may have some really tough conversations coming in our future."

We have a feeling we know who is behind the thefts, and if he thinks this is a way to renegotiate her contract with the hotel, I love her, but this isn't going to go well.

"Travis and I will be there when the police come to speak with you later today," I assure her. "We'll have a plan for you."

"I'm counting on you. I can't perform if we can't get this figured out. I may have to break my contract because I'm losing money."

Rubbing my hands over my face, I know that isn't true. I sign her checks each month, and she's fine. She makes a healthy percentage of each seat at her sold out performances.

I stay on the line with her for a few more minutes so she can feel like she's being heard. Once I extricate myself from her call, I dial Travis.

"I just spoke to Queen Diva about her ring," I tell him when he answers.

"Sorry, it's been a hectic night. I should have called you

about that. We've had a few issues in the last twenty-four hours."

"I'm guessing there are other things I need to know about?"

"Well, you know the major ones, and the others aren't pressing. The police will be here to meet with Queen at seven tonight, just before her show. If you want to meet about four or five, my team will have gone through the tape of all these different issues, and we'll be ready to update you, as well as prepare for our meeting with the police."

I agree and hang up.

I'm giving myself eight hours to shut down and block everything out. I call the front desk and put a do not disturb on my landlines, and I turn the ringer off on my cell phone. If it's an emergency, they can knock on my door. But it had better be an emergency, because I'm going to crash.

I eventually fall asleep, but when I wake up six hours later, I don't feel rested. My sleep was restless and active and not particularly helpful. I keep thinking of Maggie and the conversation we had—or didn't have. And I'm bothered by the bathrooms, the missing boyfriend, and the fact that my Queen Diva thief has moved from ten-thousand-dollar dresses to twenty-thousand-dollar rings.

I still need a whole lot more sleep, but instead, it's time to face the day—or the evening, at least. To ease into things, I leave my phones on do not disturb, check to make sure there haven't been any additional fires, and then head back to my gym.

I don't believe Queen is correct when she says the hotel is a well-oiled machine only when I'm here. Last night was an anomaly, and she has a problem all her own that we need to figure out.

When I pick up my phone after showering, I see a text message from Maggie. It actually came in a while ago. She's sorry.

I am, too, and I want so much to tell her that, but I

can't. I'm not going to be able to do this on my own, and I don't want to make it any worse. Instead, I think I finally have some clarity. I need to come clean with Christopher and recruit his help. No matter what hell is breaking loose here, this is important. I'm going to go see him in San Francisco.

Me: Hey. What do you have going for dinner tomorrow night?

Christopher: Bella has class and is working late and I was figuring on doing the same.

Me: How about I fly in and find you? We can grab dinner at some trendy spot or a sports bar. You're buying, so make sure it's expensive.

Christopher: You're on, dude. What's going on?

Me: I need to talk. I need an impartial ear.

Christopher: Great. 7 o'clock tomorrow night. I'll find a cheap spot with warm beer for you to cry in.

Me: Loser. See you then.

Now that I know my plan, I feel like I can make this work, despite the chaos surrounding me.
I think back to last fall when Maggie and I were together. After Christopher and Bella's ceremony, I'd walked her back to my apartment, which the designer hadn't even finished decorating. We were buzzing with excitement. I poured her three fingers of bourbon and sat close to her on the couch.. The room was full of electricity.
Just when I thought it was never going to happen, she turned to me and kissed me. And it wasn't slow and soft, but urgent and full of lust. Every ounce of blood in my body went

straight to my cock.

Then she pulled away. "Are you okay with this?"

I was much more than okay, though I think I just nodded, rather than actually saying something that would have helped her understand my feelings. Nevertheless, we made love three times that night. That it was incredible only cemented that we were made for each other. How I wish I'd had the guts to tell her as much way back then. Who knows where we might be now.

Chapter 14

Jonathan

A little while later, I'm dressed, and as rested as I can get. I've worked out, snacked on leftover Chinese, and caught up on my sports teams. It's time to tackle what's left of my day.

Caden meets me outside my door, and I walk with him down to see Travis in Security.

"All right, Travis, what the hell happened last night, and what did you learn over the last twelve hours?" I ask when we arrive.

"Let's start with the easy part." He gestures to a guy sitting behind a computer. "This is Kevin."

"Thanks for your help, Kevin."

Travis points to the closest fifty-inch screen, and the

feed from the bar comes up. It's high-resolution digital and they've pieced together multiple angles. We watch a customer enter, not real steady on his feet, and take a seat at a perimeter table. He seems to talk to women as they pass, but they don't appear to respond.

Karen, the server, arrives, and it looks like she takes his order.

"Can we pull the audio?" I ask.

"We're working on that," Travis says. "The guys are trying to clean it up some."

That makes sense. We don't record a lot of audio, but we do have devices set up in certain areas. Mostly they just seem to pick up a lot of background noise.

We see Karen stop at several other tables and then put an order in. Everything is going as it should. Now her tray is full of drinks, and she begins to deliver them.

The drinks she places in front of wobbly man is clear, on ice, and has a lime wedge.

"Did you see that?" Travis asks.

I shake my head. "Can you please play it back slowly, Kevin?"

Kevin rewinds the feed to where she walks up to the table and plays it in slow motion.

"Watch his right hand at the back of her leg," Travis says. "He slides it up and tries to slip it underneath her skirt."

I see the same thing, and I don't like it. "It's subtle, but she brushes it away," I note.

"She's graceful about it, which is a sign that this happens often," Travis says.

"I'll meet with the head of food and beverage and make sure we do some training on how to address this. No one should have to work that way."

We continue watching Karen help other patrons. She's happy, smiling, and seems courteous. A large group of young guys come in, and she cards them and scoots them along.

"How long until she clocks him?" I ask.

"It's coming up," Kevin says. "It's at the twenty-three-minute mark."

We're at twenty-one minutes when the man drains his drink and motions Karen over. There's talking between the two. His hands are wandering, and she keeps shaking her head.

"We need to get the audio," I say through clenched teeth.

"Agreed, and we'll get it transcribed so the video and audio match. But just wait. It gets better," Travis warns.

"I know she slugs him," I say.

Her tray is full, and she delivers drinks around the bar. When she comes back to his table, she leans over to put the drink down, and we watch him reach right into her top. You can tell she's startled, and she dumps the remaining drinks in his lap. He immediately stands and grabs her by the hair as his hand disappears down the front of her uniform.

"Holy shit," I say. We watch her nail him with a right hook.

He tumbles like a ragdoll and hits the table.

I shake my head. "Well, it appears to be a clear case of defending herself."

We watch the interaction a few more times in slow motion, double speed, and normal speed. It looks terrible every time.

"He was definitely the aggressor, but why didn't she follow protocol and call security when he sat down? He was obviously drunk. Why did she serve him?" I ask. "We need to pull his drink orders, too."

"I have that somewhere," Travis searches through a pile of paper. "Here it is. The first was a gin and tonic, and the second was just tonic. So it appears she was addressing his drink situation."

"That's good. But I still want to know why she didn't follow protocol. And it'd be great to get the audio ASAP," I tell him.

"Agreed," Travis says. "Okay, now for the missing boyfriend. It's not as climactic."

"That's good," I mumble, rubbing my hand over my face. Assault, theft, and kidnapping in the same evening is not a good night.

Kevin pulls up the new feed. "The boyfriend is playing blackjack in the third spot. He's having a good night with Tom Carpenter, the dealer at table forty-two."

We watch as the evening pit boss, Vincent, changes Tom out for a break.

"This is when his winning streak seems to falter," Travis says.

The man stands up and changes to a table where the bid increases to forty dollars.

"This is just bad luck," Travis notes.

The dealer wins two hands in a row.

"Tough for the players," I lament.

"Exactly, but it happens. You can see he runs out of chips." The feed shows him leaving the table and crossing to the ATM, but he doesn't seem to get any money from it. Either he's over his daily limit, or he doesn't have any to withdraw. He walks out of the casino, stops and looks back, and then walks to the elevator.

"Does he think someone is following him?" I ask.

"I don't think so. I think he's looking at all the activity and still wanting to participate. You'll see why I say that in just a few minutes."

Kevin fast-forwards, and the feed picks him up exiting the elevator alone on his floor. No one else is present. He lets himself into his room with a thumbprint.

"It's nine thirty-seven p.m., and he walks out at ten-oh-three," Kevin says. "No one comes after he leaves."

He zooms in on what the man is holding, and it's a pouch like his girlfriend described.

The camera follows him back to the lobby and out the front door.

"We checked with the cab company, and he caught a ride to Serena's Pawn Shop."

"Did you see him come back?"

"Couldn't find that. The room is accessed again at eleven forty-two p.m., and the video shows it's the girlfriend."

Kevin switches to that feed, and the woman I met in the lobby last night sticks her head out of the room and searches down the hall.

"In a minute she leaves her room, and she caught your attention at twelve ten p.m. in the casino in front of table thirty-two," Travis says.

"There's a distinct possibility he pawned her jewelry and went gambling elsewhere," I say. "Get this to the officer overseeing missing persons on this."

"Already done."

Kevin clicks a few keys on his computer keyboard and brings up the camera feed outside Queen Diva's dressing room.

"Now for the most puzzling one," Travis says.

Queen's shows are choreographed to the second, so we know she should hit her dressing room at nine thirty-eight, which she does. She walks with two dressers following her, one unzipping the costume and helping to remove jewelry and adornments, and the other collecting the pieces she's taking off. Her security guard, who is standing outside the room, opens the door for her. It's controlled chaos, and Frankie is nowhere to be seen.

Queen emerges with her entourage in a different costume in less than fifteen seconds, and then she's back to the stage.

"We obviously lose her each time she goes into the room, but no one else enters. I checked with the guard outside her door, and he confirmed that," Travis says. "Could she be trying to set us up? Trying to get out of her contract?"

I keep staring at the door, willing Frankie or anyone else to sneak in, but it's just the guard and an empty hallway.

"I suppose anything is possible, but I don't think so."

I ruminate over his suggestion. She wanted this. This is a good deal for her. She takes in half the money we collect on her shows, and she's home each morning to help her kids off to school and pick them up after and have dinner with them before she puts in four hours here at the hotel. She wants her kids to put down roots, not have private tutors and live out of a suitcase while she's on the road. With this gig, she goes home every night *and* makes more money than she would if she was traveling. Something's not right.

"Do you have this ready to go for the police interview?"

"Sure thing, boss," Kevin says.

"What else happened today while I was sleeping?" I ask.

"Typical stuff—shoplifter at Louis Vuitton on The Boardwalk, two card counters playing five-card stud, and a man tried to go skinny-dipping in the pool. A typical day at the Shangri-la."

I sigh. I need more sleep than I'm getting. I need quality time to sort out this mess with Maggie, and I need to get laid. "At least it's always exciting. I'm going to check in with Gillian, and I'll be back before the police arrive."

Caden walks out with me, and I text Gillian.

Me: Where are you?

Gillian: VIP room 3. Come on by and let our big spenders feel your love.

I smile. They don't care about me. It's the thrill of outfoxing the fellow players. I alert Caden where we're headed, and he leads the way.

As we pass the craps table, I notice it's three people deep all around. Someone's hot, and the crowd cheers. A tall, very sexy blonde sidles up next to me.

"Looks like someone's beating the house," she says in a sultry voice that wakes up my cock.

I chuckle. "It happens all the time." If I asked her, she'd probably join me for a drink. But I only want my Magpie. I consider texting her, but I don't know what to say. Hopefully after I meet with Christopher, I will.

Instead, I walk into the VIP room to find six tables packed with Chinese women. Smoke hangs heavily from the ceiling, and they're deep in a game of pai gow. I love watching them play. They move Chinese domino tiles around and laugh, speaking what I guess is Cantonese. The game makes zero sense to me. I can't tell which hands are high and which are low—what wins one time and doesn't the next is strange to me. There's a lot of pushing, so not a lot of money changes hands, but they've all dropped a quarter of a million to play.

I stand against the wall as Gillian explains who's here. They're a group who comes twice a year from mainland China. New money—I can relate to that. Gillian has told me before that these women easily spend six figures each between food, shows, shopping, and of course, the pai gow. This is a big win for us.

When they notice me, the game stops and thirty women pull out their mobile phones and take lots of pictures. They speak excellent English, and I smile as they bombard me with information.

"You're much more handsome in person."

"My daughter is single."

"You have a beautiful hotel."

"How do I get a discount?"

After their enthusiasm subsides, I thank them for coming and head down to Queen Diva's dressing room for our meeting with LVPD.

Travis, the police detective, and I stand around waiting. Usually people wait for me, but as usual, we wait for Queen Diva. She arrives in a flurry. She's wearing jeans and a sweater, and without her wigs and makeup, she's almost unrecognizable. But it's still as if the room was black and white and with her arrival came all the color. She shoos her entourage out, including Frankie, and the policeman gets down to business.

"Queen Diva, I'm Detective Alan Kincaid," he says, offering his hand.

"Nice to meet you," she says.

Together we watch the video. As she told us, the ring is on her hand when she goes into the dressing room and not there when she goes out. Detective Kincaid asks a lot of questions—of us and her—but no one is able to explain how the ring disappeared.

"Queen, as you know, we don't have a recording of anything in your dressing room," Travis reminds her. "It might help if we could set up a temporary camera that only you would know about. It could be positioned in such a way as to capture the whole room. The feed would go directly to a drive that is not on our main server, so it wouldn't be visible to anyone unless you permitted someone from my team or me to view it. What do you think?"

She nods. "I think we have to. My costumes are brought in by your team each day, so I only see them when I'm performing. If something's going on in the room, we need to see it."

Detective Kincaid nods. "I'm sure this is something you want to share with your family and staff, but I strongly encourage you to keep it to yourself. In my experience, these kinds of thefts are usually perpetrated by someone cozied up to someone close to you, and they don't even realize it."

I can see her wanting to fight the advice, but she nods. "I need to find out who's behind this and who's *not* behind my success."

We all agree on a timeline, thank her for her cooperation, and Detective Kincaid walks out with Travis and me.

"Is there possibly another way in or out of her dressing room that we aren't covering?" he asks.

I shake my head. "I built this place. I don't think so."

"Do you have any suspects you didn't want to mention in front of her?"

I smile. This guy is smart. "We think it might be her husband, Frankie, or someone he knows."

"Interesting. I was thinking the same thing." He smiles.

When we reach the front door of the hotel, he extends his hand. "I look forward to our next visit next week."

He heads out, Travis returns to security, and I go back to my apartment.

Through an app on my phone, I order pizza for dinner from a hole-in-the-wall place off the Strip. It's my favorite spot, and I eat and enjoy a basketball game in my underwear, sitting on my leather couch.

I'm tired, and I hope I can return to a normal sleeping schedule tonight, since tomorrow will be a long day.

∞

The following afternoon, I make myself comfortable on the plane. Squeezing ten hours of work into less than five isn't easy, but I'm a man on a mission, and I need to get to Christopher. I'm even leaving a little earlier than planned for San Francisco. One of our whales, Kevin Driscoll, was ready to return to the Bay Area, so it made sense to carpool.

"Mr. Best, so wonderful to share this ride to San Francisco," he says as I stow my bag.

"Mr. Driscoll." I extend my hand. "How was your stay at the Shangri-la?"

"Excellent. This time I'm leaving with more money than I came with."

"Great news. That's what I like to hear." Usually, whales tip my staff well and spend all sorts of money—

probably more than they ever win.

"What kind of business are you in, Mr. Driscoll?"

The flight attendant places our preferred drinks in front of us.

"I'm in semiconductors." He proceeds to talk at me, not *to* me, for the duration of the sixty-five-minute flight. After he explains his current business, he moves on to his past businesses. Then I learn why he loves poker and that he and his wife are no longer intimate.

The flight lands none too soon in San Francisco. Kian exits the plane before me and takes the keys to the waiting Range Rover. I've never been so glad to be off the plane, though it was a gift that Kevin Driscoll talked the whole way, since it kept my mind off why I'm here.

Kian navigates through traffic on the 101, and before I know it, we're sitting in front of a San Francisco row house in what Christopher describes as the Mission. All I know is they're above a neighborhood park and have a stunning view of downtown San Francisco and the Bay Bridge. The last time I stayed in their guest room on the third floor, I could see the tips of the Golden Gate Bridge on a clear day.

We've barely come to a stop before Christopher is outside to greet me and direct Kian to where he wants him to park. "I hope you're hungry. Bella made authentic tamales, chicken, and her grandmother's pork green chili. Brother, we're in for a treat tonight. We're going to eat well."

Bella comes out behind him, and I give her a hug and a kiss. "I didn't bring anything. I'm sorry. I thought I was making this guy take me out for an expensive dinner. Instead it sounds like you cooked all day, and he's getting off rather easy."

He puts his arm around her, and she smiles up at him. "I'm thrilled to cook for you. I figure you aren't served many home-cooked meals, and after dinner, I'll go up to my office so you two can have your secret conversation."

I chuckle. Bella is nothing like the girls Christopher

dated when we were growing up. She's absolutely perfect for him—an incredibly smart biochemist, beautiful long dark hair and big brown eyes, and she doesn't care a thing about the money in his bank account.

Dinner with Christopher and Bella is a lot of fun. I share plenty of his escapades from when we were in school together.

"Here we were, from two of the wealthiest families at the Carlson Academy, and rather than attend any old private university like many of our classmates, we went to a state school. Talk about blowing the lid off of their stats."

He laughs. "Well, if Hazel hadn't pushed me, and if my grandfather hadn't set up funding for my college, I'd never have been able to afford even the U. The tuition was ridiculous. My mother was so pissed at me for emancipating myself. She wouldn't pay for a thing."

This is the opening I've been looking for. "Why didn't Stevie and Maggie emancipate themselves?"

"Self-preservation," he says immediately. "My mother was not going to let that happen a second time or a third, and I'm sure she made that clear to them. Plus, we'd always known a son—well, turns out just an heir—in good standing must run the company, and I obviously wanted nothing to do with it, so she had to keep them in her clutches."

"So is Stevie going to take charge now?"

"God, no! You remember that mess with Stevie when he graduated from high school. He was wild, and that didn't go over well at all. Doesn't look good, you know." He rolls his eyes. "And he doesn't have any business training either. He's doing great, though. Genevieve grounds him, and they stay far away from my mother down in Key West. No brutal Minnesota winters for them."

"I can't blame him for that." My heart sinks. "So it's left for Maggie?"

"Well, yeah, unfortunately." He sighs. "I mean, she'll be great—she certainly knows what she's doing. We set it up so someone else is running the company, and she just has to be board chairman. She'll still be mostly focused on the Foundation. I'm sure the marriage to Alex is part of the merger with Elite, but Maggie doesn't talk to me about that kind of thing."

"You could call her and find out," Bella reminds him.

"I should, because if my mother is forcing her to marry Alex, that is truly fucked up."

Bella stands. "Jonathan, thank you for coming. I need to get some work done. She gives me a warm embrace and a kiss. "Come again soon.""

"That's your cue, eh?" I laugh as I reach for her hand and give it a squeeze. "Dinner was truly outstanding. I hope to see you very soon."

"I'm guessing we'll see you at Maggie's wedding," she says, looking at Christopher as if transmitting a message with her eyes.

My heart clenches, and I'm sure it stops pumping for a few moments. We have got to find a way out of this. If Christopher is against it too, maybe we can band together...

"Maggie's here next week," Bella adds as she goes, looking at me now. "Foundation work for Bullseye. They're working with a local nonprofit on a program they want to take nationwide. She comes out every six weeks or so to meet with the director. This time she's squeezing in some time with her big brother."

"I didn't know she was due to come out and stay."

I need to focus on how to fill Christopher in on Maggie's situation, but I'm not sure it's my place. Plus, I'm not ready to admit my relationship with her just yet. Though I don't know quite what I'm waiting for now.

"She's not just a pretty face," Bella says over her shoulder. "The guest room is ready if you need it, and the guest house has clean sheets for your team."

"Thanks, Bella, but we have a flight at eleven." I turn to Christopher. "I was out of town earlier this week, and everything went to hell in a handbasket. I can't be out of town anymore."

She waves goodbye and disappears.

"Come with me." Christopher leads me down the hall to his man cave, where we sit in two leather chairs opposite a gas fireplace. "What's going on?" he asks as he pours twenty-five-year-old amber liquid into a glass.

I take a deep breath and prepare myself for yelling and possibly a black eye. "I need some help."

"Sure, anything. What's going on?"

"You've been my best friend since we were five. Your family is my family."

"I feel the same way."

I take a deep pull of my drink and look him in the eye. "I'm in love with Maggie."

He sits back in his chair. I can see his jaw set, and he looks away. I brace myself. He slowly turns to me. "Okay, and?"

I'm so stunned that I don't know where to start.

"Jonnie, you've been in love with Maggie since we were in high school. You were more serious about keeping boys away from her than I ever was. Plus, I saw you disappear with her after my wedding. I knew you'd tell me when you were ready."

I feel my mouth fall open and quickly shut it. *He's known all along?* "Are you okay with this? I mean, I remember you threatening to cut off my balls if I got involved with her."

"You're adults, not ridiculous teenagers anymore," he says with a shrug. "She's the one you built the Shangri-la for, right?"

I nod and stare down at my now-empty glass. "She came to see me a few weeks ago, and I was ready to ask her to move to Las Vegas. I bought an engagement ring the day after your wedding. I love her, man." I sigh. "But the moment I saw her, she shut everything down and told me she was marrying Alex."

He nods soberly. "So I'm guessing my mother is behind this marriage?"

"It sounds like she waited until you and Stevie left to inform Maggie that she couldn't get around the marriage clause—and then she presented her with a ready-made solution."

"I have the most fucked-up family. How does Maggie feel about you?"

"I feel like she cares about me too. For months after your wedding, we'd been flirting and texting back and forth. We talked just about every day until she dropped the bomb about marrying Alex and ran off. Now it's hit or miss."

"What's happened since then?"

"She's shutting me out, though I'm trying not to let her. We've connected a few times, and she finally came clean about everything, but she's convinced she's the only one who can preserve the company, and she has some sort of stupid loyalty to Alex, so she's resigned herself to going through with it."

Christopher nods and looks at the ceiling for a moment. "My mother has her hooks in everything Maggie does—she always has. But she can't throw her life away, especially when she has another option on the table—you."

I almost feel relieved, but the situation still feels overwhelmingly awful. I sit back hard in my chair. "Help me talk some sense into her. We have to find another way to meet the terms of the will—or get them changed."

He gets the bottle of scotch and pours me another glass. "The wedding isn't until next month, so let me see what I can find out when she's here next week. That way we don't tip my mother off."

Chapter 15

Maggie

It's been one hell of a week, but it's finally Saturday. I'm making today a pajama day, but that doesn't mean I'm not productive. So far, I've spent the morning going through my to-do lists for the Foundation, and I reviewed the latest batch of Reinhardt Hudson P&L statements so I'm not walking in blind when I take the job of chairman.

It's late morning, and I haven't even gotten dressed. I love that I can work from home.

Or not-work from home. I pause to daydream a little. It's been several weeks since I argued with Jonnie at the spa. He didn't respond when I texted to apologize, so I've left him alone. I'm sure this is for the best, though I still think of him every day.

But I shouldn't. I lay back in bed, set aside my spreadsheets, and leaf through a magazine. It is Saturday, after all.

A few minutes later, a knock at my bedroom door distracts me from the article in *Cosmo* on "How to Make Your Orgasms Last." Just as well, as it seems a bit cliché, and thanks to my current life predicament, I won't be having orgasms any time soon.

Opening the door, I find my mother's private secretary standing with an acrylic clipboard, wearing her usual sensible skirt and shoes.

"There's a Mr. Patrick Moreau here to see you," she announces.

"Me? Why is my mother's attorney here to see me?"

She looks at me blankly. Her job is not to wonder, but to do, and do it efficiently. She waits for me to agree to meet him.

"Have him meet me in the library."

She gives a curt nod, turns, and leaves.

So much for a day in my flannel pajamas. I could meet him like this, but that's probably not the image of myself I want to project. I pick up the crumpled jeans I wore yesterday from the floor and pull them on, making sure the underwear isn't going to creep out the leg later today. I grab an Irish wool sweater to complete the outfit. My mother would turn up her nose, but I won't be caught dead in one of her St. John knit suits. He arrived unannounced. What does she expect?

As I walk downstairs, I consider what might bring him to speak to me. Maybe my mother has melted the ice in Lake Louise and drowned? Not likely.

When I enter the room, his back is to me, but I can see he's drinking coffee and studying the shelf of first editions my father collected. I've always thought he was a little smarmy. I wouldn't be surprised if he tucked a book into his briefcase before I arrived. I'll have Richard check the inventory after he leaves.

I take a big breath and paint a smile on my face. Extending my hand, I say "Welcome Mr. Moreau. What brings you to Reinhardt House?"

He's a slight man, barely equal to me in height. Rather than clasp my hand, he does what he always does and shakes my fingers. His father was my grandfather's attorney, so we inherited him, though I'm not sure why we kept him.

"Thank you, Miss Reinhardt." He opens his briefcase, which is sitting on the side table, and extracts several packets of papers. "Your mother thought you might want to go through the papers she gave you recently."

My smile is tight. I may not have gone to law school, but I've been reading contracts since I could read. I know what they say and why I'm screwed.

"I've been through them."

"Do you understand your father's will?"

"You explained his will to us when you read it after he passed."

"You understand that with Christopher not interested or able to assume responsibility of Reinhardt Corporation, and Steven unable to meet the requirements at this point to assume leadership, the company falls to you."

"That's what you explained and what I read."

"Did you read that you can only inherit the management of the company if you're married? Your grandfather was a man of a different generation," he explains.

I'm seething. "I did notice that." Does he think I'm marrying Alex because I *want* to?

"And you read the documents in which you authorized Herbert Walker of Elite Electronics to extract over a million dollars from the Reinhardt Foundation for his personal use? This action was against the rules of the Foundation and a violation of the law. You've embezzled from the Foundation."

Ah yes, here we go. "I did no such thing, as you know. And that isn't my signature." I will myself to keep my cool. My mother is trying to pull a fast one here, but I'm not going to let her get away with this. Smarmy or not, Moreau is an officer of the court, and he needs to abide by the law.

"But it *is* your signature," he counters. "I witnessed you signing that document. I told you at the time that if anyone found out, you'd be fully prosecuted by the Reinhardt Corporation and find yourself in jail." He clasps his hands in front of himself and looks me up and down like a piece of meat. "You told me no one would ever know."

That's complete bullshit. I walk toward him until I stand less than a foot away. In the sweetest voice I can muster, I ask, "What does my mother have on you to make you lie for her?"

"I was there. There's nothing to hold over my head. I assure you that would be against the law."

"You know as well as I do that I didn't sign this." *I can't lose it here. That's how she'll win.*

He shifts gears. "Did you read the paperwork Alex signed?"

I nod.

"Those documents indicate that he's stolen over a million dollars from his own family."

I shake my head. He's among the Walkers' fleet of attorneys too. "You control his accounts; Alex couldn't have done that without you."

Moreau rocks back on his heels. "He tricked me. His mother contacted me, or so I thought, and authorized the disbursements. But actually, it might have been you who called. We can't be sure, but she's made it clear it wasn't her."

After a moment, he hands me an additional stack of papers. "These will be filed by my office with the Hennepin County DA. They outline your misappropriations and malfeasance with the corporation and Alexander's embezzlement. It will no doubt result in warrants for your arrest."

He pauses, seemingly for dramatic effect. "Of course, these will never see the light of day if you go through with your wedding to Alexander and remain married to him. Any divorce will also set these documents into motion."

There it is. Blackmail, plain and simple—well, not too simple. What on earth is going on here? This is not just about the company. It can't be. My mother has lost her mind. It's finally clear that I can't just go along with this. Otherwise the whole rest of my life will unfold this way—something new and horrible waiting for me around every turn, anytime my ideas and my mother's don't exactly match up.

I need to talk to a professional of my own, but anyone here in Minneapolis will likely report that to Mr. Moreau. I need to figure this out.

"I appreciate you stopping by," I say absently, still evaluating how I'm going to move forward.

"I just wanted to make sure you understood the gravity of your situation."

He's not yet closing up his briefcase, and suddenly he licks his lips.

I want to vomit. "Thank you," I manage. "Anything else?"

He steps forward and stares me down. I flinch as he moves the hair away from my face, and I try to step back but find the wall behind me.

"I look forward to servicing you the way I do your mother." The innuendo drips from his mouth, and goosebumps cover my arms.

I'm flooded by the desire to knee him in the balls.

"You can leave now," I seethe.

He closes up his briefcase and puts his coat on, watching me.

Mr. Moreau is clearly knee deep in this mess, and once I can prove that, I will happily have his law license revoked.

He finally goes, but I remain in the library, pacing back and forth. I'm not sure what to do. I didn't sign the documents attributed to me, but I can't be certain Alex didn't sign his papers.

I've made it clear I don't want to marry Alex, but I'm still here, aren't I? My mother has to be reasonably certain I'm going to tow the line like always. Why the strong-arm tactics?

Fortunately I have a trip to San Francisco for the Foundation on Monday, because I need to talk to Christopher. He knows what kind of crap happens in our family. If anyone can help me sort this out, it's him. If I have to get married to preserve the future of the company, I'm for damn sure going to do it with eyes open. No shady business, no blackmail, and no surprises about what lies ahead.

I read through the documents again, and Moreau has included a profit and loss statement for the company as proof of my crime. I look through every line item, as my father always taught me to do. Then I spot something.

My heart beats a bit faster. The gray clouds separate ever so slightly.

Finally, a bit of leverage for me.

I hear my mother at the front door and go to greet her. "Hello, Mother."

"Hello, my darling."

She's looking way too smug.

"Your sleazy lawyer came by to see me."

She gives me a plastic smile. "I thought it best that he go through all the paperwork with you, so you knew what you were up against."

"I'm perfectly capable of reading. I'm curious as to your deal with Herbert Walker."

"He's been a long-time friend and ally to your father and me."

"He was Father's best friend. Did you fuck him to get back at Father for having an affair with Nancy and fathering her child?"

It occurs to me that if Murphy hadn't died in a car accident a few years ago, he could've been the heir to run the business. He's also the one thing my mother really resented. She never cared that my father had affairs, but the fact that his relationship with his secretary resulted in a child? That put it all right out in the open. And then Father left Nancy a quarter of his estate, so clearly he loved her. And that's not what his arrangement with my mother was supposed to be.

"Your father's relationship is none of your business." She bristles.

"Well... Patrick offered to service me *the same way* he does you," I tell her. "Do you fuck him? I wonder what Herbert would think if he knew you were screwing him, too?"

Her hand trembles, which I know is a sign she's nervous. It's her tell, as Jonnie would say.

"You know I have great respect for the company and everything Father and Grandfather built," I tell her, moving closer. "You've played on my love, knowing I'm loyal and not usually one to fight you. But you went too far when you pushed me to marry Alex in some big society wedding. You don't get to parade around like this is the fabulous event of the century. This is a business arrangement. Alex and I will marry at the Hennepin County Courthouse to meet the requirements of the will, and you'll vacate this house immediately afterward."

She shakes her head and points a finger at me. "You will have the wedding I'm planning."

I smile because I know I have her. "No, I won't. While I may be willing to do almost anything to sustain our family business and the Foundation it supports, *you* depend on the company. Your stipend comes from the corporation. You have no money of your own because Grandfather's will set it up to go to Father, the direct heir, and he kept the same structure in his will. I don't know how I missed this at the reading, but no part of it provides for you. And there are no requirements for a fancy wedding."

Her face morphs from pained to horrified and angry. I've figured her out. My mother never saw me as smart like Christopher. He went to medical school, but I went to business school, and I'm successfully running the Foundation.

I've prepared for being on the board of my family company my entire life. My ridiculous mother aside, I do believe in what my family has spent generations creating.

I take a deep breath. "If you force me into a big wedding, I promise you'll never see another penny from the Reinhardt Corporation."

Mic drop.

"Don't you dare threaten me," she growls.

"What are you going to do, Mother? Dissolve the company and lose everything? Thanks to that enlightening session with your attorney, I just realized all the money you support yourself with goes away if the company goes away. The will is clear that you didn't inherit anything. So, as I said, Alex and I will marry at the Hennepin County Courthouse when we're ready. I'll let you know the date. You will move out and go to Florida or wherever you want to go. And just remember, if you bother me, I'll make sure you don't get another penny."

I leave her standing in the foyer. I walk upstairs and feel better than I have in months. This is still a tremendous mess, but I have a little bit of autonomy. Mother inadvertently gave me all the aces in her house of cards.

I text Alex.

Me: I just learned something very interesting, and I need a high five because I actually won an argument with my mother.

Alex: What happened?

Me: I'll explain in person sometime. We'll talk soon.

Chapter 16

Maggie

"Kate, this is brilliant."

My week is off to a great start. I'm sitting across a San Francisco café table from Kate Monroe, the director of Brighter Future, the nonprofit out of San Francisco the Reinhardt Foundation is working with to roll out their Operation Happy Holiday program on a larger scale. She's just presented her latest batch of ideas about potential targets around the country.

Brighter Future's goal is to make sure disadvantaged kids stay in school and go on to get jobs or go to college. They worked with one of our San Francisco Bullseye locations this past Christmas to reward students attending school and doing well with a shopping spree. That reaches right to the heart of what I want to do with the Foundation and giving back to our communities.

"Thank you. It's been wonderful to have access to your resources at Bullseye," Kate gushes.

"I trust you're using the computers we had delivered. Are they making a difference?"

She nods. "Without a doubt. It used to take twenty minutes for the old ones to boot up, and they crashed all the time. Your gift has literally added hours back into our days."

The investment in ten computers, monitors, and software was minor for us, yet so valuable to them. I love the way small things can make a big difference.

"I'm so glad," I tell her. "Last time I spoke with the Bullseye liaison, Jennifer Chase, she said you were considering some adjustments to your program going forward?"

"Yes, she was concerned some school districts wouldn't want to *buy* the kids' attendance."

I roll my eyes. "The research backs up what you're doing. I don't think you need to change a thing. Maybe we just need to adjust your message."

Kate grins and nods her head. "I could kiss you right now. That's what I tried to explain to Jennifer, but I wasn't as articulate. You know, if the whole chairwoman of the board and head of your family foundation thing doesn't work out, let me know. We would make a spot for you at Brighter Future."

I laugh. I can see why kids are drawn to her. If only she knew how appealing her offer was.

"You never know," I say with a smile. "I might just take you up on that."

"I should warn you, the pay works out to be less than minimum wage, but when you see those smiles on Christmas Eve, it's totally worth it."

We spend another hour talking. She's getting married in a few months to a man she met when he volunteered for her.

"One of our board members gave me his name when we were short volunteers to participate in the Christmas-shopping part of the program, and he was kind enough to show up with forty people—mostly his employees. He owns a security company, so I called him when all the gifts went missing, and he worked until he found them. Somewhere in there, we fell in love."

"What a great story," I marvel.

"How did you and your fiancé meet?" she asks.

"I think we fought over the tiger costume in the dress-up box when we were in kindergarten."

Kate's eyes grow wide. "No way! That's really cool. Have you been together since you were five?"

"Goodness no. Our families are good friends, and he was my best friend all through school, so… ah, we decided to make it official."

"So romantic."

I wish it were. I envy her excitement about getting married. I'm busy plotting how to get out of my impending wedding. If only I could get out of the marriage too.

We talk a bit longer before she needs to get back to work.

She waves as she shows me to the door. "See you next month."

I have some time before I agreed to meet Christopher in a little over an hour. I'm actually going to see his office on this visit. But for now, it's nice to sit back, have a moment to myself, and take in the atmosphere of San Francisco. I order a third cappuccino and watch the busy sidewalk. Minneapolis is busy, but it's cold. We use tunnels to ferret our way through the city. Here people wrap up and walk, run, ride bikes, rollerblade, scooter, and probably cartwheel down the sidewalks.

A guy walks by with similar hair color and build as Jonnie, and when I get a whiff of his cologne, for a half-second

I think it might be him. My mind is truly at war with itself. I wonder what Jonnie's doing right now. I pull out my cell phone to stare at the pictures I have stored of him. I can't bring myself to erase them. I think of him entirely too often. I will probably always wonder what would have become of us if the family business hadn't gotten in the way. Before I can open the pictures, I see I missed a text.

Christopher: Where are you? Your luggage was dropped at the house over an hour ago.

He sent the text a few minutes after my meeting with Kate began. I need to psych myself up for our visit. I adore my brother, but I'm in knots at the thought of explaining all this to him, and ultimately I'm not sure how much help he can be. When he emancipated himself, Christopher encouraged Stevie and me to do the same. And he's been opposed to my marriage to Alex from the moment it was presented. I know he doesn't feel the same way about family loyalty as I do, and I'm prepared for an "I told you so" or two, but hopefully he'll at least have a lawyer I can contact.

Me: Sorry I was in a meeting. I thought we weren't meeting until 11.

Christopher: Since when do we adhere to a schedule? If your meeting is over, get your ass over here. I need some sister time.

Relief floods me. His enthusiasm makes me excited to see him.

Me: I'm two blocks away. Leaving now.

I chug the last of my cappuccino and leave a hefty tip before I begin the short walk to my brother's office.

I was mad at him for a long time. We were two years apart in school, but we were close growing up. He clashed often with our parents, but then he just left us and started a new life. At the time I didn't understand the handcuffs that came with being the oldest male in the Reinhardt family — expectations that would have required him to have the right friends, attend the right university, study the right subjects, marry the right person, and always put the business before himself. Christopher saw that this lifestyle had destroyed our dad, and he wasn't going to let it destroy him. Unfortunately, I see his position much more clearly now.

The elevator doors slide open, and I spot him standing at reception, talking to the woman behind the desk. Mid-sentence, he stops, rushes over, lifts me off my feet, and twirls me around. "Mag-pie!"

I laugh. "Thoph!" I used to call him that when we were kids, though he's always been Christopher to the world — never even Chris.

"Come on in." I follow him back to his office and take in the stunning open workspace with floor-to-ceiling windows and white furniture with pops of color, which ensures everyone can enjoy the bright and sunny days. Different groups are meeting in the communal open space.

Once things settle down — and I suppose depending on *how* they settle down — I want to implement these kinds of design changes at Reinhardt's offices. It's been over a decade since they've had a facelift, and it's time.

I take a chair opposite Christopher, and we talk about my flight, my meeting, and my plans for the visit. Then he launches his first attack. "How is Mother doing?"

"She's managing dad's death about like you'd expect."

"That means a strong front, nothing out of the ordinary, and zero emotion."

I nod. "I think she held back from her social commitments for about a week, and then returned to her schedule."

"Any tears?"

"None that I saw."

"They loved each other at one point."

I'm not sure they did, given what I now know about my mother's relationship with her lawyer and possibly Alex's dad. I shrug and suppress a shudder. "I think there's a lot we didn't know."

"That sounds ominous."

I laugh. "When are we meeting Bella?" I don't want to tell him what I've learned and what Mother seems to be capable of. Not yet.

"She's going to meet us at the restaurant at twelve thirty." His cell phone chimes, and he glances at it. "I'm sorry. I need to take this phone call. Will you be okay for a minute? The kitchen is right over there." He points to a brick wall at the back of the room. "Help yourself to anything you see if it doesn't have someone's name on it. I'll be right back." He practically runs out of his office and into another three doors down.

I check my email, and there are two messages from the wedding planner, but I'm not interested in managing those. I feel silly sitting here. I've already looked at all the pictures on his shelves and walls. He has his diplomas—a bachelor's degree in chemistry from the University of Minnesota and a medical degree from the University of North Carolina-Chapel Hill—hanging prominently.

I step out, see him in deep conversation, and decide to find a drink.

The kitchen area is huge, with tables and counter space filled with snacks and fruit. I look through the glass front of the refrigerator at the rows of sodas, juices, flavored waters, and a few bottles of champagne. So many choices. I reach for a diet ginger ale.

"You must be related to Christopher."

Turning, I find a beautiful, tall, blond woman with a pixie haircut standing next to me with a bright smile.

"Is it obvious?" I ask.

"Well, the diet ginger ale is his favorite, and you're the female version of him, so maybe a little bit." She says in a low voice, "I always thought he looked like a girl." She extends her hand. "I'm Emerson Healy. I work with Christopher. I think we met at his wedding."

It hits me that she was with one of the partners, but her hair was much longer. "Of course. I didn't recognize you."

"I had a baby and cut off my hair. They say women do it all the time, but I will warn you, don't. You'll regret it. I know I do."

I laugh. "At least it grows back, but I'll try to remember that. Christopher said it was okay to grab a drink."

"Absolutely. Take two." She gestures to a large, clear jar on the countertop. "Those gingersnap cookies are amazing. They were brought in this morning by someone on the team. I bet they'd be fantastic with your drink."

"You know just the way to my heart."

"What brings you to San Francisco?"

"I had a meeting with a nonprofit our foundation is partnering with."

"Brighter Future?"

"Yes, do you know them?"

"I was a mentor at Christmas. What an amazing cause, and it was so much fun, too."

"Do you have a minute? I'd love to talk to you about how it worked from a donor's perspective."

"Sure, we can sit here or head back to my office."

"Either way."

"Let's go back to my office. Our nanny is stopping by later, and it's easier if they don't have to track me down when she arrives."

I follow Emerson through the maze of cubicles and sit in an office similar to Christopher's, except the view is different.

"I love your offices."

"We're getting ready to move because we've outgrown the space."

"I hope you'll be able to replicate the openness in your new place and have these stunning views."

"That's the plan. We want to hire a few more people and have some room to expand."

I take a bite of my cookie, and the spicy, sweet ginger explodes on my tongue. "These are delicious."

"Thank you." She smiles and winks.

"You made them?"

"I did, but don't tell anyone."

"Cross my heart." I make the motion on my chest. "I would love your thoughts. Our dilemma is that while in San Francisco, and most other urban areas, we can find mentors who are able to contribute two hundred dollars without batting an eye, we eventually want to roll the program out into rural communities. That kind of donation may be more of a challenge for our mentors there. Do you have any thoughts about how to get people involved in a way they can afford?"

She sits back in her chair. "Hmmm. That's a good question. Your family foundation contributed matching funds here in San Francisco?"

"We did. When Christopher called me about what they were doing with our store here, I knew it was something we wanted to get behind. But we'd like to match the amount donors have contributed equally. Probably needs to be the same nationwide after all the publicity we've received. Ideally that would be two hundred dollars per student in every community."

"Let me think on this." A shadow shrouds the room, and we both watch a rain cloud pass over. "Are you still in town tomorrow?" she asks.

"I am. I'm here until Friday late afternoon."

"Perfect. My best friend recently joined Brighter Future's Board of Directors. Let's schedule lunch to talk about it."

"That would be great. Who's your friend?

"Caroline Arnault."

I'm stunned. She's quite a coup for Brighter Future's board. She's not only a famous billionaire, but also an accomplished entrepreneur.

"If you think she can make the time, that would be fantastic." I see Christopher looking for me, and I wave to flag him down. I stand and pull a business card from my purse pocket. "This has my cell number and email address. Let me know where and when, and I'll be there."

"Outstanding," Emerson says. "I'll be in touch."

Christopher appears in her doorway. "Sorry about that." He turns to Emerson. "We got a commitment from Fancy Pharmaceutical to buy one of my investments. It's going to be hard for the owners to say no."

She smiles. "Wonderful news. I'll wait for meeting invites when everything is ready to go."

He nods. "Are you ready?" he asks me.

"As I'll ever be."

"Be careful with this one." He nods towards Emerson. "She might try to convince you to move to San Francisco, and Mother would be really upset with me."

"Or maybe we can trade her for you?" Emerson counters.

We all snicker.

"I look forward to seeing you again soon, " I tell her.

"I'd love it if you were to move to San Francisco," Christopher tells me as we head back to his office.

"If only I could."

"Or Las Vegas might be a better place."

I look over to find him grinning at me. He's been talking to Jonnie. I don't know why that surprises me.

"Well, since you emancipated yourself and Stevie left, that sort of thing has become pretty difficult for me."

He stops short. "Maggie, you cannot give up your life for the family company. Please tell me you don't actually think that's your role. We can find you an out."

I hook my arm through his. I'm not ready to dive right into all this just yet. "Come on. We're going to be late."

I *do* think I'm stuck, but not in a way that's resentful. My brothers didn't get along with my parents. Nobody gets along with my parents. They did what they had to do to escape. Unfortunately, I'm the one left holding the bag, and it's a Reinhardt Corporation bag that weighs over seventy billion dollars annually.

Chapter 17

Maggie

When Christopher and I arrive at the restaurant, Bella is already at the table.

She stands and gives me a warm hug. "You're losing weight. You're getting too skinny."

"You always know the perfect thing to say. But I'm not sure my mother would agree."

She shakes her head dismissively. "She's a tiny waif. Ask Christopher—men like curves. It's something to hold on to."

Christopher has a look of complete terror. "Okay, we're talking about my mother and my sister. I can't go there."

We take our seats, and I change the subject. "It's my fault we're late. I got into the most wonderful conversation with Emerson about Operation Happy Holiday mentors in rural areas. She's going to arrange lunch tomorrow with Caroline Arnault."

Bella nods. "She's amazing. You'll love working with her. She's very down to earth."

"How are things going with Brighter Future?" Christopher asks.

We spend the next hour talking about all the great things going on with them, and how fearless they're being about expanding. It thrills me.

Bella's fork hits her plate with a clank. She pushes back from the table as she wipes her mouth with her napkin. "I'm so sorry to cut this short. Work is calling. You both have plans tonight, right?"

"Yes, I'll catch up with you after." Christopher winks at her, and she smiles and shakes her head.

I don't want to know what they have planned.

She disappears from the restaurant with many of the men seated around us watching as she retreats.

"We have plans?" I ask.

Christopher turns to me and clasps his hands on the table. "First, you're going to tell me why you're here," he says just above a whisper.

I sit up straight and my mouth drops slightly open; I was hoping to ease into this conversation. "You know I had an appointment with Brighter Future."

"Yeah. And you always jet home following your meeting. We might meet for a drink or a meal, but you never stay."

Could he make this any harder? "I can't want to spend time with my big brother?"

He gives me the give-me-a-break scowl. "Who do you think I am?" With his pointer finger, he circles his face. "Do I look like I'm some innocent, doe-eyed, good-looking guy?"

I snicker. "You don't want to know what I think you look like."

"I'm only teasing. But does this have to do with your upcoming wedding?"

"Why would you think that?"

"Because I had a surprise dinner guest last week."

"Who? Mother?"

He snorts. "No, Minnesota would have to fall into the Great Lakes before that iceberg would leave to visit me in California. My visitor was Jonathan Best."

My stomach drops. "What did he want?" I ask, trying to sound innocent.

Christopher gives me the side-eye. "He finally confessed what I'd figured out years ago."

I'm completely confused. "And?"

"He's been into you since high school."

I sit back hard in my seat. That was the last thing I expected him to say. "Did he tell you that?"

Christopher nods. "Are you into him, too?"

I nod and feel tears form in my eyes. "But it doesn't matter."

"What do you mean? Of course it matters. All the more reason for you not to give up your life for the company. Why didn't you tell me what Mother is trying to pull? Reinhardt doesn't need Elite Electronics, and if you don't want to marry Alex, don't."

I take a file folder from my purse and push it across the table. I look around to make sure no one is obviously listening. "The situation has been crazy from the beginning — all hell broke loose right after you and Stevie left town, and I don't have a good answer for why I didn't tell you. You guys have made it clear you don't want to be involved with the company, and you'd already gone out of your way to help me address the situation by hiring George Dayton, so I just thought I'd step up and do what needed to be done. But there's something even weirder going on now. I need to meet an attorney here in San Francisco — someone who won't tell Mother I'm investigating her claims."

He doesn't open the file, just stares at me. "What claims? What's going on?"

In a small voice, I walk him through what I learned during my meeting with Patrick Moreau. He grinds his teeth and doesn't make eye contact with me as I speak.

"Did you sign the paper Moreau says you did?" he asks.

"No. I would remember committing fraud and embezzling money for Herbert Walker. I have no relationship with that man, and he makes me incredibly uncomfortable. I checked my calendar, and the last time I met with Moreau, we were going through the estate. I'd never met with him alone before Saturday."

"So the document is a forgery?" Christopher presses.

"That's correct. I believe it's a forgery. Patrick Moreau says otherwise, but I swear to you I didn't do it. What would I have to gain?"

"Did Alex sign his?"

My shoulders fall. "I don't know. Maybe? I haven't asked him about it yet, and I honestly don't know who to trust with anything at this point." I sigh. "But I did find one small bit of leverage."

Christopher finally looks at me.

"I figured out that if I don't get married—or if those documents send me to jail—and the family sells the business, Mother loses even more. Dad's will left her nothing. The house goes to the board chair, and the company shares were divided among the three of us kids and Nancy. No part of the business is in her name, because Grandfather wanted it to be direct heirs inheriting only. As it is, she owns nothing, but gets a stipend from the company. However, if we're required to sell the business because we're in breach of the will, the new owners aren't going to keep her on the payroll, which means she'll have nothing. And, if she forces me into a big society wedding, I told her I wouldn't give her a dime either." I laugh, my eyes wide. I can still hardly believe I managed that.

Christopher sits back in his chair and laughs so hard people turn and gawk at him. "That's classic!" he says when he finally catches his breath. "It explains so much."

I wish I found this as humorous as he seems to. "Christopher, I'm certain she and Herbert Walker are up to something and have been having an affair. I don't know why she'd be threatening me with all these documents if there wasn't more to this."

He shudders. "That frigid bitch has sex? I find that unlikely, but I wouldn't blame her. I mean, at the funeral Nancy cried harder than we did. She loved Dad, and I believe he loved her. But you're right. Mother is definitely is up to something."

He sits for a few minutes and taps the folder, still not opening it.

The waiter tops off our water glasses and sets down the check.

When I reach for it, Christopher stops me.

"I've got this." He takes out a black American Express card and places it on the bill. He doesn't say anything else.

I watch the people on the sidewalk outside of the restaurant scurry by to get to their destinations.

Finally, Christopher looks up and focuses on something over my shoulder. "We're going back to my office." He picks up his phone and sends a message.

I'm confused. I open my mouth to speak, but he holds up a finger to stop me.

"Do not say anything."

When the server returns with the credit card receipt, he signs it, and I follow him out the door. I'm not sure what he's done or what his plan is, but I try desperately to keep up as he walks swiftly to his office.

I'm in three-inch heels and struggling with this pace. I trip over a piece of uneven sidewalk and stumble to a halt just before I fall down. "Christopher, stop!"

Circling back to me, he takes my arm. "We need to

hurry. We're meeting with Sara in my office. I want her thoughts, and then we'll find you a lawyer you can talk to and get to the bottom of this bullshit your mother is pulling."

"That's fine, but I can't walk this fast in these shoes."

"I recognized someone in the restaurant, and I'm fairly certain you're being watched," he murmurs.

I'm sure I misheard him. "What?"

"Let's go to my offices, where we can talk."

Arm in arm, our pace slows. I'm beginning to hate these shoes. When we step into the elevator in his building, he turns to me. "I'm fairly positive I saw Vanessa Locklar's father in the restaurant. He was dining alone and watching you very carefully."

My hand goes to my mouth. I'm sunk. I'm going to jail. When the elevator doors open, Christopher steps out, grabbing me by the hand, and I follow him to a small, windowless room in the back of the office space. When I enter, a pretty dirty-blonde is sitting and waiting for us.

"Sara, this is my sister Margaret," Christopher says.

She stands and extends her hand. "It's lovely to see you again. I believe we met at the wedding."

"Yes, I remember. It's nice to see you again, but please call me Maggie."

"Show her what's in your file," he says. As I take the folder out of my bag, he adds, "I'm also sure a private investigator from the Twin Cities was following her."

Sara looks up. "How do you know this private investigator?"

"He's the dad of a girl I dated in high school. He cornered me and threatened me with a gun when I was sixteen. He's not a face I'm likely to ever forget."

Sara begins to leaf through the documents. When she's done, she stares up at me. "First, I should make sure you understand that this is probably outside of my wheelhouse. A lawyer's education is broad. We learn the generalities and specialize afterward. And this is not where I ended up."

"I understand. But I don't have anyone I can trust in Minnesota. I worry anyone I meet with could talk to my mother or her lawyer. We have sort of a well-known name there."

She nods. "I think Reinhardt is a well-known name everywhere."

"Here are a few things that may add to your understanding of the documents you just read, I begin. "My father maintained the will that my grandfather set up, with a small adjustment after Christopher emancipated himself." I pause to give him the side-eye. I can't help it. "It says a married Reinhardt family member must run the company. My father had a thriving law practice, but my grandparents pushed him to marry my mother, whose family owned the Hudson company and were of a similar social station. This allowed for a company merger without an actual sale. When my grandfather died, my father stepped in reluctantly to take over the company. It had never been something he wanted. Anyway, my parents had an arranged marriage of sorts, and they were never faithful to each other. My father eventually built Murphy's and named it for a son he had with his secretary."

I pause and clear my throat and explain that the pattern is now repeating itself—or at least my mother would like it to. Having me marry Alex brings Elite Electronics into the Reinhardt Hudson fold, and she seems willing to stop at nothing to make sure that happens.

I pull out the loan authorization form. "My mother and her attorney presented this to me as something they'd take to the authorities if I don't marry Alex Walker." I point to my signature. "This is a forgery. I did not arrange this loan or sign this document. But if they present this to the authorities as real, I'll go to jail for embezzlement and fraud."

Sara nods. Pulling out the page with Alex's signature, she asks, "And this one? Do you know if this is a forgery?"

"I haven't asked Alex, but that appears to be his

signature. I'm hopeful his is also a forgery, but I'm less confident that's the case."

"Why is that?" she asks.

"Alex's father has told him if we don't marry, he'll lose his inheritance, and Alex believes this will ruin his life. He has expensive taste, and he doesn't work." I look down at my manicure and pick at the chips in the polish. "He tends to date men who like him for his money."

"I see. And for your mother, this is about growing the company?" she asks.

"I can only speculate..." I wait for her to ask her next question.

She and Christopher stare back at me.

"So speculate," he says.

I close my eyes a moment. "The merger would add a huge electronics section to Bullseye. Electronics hasn't traditionally been an area where we've excelled, but if we were to rebrand the Elite stores, that would be a huge win. Not to mention there is a sizable real estate acquisition that would come with the company. My mother's fortune is dependent on the continued success of the Reinhardt Corporation."

Sara goes through the paperwork several more times. "Christopher, do you know Marci Peterson?" she finally asks. "This level of embezzlement would be federal. She knows people and helped William with his family's business in Philadelphia. I think we need to start with her."

Christopher nods. "That's what I was thinking, too. And if Maggie is being tailed, we don't want to tip our hand that we're aware of what's going on. That could set off a chain of events that will take time to unwind."

"I think that's smart." Sara opens her cell phone, pushes a few buttons, and places the phone on the table.

"Peterson Kelly Lively," a voice calls through the speaker.

"Marci Peterson, please. This is Sara Arnault."

"Just a moment please."

We wait while soft music plays.

"Hi, Sara," comes a gentle voice over the phone.

"Hey, Marci. How's your day?"

She chortles. "I have a feeling it's about to become more interesting."

"For various reasons I can't go into over the phone, I'm wondering if you have time to come to our office this afternoon," Sara asks.

"I have a depo tomorrow I was going to prepare for…" Marci notes, and I know she's politely asking how important this meeting is.

"My client is only in town a few days, and we think she has a private investigator following her," Sara explains.

"A private investigator?" Marci takes an audible breath. "Can you give me an hour? I'll give some of my work to a paralegal. I can sleep when I die, right?"

"Thank you," Sara says. "I will owe you big time."

"Agreed," she teases.

Sara sits back in her chair and picks up the documents again. "Anything you need."

"See you shortly," Marci says before disconnecting the call.

Sara picks up her phone and makes another call before setting it back down.

"Jim Adelson," sounds a rich, deep voice from the speakerphone.

"Hey, Jim."

"Sara. What's up?"

"What do you have going on? Are you free this afternoon?" she asks.

"For you, anything."

"Wonderful. Marci Peterson will be here at our offices in an hour. Can you join us?"

"I'll leave in five. Anything I need to bring with me?"

"I don't think so. Christopher Reinhardt is here with

his sister, and they have an issue and a professional stalker."

"Are we sure?" he asks.

Sara looks at Christopher. "What's the name of this PI?"

"He's from Minneapolis, and his last name is Locklar." Christopher spells it for him. "He was always Mr. Locklar to me, so I'm not sure of his first name."

"I'll do some research and bring what I find," Jim says. "See you shortly."

Sarah is quick and efficient, and I'm impressed.

"Marci can advise you on the forgery and next steps," she tells me. "She's super strong with corporate governance, and that's what I think you need. If she thinks something else, she may direct you elsewhere."

I nod. Christopher puts his arm around me, and I feel strangely assured by my older brother.

"Like I keep telling you, we're going to figure this out," he says.

"Jim will be ideal for helping Marci with any research but more importantly for your physical protection," Sara continues. "Where are you staying tonight?"

"At my house," Christopher says.

She nods. "That's good. You can make room for the guys."

"Whatever it takes," he confirms.

"I'll leave you to it. This will quickly be a very crowded room. I'll have Marci and Jim shown back as soon as they arrive."

When she steps out, I turn to Christopher. "Wow. I didn't expect the cavalry."

He smiles and wraps me in a hug. "I'll always be here for you; remember that."

I wipe my suddenly wet cheeks. We don't always see eye to eye, but I know my brother loves me.

The hour wait seems to take forever. I play on my phone and continue to destroy my manicure until Jim arrives first.

Christopher introduces us. Jim is a huge man at over six and a half feet tall, and he carries himself like he was in the military. "It's so nice to meet you." He extends his large hand. "I've heard a lot about you from my fiancée."

I'm confused. "Fiancée?"

"Kate Monroe."

I smile and nod. "She told me all about you being her knight in shining armor when you saved the Christmas gifts for the children last year."

He blushes. "I was happy to be able to help. While we wait for Marci, let me tell you about Kevin Locklar." He glances at Christopher, who nods. "His license was revoked over three years ago. He does some minor work for some less-than-savory clients with one common thread: the Kryetar, an Albanian organized crime family."

My heart sinks. Could my mom be involved with them? I glance at Christopher, and his brows knit. Having leverage on Mother is one thing, but if she's backed by an organized crime family, that takes this to a whole new level.

Now I really am scared I could go to jail, not for fake embezzlement but for trafficking goods or laundering money for the mob or whatever they've got their talons in with the Reinhardt Corporation. I can feel my throat constricting.

Before Christopher can say anything, Marci arrives. I paint a smile on my face and hope she has some way to help me.

Christopher greets her and again makes the introduction.

"So wonderful to meet you," she says to me. Turning back to Christopher, she adds, "Sorry it's not under better circumstances." Then she smiles at Jim. "We meet again. We need to stop doing this."

"It's always something with these guys," he teases.

"I take it you're involved because of the stalker?" she asks.

He nods as we once again take seats around the table and slides a file folder over to her. "Here's what I've learned about the stalker after a quick search. You can keep that."

She opens the file and looks through it.

"He's involved with an Albanian organized crime family," Jim says.

"The Boss family?" she says.

I must look confused.

"*Kryetar* in Albanian means *boss*," she explains.

"Do you know them?" Christopher asks.

"Not directly. I've seen sealed documents running through the federal courts, though. I can say that they don't mess around, but I didn't realize they were doing much in the Midwest."

Jim shrugs.

Marci has me start at the beginning, and she asks multiple questions as I work my way through the story and examine all the documents. We spend the next two hours going through everything.

"And this lawyer, Patrick Moreau, told you he witnessed you signing this document?" Marci asks.

"Yes, but I swear I had never seen this before, and that's not my signature. When we met, he was careful to tell me all about how he had previously spelled out the ramifications and counseled me against it."

"Have you signed other documents?" she probes.

"Easily a thousand of them..." Looking at Christopher, I add, "We all did after our father died."

"And to be clear, he didn't casually say, 'Hey don't you remember on X date you signed this?'" she pushes.

"No, he was just very clear to spell out what he'd said and what exactly I did on the day I supposedly signed it," I say.

"Was there a recording device?" Jim asks.

I sit up straight. "No. Not that I could see."

Marci glances at Jim. "Sounds like that might've been

recorded. Do you agree?"

He nods. "It sounds awkward the way he said it. Just an FYI, he was admitted to the bar in Minnesota in 1985, and he's in good standing."

My heart sinks. Recording devices? An Albanian crime family? What has my life become? The only thing holding me together is knowing I have Christopher here with me. He's upset too, but each time I look at him, he gives me a reassuring smile. I'm not alone. I have to remember that.

Chapter 18

Maggie

Late in the afternoon, Marci leaves to go back to her office. We have a plan. Some other men from Jim's office arrive, and he introduces me to Zack and Thomas. "Zack's going to be with you a while. He's from the Twin Cities, so he knows the area if you go home."

If I go home? Why would I not go home? My pulse picks up, and I feel sweat prickling along my hairline.

Christopher puts his hand on my leg. "Don't panic. You're okay. We just need to be cautious until we understand what's going on. Are you ready to head back to my place?"

I nod. Thomas gets behind the wheel of the Suburban, and I'm in the back of the car, sandwiched between Zack and

Christopher. I rest my head on the back of the seat. "God, I'm exhausted. I'm going to bed early tonight."

"I actually have a surprise for you," Christopher says. "I don't want you to be angry with me. I made these plans before I knew we'd be spending the afternoon with Marci and Jim."

"What's the surprise?"

"You'll see." He's silent a few moments. "I'm having a hard time processing everything I learned today, so I know this must be overwhelming for you. But so much more makes sense now that I know the whole story. You can't marry Alex."

"It's the only way to ensure the future of Reinhardt Hudson. And Alex needs the merger, too." I sigh.

"This can't happen," he says with determination.

"Alex and I are friends. I don't want to leave him with nothing."

"Don't give up. You deserve better than this, and if anyone can figure a way out, it's Marci."

The car pulls up in front of Christopher and Bella's home. Christopher is out the door before we come to a complete stop. I'm so busy gathering my things and trying not to bump into Zack that I don't notice someone sitting on the front steps.

But I snap to attention when a familiar voice says, "It's about time."

It's Jonnie, and my breath hitches in my throat.

"Sorry. We got hung up at the office," Christopher says.

"Maggie, it's nice to see you," he says as I emerge from the car.

My heart is beating triple time. I stare up at Christopher. What was he thinking?

My mind is racing. He can't be here. Why is he here?

"Let's go in," Christopher offers.

Zack and Thomas walk with us up to the door. Zack

goes in first, and we follow with Thomas at the rear.

"You have security now," Jonnie teases Christopher.

"They're actually for Mags,"

Jonnie stops short. "What? Why?"

"Let's get inside. We have a story that might interest you."

Thomas goes back to remain with the car, and the rest of us make our way into the living room. Zack wanders around with some sort of device in his hands. It takes a few minutes for me to figure out it's looking for things sending an RF single signal—listening devices.

Christopher busies himself pouring drinks for the three of us, and he and Jonnie talk about the Minnesota Wild hockey game last night. I take a seat next to the fireplace. The room is chilly. I can almost see my breath as I fight to remain calm. Rubbing my arm for heat, I debate grabbing my coat I just left hanging on the rack by the door.

Christopher sees me and stops mid-sentence. "Sorry you're cold, Mags. These old houses can be drafty." He flips a switch next to the gas fireplace, and it lights up immediately.

Zack returns, places something in the window, and nods at Christopher. "Okay, now we know there are no listening devices, and the parabolic mic will be on scramble so no one can pick up our conversation. We can talk freely."

Jonnie's eyes dart between Christopher and me. "What's going on?"

Christopher looks at me, waiting for me to unload the afternoon's news. I take a deep breath. "We've uncovered some unsavory things. I'm being followed by someone who's associated with the Kryetar."

"Who are the Kryetar?"

"Albanian organized crime."

"From Minnesota or here?"

"Minnesota."

He tilts his head up and takes a deep breath. "Are you okay? Has anyone threatened you?"

I shake my head and then laugh. "Well, mostly just my mother. She's forged some documents to make extra sure I marry Alex."

"How's that even possible?" Jonnie asks.

I'm not sure how much Christopher wants shared with Jonnie. He raises his eyebrows and gives me a small nod—confirmation to continue. So I walk Jonnie through the whole saga—from the slimy meeting with Patrick Moreau to the Albanian mob-affiliated PI.

"The lawyer said he was there when you signed the paperwork and warned you of the repercussions, but you signed anyway?" Jonnie asks.

I nod. "Yes."

"That's ridiculous. You would never do that." He turns to Zack and Christopher. "So what's the plan?"

"I've hired a lawyer here in San Francisco and a security company," I explain.

"Clear Security," Christopher adds.

Jonnie nods. "I use them at the resort. They're the best in the business. And what else?"

"The lawyer is going to do some research over the next day or so, and Clear is going to do some investigating into Elite Electronics and Reinhardt Corporation, looking for connections to the Kryetar. Meanwhile, I'll go on with my meetings in hopes of not raising too much suspicion," I say.

Jim steps into the room. *Where did he come from?*

"Is she safe?" Jonnie asks him immediately.

He's talking about me like I'm not in the room, and my blood pressure begins to rise. "I'll be fine," I stress.

Christopher looks at me. "I thought I heard something a little different earlier—not to go to your meetings, and to keep a low profile."

"Do you have cameras and a strong security system—motion detectors, window alarms, video camera surveillance, and night vision coverage?" Jonnie asks.

Christopher shakes his head. "No cameras, but I have a

strong security system, and we'll have two men with her at all times."

I shut my eyes and take a few deep breaths as I put a death grip on the arms of my chair. Don't they understand I'm alarmed, too? One bodyguard is too many. How is this going to fly at home in Minneapolis?

"What's the big-picture plan here?" Jonnie asks, finally looking at me.

"The wedding has been reduced to a courthouse affair suitable for the business arrangement it is, and I've made it clear to my mother that it will be on my terms. It won't be the giant society event she's trying to have. Although I'm not sure she's notified anyone of that change, because I'm still getting emails from the wedding planner and some of the vendors."

"But why are you going through with the wedding at all?" Jonnie asks. "I know you feel it's what's needed for the business, but it sounds like your mother isn't arguing in good faith. There's something shady here."

I shake my head. "I just don't know what else to do. The wedding is still a few weeks away. Maybe one of these attorneys will see something workable—and also a way to invalidate those fake documents and keep Alex and me out of trouble."

Jonnie doesn't look thrilled, but he nods, squeezes my hand, and stays silent for now.

A little while later, Christopher says, "You and Jonnie have a dinner reservation at Bix in about an hour. You're going to need to get a move on if you don't want to be late."

"That doesn't sound like keeping a low profile," I point out.

"It's a small restaurant, and you'll go with a team. I was just there getting it all taken care of," Jim says.

I gasp. *This is really happening?* "What? I'm not dressed for a fancy dinner."

"You look beautiful, and frankly, if you were wearing a potato sack, I wouldn't care as long as you join me," Jonnie says with a smile.

"At least let me freshen up," I implore.

Christopher turns his wrist to look at his watch. "You have ten minutes."

I jump up. "I'll need everyone." I begin to search for my suitcase. The car service dropped it off this morning while I was at my breakfast with Kate.

"Your bag is already upstairs in your room," Christopher informs me.

Dashing up the stairs, my excitement pushes past all the fear and uncertainty of today—and the past months. A date with Jonnie. We've never had a real date. I quickly change into something other than dark pants and a peasant blouse.

"Time's ticking!" Christopher yells upstairs to me.

I roll my eyes. He gave me ten minutes, and I intend to use them. "Be right there!" I wish I had time to curl my hair, but at least I can wash my face and apply fresh makeup. After a lighting-fast transformation, I rejoin the guys downstairs a little winded.

"Okay, Zack and Thomas will be seated at an adjacent table," Jim tells me. "You'll be at a corner table on the second floor. If at any time you see something strange or someone you don't know attempts speak to you or join you—or you just don't feel comfortable—you need to use your safe word."

"Safe word?"

"You'll say a unique word only your security detail will know. And they'll only allow the staff at Bix to approach your table. We need to choose a safe word you won't forget."

"Having a safe word makes it sound like Bix is an S&M club," I quip.

My brother's eyes bulge. He isn't appreciating my sense of humor.

Jim smirks. At least I entertain someone. "It's just a word that will put the team on alert. We don't want to be a distraction to your dinner."

"I understand. My word is *glasswing*," I tell him.

"Glasswing?" Christopher gives me a strange look.

"Yes. It's a butterfly from South America. They're rare." I shrug.

My brother expels a breath of frustration. Despite our ages, I still take extreme pleasure in irritating him.

I wrap a pashmina around my shoulders to keep the cold away. "All conversations about rare butterflies are off the table during dinner," I tell Jonnie.

He salutes me. "No problem. Perhaps next time."

We pile into the Suburban with me in the middle of the back again, between Zack and Jonnie. Thomas drives, and Jim sits next to him in the front seat.

"I feel quite important," I announce. I'm nervous-talking. Whenever I do this, I think I'm funny, but no one else seems to.

"Do you know a lot about rare butterflies?" Jonnie leans in, and his warm breath on my neck sends jolts to my core.

I laugh. "No, and before you ask, I don't know much about S&M either."

"That's too bad." He grins and reaches for my hand, giving it a reassuring squeeze.

The restaurant becomes a circus when we arrive. People turn to gawk at the three absolutely gorgeous men with me. I chuckle. If they only knew. We sit down at a private booth upstairs in the corner. Light jazz drifts up from the quartet downstairs. I really like this place. The Art Deco ambiance makes me think this restaurant—which is hidden down an alley, away from the busy downtown streets—must've been a speakeasy in a previous life.

Jonnie puts his arm around me and pulls me in close. His touch sizzles my skin with electricity. It feels so right to be here with him. Despite everything else going on, I somehow know I'm just where I want to be. I'm not sure I've ever felt this way before.

He leans in and asks, "What was so funny downstairs when we arrived?"

"I'm sorry?"

"When we walked in, you laughed. How come?"

I shrug. "Everyone turned to stare at us. I'm the envy of every woman and gay man in here."

His brows furrow. "What makes you say that?"

"I have three hot guys with me."

He grins. "So you think I'm hot?"

I can't help but smile. This is the guy who had every girl in school chasing him, and he's here with me. I'm going to have fun tonight and pretend I don't have an arranged marriage looming and people—possibly led by my mother—tracking my every move. I can deal with all the crap tomorrow. Fuck 'em.

I lean in and put my hand on Jonnie's upper thigh. "I think you're hot with clothes on, and definitely when you're naked."

"Outstanding, because my flight doesn't leave until morning, and I plan to refresh your memory tonight."

I shake my head. "Sorry, I'm staying at my brother's."

"I'm well aware, and it doesn't change my plans," he says with surprising confidence.

"Well, for your safety, I don't think you'd want to risk Christopher hearing us," I reason.

"It's only a sign of two people having fun." He shrugs.

"I'm not sure my brother would see it that way."

A man approaches the table. "Jonathan Best," he exclaims.

"Doug? I didn't know you were working tonight." Jonnie stands and extends his hand.

"This is my restaurant. I'm always working. The real question is what brings you to San Francisco and my humble restaurant."

Jonnie lets out a loud laugh. "Doug, let me introduce you to my girlfriend. This is Margaret Reinhardt."

Girlfriend? I put on the best smile I can and extend my hand.

Doug grasps it, turns it, and brings it to his mouth for a soft kiss. "Welcome to Bix, Margaret. You're in for a treat." He winks at me, and I watch Jonnie bristle.

"I'm thrilled to be here," I tell him.

"I know you have menus, but Bruce and I thought we'd do a tasting menu, special just for you. You know, we were very disappointed we weren't invited to be a part of The Boardwalk at the Shangri-la."

Jonnie grimaces. "I'm sorry. I didn't think you'd want a restaurant outside of San Francisco."

"So many of our customers go and stay with you. I hope you'll consider us if something opens up or you expand."

Jonnie nods as he sits down and reaches for my hand. "We look forward to the tasting menu."

"May we add the drink pairing?"

Jonnie glances at me, and I nod.

"Sounds wonderful," he tells Doug.

"Then I'll leave you to it. If you need anything, do not hesitate to have your server come find me."

"Excellent. And I'd love to see Bruce before we go," Jonnie says.

Doug grins. "I'll make sure that happens."

After he retreats, I ask, "Who's Bruce?"

"Doug owns four restaurants here in San Francisco, and Bruce is his partner with Bix. Bruce also owns another restaurant. They're a real business power couple."

Over the next two hours, we enjoy an amazing five-course meal, and Jonnie has me laughing all the way through. I swear I even snorted, and I normally avoid that at all costs. He's kind and considerate, always asking for my opinion and letting me talk. Each time my wine glass gets low, he fills it. And thankfully he never brings up Alex, my mother, our last meeting in Minneapolis, or our current situation. This is more fun out than I think I've ever had, and I don't want it to end.

When I take my last bite of the chocolate soufflé, I moan my appreciation.

Jonnie picks up my hand and places it firmly on his crotch. His hardness is prominent through his pants. "This is what you're doing to me," he rasps.

I smile and stroke him. Thoughts of our previous time together run through my head. I bite my lip, and he watches me intently. "You're very naughty," I whisper.

"I can be extra naughty, and we can break out your safe word," he growls.

I stare down at my plate, and I'm sure I turn a nice shade of crimson. He kisses the most sensitive part of my neck and whispers, "There's nothing wrong with doing something that feels good."

A flood of wetness dampens my panties. I'm grateful for my padded bra because my nipples are so erect, they hurt. But I put my excitement on hold when Doug returns with a man dressed in the kitchen chef's shirt and matching pants.

"So what did you think?" he asks.

"Absolutely outstanding, Bruce," Jonathan confirms.

Doug and Bruce turn their attention to me.

"Perfection" I assure them.

They talk about the dinner, and then the conversation moves to the Shangri-la. I feel like I'm intruding on their proposal. I excuse myself and head to the ladies' room with Zack at my heels.

When I return to the table, Doug and Bruce make their apologies for running me off.

I shake my head. "Please don't worry about me."

"We're sorry to intrude on your evening," Bruce says.

"You'd fit in well on The Boardwalk at the Shangri-la," Jonnie assures them, and they light up.

After a little additional small talk, they make tentative plans for a trip out to Las Vegas, and then leave us to finish up.

"I'm really sorry about that." Jonnie pushes a wisp of hair behind my ear, and his hand on my leg moves closer to my center. "You look absolutely amazing tonight."

"I wasn't kidding about my brother's house. I can't have sex with him one floor below me."

Jonnie stands and reaches for my hand. "Your brother already told me he won't be home tonight. We have the house to ourselves."

My breath hitches.

"You'll be needing that safe word." He grins and my nipples pebble all over again.

Chapter 19

Jonathan

The security team drops us off at Christopher and Bella's and does a quick sweep before they head out to the guest house for the night. We move upstairs, barely making it to the third floor and Maggie's room before our clothes are off, and I've got her up against the wall, massaging her glorious tits. I've missed them. I trace a finger around her areola, and her nipples tighten to hard points. I lick and suckle. Her breasts are so soft.

Maggie reaches for my cock and strokes it. Then she moves farther down and caresses my balls. She returns to my shaft with a firm yet delicate touch. Her fingers find my pre-cum, and she wipes it around my head, sending shivers through me.

I suck her nipple into my mouth, and she places a hand behind my head to keep me there. I reach down and slip a hand over her mound, dipping a finger into her slit. She's wet, and I slide into her opening. She presses my head to her nipple, and I gently bite down. She gasps, and her pussy contracts around my finger.

I take my mouth off her nipple and kiss her. Her lips are hungry against mine, and she drives her tongue into my mouth. I suck on it, and she presses herself up against me. My cock presses into her stomach and she continues to rub it. She drops her hand from the back of my head and grabs my left ass cheek, squeezing and pulling me in tighter. My finger drives into her pussy, and she moves her hips with me.

"Please, Jonnie," she whispers into my mouth. "I need you inside me."

Still kissing her, I look past her and spot a large soft chair across the room. I steer her backward, and when her calves touch the chair, she lets go of me and sits back. She lifts her legs and spreads them. She keeps her eyes locked on my erection and licks her lips.

I take a moment to admire her. Her breasts are pushed together by her upper arms. Her hands cross over her stomach and her fingers splay her pussy lips apart. I can see her clit is swelling, rising hard and prominent. It's beautiful and glistening.

She's so open and ready for me. I sink to my knees and behold the beautiful sight. I kiss up her thighs as she leans her head back and moans. Her fingers find her nipples, and she twists and pulls. I lick and suck on her clit. My fingers pivot in and out of her.

"Right there... Yes..." Her breathing increases, and her internal muscles hold me tight. "Jooooooonnie."

She reaches for my wrist, holding me deep inside her. My cock is standing at attention, begging for its turn.

The gush of her excitement coats my hand. Her head lifts, and she's orgasm drunk. I continue to lap up her juices.

"You taste sweeter than fruit."

"It's your turn," she rasps.

She takes my cock deep in her mouth, and I'm not going to last long if she sucks me off. I help her stand and move her to the bed behind us. It's tall enough that I can stand between her legs. She positions herself on the edge of the bed, and I line myself up with her opening. I hold my cock as I run the head between her pussy lips and up and over her clit. She moans her appreciation and thrusts her hips. It's tempting to just plunge in, but I resist her and keep rubbing my cock along her wet pussy and clit.

"I need a condom," I grumble.

She nods.

Scrambling to my pants pocket, I find a condom and feel victory. I turn and she's moved up into the bed.

She locks eyes with me, and I enjoy the look of wanton lust she sends my way. This woman wants me bad—me and my cock. I'm a man deeply desired, and she is a woman wet and open, willing and equally desired. I cover my cock faster than I think I ever have, press my swollen head to her opening, and push in. Her eyes plead with me to continue, but I withdraw and run my cock back up and over her clit.

She makes an angry noise, but her head falls back as I continue to circle her clit with my cock. I tap my cock against her, and she rewards me by sucking air in past her teeth. I rub her clit harder, enjoying the electric shocks running down my dick.

I press my cock against her opening and push it in just past the head, then pull it out again. She makes an exasperated noise and looks down to watch my cock play with her pussy lips and clit. I tap her clit again, and she smiles.

I can do this all night. I probe her lips, run my cock head up through her swollen inner labia, and circle her clit hard. She's breathing heavy now and can't tear her eyes from what I'm doing. Her clit is swollen and standing tall. I'm mesmerized by it. Her pussy is dripping now, red with excitement. Her upper chest is flushed as well.

Our matched desire overtakes me. I'm rock hard. The wet sound of my cock rubbing against her fills the room. She reaches up to pinch and twist her nipples again.

She's getting close to a powerful orgasm—and so am I. This time when I push against her opening, I go all the way in. The feeling of her pussy wrapping around my shaft is heaven, and I almost come from the sensation. She throws her head back and cries out loudly. My balls press against her, and I then slowly pull back.

I push back in slowly and then withdraw. I keep up this agonizing pace, though I want nothing more than to thrust wildly. She doesn't move. She lets me set the tempo. She lowers a hand and circles her clit. I watch, amazed as she touches herself with thumb and forefinger, stroking. It's an amazing sight to see. I almost lose my rhythm and falter for a moment before resuming.

I continue to fuck her slowly, and my orgasm begins to crescendo. She's close again. Her eyes are screwed tight and her mouth is open in a little O. I thrust harder, and her eyes shoot open. I thrust three times hard and fast, and she comes, screeching my name again.

I feel like a superhero as she loses control, bucking and thrashing. It's all I can do to stay inside her. Her pussy's clenched so hard on my cock I can barely move it. I need to come, but hold off to watch her. She's beautiful. A flood of liquid surrounds my cock and trickles out to run down her ass. I keep thrusting, and she keeps coming.

I don't know if she has one or many, but I'm in awe as this woman simply gives in to her pleasure. She's breathing quickly, and her pussy clenches and unclenches, holding me as my orgasm surges.

I've never had sex like this before. I've never felt so in tune to the needs of my partner. We've synced our desires perfectly. I fall forward against her, and she wraps her arms around me and holds me close, the wetness between us a symbol of our enjoyment. I collapse beside her and lie gasping.

"That was amazing, Jonnie," she whispers. "Thank you."

I grunt in reply, unable to form words. I'm exhausted and spent.

She strokes my back and runs her nails over me, causing me to shudder.

There isn't anything I wouldn't do for this woman. We have to find a way.

Chapter 20

Jonathan

"You're amazing," I gasp between breaths.

"We're even better than I remember," Maggie says shyly.

I chuckle. "We need to do this more often."

"When are you going back to Las Vegas?" she asks after a moment.

"In the morning. You should come with me. I have plenty of room in my apartment, and I'd love to do a lot more of this."

She stiffens. "I have meetings with a board member of Brighter Future, and I suspect I'll need to meet with my lawyer again. I can't leave San Francisco."

I'm disappointed, but I worry if I push too hard, she'll run away, and I want her to be assured I'm here for her.

"Okay. But this was a lot of fun," I offer as I caress her arm.

"Let's not worry about tomorrow quite yet..."

Barely able to complete her thought, she falls asleep in my arms. We're supposed to be together — this only proves it.

Christopher told me he and Bella would meet us in the morning. And even when her work is done in San Francisco, Maggie can't return to Minnesota. Not with everything going on. Maybe with their help, I'll be able to convince her to come to Las Vegas.

It would be wonderful to have her with me. I've loved her since we were kids, and now that I can tell she feels the same, I'm impatient. I've waited long enough.

If we can just sort out this current mess, surely we can find our way to the future. I think of parties with her beautiful body by my side — and naked in private. I think of the time we could spend together — not all of it naked. There are so many fun things we could do together and enjoy. I finally fall asleep, dreaming of what I hope is to come.

∞

I smell coffee before I open my eyes. The bed is cold. I roll over, and I'm alone. So much for my morning wood.

I pull on pants and a shirt and head downstairs. I hear Maggie laugh, and it occurs to me that I don't hear that nearly enough. Then Christopher and Bella laugh. I realize I'm not sure what time it is.

Following the noise, I find my way to the kitchen where Maggie and Christopher are listening to Bella tell an animated story. I hang back a moment and take it all in. Bella's arms are flailing as she talks a mile a minute.

In this moment, Maggie is almost the same girl I

remember from my childhood—carefree, bright smile, and joy emanating from every part of her.

Bella sees me, and our eyes lock. "Hey! There he is," she announces.

I walk in and join them.

Christopher pours me a cup of coffee. "Did you get any sleep last night?"

Maggie turns scarlet and looks away.

"I slept better than I have in months," I tell them.

Bella gives Christopher a death-ray stare as he's about to quip something, and instead he closes his mouth.

"What's for breakfast?" I ask.

"I made *huevos rancheros*," Bella says.

"Sounds delicious." I take my seat next to Maggie and kiss her temple.

She gazes up at me and gives me the doe eyes I saw last night. We really did connect. I hope that means progress. I want her to understand what she means to me, that I'm here for her as she finds her way through this.

Bella serves up heaping plates of corn tortillas covered with her grandmother's refried beans, two eggs sunny side up, cheese, homemade salsa, and sliced avocado. I didn't realize I was hungry until the mix of spices permeates my brain.

I take a bite and moan my appreciation. "What are you doing toiling away at some startup? You should be sharing your cooking talents with the world."

She shakes her head. "I can only make three things."

"She's an amazing cook. Don't believe her." Christopher smiles at her adoringly.

"How do you keep your figure with these meals? I'd weigh three hundred pounds," Maggie says. "This is amazing."

We hardly talk as we devour our breakfast. I have a second helping and struggle to finish.

Pushing back from the table, I groan as I enter a food

coma. "That was delicious."

"When's your flight?" Christopher asks.

"I told them we should aim for ten, but we'll leave when I get there." I look around at the group and add, "I think Maggie should come with me, but she doesn't want to. She'd be safe with me. Her team can join us, and she could be in seclusion without anyone knowing where she is until we find a clear path forward. What do you guys think?"

Christopher turns to Maggie. "I could see how that might work. Why do you believe going to Las Vegas is a bad idea?"

"Well, for starters, I'm supposed to meet with Emerson Healy and Caroline Arnault *here*."

"What's the meeting about?" he asks.

Maggie shrugs. "Foundation stuff."

He raises his eyebrows and waits for her to continue.

"We're brainstorming ideas on how to manage mentors and funding for rural areas when we expand Operation Happy Holiday," she says with a dramatic eye roll.

"Kate is busy rolling out to sixty *inner* city locations this year," Christopher stresses.

"It's actually sixty inner city school *districts*," Maggie corrects.

"But are you doing any rural locations in this phase?" he presses.

"No, that's phase three," she mutters, not looking at any of us.

"So it isn't urgent?" he asks.

"Christopher! Please don't discount my work. And besides, a meeting with Caroline Arnault doesn't happen every day."

"Maggie, trust me. I get it, and I'm not discounting anything, but your access to Caroline is not going anywhere. Right now you've piqued the interest of an organized crime group, so it might behoove us to put you into hiding until we can figure this out."

She shakes her head. "I'm not going into hiding. They win that way."

I can almost see the steam coming from Christopher's ears. No one has ever been able to get him angry like this in all the years I've known him except for Maggie—or maybe his mother. Normally I'd find it hysterical, but now I'm right there with him.

I reach for Maggie's hand as a show of support. I've said all I can say. Now it's up to them.

"Maggie, you've been managing all of this by yourself for some time," Bella says. "I'm sure it feels like you're all alone, but please reconsider. Let these people help you."

"I am committed to doing what I need to do to keep the family company intact, but I have control over almost *nothing* in my life at this point—nothing! I'm tired of sacrificing everything and having everyone else make choices for me." Maggie breaks down in tears.

We rush to comfort her.

"We just want you to be safe," I implore. "And we're going to get you back in charge of your life. You told me you hired the best attorney in San Francisco to help, along with Clear Security, and those are fantastic choices. But let's not race back to the Twin Cities where you don't have any cover. With me, you can hide in my apartment while we figure out what's actually happening, and what we're going to do about it."

She looks less certain, and her tears have slowed. I think we're making some headway with her.

"We can fly you in under the radar, and you can stay there with Jim's team close by while we let Marci do her job," I add.

Maggie starts crying again. She's scared, and I know she's also overwhelmed.

I pull her in close and hold her while she weeps. Christopher and Bella move in, and soon she's getting a hug from all sides.

"We're going to get through this, I promise," Christopher says.

When the tears stop, we give her some room and she takes a deep breath. She bites her lip and twists the ring on her right hand as she visibly weighs everything we've said.

"I guess I can go to Vegas," she finally says. "But I have to cancel my lunch with Emerson and Caroline."

"Excellent, and I already have a plan," I inform the group. I take a few minutes to walk them through my thoughts, and in the end, everyone agrees.

"You know, if you were to become a criminal, you'd never go to jail. You're way too slick." Maggie says.

I grin. "How do you think I got my hotel built on prime Las Vegas property in the middle of the Strip?"

Maggie shakes her head. She's wearing mascara streaks and a smile, and she looks beautiful.

"Well, let's hope your approach works in this situation," Bella says.

"It has to," I say, squeezing Maggie's hand.

∞

A little while later, Maggie and I have packed our things, and Jim and his team arrive with six black Suburbans, lining them up at the curb. It's time to implement the first phase of my plan: getting Maggie to the airport unnoticed.

In less than a minute, the four of us each take a seat in a different vehicle. As we pull away, it becomes a giant game of three-card monty. The cars all appear identical, with the only difference being a number in the middle of the license plate.

We traverse the city in various ways, moving around and switching positions. The dark windows make it difficult to discern who might be inside any of the cars. When Maggie's car gets on the highway to drive to the airport, the other five cars are left continuing down the street. Eventually most of them also enter the highway, but they get off at different exits and move around.

The shell game hopefully made it difficult to determine where we were headed, and we should have thrown off any tails. In the end, Christopher's car goes to his office. One of the cars goes to Jim's office. Bella goes across the Bay Bridge to Berkeley. One of the cars heads over the Golden Gate, and the cars carrying Maggie and me head down the peninsula on different highways, each making its way to the private airport entrance.

Maggie will arrive first at the airport. She's wearing a bright red wool coat and has a green hat. The plan is for her to exit the car without the hat and look around as if she's searching for me. Then she'll put the hat on and walk up the stairs to the plane to wait.

When my car arrives, I don't see her anywhere, so I bound up the stairs to the plane. We've registered the flight plan to drop me in Vegas and then go on to Minneapolis. When I arrive, Amanda, one of my staff members from the hotel with a similar build and hair color to Maggie has flown in with the plane and crew. She's significantly older than Maggie, but they shouldn't notice that. Maggie gives her the red coat and green hat, and she lifts it onto her shoulders.

"Amanda, you'll have a bodyguard with you. You have nothing to worry about. Enjoy a few days in San Francisco on me."

She cinches the belt of the coat, kisses me on the cheek, and hugs Maggie. "Whatever you two kids are up to, have fun and be safe. I'm going to go see my son." She puts the hat on and walks down the stairs to the waiting car.

"I hope this works," Maggie says.

We settle into our seats, and the flight to McCarren Airport in Las Vegas is short. Maggie bounces her foot the whole time, crossing and uncrossing her legs. Her brow furrows as she stares out the window of the plane.

"We're going to be fine," I assure her.

She nods. "I know. I just don't flake out on people, and I hate doing that to everyone back in San Francisco."

"You have the burner phone we picked up, don't you?"

"Yes, my phone is at Christopher's, as if I never left, and it will forward calls to this number."

"We've got this." I hold her hand tightly. "Christopher will let everyone know you can't make your meetings. I'm sure they'll understand."

"I just hate being the center of attention, I guess."

I kiss her on the forehead, and the plane begins its descent.

Once we land, we deplane in our hangar, and the plane is on the ground for less than five minutes before it takes off again for Minneapolis. The car waiting drives Maggie and me to my hotel and into the parking garage. I take Maggie up to my apartment via the back stairs, where there are no cameras, and get her settled.

I give her a quick tour and put her things in my bedroom. If she isn't comfortable with that, we can talk about it, but I've waited too long for her to be in my apartment to have her in the guest room and not next to me.

"I'm going to check on how things went while I was away," I tell her. "Unpack. Get comfortable. Zack is remaining for a few days until my team gets onboard."

"Thank you." Maggie stands at the windows overlooking the desert with her arms wrapped around herself.

I gather her in my arms. "We're going to get through this together."

She gives me a half-smile. I tilt her head, and our lips meet. Our kiss is hot, aggressive, and full of need.

"I promise I won't be gone long."

It takes all my will power to leave. But if I don't, they'll interrupt me all afternoon. Closing the door behind me, I step into the elevator that will take me to the lobby with Caden on my heels.

"You're back," Connie, our head concierge, greets me

as I step out.

"I am."

Crowds wander the hotel, and the foot traffic is busy but not overwhelming. It's typical mid-week, mid-day chaos.

"Anything exciting happen in the twenty hours I was gone?"

"Travis will have a report for you," she says.

I stare at her. "That bad?"

She shrugs. "Something's going on, but he knows more than I do."

I nod and walk the long way through the casino to the security team's nest and Travis's office. He's waiting for me when I enter.

"How bad was it?" I ask, not sure I really want the answer.

"We had another issue with Queen Diva."

My heart stops. "What the fuck? What happened this time?"

He laughs. "Actually this time it was her. One of her shoes—you know the ones with the Swarovski crystals?"

I nod slowly. Those shoes are worth more than some people make in a year, and I do not want to hear they're missing.

"Mark Butler was in her room the entire show," Travis continues. "She wears them for the opening and the closing."

I nod.

"She removed the shoes after the first act. And throughout the show, everything went well. There was a VIP birthday, and she sang to them. But then she ran back to put on her shoes, and her fitters couldn't find them."

My pulse quickens.

"They were in a panic. She was upset that she had to do the last act in a clear pump—whatever that means." Travis rolls his eyes. "She does three encores before Frankie stops it and has the house lights go up. By this time, they've called me and Detective Kincaid."

Now Travis seems to be fighting a laugh, and there's a giant smirk on his face.

"We arrived within seconds of one another. I had the footage of the evening coming to my phone as soon as it was ready. I figured I'd be calling you to tell you she's breaking her contract. Then Frankie sits down hard on the couch, and Kincaid notices it moves."

I'm waiting for the punch line, and my palms begin to sweat. I'm not sure if I'm going to vomit, shit my pants, or both.

"Kincaid asks Frankie to stand, and of course, he puts up a fight and doesn't do it. But when Queen Diva screams at him, he does. We move the couch back to where it was earlier in the evening, and there are her shoes."

"You've got to be kidding." A wave of relief settles over me. "What else was under the couch?"

"Not what we were hoping for—no dresses or ring. We did find a condom wrapper, which we covered pretty quickly, although I'm positive Queen saw it."

My sense of relief dissipates, and I stare up at the ceiling. Trouble between Queen Diva and Frankie could spell disaster for us.

"Well, it might not be Frankie's," I offer.

"Yeah, right."

"At least that's some positive news," I try to rationalize. "What about the rest of last night?"

Travis shrugs. "Typical weeknight. LVPD was here for a drunk and disorderly and for two shoplifting events on The Boardwalk."

He glances at the monitors on the wall. "How is your friend doing?"

"You've talked to Jim at Clear Security?"

He nods. "I have facial recognition software running on all the people in the hotel at all times. We're looking for members and anyone else associated with the Kryetar."

"No one should know she's in the hotel," I warn.

"I get it. Those are some nasty guys."

I nod. "I'm already wishing all we were dealing with was drunks, gamblers, and a few missing expensive dresses."

Chapter 21

Maggie

I take in the vastness of the apartment for a little while after Jonnie leaves. I wish he could just hole up in here with me, but I focus on being grateful for what I have. At least I'm here at all.

The burner phone chirps and vibrates as it sits on the coffee table in the middle of the room. I haven't spoken to Mother since our blow up before I left. My heart races, and my palms begin to sweat. Zack stares at his wrist and nods.

"Hello, Mother." I take a few silent deep breaths and will myself to sound aloof and calm while I wait to see which one of her many personalities she will present. Will she be angry, worried, or sickeningly sweet?

"Darling, where are you?"

Sickeningly sweet it is. *Could she be tracking me?* I hoped we were overreacting.

"I'm in San Francisco. Don't you remember?"

She's quiet a moment. "Oh, yes of course." She's quiet again. "But I thought you were due home today."

"I'll be home in a few days. I'm enjoying my time with Christopher and Bella. Plus, I'm working on some Foundation things while I'm here."

"You really need to come home soon," she presses. "I'm sure Alex misses you. And we need to work on your wedding."

"No, we really don't. I told you, I won't be having a high-society event." I glance over at Zack, and he warns me we're approaching the two-minute mark, which makes the call traceable. "Listen, I've got to run. I'll call soon," I tell her and disconnect the call.

Uneasiness grips me. "Did I make it in time?"

"Yes." He nods, looking at his phone. "Jim wants me to take the SIM card out of the burner and replace it with this one." He holds up a little electronic card smaller than a dime. "It has a different phone number."

"How will I talk to my mom and convince her I'm still in San Francisco?"

"We're converting it to a VoIP, which will scramble the location with the help of a VPN."

I look at him, confused.

He smiles. "The VoIP is an Internet-based phone number, and the VPN will have it jumping to multiple servers all over the globe. So the next time you talk, you can talk a little longer. It'll jump every thirty seconds. But at some point, we'll have to change it up again."

Zack heads off with my phone, leaving me alone. I don't know what to do. I don't want to wander through the apartment, snooping, so I stay put in the living room. I stare out the window at the desert. The last time I was here I told Jonnie I was getting married. I hurt him. I didn't want to…but now I have no idea what's going to happen.

My mind is like a pinball machine, bouncing from one thing to another. This happens when I don't sleep well—and probably also when my life is crazy. Last night was amazing, but we didn't sleep. My mind goes to what we *did* do. I'm a little sore, but in a good way. The mental ping-pong continues as I lie back on the couch.

I really didn't expect Jonnie to want anything more to do with me after I told him I was marrying Alex. His reaction makes me realize I don't have many true friends in my life. But I think he's one.

I loved having dinner with him last night. The food was amazing. I think my pants fit a little tighter today. I can't eat like that very often.

My brother and Bella are so happy together. I've never seen Christopher so relaxed and calm. It makes me feel sad all over again at the prospect of marrying someone I'm not in love with. Also, Christopher is truly happy in San Francisco, and it's great to know that's possible, even for a Reinhardt. I don't want to drag him back into this disaster at home. I just don't have much choice.

I wonder what Alex is doing. I should talk to him…maybe. I just don't know if he's also being hung out to dry, or if he's somehow involved in this.

The sex last night was mind-blowing. I've never had that intense of an orgasm, let alone that many. Jonnie has ruined me for all other men.

I turn my Kindle on. I only feel safe doing so because we turned the Whispersync off. But I can't concentrate long enough to read. I keep looking at the same two sentences over and over. Nothing grabs my attention.

I pace in front of the windows, and then worry I'll wear a hole in the floor coverings. Is this considered carpeting? Or a woven grass?

After a while, I don't know how much more I can take. Then just when it seems like forever, I hear the door, and it's been less than two hours Jonnie was gone. My anxiety dissipates as he walks over and kisses me.

"You look beautiful. Las Vegas suits you."

"Thank you. I would have changed, but I didn't know where my luggage was and didn't want to snoop around."

He smiles. "I asked them to put it in my room."

My eyes go wide, and my pulse quickens.

He holds me tight and kisses the top of my head. "I understand my feelings are new to you, but I've spent every day since you told me you were going to marry Alex telling myself that if I ever got a second chance, I was going to be honest." He takes both my hands in his and looks at me. "But at the same time, I don't want to scare you. Just know that I love you very much, and I will take this at whatever speed you need me to."

He loves me? My heart breaks a little bit. I don't want to think about what's going to happen when everything falls apart. I just want to hold him close. I step in and kiss him, our tongues tasting and growing anxious with each passing second.

I bite my lip and stare up through my eyelashes. "I haven't had a tour of your place since it was decorated."

"Then what are we waiting for?" He holds my hand and escorts me down the long hallway. "This is our bedroom."

It's beautiful, done in various shades of lavender with a king-sized, four-poster bed. "I love it." I turn to him, and he begins to unbutton my blouse.

"Do you know how many times I've fantasized about you being here with me?"

I shake my head. "What did you imagine doing in this beautiful bedroom?"

His kisses are soft, and his hands explore. Soon I'm standing in my bra and panties.

"I've wanted you for so long," he whispers.

I feel the hardness against my stomach grow. I want to

taste it, to feel it. I move to get on my knees, but he stops me.

"You first," he says.

He steps away and examines me. I think of the roundness of my too-big breasts, my too-wide hips, and my straight blonde hair. I half worry he's going to run out of the room, never to return.

"You are stunning," he sighs. "Your skin is glowing in the orange light of the sunset."

Bowing my head, I reach for Jonnie's belt. I contend with the buckle as I stare into his eyes. His gaze doesn't waver as I slowly loosen his trousers and they fall to the floor. Once I unbutton and remove his shirt, he kicks away his pants and socks, and we fall together, as one, onto the bed.

Jonnie's lips crash urgently onto mine, needing, taking. He maneuvers his body so he's lying above me, and his naked chest slides across my skin. I think I may pass out from the adrenaline high. The weight of his body traps me, and I never want to escape. My breathing speeds up, and I can make out his smell of citrus and clean. My hands roam his hair and across his muscular shoulders and back, and all the while I'm kissing him back with fervor. When my hands drop to stroke across his well-muscled ass, still covered by a pair of cotton boxer shorts, a groan reverberates in his throat.

Breaking away, he places soft, light kisses over my neck, across my collarbone, and along the edge of my bra. Gasping for breath, my eyes roll back as he changes direction and places his mouth directly over my nipple. He gently clamps his teeth around the sensitive flesh, partially protected by my silk bra, until my body hardens beneath his touch.

"Oh, fuck," I groan. A strong pulse beats between my legs, and a white spark of light flashes across my eyes, even though they're closed. I feel ridiculously turned on, with liquid pooling in my swollen pussy. Jonnie's hand migrates to my back, and he releases the catch of my bra. Stroking the straps from my shoulders, he removes the offending article, allowing the warm air to caress my naked breasts.

"Mmmm," he murmurs as his lips wrap around my erect nipple.

A thrill passes through my body as his tongue darts over my skin. After ensuring the other nipple isn't left out, he migrates farther down my body.

"I need you inside me. Please," I beg.

"So demanding," he says, looking up at me, his tongue lazily circling my bellybutton. Hooking his thumbs inside my silk panties, he slowly pulls them down my legs, eventually casting them aside, onto the floor.

"You're incredibly sexy, Ms. Reinhardt." His lips drop to my bare pussy, and he inhales deeply.

"I need you," I reply, pulling him up until we're face to face.

I bite him softly on the shoulder and push him back into the duvet. I caress my way down his body, over his taut stomach and down the line of downy hair that eventually disappears into bare smoothness under his boxer shorts. Pulling his last remaining garment down and away from his body, I'm thrilled to uncover his sizeable erection. Using the tips of my fingers, I take my time stroking up his thighs and over his balls, reveling in his sharp intake of breath as my hand moves up his thick, solid shaft. I close my eyes and moan softly at the feel of Jonnie's incredible cock, which I stroke softly with the palm of my hand.

When he places his hand on the inside of my knee, I jump. But this quickly turns to anticipation as he encourages my legs to move farther apart.

"I've dreamed of you splayed out like this in my bed, and it didn't do you any justice." He groans as I circle my wet thumb over the engorged head of his cock.

With the lightest of touches, he runs his fingers along my inner thigh, the look on his face telling me he's fully aware of the desperate tension he's causing in my body. When he reaches my swollen lips, he brushes across them before caressing the opposite thigh. I'm panting noisily now, and my grip around him tightens.

Jonnie gradually trails his fingers toward the pool of liquid between my legs. As he pushes one finger deep inside, I cry out. He slides his finger forward until he reaches the base of my clit. He holds his finger in place, applying exquisite pressure and allowing the tension to build.

"Fuck me." I exhale through gritted teeth.

"Expletive or request?" he asks.

"Either...both—" I cry out as Jonnie adds his thumb to the mix, positioning it at the top of my clit and making a small circular motion.

"I'm on the pill," I gasp as he begins a set of slow strokes.

"I'm clean and have paperwork somewhere here to prove it." He begins to ramp up the pressure, and I can feel the early signs of an orgasm building inside my body.

"I need to feel you," I demand.

Suddenly, Jonnie's hand clamps tightly around my wrist, preventing me from stroking him any further. He maneuvers me back on the bed, leaning over me. As he drops his mouth to mine, I wind my legs around his waist, pulling him closer. Moving his hand between our bodies, he positions himself and pushes a little inside me. I feel so full.

Breaking our kiss, he pulls slightly away and gazes into my eyes. Without a word, he begins to slide into my tight, desperate, quivering body.

"Oh...my...God," I groan as he buries himself within me, every wonderful ridge and curve of him feeling gloriously magnified. I close my eyes and take in the sensation.

"Look at me," orders Jonnie. "I want you to keep watching." He smiles as he continues to sink into my tight, twitching body until he's buried to the hilt. I take a sharp breath, aware that I'm currently being stretched wide and loving every second of it. Rocking his hips, Jonnie pulls partway out before pushing himself forward once again.

I groan as my internal muscles clench around his solid

mass. Once again, Jonnie retreats, pausing for a short time before thrusting himself inside once again. I cry out, a ferociously strong orgasm building inside me with every stroke.

"I want to see you lose control," breathes Jonnie, partly pulling out once more, forcing me to wait for the overwhelming sensation I know I'll feel when he plows himself back into my body. "You," he says, slamming himself into me and pulling back. "Are...so...fuck...ing...sex...y." He thrusts his hips with each syllable muttered.

"Oh, God! Please don't stop!' I beg as I begin to scale the heights of my orgasm. "Please. Please."

"You like it hard?" grunts Jonnie.

With a pleading groan, I nod, unable to find the words to respond.

"Hold tight, then."

With a hand out to brace himself, he hooks one of my legs over his shoulder, opening my body wide to him. He thrusts long and hard with a rhythm that makes me cry out and pushes me toward the dizzy heights of my all-consuming orgasm. Just before my release, when my body is tense and set to explode, Jonnie sucks his thumb into his mouth and then rolls it gently around my clit. At the same time, he speeds up his thrusting hips until I'm pushing effortlessly into a noisy, violent orgasm.

As pleasure crashes through my body, Jonnie lays still, allowing my internal muscles to contract in waves around his rock-hard cock. Then just as I'm starting to recover, he resumes circling his thumb and rocking his hips.

"Oh, no! No!" I moan as Jonnie pushes my body immediately back towards a second orgasm.

Showing no mercy, he pushes me beyond the boundaries of any pleasure I've previously experienced. When I begin to tire, he drops his mouth to my nipples and clamps down. I roar in response, the sensation a jump start to my fatiguing body. A short while later, his thrusts become more random and much less controlled.

"I'm sorry, I'm going to come…"

He groans, and despite my exhaustion, I can feel a change in his thick cock within me. My body clenches even more tightly around him in response.

"Oh, God!" I shriek as he slams himself harder and harder into me and my muscles spasm into yet another orgasm. With a final thrust, Jonnie roars as he pumps his cum deep inside my body. We collapse back onto the bed, and he drops his lips to mine and kisses me tenderly, on and on.

We're both beyond spent and breathing raggedly. Jonnie pulls a blanket over us, and I spoon against his body.

"Always and forever," I hear him mumble as I drift off to sleep.

Chapter 22

Maggie

It's day three, and I've been reduced to watching reruns of *America's Top Model* — the season Sophie Summer wins. You can tell her designs are far better than anyone else's. I've watched six episodes back-to-back, and I can't take another one. I've paced the apartment, worked out, and am planning my lunch — all before ten.

Jonnie and Jim don't think it's a good idea for me to leave the apartment. I understand this in theory, and I've only been here two days, but I wonder if it's possible to die of boredom. Nothing holds my interest — I can't work, and while Jonnie's busy, I can't play. I want to explore the city and get lost.

I don't quite understand it, actually. I spend many days

not leaving my room at home during the winter, and I love it. It's probably because I *can't* leave that I feel so boxed in.

I check my email, and again I see messages from the wedding planner. She's sent a half dozen this morning. I'm tired of this. My mother should have told her by now, but obviously, she's not going to, leaving it to me.

I fire off an email to Veronique and carbon copy my mother and Alex.

> *I truly appreciate all you've done for the wedding on Alex's and my behalf. However, we've decided to go a different direction. Thank you for all your beautiful designs. We'll be sure to recommend you to anyone looking for a wedding planner.*

I push send and feel like I got something accomplished today. Wandering into the kitchen, I open the fridge for the twentieth time. I'm not much of a cook, but the freezer is full of options.

I hear a phone ring, but it's not familiar, so I ignore it. It stops and starts again. I realize it's the ringtone to my new burner phone.

Oops.

Racing over to answer it, I expect my mother, but it's Alex. I feel better about this, although I'm not sure I should.

"Hey, you," I answer.

"Where are you?" he asks immediately.

I don't answer that. "Did you read my email?"

"Yeah. What the fuck? You're canceling the wedding? My father is going to go apeshit."

I'm a bit taken aback. I would have thought he'd be thrilled.

"Well, my mother's not thrilled either," I say with as much indifference as I can muster. "This is what I was going to tell you the other day. I figured out a small way to do something for myself—for us. I didn't think you were into a big production either." When he says nothing, I continue. "I'm not canceling the marriage, only the outrageous shindig. I told my mother we'd get married at City Hall. Isn't your friend Edward a judge?"

"Maggie!" He's near hysterics. "You can't cancel the wedding without talking to me!"

"What's the big deal? I didn't think you'd care."

He inhales a big breath. "I don't, but I'm also not interested in the hellfire my folks are going to rain down on me. Where are you?"

"I'm still in San Francisco. You know that."

"Your mother told me you left San Francisco."

The hair on the back of my neck stands on end.

"Where did she tell you I was?" I ask, trying to sound normal, though alarms are going off in my head. What is Alex's angle here?

"She didn't say. She only wanted to be sure I was talking to you regularly, and I assured her I was. Now not knowing about the wedding being canceled makes it seem like we're not talking."

I don't know why it matters to anyone if we're talking, and I'm still not sure whose side he's on.

"Please tell her I'm at my brother's, if she asks. Remind her I'll be home late tomorrow night as planned. Jeez, it's like everyone is freaking out. I'm in San Francisco, taking meetings about Operation Happy Holiday, as I told everyone I would be doing before I left. I discussed the change in the wedding with my mother before my trip, and I was tired of waiting for her to tell Veronique. She kept emailing me. We pay for Veronique's time, but I felt bad that we were wasting it."

"Your mother's going to come unhinged when she reads your email."

"Well, she came unhinged in person when I talked to her about it, but I'm used to that," I remind him. "This is better for both of us."

"We just need to talk about these things," he insists.

Something's not right. But I'm over the two-minute mark, and I need to go. "Hey, I've got to run. Bella promised me a class at her yoga studio. I'll be home on Friday. See you then."

"Bye, hon. I guess I'll check to see if Edward can marry us this weekend."

My stomach turns. Why is everyone in such a hurry? "How about next month? Let's make them worry a bit."

"You're making me worry," he quips.

"Don't be silly. I've gotta run."

I disconnect the phone and pull the SIM card before I call Jim from the landline. I tell him about my conversation with Alex.

"My mom knows I've left San Francisco."

"We have her under surveillance," he says. "I don't think she does. Tell me more about Alex."

"About the phone call?"

"About him personally," he explains. "How did you meet? Tell me about his social life."

I walk through everything I know about Alex, his family, and the men he's dated. It doesn't paint a very pretty picture, and it makes me a little sad.

"What did Christopher being emancipated mean to the family? Why didn't you and Steven emancipate yourselves?" Jim asks.

"Well, we were both younger, and at that point, we weren't under the same kind of pressure Christopher had been. Plus, once Christopher did that, my mother worked hard to remove friends from our lives she didn't approve of. We didn't have any friends to fall back on that weren't in her social circle—which meant they'd never cross her by opening up their home to Stevie or me. She made sure we knew what happens when you turn your back on family."

"What about your housekeeper and her husband—did she fire them?"

"Surprisingly no. They hate each other to this day, but

they remain employed. There's something there, some reason why, but I don't know what it is."

"All right. That helps a lot. Thank you. I'm beginning to look at some of these characters, and I'll have a new SIM card brought up to you shortly. Be sure to check your voice mail. It looks like you have five messages..." He pauses for a moment. "The number is your mother's."

I breathe a deep sigh. "That's not a surprise. I upset her this morning."

"What did you do?"

"I canceled the wedding planner. I discussed changing the wedding with her before I left — we argued, actually — and I hoped she would do it. But she didn't, and the poor wedding planner was freaking out and robo-emailing me. So I emailed her and cc:'d my mother and Alex."

"Is this why Alex called you?"

"Yes. And he was more upset about it than I thought he'd be. I can't quite figure out what's going on there either."

"All right. Keep doing what you're doing." We disconnect.

There's a knock at the door, almost as if they knew I was off the phone. I check the peephole and see Travis.

When I open the door, he hands me a small plastic box no bigger than my thumbnail. "Jim texted and asked me to deliver a new SIM card."

I nod. "Thank you."

He offers to put it in my phone, but I decline and quickly pop it into place with his supervision.

Travis waves as he heads down the hall, and Jonnie calls just after the phone boots back up.

"I hear you had an exciting morning," he says.

"I'm not sure about that." I tell him my concerns about my conversation with Alex. "I think I should go to San Francisco and be seen and then come back. You know, an in-and-out-in-one-day trip."

"Absolutely not," he says firmly. "That's a bad idea."

I'm surprised. I thought we were trying to keep them off my trail. If I'm seen with my bodyguard, they'll think I'm keeping a low profile and back off, won't they? "My mother has left five messages since I sent the email this morning. What do I tell her?"

"Just what you told her before—that you'll be home late tomorrow night," he says.

"What are we going to tell them when I *don't* fly home in two days?"

"I'm not sure yet, but I'm working on a plan that will help us make sure they don't know you're here."

He's silent a moment. The sun is nearing its highest point in the sky, and the weather looks perfect. What I wouldn't give for some quality time outside in the fresh air.

"I can tell you're feeling a little cooped up at the apartment. Give me an hour," Jonnie says. "I'll take you out for lunch, and we can go over to my friends' place. They live on the outskirts of town and have a pool."

Yes! I resist doing a dance of joy. That sounds fantastic. "I'll pack a few things and call my mom. I'll be ready when you arrive."

"Don't let her get to you. Remember, we're in this together."

"Okay." I stand straighter, knowing he has my back.

I pull a bikini Bella insisted I take from her out of my suitcase, find a towel in the bathroom, and put some of my toiletries in a bag, along with a change of clothes. Perhaps we'll go out for dinner, too.

When I've stalled long enough, I open my voice mail and listen to my mother's messages. They grow more and more urgent, wondering why I have canceled Veronique. *Because you didn't?*

I spend a few moments psyching myself up for the call. There are normal parents out there. Why couldn't mine be one of them?"

I dial her number. The phone rings for a fifth, and then

a sixth time. She's not answering. The stress between my shoulders dissipates with each ring. I'll be able to just leave a message... But my excitement evaporates when she picks up. *Crap.*

"There you are," she singsongs.

"Sorry, Mom. I was in a meeting when you called."

"Where are you?"

"Still in San Francisco. I'll be home late tomorrow night."

"You're not in San Francisco. I was at Christopher's house this morning, and you weren't there."

Rather than deny, I ask her a question. She does this all the time, and I've learned from the best. "What are you doing in San Francisco?"

"I came to talk some sense into you. Why did you email Veronique? We need her for the wedding."

"Mom..." I count to five, making sure I can speak coherently. "I told you the society wedding was off. I'll marry Alex, but with a judge at City Hall. No big production."

"I put hours into this wedding," she whines.

"I don't care. It's my way or no way. You're single. If you want a society wedding, you find someone to marry."

She sighs in irritation. But I still have the upper hand. "Where are you?" she asks. "We need to talk about this."

Why does she continue to push this? She's still getting what she wants from me—isn't she?

I cover my eyes for a moment, but then Jonnie walks in, and I find the strength to move forward.

"Mom, my next appointment has arrived. I'll see you Saturday morning after I wake up at the house."

"Does Richard know when your flight is arriving?"

"I'll just take a rideshare. See you on Saturday." I disconnect the call. Under two minutes. Not bad.

Jonnie leans in, and I kiss him. He tastes so good.

"What's wrong?" he asks.

"She's in San Francisco," I breathe.

"Shit. I thought we'd have more time. I need to let Jim know."

"Okay, and I'll call Christopher to get the low-down on what happened. I can't believe he didn't call and tell us."

While Jonnie steps into the adjoining room, I call Christopher on his office line.

A female voice answers, "Sullivan Healy Newhouse." It sounds like a law firm instead of a fancy venture capital firm.

"Christopher Rinehart, please."

"May I tell him who's calling?"

"Tiffany Daniels." She's a mean girl we went to school with and my recently decided undercover name. There's no way she would ever call Christopher, so he knows when I use that name, I need to talk to him immediately.

I wait a few moments and hear, "Is everything okay?"

"I just spoke with Mom. She said she's in San Francisco and was at your house this morning?"

"No, she wasn't, at least not that I'm aware of. Are you okay?"

"Yes. I'm going a little stir crazy, but Jonnie's taking me to a friend's place where they have a pool."

"Sounds fun. Listen, things are tough right now, but you need to stay in hiding. You can't fix this by reasoning with Mother. She's not listening. I love you. Stay strong."

"Thanks. Love you too." We hang up, and when Jonnie appears, I mouth at him, "My mother was not at Christopher's this morning."

He nods. "Okay, great. We'll see you then." He disconnects his call. "Jim's team has Christopher under surveillance, and they had a quiet night and morning. No sightings of your mother."

Now I'm angry. First the pressure, and now the lies. "She's trying to catch me in a lie, that bitch!"

"I like it when you talk dirty." He puts his arms around me and rubs his cock against my core, and despite the layers of clothes between us, I feel his hardness.

I blush. "Are you packed?"

"I am." He holds up a bottle. "I'm just bringing sunscreen. We'll be alone, so we can go skinny dipping." He wiggles his eyebrows suggestively.

"You've seen this," I motion to my body. "I've spent thirty-one years in Minnesota. You know full well there are many parts on this glow-in-the-dark body that have never seen the light of day."

"That's why I'm bringing sunscreen."

"You're too much." I shake my head and smile.

"Let's get you some fresh air and nourishment."

Chapter 23

Jonathan

Queen Diva was so generous to allow us to use her second Las Vegas home. This afternoon I'm grateful we're able to escape the Strip, the hotel, and my apartment. Maggie was beginning to go a little nuts. And while the security team isn't physically with us as we drive, they'll be strategically around — within seconds of assisting us, if needed.

When we arrive, Maggie and I take a quick tour. I notice the plush king-size bed and the shower that easily fits two people. Maybe later.

"You can change if you're not comfortable skinny dipping," I tell Maggie with a wink. I'll talk her out of her suit eventually.

She smiles. "I'll meet you outside in a few minutes. I

should at least try the bikini on."

The weather is neither too hot nor too cold. Las Vegas in the fall is my favorite. The desert gives us spectacular sunrises and sunsets, but it's the lack of humidity and the moderate temperatures that really make a difference.

I check the fridge, and everything I ordered has been stocked. I pour us each a glass of wine and go sit in the cool saltwater pool. Leaning back against the wall, I let my feet float to the top and the stress of my crazy morning leaves me. Then, out of the corner of my eye, a flash of skin catches my attention. It's Maggie in a beautiful dark pink bikini.

My cock comes to immediate attention. She's not allowed to wear that in public. "You look hot."

"Thanks. Bella tucked the suit into my suitcase before I left. She said Christopher wouldn't let her wear this in public."

She models for me, and I can't get past her hard nipples. I'm tempted to undress her and let my fingers explore.

"I can see why," I say dryly.

She rolls her eyes and puffs out her chest. "It covers all the important parts."

"That top is like little eye patches."

She walks into the pool with my eyes glued to her most private spot. The bottoms hang on her hips, leaving nothing to the imagination.

"Don't get me wrong, but you are a felony in that swimsuit."

She turns almost the same shade as the fabric. "You're the one who talked about skinny dipping."

"I didn't realize someone could see you here."

She walks over to me in the pool, stopping long enough to go under the water and wet her hair. She backs me into the corner. "Who can see us?" she rasps as she rubs her hands over my pecs and nibbles at my neck.

The idea of public sex has never excited me, but right

now I'm so aroused I don't care who could be watching. I've lost my voice, so I motion to the neighboring houses on each side.

Seductively she whispers, "I doubt they can see us, so you're safe on that one, but *you* get to see me in Bella's swimsuit."

I take her hand and move it to my rigid cock as I find my voice. "You're beautiful in everything you wear, but this suit says you're begging to be fucked."

She steps in and kisses me. Our tongues are aggressive. "I do want to fuck you."

"I'm sure I can make that happen."

She bites her bottom lip, and I'm close to taking her right here, right now in the water, but I want to enjoy some fresh air. If I take her now, we'll be in bed all afternoon. She needs the break, and we can have sex in my apartment any time.

I reach over to the ledge where I put our wine and hand her a glass. "Here's a sauvignon blanc. The caterer dropped off some snacks and dinner we can eat later. Queen Diva has offered us the house tonight, if we want to stay. We don't have to make up our minds now."

"Where does *she* live?"

I point to the house next door. "She has a lot of houseguests. Some stay at the hotel and others stay here."

Maggie gazes back at the house. "This is quite a spacious guest house."

"I know. It's over fifty-five hundred square feet." I study her as we talk and try not to think about the look of ecstasy that crosses her face when she comes. She really has no idea of how she affects me. I want to spend the rest of my life showing her.

She leans in close. and her breast grazes my arm. Again my cock, which had started to deflate, is back at attention.

She smiles. "You're thinking about sex, aren't you?"

I nod. "It's hard not to when I'm with you."

"Next time I'll wear a burka."

"Trust me, it doesn't matter."

She rolls her eyes and grins. "What's going on at the hotel?"

"Nice segue. There are always a thousand things happening. Currently, the biggest distraction is that someone is stealing from Queen Diva."

"You're joking."

"Nope. She's had two dresses stolen. We changed the way we store her costumes, so the thief moved on to an expensive piece of jewelry."

"I thought essentially everything was watched in the hotel?"

"It is, but not her dressing room—for privacy. Although right now, we've added a camera even there. Only she knows where it is, and we can keep an eye on her valuables when she's not there or on stage."

"People have stolen from her while she's on stage?"

"Yes, an amethyst ring was stolen last week during the second act."

"That's awful. Those dresses she wears are stunning."

"And expensive."

"I'll bet." She thinks about it a few moments. "I'm assuming you checked the vents between that room and the next?"

I nod, distracted by her nipples, which scream *I want to be played with*.

"Is this what keeps management so busy at a large hotel?"

"There are several things on my plate right now, but that's the big one. We're also dealing with a prima donna on our catering team. He's good, but I'm close to terminating him. He keeps berating his staff and they're dropping like flies and going to our competitors. You need to be respectful, and that trumps talent."

"Makes sense."

"And there are daily issues like card cheats and people who try devices that throw off our machines, but the one we're spending a lot of time on is a group of college-aged students. We never see the same players twice, so it's hard to catch them, but they use hand gestures to tell each other what they have, which helps them win. It's called collusion. We can actually have them arrested, if we catch them. A few of our dealers may also be involved. They might even be marking cards."

"People do that?"

"Yes. There are all kinds of cheaters out there."

"Do you ever have a night when the house loses?"

I shake my head. "Not really. Even when we have a high-value game going in the back rooms and someone wins a multimillion-dollar pot, we come out ahead."

"What about nights when it's all small games going and someone wins big?"

"The thing is, everyone plays to win in Vegas. Very few stop when they're ahead by even one hundred dollars. Psychology says they determine their budget, and they will lose until they win big. Most lose what they've allotted to spend."

"But what's big to one person is different than another."

"Exactly."

She swirls her hands through the water for a moment. "What made you want to do this? I mean, it's so different than anything we grew up with."

"Actually, in undergrad I developed some software for hotels. And over time, as it grew, I decided I needed a hotel to test it on, but no one was interested. Christopher and I came out here to Las Vegas, and I saw a lot of potential. So I went to grad school to figure out how to build my idea and talk some guys into investing."

"You built a hotel to test how your software could work?"

"Yes and no..." I built the hotel for her, but I don't want to drive that home until she's free of the mess she's in. "I also enjoy the business."

"You make it sound so easy," she teases.

I smirk and shrug.

"What happened to your software?"

"It's up and running in the hotel, managing all the guests. It moves things around without anyone knowing and makes the Shangri-la *the* place for the best customer experience anywhere in the state of Nevada."

"You must have a software team. Are they in the US?"

"My team actually works in the building. They have offices just down from the hotel business office so I can drop in on them when needed. Overall, it's coming together nicely. Christopher recently talked me into considering a partner who can help sell it to other hotels and chains. The software has a variety of applications."

"Are you interested in giving up that profit?"

"I'm not sure yet. I told him I'd consider it. Currently, I'm thinking half of something is better than all of nothing."

"You could hire a team to sell the software."

"True, but it would take time to get a sales team up, which might allow someone else to come in and beat me to market."

"Sounds like you're considering selling some of it."

"I haven't decided. I'll just see what Christopher comes up with. These days my priority is the Shangri-la."

When we start to look like prunes, we get out of the pool, and I cover Maggie completely with sunscreen. It takes all my willpower not to take advantage of the situation, but instead we enjoy the afternoon sunning ourselves. I do a little bit of work, and she reads on her Kindle. I could get very used to this—pure luxury.

"I love my apartment, but it's nice to get offsite and relax."

"That's true," she murmurs, sounding half asleep.

I decide it's time to broach the subject I've been reluctant to bring up. "Maggie, I know you think being seen in San Francisco might put whoever is watching you off your trail…"

She sits up and looks away.

I try again. "Jim is flying in. He's going to join us tonight for dinner. It's not the romantic evening we were hoping for, but he's learned something, and I think we need to talk next steps."

"That sucks, but I get it. When will he be here?" She drops her voice. "I know you don't want him to see me in the suit."

"No. I would prefer not. I'd hate to have to take him out."

She grins and gives me the side-eye. "You're quite confident in your abilities."

"You doubt my sincerity?" I laugh a deep belly laugh. "I could totally do it if it came down to fighting for you."

"That would be quite a show, but I'll pass. When is he due to arrive?"

I glance at the time. "He'll be here in about two hours."

"Good." She stands, and our eyes lock. Reaching behind her back, she unties her top and it falls, exposing my favorite tits. Hooking her thumb in the sides of her bottoms, she slowly drops them to the pool deck. Standing in the low, afternoon light, her naked body is pristine. "You promised to fuck me, and I've never had sex outside."

We make love on the chaise lounge. It's slow and luscious and incredible. I now wish I'd told Jim we'd meet him another time, as I'd much rather do this for the rest of the evening and however long she allows.

We take a break with enough time for her to shower. "There's enough room for both of us," I tell her.

"But then we'll never be ready when Jim arrives."

"I'm glad someone is looking out for us," I tease.

When Jim gets here, Maggie is a different person than

the woman who arrived. A few hours of fresh air, sun, and two orgasms have left her relaxed, with a little bit of color.

"Thanks for joining us tonight," Maggie says politely as she leads Jim to the dinner table.

We make small talk as I serve the spinach salad and mushroom risotto with lamb. And no one says too much during dinner—our focus is on the fantastic food.

But after we've finished our meal, Jim clears his throat and begins. "I shared this with your lawyer this afternoon, Maggie. She's still working on some things, but this is what we know." He pulls out a sheet with some notes on it. "The Kryetar has infiltrated the Reinhardt Corporation. Their operations have been somewhat low-key in the Midwest, but they're definitely a presence. We believe they probably got in with Reinhardt through the unions when they were Hudson's back east."

"Does my mother know they're involved?" Maggie asks.

"We believe so, yes. It appears her father was working with some sort of mafia presence back in the Hudson's days," Jim says.

"Hudson's became part of Reinhardt from the merger when my mother and father got married," Maggie shares, her eyes going wide.

This is going to get interesting fast.

Chapter 24

Maggie

I sit back in my chair and look from Jim to Jonnie. We're only beginning and already my head is spinning.

"The Kryetar are also active at Elite Electronics," Jim continues. "In fact, we believe one of their board members is a Kryetar member."

Jonnie reaches for my hand, and our fingers intertwine. I take comfort in his touch.

"We believe there may be some ongoing financial malfeasance with corporate funds at Reinhardt," Jim explains.

"Meaning embezzlement," I clarify.

Jim nods. "Yes, and it seems that marrying Alex would not only cement you as chairman of the board, it would lay the groundwork for your guilt in the embezzlement."

"What do you mean?" Jonnie asks.

"It looks like Maggie signed the document, and she's now marrying to move up within the company with the goal of hiding her criminal activity."

"But that's not what happened," I assure him.

"We understand that, and that's why your lawyer is looking for some additional information."

"Do you have any idea why my mother would care if I was married in a civil ceremony or a big social ceremony?" I ask. "I can't figure out if that's just her ego, or something more."

Jim shrugs. "We're not sure. Maybe the scandal would be bigger after you'd been splashed all over the society pages? But we don't have enough data points yet."

I can feel my contempt for my mother growing. We've struggled over the years, but I've never wished harm for her. That may change.

Jim clears his throat again. "We've also found that your mother has private accounts in Cayman, Nevis, and the Cook Islands, totaling several billion dollars."

I sit up straight, and I'm sure my eyes bulge.

"Given the account balances, she's likely been putting money into them for a while. She made a five-hundred-thousand-dollar deposit last month in the Nevis account."

Now I'm mad. "What about the Walkers?"

"Herbert has significantly decreased the value of Elite Electronics. He has close to a billion dollars in Nevis. We didn't find anything in the Cayman or Cook Islands in his name. But that doesn't mean he doesn't have money stashed elsewhere; we just haven't found it yet."

I'm afraid to ask, but I need to know. "And Alex?"

"We believe the documents he signed are most likely genuine. Alex's trust is gone, and Herbert has heavily embezzled from his own company—"

"Why embezzle from himself?" I ask, bewildered.

"Great question. He doesn't actually own any of the

business. Elite Electronics is wholly in his wife's name. If they divorce, he has nothing."

This is mind-blowing. How did I miss all of this going on? "I interrupted you when you were telling us about Alex," I prod.

"Herbert legally cut Alex off when he turned twenty-one because Alex received access to his trust fund, provided for him by his maternal grandfather. At that time Alex was seeing a man named Michael Corwyn, a known con artist. Mr. Corwyn told Alex he was a doctor, but his ex-wife had taken most of his money. While they were together, Alex went through about twenty-five million in less than three years. Once the money was gone, so was Corwyn. It looks like Alex then dipped into his anticipated inheritance he'd get from his mother."

"I can't believe this. Why didn't he tell me?"

Jim looks at me and then at Jonnie. He seems to be choosing his words carefully. "I believe his financial problems are even bigger than you knew. It looks like Alex might've been paid to marry you."

My hand goes to my mouth. *What?* I trusted him. He's been my best friend for most of my life. Or so I thought. Have things gotten that desperate for him? I shared my secrets with him, and suddenly I feel dirty and used.

Tears fill my eyes, and Jonnie puts his arms around me.

"I'm here for you. Don't worry. You're going to be fine. I promise."

He lets me cry.

Why would my mother do this to me? I ask myself that question over and over.

Jim and Jonnie let me move through the storm of my emotions, waiting patiently. After a while, Jonnie hands me a handkerchief. When I can finally see through the fog of my brain, I ask the question I dread most. "What else haven't you told me?"

"The Kryetar have you and your brothers under

surveillance, but we haven't ascertained why yet."

"So what are the next steps?" Jonnie asks.

"Are you okay staying here in Las Vegas for a while longer?" Jim asks me.

I look at Jonnie, not sure how to answer.

"She can stay as long she wants, and I'm fine with forever."

Jim's eyes widen, and he smiles. "Good. We need to give you and our teams more time to get up to speed before everything goes crazy. Right now the Kryetar aren't sure where you are. We have a plan to have someone from my team board a plane with your ID, disguised as you. She'll go back to Minnesota on Friday. When she arrives at the Twin Cities airport, she'll go into the bathroom and change. She'll lose the wig and dress much more sedately so she blends in and will be harder for them to follow. On the off chance they do, she'll take a rideshare to the Le Meridien downtown where she'll meet her actual husband and another member of my team. They'll go out for dinner and a night on the town. The next morning she'll fly home with her own ID. The subterfuge should buy you some time."

"And I need to stay cooped up in Jonnie's apartment?"

"Or you can stay here," Jonnie offers. "I don't think Queen Diva will mind."

"I understand all this seclusion will be difficult, but in the long run, I think it's best."

"For how long?" I ask, my mind racing. "A week? A month? Forever?"

"I think much of it depends on what they do next and what we're able to find out. We believe the Kryetar will eventually go to the press about your embezzlement, but they may not right away."

"You've lost me," I confess, throwing my hands in the air. "What does that do?"

"They may not be willing to risk surviving the transition of power again," Jim says. "They've kept track of your family affairs, so they're likely realizing you have different goals and ambitions than those who came before you."

"Could they be making my mother do this? Maybe it's not what she wants…" I realize how ridiculous that sounds. In my experience, my mother doesn't do anything she doesn't want to.

"Your mother is likely doing what they ask to protect herself—keep their attention elsewhere," Jim says. He hesitates. "She also has a flight to Cuba booked for the Monday after the weekend your wedding was supposed to be."

The news hits me like a slap in the face. "She intends to feed me to the wolves and disappear with all the money?" I pound my fist on the table. "Why doesn't she just run and leave me to pick up the pieces? Why is she determined to ruin my life first?"

"I can't answer that yet," Jim says with a sigh. "We think the Kryetar may be a factor in her decisions at this point. We're still working on this."

We talk a bit longer, but I'm physically drained. I'm not sure I'm processing much information anymore. I thank Jim, excuse myself from the table, and go back to the main bedroom to collect my things. Suddenly it seems too wide open here. I know I'm being paranoid, but I guess it's time to return to the apartment. I need some rest, and I need to think.

Chapter 25

Maggie

In the morning, back at Jonnie's place, it's back to business. I worked out to clear my head, and then procrastinated a little by giving myself a mani/pedi. I haven't painted my own nails since I was probably six and turns out I'm terrible at it. Jonnie offered to have a nail tech from the spa come up, but that made me nervous. I want as few people as possible to know I'm here, or even that there's somebody staying in his apartment. Any innocent slip could ruin everything.

Shortly after that, Jonnie was out the door. He's been busy preparing for a poker tournament with a bunch of major tech guys coming in. Christopher would normally be a part of the group, but Jim and the team decided he should stay away this time; that way those watching us don't get any bright ideas that I might be with him and come here.

I check my messages and realize I need to make a few calls before I go totally radio silent. I mostly need to touch base with Christopher and Stevie.

When I call Stevie, before I can even say hello, he asks, "Why is Mother freaking out?"

I brush it off as if normal pre-wedding jitters. I'm careful what I tell him since he's on his cell phone and I'm on the burner, and I can't be sure his phone isn't bugged or someone's tracing our call.

"At some point you're going to have to explain why you're marrying Alex," he tells me with a sigh. "The family business can't be worth all that. Genevieve and I think there's something hinky going on."

I open my mouth, but close it again. I can't get into it over the phone, and at this point, I'm not sure where I'd begin anyway. "I'll tell you everything soon enough."

"Continue to ignore Mother's calls," he says. "I do."

"Clearly that's the best plan." I manage a laugh.

"I'm thinking about you," he says. "I hope everything's okay."

My call with Christopher is much more honest. Jim has provided him with a burner phone, too, so I have more freedom to talk, as I know we're not being traced.

"What did the lawyer say?" I ask him.

"Nothing new yet," he reports. "And Jim's trying to find Moreau's client list but hasn't located it, yet. How are you doing?" His voice softens.

"I'm getting used to captivity," I grumble.

"It won't be for long."

I wish I knew he was saying that for certain. "I hope not. As you know, shit hits the fan late tonight or early tomorrow morning," I warn. "Be ready for some phone calls."

"So far I've ignored them. I'm turning your phone off and removing the SIM card after we hang up, so you won't hear from her. Once your voice mail fills, it won't even matter, and knowing Mother, that will be by noon. She'll be stuck and frustrated, but you won't have to know about it."

"True, but I'm worried about this phase of the plan."

"Why?" he asks.

"Mother's in deep, it sounds like, and as of yesterday, we don't know all the players. Every one of us has some sort of surveillance. Oh, also, Jim has a theory that because I'm not being cooperative with Mother's demands, the Kryetar see me as a threat to their power—hence the fake embezzlement documents."

"Well, I'm sure he has reason to believe that," Christopher says. "But I know he stepped up our personal protection, so please don't worry. Bella and I have friends with a beach house just north of San Francisco, and our plan is to head up there for the weekend. We'll be fine. Between our security team and burner phones, the paparazzi can't get to us, so I highly doubt some super-muscle dimwits can."

Somehow, I doubt these guys are dimwits, but it's not worth debating. "Just use your beach house weekend trying to make me an aunt."

"That's my plan. Bella may have some other ideas." He's silent for a moment. "I love you, Mags. I'm here for you. Promise."

"Thank you. I love you, too."

I pick up my Kindle to read, but when my burner phone rings a little while later, my stomach tightens. Curiosity gets the better of me.

"Hello?" I say cautiously.

"Margaret? This is Marci Peterson."

Oh, thank goodness. My stomach immediately releases. "Hey, Marci, I hope you are the bearer of good news today."

"It's not bad news, but it's not really good news, either," she says. "Just a bit of an update."

I take a deep breath. "Lay it on me," I say, trying to be more chipper than I am.

"We're all set up for this afternoon. Our plan is a scheduled departure from SFO at three twenty. Your ID will arrive in Minnesota just after nine, or seven o'clock your local time."

"Okay, that sounds like what Jim explained yesterday," I tell her.

"We believe you'll have until maybe midnight their time until they figure out you're not in town—or at the very least that they don't know where you are."

"What do we do if they file the papers for my arrest?" I look down and my hands are shaking.

"You're staying put. I suspect this weekend will be quiet on that front. The courts will be closed, and they'll need a judge to sign off on a bench warrant. I'm not legally able to practice law in Minnesota, but I have someone in my firm who is, so we'll be fine if and when it happens. This is a white-collar crime—or it would be if it were real—so we're in a strong position if it goes federal, as I can manage that. Plus I have a good contact here in the US Attorney's office. We'll talk regularly, but for this weekend, I think staying put at the Shangri-la is your best bet."

"Don't worry, I have no plans to leave the apartment."

"Excellent. Try to stay off the phones if you can, and in particular, don't call your brothers this weekend."

"No problem. I already spoke to them."

"I understand you're worried, but you've got this."

Strength rolls over me like a warm blanket. She's right. I've got a wonderful team in place. "Thanks, Marci."

"We'll talk soon, and if you discover any surprises, please call me. You have my cell number."

"I promise, I will. Thanks."

After we hang up, I go back to my book. I found one that finally grabbed me, and I settle in on the couch. I'm not sure how much time has passed, but I'm so engrossed in the story that when the landline rings, I jump. The caller ID confirms it's Jonnie.

"Hey." I smile as I answer.

"I've got a surprise for you."

I remember our time at Queen Diva's, and my pulse quickens. "Really? Does it include fresh air?"

"Nope," he says. "But it does include company."

"Are you sure it's a good idea? What is Jim going to say? I just promised Marci I'd keep a low profile."

"Relax," Jonnie says. "Jim has a client in town for the poker tournament tomorrow, and he gave me the idea. Do you remember Nate and Cecelia Lancaster from Christopher's wedding?"

My brain goes a bit crazy. Nate's listed as one of the richest men in the world. I met him briefly at the wedding and was so starstruck that I got cottonmouth and couldn't do more than squeak. Hopefully he won't remember that.

I swallow my pride. "I do."

"Great. He and Cecelia will be coming up to the apartment for dinner. They don't eat in restaurants too often since they're so recognizable, but I offered them dinner with us, and they accepted. Cecelia requested salmon; I hope that's okay."

"I love salmon, and it will be fun to have new people to talk to. What time will they be here?"

"About eight. The catering company will bring dinner up about seven forty-five. I should warn you, Cecelia is always on time. I'll try to arrive before them, but if I make it, it won't be much before."

I have just over two hours. "I'll be ready."

"Great. I think you'll really like them."

"I'm looking forward to it."

"We're going to have fun tonight," he promises as he rings off.

I can't wait. I change into a sundress with a sweater to push back the bite of the air conditioning. I haven't been wearing shoes since I arrived, and my feet aren't very happy with me when I squeeze them into come-hither sandals, but they look sexy, and I feel a little more like myself.

Once I'm ready, I return to my book, but when the front bell rings and it's the catering company, the butterflies in my stomach begin to flutter. *People. Conversation. And most importantly a distraction.* In the back of my mind, that woman who works for Jim is putting her life at risk, pretending to be me and flying into the lion's den.

The chef who drops the meal off gives me directions on how to heat it when we're ready. I can tell he's unhappy—he's an artist after all—but he isn't serving us. We're serving ourselves for privacy, and he'll get over it.

"This is your appetizer plate," he explains. "It's all antipasti. The wine is to be served with dinner, not with the appetizer."

He would never be the wiser if I did serve it with the first course, but I'm not going to tempt fate. He places the tray on the center table in the living room, and I study the liquor cabinet. We have a pinot gris for dinner, but I need to think of a mixed drink that won't overpower the antipasti. I may not be the best cook, but I'm an outstanding bartender. My dad used to say, *You can hire people to make your food, but being a hostess requires making drinks.* I spot gin, triple sec, and fresh lemons. And then I know what will be perfect for us: a Chelsea sidecar—not too sweet, not too fruity, and the lemon will go well with our snacks. Plus, the most important thing, it's easy to make a batch in a pitcher.

I hear them before I see them. "Sweetheart, we're here," Jonnie calls.

The timing is perfect, as I've just finished the drinks. I walk out of the kitchen, and Jonnie is standing with technology rock star Nate Lancaster and his wife, Cecilia. After a career in the military, Nate founded a company that makes high-tech artificial limbs. Jonnie told me Nate was Jim's first security client, and they've been friends for a long time.

"Jonnie, your apartment is amazing." Cecelia gushes. "It's like an oasis hidden in the back of your hotel. I bet the views during the daylight are spectacular." She looks out into the blackness of the desert.

"Thank you," Jonnie says. "I do enjoy looking at the desert."

I approach with a pitcher of Chelsea sidecars, and Jonnie says, "Nate, Cecelia, please meet the woman I built and designed my hotel for, Margaret Reinhardt."

I'm stunned by his statement. It has to be hyperbole...doesn't it? Nothing in my life makes sense right now.

I place the pitcher on the table next to highball glasses I set out and extend my hand. "Please call me Maggie, all my friends do." I gesture to the drinks. "I made some Chelsea sidecars to go with the appetizers. Please help yourself."

"So wonderful to meet you," Cecelia says as she approaches me with her arms wide.

And then I'm locked in an embrace with *the* Cecelia Lancaster.

"You're my new best friend," she says. "You have drinks and food. I'm famished. I can't eat in public with everyone having a camera in their pocket these days. They always get the worst picture of me stuffing my face, and I show up on the cover of some stupid tabloid."

My wits return. "Well, no camera here, and at least it's a short walk to your suite if I tempt you to overindulge."

"Tempt away." She covers her mouth and mock-whispers a comment. "I'll tell you a secret. When I get tipsy, Nate tends to get lucky."

I blush at her openness.

"Keep them flowing." Nate grins at his wife. Pure love.

We pour drinks and sit in the living room. I settle on the love seat with Jonnie next to me. His body is warm, and he drapes his arm around me. "You look beautiful," he says, winking. He raises his glass to the Lancasters across the room. "I'm so glad you could join us."

They raise theirs in return, and then Nate says, "Please

don't be upset with Jim, Maggie, but he shared a high-level view of what you're dealing with. We're sorry."

I nod my thanks.

"But then again," he adds with a laugh, "we're not sorry, because this way we can spend the evening with you."

I laugh too. The sidecar is helping me make light of my plight—at least for the moment. "I'm glad to be here, and I'm grateful Jonnie has been so kind as to offer me a place to hide while the lawyer helps me figure it out."

"If the papers report anything other than she's been named chair of the Reinhardt Corporation board of directors, be assured it's all lies," Jonnie adds.

"We've been there," Nate empathizes.

"I love Bullseye," Cecilia says. "I don't understand how anyone can escape without spending a hundred dollars every time they walk in the store."

She's hard not to like, so genuine. I smile as I imagine the circus that breaks out when she shops at Bullseye.

"I've seen big bills from Reinhardt Hudson's, too," Nate notes. "You're spending all over the company."

"When you find I'm not looking my best, then you can complain about my bills," Cecilia retorts.

Nate and Jonnie start a conversation about tomorrow's poker game, and Cecilia leans over. "What are you doing to keep busy during your sequestration?"

"Not much," I tell her, rolling my eyes. "My goal is to keep a low profile. I don't want someone to slip and give me away, so we're rarely even ordering in, and I stay here all day. Jonnie has a home gym, and I read. Daytime television is worthless."

She nods. "When Nate's business took off and we went from a man with an idea to being household names, the threats started. Our oldest daughter, Grace, was even kidnapped. She was only gone for three days, but I didn't leave the house for over a year after that. I know it sounds like complaining, and this really is a one-percent problem, but I know it's hard to stay within the same walls every day — day in and day out."

I'm so relieved to have someone who understands this. "It's been less than a week, but already I'm feeling trapped. What did you do to keep your sanity?"

"I read a lot of books, organized my closet, and eventually started entertaining myself by cooking."

That surprises me. She doesn't look like she ever eats much of anything.

"I learned to make macarons, roast the perfect chicken, and blend the best tomato sauce."

"She also started our foundation," Nate adds.

"Well, that's true," she says. "We didn't feel our kids needed all the money we were making. They need to be productive members of society, and a generous trust fund was more than enough for them, their children, and grandchildren. There are so many people in need out there, and we know we're incredibly lucky. A lot of good ideas never reach fruition due to funding."

I nod. "I oversee our family foundation. It feeds your soul to give back some of your good fortune."

"Exactly," she says. "You're launching a project we gave some money to last year — with Brighter Future?"

I light up. Cecelia and I spend most of the rest of the evening talking about our causes and enjoying a fantastic dinner. Their foundation is significantly larger than Reinhardt's, but it inspires me to do more. And she invites me to hang out with her again tomorrow, once she's a poker widow.

It's midnight when Nate and Cecelia prepare to leave. "Should you have one more drink before we go?" Nate teases.

She grins and places a chaste kiss on his lips. "I'm sure I'm tipsy enough."

"Then what are we waiting for?" Nate exclaims. He turns to me and extends his hand. "Maggie, you were pure delight tonight. I hope we see you again soon."

"Thank you, I hope so, too."

They pick up their team outside the door, and Nate turns and waves. "I'll see you tomorrow at three, Jonnie. I'm ready to win a small company this weekend."

Jonnie laughs. "Who's betting a small company this time?"

He shrugs. "Who knows. Someone always puts one on the table at some point. That's how I got Syllabus last year. They went public a few months ago for three times their market projection—after I made a few tweaks, of course. Landon thought it was dead. I sent him a magnum of Cristal to celebrate."

"You're bad." Jonnie laughs and shakes his head.

"I'm going to show her how bad I am." Nate hooks his thumb toward Cecelia.

Her eyes light up. "Bring it on."

We close the door behind them, and Jonnie steps in close. "That was fun."

"It was. Thank you."

"I'd love to take credit, but it goes to Jim. Clear Security got started because of Nate, and he knows what happens when you can't leave your home for extended periods of time."

"Yes, Cecilia and I discussed that a little. This was a nice change. Good to have new people to talk to."

I give him a hug and walk into the living room to clear the used glasses. "Why did you tell the Lancasters you built the Shangri-la for me?"

"Because I did," he answers.

"How is that even possible?" This seems a bit extreme.

His arms circle my waist. "You're right. I didn't look at you when I was fifteen and think, *I want to move to Vegas and open a hotel for her.* But I did know I wanted you in my life, and I spent years figuring out how to make it happen. It was little things. Christopher and I stayed here in Vegas one spring break in college, and I really liked the place, from a business perspective. I wanted to be self-reliant, so I could take care of you. So this is the perfect world I've created for you. This is our Shangri-la."

Wow. I don't really know how to respond, so I lean in and kiss him. It quickly becomes an aggressive tango of our tongues. "Thank you for telling me. I don't quite know what to say. I... Like always, I wish things were different."

"We're working on that, okay? Speaking of which, did you talk to Christopher or Bella today?

"I talked to both my brothers this morning, and I got a text from Christopher this afternoon. He wished me luck. And then Bella called while she drove from Berkeley to The City." I'm normally a vault when it comes to secrets, but I have to tell him. "I'll tell you what she told me, but you have to act surprised when they tell you."

He smiles. "I think I have an idea of where this is going."

"They had an appointment with the OB/GYN this afternoon—and she's pregnant."

"I knew it! That's fantastic. Christopher must be so excited. They've wanted this for a while."

"I know, it's still early, but it's fantastic news." I sit on the couch and put my feet up on the coffee table. I glance at the time and think about all the things probably going on by now in Minnesota. *How many times has my mother called my phone?*

Jonnie sits down next to me and pushes the hair from my face. "You can't worry about what's happening elsewhere. You're perfectly safe here." He kisses me, and I wrap my arms around him. "I heard you make plans to meet Cecelia tomorrow."

"Yes, she's having a few friends over during tomorrow's games. We're meeting in her suite for spa treatments—massages and I think some nail techs are coming. She mentioned that Emerson Healy and Caroline Arnault will be there, and she told me Jim signed off on this. Are you okay with me going?"

Jonnie nods. "Jim ran it by me. The women have been briefed, and they're his clients, too. Jim's team will escort you down, so no wandering or going anywhere without your guys. Promise?

I kiss him softly on the lips. "I guess I should show you my appreciation for taking such good care of me." I unbutton his pants and can feel the bulge growing more pronounced.

He flips me onto my back. "Not until I show you my appreciation first."

Chapter 26

Jonathan

Maggie has a spring in her step this morning, which I'm thrilled to see. Our adventures the past few days seem to have pulled her from the brink of feeling too confined. Now I just have to keep her from panicking about all the aspects of her life that are up in the air.

I take a sip of orange juice and catch her peeking at her burner phone. "Any news?" I ask.

"No, and it's making me nervous."

"I can understand why. It's making me nervous, too. Let's check in with Jim." I pull my phone from my pocket, and he answers on the first ring. I greet him and tell him I'm putting him on speaker. I set my phone on the table between us.

"You must be psychic," he teases.

"Maggie is sitting here, and we're a little nervous that things seem so quiet. Is there any word?"

I reach for Maggie's hand and kiss her delicate fingers. She takes a deep breath and gives me an encouraging squeeze.

"It's been an exciting night and morning," Jim says. "The police just left Christopher's home."

Maggie drops my hand and sits up straight. "Is everyone okay?"

"Christopher and Bella are up in Stinson Beach, north of San Francisco."

Maggie nods and smiles. "He told me when we spoke that he'd be at a friend's beach house."

"Correct. As predicted, the men watching your brother's home started to multiply about eight thirty last night, and once it was dark at ten thirty, they wandered around the front of the house and jumped the fence in the alley to access the backyard. We have on tape that they knocked on the door. My team was watching from both the street and on closed-circuit TV."

"They didn't see you?" Maggie asks.

"No. We were in the park across the street hiding in a homeless encampment we created. We notified the police as soon as they put a pick in the lock. San Francisco Police arrived eight minutes after they gained access to the home and caught them in the middle of their search. Nothing was taken. They were arrested, but they're not saying anything."

"I'm so glad Bella and Christopher weren't home." Maggie presses her hand to her heart.

"Agreed," Jim says. "We also tracked my employee who traveled on your ID. We spotted someone at the airport who we were fairly certain was following her. Thankfully, her tail was a man who couldn't follow her into the ladies' room. He waited for you to exit, but instead Lindsay did, and she walked right by him. He didn't recognize her and didn't follow. He waited thirty-five minutes before he asked someone to go in and look for his daughter. When they reported her not there, he looked around the terminal, and forty-eight minutes later he called a number—which we were able to capture on a security camera—to report her missing."

I give Maggie a thumbs up. She's all smiles.

"My team made contact with your brother Steven in Key West," Jim tells Maggie. "We moved him and his girlfriend to a safe house. Christopher and Bella will remain where they are through tomorrow, and then they'll go on a boat tour that will move them to a safe house farther north in Mendocino."

"What about Bella's family?" Maggie asks.

"We're keeping an eye on them. We're also watching Alex. The guys following him pulled him out of a sex club shortly after midnight. They talked to him on the sidewalk out front, so my team was able to hear the exchange. He denied knowing where you were, and they left him there. He left two hours later with a friend and went back to his place."

"Is he safe?" Maggie asks.

"We think so. The good news is what we observed at your family home."

Maggie and I move to the edge of our seats.

"Herbert Walker joined your mother at eleven thirty last night. By midnight, six more cars had arrived. We photographed their occupants. We didn't have access to their cell phones when they spoke, but we did have parabolic mics working and could hear half the conversation. They're looking for you, and they're panicked."

I can't help but smile. "Did your team recognize anyone?"

"No. But we have a contact at the FBI in organized crime. We sent them the photos and should hear back shortly. I'll keep you posted."

"I'm so glad they haven't figured out where Maggie

is," I say. "As you know, we have a poker tournament starting today with our tech billionaires. Maggie will join Cecelia and two other friends for a spa day."

"Maggie, did you enjoy your evening with the Lancasters?" Jim asks.

"I did. I can't thank you enough for setting that up."

"Cecelia went through a tough time when things went south with her daughter," Jim says. "The FBI was lost, so the Lancasters brought me in, along with two other guys Nate had worked with during his stint in the Marine Corps. We couldn't determine how to manage Cecelia's risk in public, so she was stuck at home. Granted, she wasn't hiding, but we've used some of what we learned there to make sure your stay feels less like you're a captive."

"I appreciate that," Maggie tells him. "But I don't want to put myself at risk just to get a massage or breathe of fresh air."

"I'm glad you feel that way, and I appreciate you being cautious," Jim says. "We'll find a light at the end of this tunnel. We just don't know how long the tunnel is yet."

"Thank you for the update," she tells him. "I'm glad you have Stevie and Christopher."

"Of course. I'll stop by sometime this weekend since I'm coming in this afternoon for the poker tournament."

"You know where to find me," she says.

"And I will," he assures her.

Once I end the call, I lean over to kiss her forehead. "What's your plan today?"

She stands and picks up our dirty dishes, "I'm going to work out in your gym, and then I'll finish my book. I meet the girls after lunch. Next time you see me, I'll have pretty fingers and toes and be as relaxed as jelly."

I lean in close and murmur, "You taste as sweet as jelly."

She looks down and blushes.

I hate to leave her, but it's possible the Kryetar are in

Las Vegas and watching, so nothing should be out of the ordinary. I feel confident that they can't detect us moving around the hallways, so Maggie will be able to enjoy her afternoon.

I gather my things to leave and give Maggie one last squeeze goodbye. I won't be back until the game closes tonight, and I let her know I expect to be very late.

I pick up Caden out in the hallway and snap into business mode.

When we reach Gillian's office, she informs me that everyone has arrived for the tournament and checked into their suites, which give them a view of the fountain and the light show that displays every half hour. It's quite spectacular.

"Do they know where we're playing today?" I ask. "The room is different this time—it's waterfront."

"Of course," she says, "as do their escorts. Each one is being met at their room at a quarter to three and brought in through catering. This addresses our issue from last time when several players were recognized and it created problems."

She hands me a timetable. "This is probably the sixth iteration of the plan, so it should be accurate. We're scheduled until midnight, and we can go into expansion for up to four hours. We have a dozen gamblers, two tables going for dealers, food arriving, a cocktail waitress for each table, and a bartender in the room."

I peruse the schedule. "This looks amazing. Let's hope everything goes to plan." It's amazing how much work it takes to make something appear so effortless.

"Don't put any bad karma out there," she warns.

Travis gets into my line of sight and motions for me.

"Excuse me," I say to Gillian. "I'll be back before the game starts."

She nods, and I walk over to Travis. "What's up?"

"Do you think you can step out about five?"

"Probably," I tell him. "What did you find?"

"We need to meet with Queen Diva."

"Is she requesting the meeting, or are we?"

"We are." Travis turns his tablet toward me. "Check this out."

It's a split-screen video. On the left side is the hall that runs outside Queen's dressing room, on the right is a dark room. Both timestamps are running identically. Suddenly a small light appears in the room.

"Where did that come from?" I ask.

"Just wait," Travis warns.

The light flips on, and it's Queen Diva's assistant. She's opening drawers and searching for something.

"What's she looking for?"

"Just wait," Travis warns me again.

We watch her pull a bustier out of the drawer, shimmy out of her clothes and lay provocatively on the couch. On the left screen, we see Frankie wander down the hall and enter the room. They fall into a romantic embrace.

My heart stops. This is going to create more drama than I care to admit. "Fuuuuuck," I mutter. "It's exactly as we thought, except how the hell did she get in the room without walking down the hallway?"

Travis points to a large vent in the wall. Its cover is askew.

"Did this happen today?" I begin thinking about how to manage Queen's fans tonight when she cancels her show. I may very well be bailing her out of jail after she beats Frankie to a pulp.

"This afternoon. Once we saw him go in, we checked the feed in her dressing room."

I watch the video of the assistant coming in a few times. "I'm not sure I want to be there when you tell her."

"*I'm* not going to tell her her husband is having an affair," Travis says, his eyes wide. "You own the joint. As far as I'm concerned, this is your job. She's been riding my ass about this."

"Shit! This is not a conversation I'm looking forward to. She's expecting us at five?"

"Actually, five fifteen. I thought we'd check out the vent first."

I think for a moment. "Do we need to show her the video past who broke into the room and how?"

He stares at me a moment and shrugs. "I guess not..."

"We're reporting on the theft, and she pulled the lingerie out of her drawer," I say, thinking aloud. "We can stop after she puts it on? I mean, we see her ass, but it makes our case. We can stop it there."

"What will you do if Queen Diva wants to see what happens next?" Travis asks.

I look back at the paused video of Frankie feasting on Queen's assistant. This could get really ugly. "I guess I'll show it to her."

"Do you think she'll cancel tonight's show?"

I nod. "This will be a big blow. This is not the time of year I need this to happen."

"Is there ever a good time?" Travis wonders.

I shake my head. "No, you're right." I take a deep breath. "Please come get me at five. See if you can find the dresses on any online auction sites or fan sites."

"We're on it."

This is all sorts of fucked up. Maybe I should throw my hat in the ring at the poker tournament and lose the Shangri-la to someone who wants to deal with this shit. I glance at my watch, and it's almost go time. The players should be beginning to assemble.

I spot Walker Clifton on my way back to the private room we've set up for the game. "Hello, Walker. So glad you could make it."

"Thanks for including me. I'm hoping tonight is my lucky night."

"I hope that for you, too."

I turn and Jackson Graham walks in. He nods his

greeting to me.

"Welcome."

"Hey, Jonathan. I brought my girlfriend. Is it okay if she sticks around and watches?"

Nate walks up just in time to hear Jack's question. "She can stay," he says. "We'll try not to embarrass you too badly."

"She's my lucky charm."

"You'll need more than luck. I hope you enjoyed the Cristal I sent over," Nate needles.

"We both did, as I licked it off her nipples."

The conversation is going downhill fast. I see Mia Couture arriving, so it's a good excuse to leave them to their ribbing.

"Welcome, Mia."

She lights up and gives me a hug. "Great to see you."

She immediately settles in and watches the room and the players as they arrive. I'm sure the reason she does well is not just because she manages the odds, but because she can assess people and their tells.

"You look ready to play," I note.

"I flew in from Aspen," she says, looking in Nate's direction. "The snow was incredible."

Nate heard her jab. She won the chalet from him. "I got in some major trouble on that one."

"You tell Cecilia she's welcome anytime." Mia points at him. "You, on the other hand, are not."

Mason Sullivan slaps him on the back and warns, "Don't go there."

A moment later, Gillian appears with a velvet bag. "It looks like everyone has arrived," she announces. "The buy-in this afternoon is five million. We'll play down to five players and then pick up again tomorrow. You can increase your spend if others at the table agree, but only after nine this evening."

"Mia, I plan on winning my Aspen chalet back," Nate warns.

Snickers filter through the room. "Good luck," she says. "I've become rather fond of it, so I don't think I'll be betting that this weekend."

The laughter grows louder.

"Mr. Best, can you please help me pull names from the bag for our seating arrangements?" Gillian asks.

"Of course." I make my way to the front of the room.

Gillian holds the bag up, and I pull each name out one at a time. Everyone takes their designated seat.

"As Jack London said, 'Life is not always a matter of holding good cards, but sometimes playing a poor hand well'," I tell them. "Good luck, ladies and gentlemen."

The games begin, and the players seem more cautious as they start this time. I watch for a while, but nothing earth-shattering has happened before Travis pokes his head in to grab me for our meeting.

My stomach tightens as we walk down the hall, past the main auditorium dressing rooms, and towards Queen Diva's dressing room. When we arrive, we inspect the vent, and its cover pops off with a solid tug.

"We would have seen her come in next door, so the question is, how many rooms is she sneaking through?"

"You know, Maggie asked me if we had checked the vents. I thought she was crazy. Now I know better."

Travis pushes through to the next room, and I can hear him push through and check several more.

Queen Diva arrives and smiles. "What brings you down here?"

"We've made some progress," I tell her. "Someone was in your dressing room this afternoon."

"Did you catch them?"

Travis walks in, holds up six fingers, and hands me the tablet.

"Let's watch this," I suggest.

I push play, and Queen peers over my shoulder to watch the split-screen video.

When the light comes into the room, she asks, "Where is that light coming from?"

I pause the video. "I believe it's a flashlight, and she's entering through the vent. We think she came through six rooms, Travis?"

He nods. "Yes. The perp enters at the end of the hall in your business office and works her way through the vents of six rooms." I walk over and remove the vent cover, and Travis squeezes out of the room.

"Who is it?" Queen demands.

I push play again and know the moment Queen Diva recognizes her assistant, Renee.

"Oh, you've got to be kidding me!" She stands with her hands on her hips and her eyes locked on the screen. Once we watch her assistant wiggle into the bustier, I stop the show.

"Do you want this splashed all over the news? That's what will happen if you press charges," I warn.

She squints at me and breathes in short, staccato bursts through her nose. "Who does she meet in my dressing room?"

"I'm sorry?" I try to play dumb and pray she doesn't want the video to continue.

"If she was only stealing the bustier, she'd grab it and tuck it away, but she was putting it on. Who is she meeting?"

I take a deep breath. "You're not going to like the answer to that question."

"Play it," Queen Diva demands through clenched teeth.

I push play. She watches it and remains surprisingly calm.

When it's over, I ask, "What do you want to do?"

"I have a show tonight," she says. "Please contact Detective Kincaid and ask him to make the arrest after the show. Please also warn him he'll most likely be arresting my husband as well."

"We didn't see him take anything."

"I guarantee she'll implicate him. I'll let the lawyers figure it out, because I have a show to put on. If you can ask him to be discreet, I'd appreciate it, but I've got to get ready for tonight's performance. These ticket holders paid good money."

Her professionalism has blown me away. Of all the times for it to kick in... I nod, knowing she must be dying inside. "We'll make the calls and be ready at the end of the show."

"Thank you." We walk out, and she yells after us, "And thank you for figuring this out for me."

"Of course." I turn back to give her a smile.

I walk Travis back to the NOC. Neither of us says anything until we're firmly behind the security of the room.

"She took that better than I thought she would," I finally say.

Travis speaks to Luke at the corner monitor. "Let's put Queen Diva's dressing room feed up for the night. I want to know if all hell breaks loose."

"Yes, sir," Luke says.

"I'll call Detective Kincaid," Travis tells me. "I assume you want to be there when this goes down?"

"Yep, this is a train wreck. It's too bad he's doing this to her."

Travis nods, and I let him know I'm headed back to check on the tournament.

When I return to the game, the first player is out.

"Dillon, what happened?" I ask.

Dillon Healy is a business partner with Mason Sullivan and Christopher, Maggie's brother.

He shakes his head. "I had a full house of aces high but ignored all the royalty on the board. Viviana had a royal flush."

"No! Oh man, that's pretty rough."

"Tell me about it." He plops into a chair and downs his drink.

Chapter 27

Maggie

"You have a lot of knots in your back," Olga the masseuse says in a deep German accent.

"Ugh," I groan in response.

"You need to drink more water," she informs me as I swear she's working on my back with an ice pick.

When the ninety-minute torture—I mean massage—is over, I thank her kindly as she hands me a glass of water with cucumber.

"You have too much stress. It must go away. Drink all this water and two more. No alcohol."

Her tone makes me want to click my heels together and salute her, but I refrain. I actually can't. My muscles have revolted, and I'm bent like an old woman. I worry if I stand straight, every muscle will rip and I'll be permanently crippled.

In addition to the massage, my toes are deep red, and

my nails are subtle pink. I feel pretty.

I make my way back to the main room, and Cecelia hands me a large glass of white wine. "What did you think?" she asks.

I cautiously glance over my shoulder. Olga is gone, thank goodness. "It was fabulous," I say as I take a big sip of the crisp wine. "It was wonderful. And I know I monopolized most of the conversation this afternoon, but I couldn't help it. I've only spoken with Jonathan and my brothers for the last week, and I'm a bit lonely."

"Don't worry about a thing," Emerson and Caroline assure me.

"I've been there," Cecelia sympathizes. "There are days where it's lonely and others that you don't want to spend time with anyone."

I'm grateful she understands. Jim was really smart to put us together.

I lean back carefully into the couch and something on the television catches my attention. It's on mute, but I recognize Patrick Moreau, my mother's sleazy lawyer, behind a podium in the Reinhardt Corporation press room. I reach for the remote and turn the volume up. Everyone turns to listen.

"...Reinhardt was last seen in San Francisco," Moreau says. "She was staying with her brother, Christopher Reinhardt, and his wife, Isabella Vargas Reinhardt, and they are also currently missing. The third sibling, Steven Reinhardt, and his live-in girlfriend, Genevieve Caprice, reside during the winter in Key West, Florida, and their whereabouts are unknown at this time. We're concerned about foul play."

The camera moves to poster-size pictures of my brothers and me.

My palms begin to sweat. I shut my eyes and take a deep breath. "Holy shit," escapes from my mouth.

"I think we should call Jonathan," Caroline suggests.

"No, please don't. The poker tournament is important, and he has stuff he's working on with Queen Diva. I don't want to be a further distraction."

"Are you sure?" Emerson asks.

I nod. I need to call Christopher and make sure he's safe and aware of the threat my mother has just lobbed at all of us. She knows we're not where we should be.

But I need to be polite to my hostess. Standing, I regain my composure. "Today was positively wonderful. Thank you so much for including me."

Cecelia brings me in to a warm embrace. "I know you have a lot going on. While our circumstances were different, I do understand what it's like to be vilified by people you thought loved you. Stay strong and get some rest." In her best German accent, she adds, "And drink your water."

I can't help but smile. "I'm so grateful Jim suggested this. Thank you."

"Anytime. Nate texted me about an hour ago, and they're going strong at the tournament. The girls and I are going to meet for dinner. We can order in tonight, and you could join us?" Cecelia offers.

"Not necessary. Jonathan is planning on a dinner break with me, so I'm good. You guys have a great time. Where are you going?"

"We have reservations at the Asian fusion place. Have you been?"

I nod, smiling wide. "It's fantastic. Be sure to try the pad thai tacos. They're outstanding."

"I will, and I'll let you know what I think. They sound delicious."

I wave my farewell and walk back to Jonnie's apartment through the back stairwell. It's really well hidden. Nobody has much chance to see me coming or going.

As soon as I enter the apartment, I grab the burner phone and see multiple texts.

Jonnie: I love you. Don't worry. Call Jim if you have any questions.

Christopher: We're fine hiding in beautiful Mendocino. Don't do anything. Running home will only land you in jail. Love you. C & B

I sit back and reread Christopher's text. He knows me so well. I'd love to run back home and tell the media I'm fine, not to mention alert them that this is a smear campaign, but Christopher is right. That's not a great plan in light of all that seems to be going on. Instead, I decide to take Jonnie's advice and call Jim.

"Hey, Maggie. How was your afternoon?" he asks in greeting.

"It was good. I relaxed and caught up on all the latest gossip."

"I assume you're calling because you saw Patrick Moreau's news conference?"

"I did, but I only caught the last few minutes. What did I miss?"

"It started with the announcement that you were the future chairman of the board at Reinhardt Corporation. Then they said you got on a plane yesterday in San Francisco and somehow disappeared. Neither Christopher nor Steven can be located either, so they've told the public there's a national manhunt."

I groan. Such a waste of manpower. "The FBI is involved?"

"They are. Don't stress about it, though. It's all designed to flush you out."

"Christopher told me not to rush home to Minneapolis."

"He's right. Stay where you are. We've seen an uptick in the Kryetar's presence at the hotel and throughout Las Vegas. Since the last person they saw you with is Jonathan, they're snooping around. It's important you keep a low profile."

My stomach drops to the floor. I can hardly breathe. It takes a few minutes to process that Jonnie is not safe with me here.

"Your team is well equipped to deal with this," Jim assures me. "And Marci's working on the legal situation. Please try to avoid the news. The press conference is going to replay often, and it will only further upset you."

"Thanks for that advice. I'll touch base with Marci and get some direction from her."

He offers a few additional updates about my security detail and his plans to increase the coverage. He alludes to possibly having someone inside with me, rather than down the hall.

I hang up the phone and pace in front of the big windows. I pick at my newly polished nails and peel off the light pink polish, cursing myself even as I do it. Jonnie is in trouble, and Christopher and Stevie are in hiding — all because of me. What will I do if I'm the reason Bella loses her child?

What if there's something more I could do about this — rather than just sitting around? I need to take some kind of action… I start by calling Marci's personal cell. She answers before it even rings.

"I'm so glad you called," she says warmly.

"I couldn't help myself after my mother plastered a poster of me and my brothers all over the news as if we've been kidnapped. They only 'lost' me maybe…" I glance at the wall clock. "…twenty hours ago. It seems a little overboard, don't you think?"

"It would seem the actions of a desperate woman," Marci replies.

"Jim tells me the Kryetar have stepped up their presence here at the hotel."

"That's alarming," Marci says. "But you're hidden away, and you have the finest group of protectors."

"Maybe if I make my case to the public, I can show them my mother and her lawyer are lying," I offer.

Marci's quiet a few moments. "Right now I don't have anything to prove your signature isn't a forgery, and it would be your statement against theirs. And if Mr. Moreau, who is an officer of the court, lies and says he advised you not to do it but witnessed you taking the money, the court of public opinion will be against you."

My stomach ties itself in knots." So you're telling me they hold all the cards here."

"I like your Vegas analogy." She chuckles.

I smile. "I didn't know that was a Vegas analogy, but the cliché fits."

"I want to assure you that I'm working on this through back channels and remind you that all of our discussions are privileged. So call me if you learn anything or something happens," she says.

I hesitate. I know if I tell her I'm going to commit a crime that may harm someone, she has to share that. That isn't my plan, but it could go sideways, and she might recognize that and alert the police. I debate all the things that could go wrong, and it's a few moments before I decide to tell her what I'm thinking. But I take a different tack.

"Marci, I'm worried Jonnie is in danger. The Kryetar has increased its presence at the hotel. What if they make a move?"

"What do you know about Jim Adelson and Clear Security?" Marci asks.

"Not enough, apparently."

"These guys are all top-notch former military, FBI, and police. They're willing to put their lives at risk for you. Don't let a little bit of fake news get to you. Keep doing what you're doing. You can't allow them to scare you."

"But they are," I whisper, fighting back tears.

"It's probably going to get worse," she warns. "But once they announce a warrant for your arrest, I've got a plan. Don't you worry. An old friend from law school lives in Chicago. She's going to reach out to whoever has issued the warrant and act as our intermediary. That will move the search for you away from Las Vegas and the West Coast, and it will also give me room to work behind the scenes with local federal prosecutors. I've worked with them before, so that's helpful."

"All right. I'll be patient," I tell her.

I sigh. The calls to Jim and Marci were supposed to calm me, but instead, they've ratcheted up my concern.

"Thank you for all your help, Marci. I really appreciate it. I'll remain in touch."

The sun has set, and I stare out over the dark desert. *I have the truth on my side. People will believe me.* They have to. I begin to formulate my plan.

I'm still pacing when the front door of the apartment opens, spilling light into the living room.

Jonnie steps in. "Why are you in the dark?" He approaches and puts his arms around me. I immediately feel better.

"I didn't want someone who may know this is your apartment to see lights turn off and on while you were downstairs," I explain.

He studies me. "You can't sit in the dark just because I'm not here. I want you to know, we're going to weather this. Do not let today's press conference upset you."

"Have you seen it?" I challenge.

He nods.

"You don't think seeing a poster-size image of your face behind a man who is lying about you might be upsetting? What about the fact that the Kryetar have descended on the hotel? It's making me question my decisions, which could bring harm to people I care about.

"I'm here for you. Emerson, Caroline, and Cecelia are not going to let anyone know where you are."

"I believe that." I kiss him, and it quickly becomes deeper. The air in the room grows thick with the passion between us.

My heart explodes, racing faster, not knowing how far he'll let me go. I want him. I need him. I step out of my yoga pants, pull my T-shirt over my head, and stand before him in a lacy black bra and matching thong.

He hasn't had a chance to move before I take over, removing his shirt and jacket and tossing them over the sofa. Our eyes lock before he leans down and his lips touch mine. He rubs his thumbs over my erect nipples, my breasts straining against the tiny black lace bra. I reach back and quickly unhook it.

He catches his breath and mutters, "Magnificent."

I smile.

He fumbles with his buckle and pants, and I slip my thong over my hips and stand naked before him, ready and waiting. When he kicks them free, his eyes are hooded and his glorious cock bobs at full mast, aching to be touched.

He steps back and licks his lips. "You're positively beautiful." He kneels to stroke my legs and caress my hips as he whispers, "You have the most perfect heart-shaped ass."

His hand grazes my core, and I move my hips to beg for more. He reaches for my breast and his thumb rubs over my nipple, which is just begging to be sucked.

I begin to kneel, but he stops me and tells me in no uncertain terms that he needs to taste me. We move to the couch and he drops to his knees, putting my leg over his shoulder. I can see him take in the sight and smell of my pussy through the reflection of windows. He licks around my clit, lapping up moisture and sucking as his fingers explore me from the inside. My breathing increases, and a deep moan escapes as I push my pussy deeper into his mouth. Flicking my clit with his tongue, he increases the pressure. My breathing becomes labored and my legs stiffen as I reach my peak, groaning as I fill his mouth.

"You taste amazing," he breathes.

I sit up to kiss him on the mouth, tasting myself. It turns me on even more.

"You do that so well," I tell him.

I will now thoroughly enjoy giving him his much-desired attention. Leading him by the hand, I move past the living room to the bedroom, where I lay him on his back. Kissing him deeply, I kneel between his legs, taking his cock into my mouth. I work magic with my tongue as I swirl around the head, holding firm at the base of his cock and stroking to match each head bob. I suck and stroke a steady rhythm while rolling his balls in my palm. His breathing becomes labored, and when I look up at him, his eyes are glazed over in ecstasy.

"I don't want to come in your mouth. Can I come inside you?"

I look up at him, his cock still deep in my mouth, and think about it. I enjoy drinking from him so much. He gave me pleasure with his mouth, and I want to do the same. However, the idea of having him inside me is even better. He pulls his cock from my mouth with a pop.

With a wicked smile, I climb on top of him. He's so big that it takes a few strokes for me to fully accommodate him. I can't decide if I like sucking him or fucking him better, but regardless, an electrical current spreads through my veins as I feel his hardened cock penetrate me repeatedly. God help me, it feels good.

My tits bounce in front of him, and I begin to fondle them and pinch at the nipples. His hands quickly cover mine and then replace them entirely as he works my nipples while I continue to move up and down on his length. After a moment his hands move to my hips, guiding my pace as I ride his cock so we can both enjoy every minute.

He looks me in the eye, and I lick my fingers as if they're his cock. With those same wet fingers, I strum my clit, fast and hard. My insides respond, and I clamp down on him.

He's loud when he comes, calling my name as my pussy clenches his cock, milking every last drop of his cum.

I collapse on top of him, breathing heavily, and ask,

"Was that okay?"

"Ab-absolutely!" he stammers with a silly grin. "That was so much better than okay."

I giggle, and we curl into each other. I feel a sense of peace for the first time since the news conference this afternoon. "Thank you for everything," I tell him, nearly asleep.

He holds me tightly. I can hear his heart flutter.

"You should probably head back," I murmur.

"I won't if you need me." He kisses the top of my head.

I shake my head. "I'll be fine. I don't want you to raise any suspicion. Go."

He kisses me goodbye, and I hope he can forgive me for what I need to do.

Chapter 28

Jonathan

"Are you ready?" Travis asks.

He's materialized next to me like a ninja. I knew he was coming and still missed him entering the room. I take a deep breath and look at my watch. Queen Diva is in her last set before the encore. It's ten fifty p.m. We meet the police in ten minutes.

I nod to Gillian across the table. She knows I'll be back after this is finished. All indicators point to this game going strong, as there are still five tech billionaires at each table. They're playing conservatively tonight.

Caden and Kian escort Travis and me as we go to meet Detective Kincaid. When we reach the lobby, I spot him standing beneath the vibrant Dale Chihuly chandelier, looking like a lost tourist. He's taking in everything going on around him as he waits.

"Did you come alone?" I ask, though I'm relieved that there isn't a group of uniformed officers with him.

He shakes his head. "We've got three squad cars around the back. They'll come in on my signal."

We walk and talk in hushed tones. "My team has eyes on backstage and the surrounding area," Travis says. "Queen Diva's assistant, Renee, is hovering in her dressing room. During the last set, she blew Frankie on the couch."

This is going to be awful. "Is she going to say she was coerced by Frankie?" I ask.

"That's for the courts to figure out," Detective Kincaid says. "But while the sex may be coerced, I don't think the theft is."

"My gut says yes, but I still can't figure out for sure if Frankie is involved. He was visibly upset that the dresses were missing, and he received most of the blame," Travis notes.

"He's also in debt to a few bookies here in town," Detective Kincaid adds.

"Are you going to be able to arrest him?" I ask.

"Well, this is our trick. We'll read them their rights, and sometimes while we're going to go through the motions, they shower us with the incriminating evidence. It's always interesting the way things play out. We may find that he didn't know about the dresses, but we're confident he knew something. Let's see what we learn."

When we reach the auditorium, backstage is a flurry of activity. Queen Diva has completed her final change and started the encores. The crowd is on their feet and singing along.

"She's amazing. So much talent." Detective Kincaid claps loudly, enjoying his VIP view of the show.

"I'm sure she'll give you an autograph," I offer.

He shakes his head. "I wouldn't dare ask." He stops

dancing and looks at me. "Maybe I can get a discount on some of the cheap seats for my wife and two daughters for a future show."

"You can go to my box seats. You name the date," I tell him.

"Can't accept that. It could be construed as bribery," he says.

I'm stunned. Free tickets, comped meals, and essentially anything that can be given in this town are usually expected, not considered bribes.

"We'll make it happen," I assure him. "Separate from any of this. You name the day."

"My wife's birthday is coming up..." he says, thinking out loud.

"Consider it done." I'll upgrade their tickets, and I'm sure Queen Diva will want to gush all over him and meet the family after the show. She's always happy to do those types of things. Always looking out for others. How she ended up with the likes of Frankie I'll never understand.

Queen Diva finishes with her third encore and marches right up to us. Her stage smile disappears as soon as she's out of sight from the crowd.

"Let's get this done. I've never been so angry," she hisses.

She rushes back to the dressing room, and we follow along. Frankie's sitting on the couch, very close to Renee, and he scrambles to stand.

"I know all about you two. No need to hide it," Queen Diva announces.

"What?" Frankie looks from Renee to Queen, and then to the three of us. "No-nothin's going on here." He wipes his pants as if there are crumbs, but I suspect he's wishing his erection away.

"I'd kick your fat ass out of my dressing room, but the police here are gonna take care of that for me," Queen Diva declares.

Detective Kincaid steps up with two uniformed officers standing behind him. "Francis Michael Lowell, I'm with the Las Vegas Police Department, and I have a warrant for your arrest."

"Arrest? Wh-what?" Frankie stammers.

Detective Kincaid turns to Renee, holding a piece of paper. "Renee Samantha Hawthorne, I have an arrest warrant for you as well."

An officer begins to read their Miranda warning.

Renee jumps up and attempts to run out of the dressing room. "You can't arrest me for having an affair."

Frankie continues to protest as the officer speaks. Queen Diva sneers in disgust and walks out of the room.

"He forced me to have sex," Renee whines. "If I didn't, he told me I'd lose my job."

"That's bullshit," Frankie roars. "I love my wife; I did no seducing. You were the one seducing me. Who got down on their knees only an hour ago? I don't think so."

"He... He... He made me." Renee dissolves into crocodile tears. "I love Queen Diva. I'd never do anything to hurt her."

"That's why you stole her dresses," Frankie says with contempt.

We got what we were hoping for. I'm impressed.

Renee whips her head toward him with a look of shock. "I did no such thing."

"She has them listed on eBay," he tells us. "I saw them there today. I was going to call you tomorrow to let you know."

"He's lying!" Renee screams. "The eBay account is his."

"Don't worry, we'll get this all straightened out." Detective Kincaid opens the dressing room door, and four police officers enter.

"You cannot arrest me," Renee yells. She tries to push the police officers away.

"Ma'am, we can add resisting arrest if you'd like," one

of the officers says.

"But I didn't do anything," Renee begs.

She's in for a real surprise. I know Travis had the vents brushed for fingerprints, and hers were all over them—only hers. The video makes it clear she was heavily involved in the theft, but tying Frankie in may have just gotten easier if the eBay account really is in his name.

Frankie and Renee are screaming at each other as they're led out the back. I stand there, staring. It's like a train wreck—you can't help but watch.

I hear rustling behind me and turn just in time to see Queen Diva go into her dressing room and close the door behind her.

I lean over to Travis. "I'm going to see how she's doing."

"Got it, boss." He mock salutes and begins to walk away. "I've got the VIPs in the private poker tournament, plus all the other typical Saturday-night craziness. Caden and Kian will remain with you."

"Thanks."

The guys take a post on each side of Queen Diva's dressing room door. I knock softly. There's no answer. I knock again, much louder.

"Dana?" I call her by her legal name. "It's Jonathan. May I come in?"

I can hardly hear her yes.

I peek inside without entering. Queen Diva's dressed in jeans and a T-shirt. Her wig is on a mannequin head, but she still wears a wig cap, and her feet are bare. I watch her wipe streaks of makeup off her face.

She sees me in the mirror, and I open my arms. She turns and almost runs to me. She's crying.

I rub her back. "I'm so sorry," I keep repeating.

When she can't shed another tear, she breaks our hug. "I'm sorry."

"Don't be sorry. They took them out the back. There

was no press, so you're good for a day or so."

"I really appreciate that." Tears sit heavily in her eyes but don't fall.

"Do you want to take a few days? Maybe a week or two to deal with your kids and manage this?"

She places her hand on my chest. "You're too good to be in this business."

"I treat people like I want to be treated. Plus, if you need to take the time, I'd rather you do it than be here doing a half-assed job because your mind is on your kids and their welfare."

"I'm a professional. We go on with the show—no matter what." Her voice softens. "I'm sure the media will have this plastered all over for the next few months. They're going to be hard, but I need to work. Right now I'm broke. I learned today that Frankie has drained our accounts."

"Oh, Dana. I'm so sorry."

She gives me a sad smile. "He's a gambler. What can I say? I guess you're stuck with me."

I reach for her hand and squeeze it. "I can't imagine anyone I'd rather be stuck with."

She takes a deep breath and then Dana is gone. The Queen has returned. "Tell me about your friend staying in your apartment. Is she gone? I haven't seen her. When are you bringing her down to pass my inspection?"

"I will when the time is right. She's dealing with some family things."

"Hopefully they're not as bad as mine."

I can't tell her it's worse without outing Maggie, so I just squeeze her hand again and glance at my watch. "I better run." I look at my watch, and it's after two. "I still have ten tech billionaires playing poker in the Waterfront Room."

"I thought I heard they were here in the hotel."

"It's the most surreal game. Neither Gillian nor I have ever seen anything like it. Go big or go home means something very different to these guys."

"I'll bet. Let me know if you want me to stop by before my show tomorrow night," she says.

"Let me check with Gillian," I tell her on the way out. "But that sounds great. And Queen, we're going to get through this."

She nods, her brave face firmly in place. She has been a gift to the Shangri-la since she agreed to make Las Vegas her home.

As I head back to the poker game, I call Maggie. It's late, and I don't want to wake her, but I'm secretly disappointed when I get voice mail. Hopefully, she's getting the rest she desperately needs. "I'm thinking about you," I tell the machine. "I love you. Let's do something special tomorrow, just the two of us."

I walk in and the tables are getting smaller—one is down to four players and the other's at three. Mason's standing to the side watching.

"You're out?" I ask.

He nods. "I had three Jacks and was feeling good, but Walker had a straight."

"No!" I say.

He shrugs. "It happens. I think Viviana is almost done. She's down to two thousand dollars, and Marcus is on a roll."

We stand and watch as she wins two small pots. She's at three hundred thousand. Marcus pushes her to go all in, and she smiles. The pot is pretty rich, and he's sure he has her.

He flips his cards with a pair of eights. Her grin erupts, and she throws out two Kings. The table explodes. Marcus is on the ropes, and Viviana is back up over a million dollars.

"I stand corrected." Mason smirks. "I'm going to go find my girlfriend. Enjoy your night." He shakes my hand.

"Are you going to come by tomorrow to watch?" I ask.

"Probably, tomorrow is when things get really interesting."

"See you then. Have Caroline come with you, and she can meet with Gillian. We would love to have your wedding here," I tease.

He grins. "I think Caroline's booked something in Italy, but I do believe she's looking for a place for her company-wide meeting."

"We'll take whatever she wants to give us. See you tomorrow."

Viviana finishes off Marcus with the next hand, and the game finally draws down to five players. It's after five in the morning, and everyone is exhausted.

"I'm impressed," I tell Viviana.

She leans in close. "He has a tell when he bluffs."

"Really? Do tell!"

"I almost lost all my money figuring it out." She leans in close. "He taps his toes, which makes the table vibrate a tiny bit. Mason's breathing increases slightly, and Jackson touches his ring. I'm going to take it all tomorrow."

I laugh. She's incredibly perceptive. "I can't wait to see it."

The room quickly empties, and soon Gillian and I are the only two left.

"I love that everyone thought Viviana was out and all of a sudden she came back with a vengeance," Gillian says.

I laugh. "She figured out Marcus's tell."

"That's awesome." She leans against a table. "I need to get out of these shoes. I'll be back here at about three tomorrow. Play starts at seven. Don't be late."

"I promise." I salute her, and Caden and Kian walk me back upstairs.

I'm going to sleep and hopefully have morning sex with my woman and go back to sleep. I let myself into my apartment. Everything is quiet. I'm glad Maggie isn't still pacing by the window, worrying about the press conference and what it could mean.

I kick my shoes off next to the door. Trying to be as quiet as possible, I half undress in the living room and head into the bathroom in my boxers. I don't want to wake her.

Once I turn the light on, I glance back at the bed. She's not there. I walk back out to the living room, but she's not there either.

"Maggie?" I yell. But there's nothing. No sound. Crickets.

I look around wildly, and finally see the note on the kitchen counter.

Jonnie,

I waited my whole life for you. You are my everything. I can't put you in danger. I couldn't live with myself if anything happened to you. I need to get this fixed. I hope you can understand. I love you more than I can say. I'll try to get this figured out soon.

Maggie

Immediately I pick up the phone and call the NOC. "Yes, Mr. Best."

"Who is this?" I ask.

"Lucas, sir."

Good. I know Lucas. "My houseguest left unexpectedly," I tell him. "Can you tell me when my door was last accessed?"

I hear the computer keys clicking away. It takes a few moments, and the knots in my stomach are getting bigger all the time.

"It appears the door was opened at nine thirty-six — that's excluding the entrance eight minutes ago."

I sit back hard. She left just after I left last night. That was almost nine hours ago.

"Thank you," I murmur into the phone and hang up.

I call the burner phone, and it rings here in the apartment.

She's alone, with no support, and it's dark.

I do the only thing I can think of. I dial the phone again.

"Hello?" a groggy voice says.

"Jim, she's gone. She left me a note and snuck out."

Chapter 29

Maggie

After leaving the apartment, I move down the back stairs. When no one stops me, I know I'm clear for a few hours. Jonnie is tied up and won't know I'm missing until at least midnight, or hopefully much later. The more time I have, the more I can get accomplished.

There are many used car lots close to the Strip, so I start walking. I'm wearing a hoodie and jeans and carrying a duffel bag, and after walking past three lots, I spot a gray Honda Accord at the fourth. As soon as I step on the property, a salesman approaches. The price listed on the car is eight thousand dollars. I brought ten thousand dollars with me that I'd been hiding from my mother at home. I don't know why, but I thought I might need it some day. I'm glad I have it, but I don't want to spend it all on my car.

"Nice-looking car," he says when he sees what I'm interested in. "It just arrived on the lot a few hours ago." He's pretty slimy and gives used car salesmen a bad name, but I need this car, so I swallow my pride and bite my tongue.

"What's the history on it?" I ask.

He opens the driver's side door. "Why don't you have a seat in the car?" He reaches into the glove box on the passenger side. "Here's the AutoFax. It's never been in any accidents, though the mileage is a little high for a five-year-old car. How does it feel?"

It'll get me where I need to go. "I have sixty-five hundred cash to take it now."

He looks at me, beginning his process. "Well, I don't know. This car just landed on the lot, and I'm going to take a loss."

I look at him. "On the three neighboring lots, there are a combined six Honda Accords roughly the same age and probably with similar miles. This car is worth sixty-five hundred in perfect shape, but this one has a few dents and the tires need replacing. You can take my offer, or I'll go to one of the others and drive off their lot. Tell me what you want to do."

He holds his hands up in mock surrender. "You got me." He shoots his hand out and shakes mine a little too aggressively. His sweaty palms give me the creeps. "You've got a deal."

We walk into the trailer, which has a television running, and I take out sixty-five hundred-dollar bills and count them.

"Looks like someone won today."

"That's right, and rather than wait to fly home, I'm going to drive back to San Diego."

He hands me the keys, and I head away from Las Vegas and San Diego.

There's enough gas in the tank to make it about an hour

outside North Las Vegas, where I stop and pick up a burner phone, snacks, and two large black coffees. That should keep me awake tonight as I drive through the dark desert.

I drive and drive, and hours later the sun crests the horizon outside Moab, Utah. It fills the sky with gold and pink and reminds me that this is a beautiful part of the world.

When I enter Colorado, the orange foothills and Book Cliffs begin to rise out of the desert. It's almost as if they were dropped in the middle of nowhere.

Not long after that, exhaustion creeps up on me, and I'm concerned I might make a mistake. I can't go any farther. I need to stop before I do something stupid, so I pull into a roadside hotel in Grand Junction, Colorado. It's clean, and once I've checked in, I put the Do Not Disturb sign on the door.

I lie down on the bed and listen to the constant hum of the traffic from the nearby interstate. Most people are getting up about now, and the other guests are walking and talking loudly as they make their way down the hall, with kids running and yelling. Though I have been awake for way too long, it is difficult to relax.

I turn the TV on to drown out the noise and finally slow my mind enough to fall asleep. But I wake when I hear a voice I recognize on the TV: Patrick Moreau's.

I sit up, forgetting where I am for a minute. Clearing the haze from my head, I concentrate on what he's saying. He's once again in the Reinhardt Corporation press room. Standing behind him are Herbert and *Alex* Walker, and my blood boils. *Traitor!*

"Ms. Reinhardt is suspected of embezzling over five million dollars from the Reinhardt Foundation, and her whereabouts are unknown. She's considered armed and dangerous, as she has a collection of firearms..."

What? I've never held a gun in my life, much less owned a firearm. What. The. Hell?

"If you see her, do not approach, and call the number

printed on the bottom of your screen. There is a hundred-thousand-dollar reward for any information that leads to her arrest."

Holy fuck!

I pick up the phone and debate outing myself. I remember Jim suggested keeping all calls shorter than two minutes. I dial and start the timer.

"Maggie? Where are you?" Marci asks as soon as she answers the phone.

"I'm fine. I've not been kidnapped, and my love of firearms has been grossly exaggerated."

"Where are you?" she presses.

"I'm off the grid, but I promise I'm okay. I'll keep in touch, but I can't put Jonnie in any danger."

"Why would he be in danger?"

"Jim said the Kryetar activity picked up at the hotel. They're there looking for me."

"Jonnie is going crazy with worry."

This makes my heart hurt, and I close my eyes. Part of me wants to turn around and go back to him, but I know I have to keep going.

"Marci, please," I beg. "Tell him I have to do this to protect him."

"Can I at least have someone from Jim's team join you so you have some sort of protection?"

"No." I look at the timer and see I'm approaching the end of my time. "Let everyone know I'm okay and I'll check in."

I disconnect the call and pull the SIM card. Our call was less than two minutes, so even if she wanted to track me, she shouldn't be able to.

I can't stay long here at the hotel. I didn't use my real name when I checked in, but people begin to have better memories after they're enticed with a hundred thousand dollars. I've come this far; I can't do anything to mess this up now.

I take a quick shower and gather my things, and I'm out the back of the hotel within twenty minutes. I hit the road about eleven am and drive a few miles before I stop to get gas and buy more convenience store snacks to hold me over until I head into the mountains. I have about a two-hour drive to my destination, and I can only hope things work out after I arrive. *I can do this.*

Despite my rush, I'm struck by the beauty of the Colorado River weaving its way through the Rocky Mountains along the highway. The land changes from jagged mountains to open valleys of farmland sprinkled with oil pumps. I wouldn't mind living here. I periodically exit the highway to see if anyone is following me, but no one exits with me or seems to be waiting when I reenter the interstate.

I drive into Glenwood Springs and check my rearview mirror one last time as I exit towards Aspen. I stop for some fast food and again pay attention to the cars around me. This is where a mistake could be bad.

In my mind, I carefully work out what could be going on and what I'm going to say when I arrive. I hope I can be compelling enough.

Basalt is a small community outside of Aspen. At one time it was where the workers and those that served the wealthy in Aspen lived. Now the wealthy live there, leaving most of Aspen to tourists.

I pull off the two-lane highway, still watching my rearview mirror carefully, onto an unmarked gravel driveway. I know the dust cloud behind me will announce my approach before they see or hear me.

When I arrive, he's standing on the wraparound porch, and four labs rush to meet me. He looks like my father — if my father had spent his winters doing ski patrol and his summers doing construction.

I step out of the car and his eyes go wide when he recognizes me. "What are you doing here?"

"Aren't you happy to see your half-sister?" I ask.

He crosses his arms. "Depends. The news says you're armed and dangerous." He watches me exit the car and doesn't make a move to approach me.

The dogs greet me with plenty of excitement, and I bend down to lavish them with the attention they're begging for.

"Since when do you believe everything you hear on the news?" I ask as I walk up the stairs toward him, hesitantly. "They said you died in a car accident."

Murphy's been off the grid for over a decade, and I don't want to screw this up for him, but I need his help.

He opens the front door and ushers me in. He's being cautious, and I can't blame him. He leads me into the kitchen where I spot a blond-haired, blue-eyed woman in jeans and a turtleneck with a wool sweater. I wasn't expecting her. I'm nervous and reluctant to increase the sphere of people who know where I am. If there are kids here, I'll have to keep moving.

"Anna," Murphy says, "this is my sister, Maggie."

She smiles and immediately stands to hug me. I didn't realize how much I needed this, and a sudden sense of relief wraps me like a warm blanket.

"I recognize you from the pictures," she says. "Welcome to our home."

"Where are your keys?" Murphy asks. "I want to move your car into the barn and out of sight."

"This may be a bad idea..." My relief dissipates as suddenly as it arrived.

"It is a bad idea, but you haven't told anyone else I'm alive, so there isn't much I wouldn't do for you."

I hand him the keys, and he disappears.

I feel tears building. "This is such a mess."

Anna pats my hand. "We want to hear all about it and see how we can help. Let's start with a cup of tea while Murphy moves your car."

"Thank you." I sit down at the table and try to breathe

slowly and evenly.

When Murphy returns, Anna is serving tea, and I pull a file folder from my bag.

"I'm sorry I didn't make it to Dad's funeral," Murphy says.

I snort. "You didn't miss much. It was more of a show than anything else."

"That's the same thing my mom said."

"Your mom and I were the only ones upset."

"He often made it hard to love him," Murphy says.

Anna reaches for his hand and gives it a squeeze.

I take a sip of my tea.

"He came out to visit when things started going south," he tells me. "He and Mom were at our wedding. He explained what he wanted for me. I kept telling him I didn't want anything from him or his crazy family."

I nod. "I'm sorry, and now his crazy family needs your help."

His eyes soften. "Neither you, Christopher, or Steven is crazy. Your mother, well, that's another story. I'm guessing she's behind this farce with you being all over the TV and Christopher and Steven in hiding?"

"I think so." I pull my dad's will from my bag and walk Murphy through it. "The will says a Reinhardt must run the company or we have to divest and sell. It also says that person must be married. Although Christopher is still part of the family, he's emancipated, so he has no ties to the business, and Stevie has no interest or qualifications for the job. That leaves me, and my mother is insisting that we comply with the terms of the will immediately, which means she expects me to marry, and she's decided it should be Alex Walker." Finally, I tell him about the forged promissory note Mother showed me. "I think she started out using it to blackmail me into getting married, but now she's made it part of the media blitz, so she seems to have another objective."

"I don't understand why she'd care if you're married,"

he says. "Or if she cares so much, why she'd give up her leverage."

"I believe it's because the Kryetar, which is an Albanian organized crime family, are connected to the company. They may be calling some of the shots."

He sits back in his chair and clasps his hands behind his head. "And you didn't know anything about that?"

"No. This is all news to me. And it seems they're involved with Elite Electronics too—that's the Walker family's company. I have a lot to sort out."

"Better you than me, sister." Murphy shakes his head. "Why would your friend Alex want to marry you? What does he get out of it?"

I shake my head. "When we first talked about it, I thought he was helping me solve a problem and keep the Reinhardt Corporation together. But he's also in a bad financial place. The more I learn about this, the more I think it's just about money."

We sit for a few moments drinking our tea. A deer walks through the backyard with her fawn.

"Where do Christopher and Steven think you are?"

"On the run," I say.

"But your lawyer in San Francisco knows where you are?"

"No, not really. She just knows I'll be in touch." I hand him the SIM card and phone. "This is my burner phone. She can't track me, but she knows I'm safe."

"We should call your brothers."

"I only have the number to Christopher's burner phone. He's in a safe house north of San Francisco. Stevie is in a safe house in Miami."

Murphy gets up and returns with a phone. "This will route your call through Paris."

"I'm impressed."

"We have the same family." He grins. "I talk to my mom weekly, and we do it under the radar for her safety and mine."

"Why does she stay in Minneapolis?" I ask.

He shrugs. "Better to keep your friends close and your enemies closer, I suppose." He thrusts the phone at me. "Call Christopher. Try not to be longer than ten minutes but be sure he knows you're safe."

I dial the number, and it gives the fast double-ring, as if I'm calling from Europe.

"Where the fuck are you?" Christopher growls without saying hello.

"I'm in France. And hello to you too. How are you doing?"

"Frankly, Maggie, I'm pissed. You were safe with Jonnie."

My lip starts to tremble, and my voice breaks. "Christopher, I couldn't bear the thought of anything happening to him."

"How do you think we feel with you out there on your own and no one to protect you? Jonnie is a mess."

"Please tell him and Stevie I'm working on this and I'm safe."

"What's in France?" he asks.

"Distance."

"Can we use this number to call you?" he asks.

I look at Murphy, and he shakes his head no. "I'm moving around," I tell him. "This isn't permanent."

"I want to hear from you regularly. Marci has a lawyer in Chicago working with the US Attorney. The Kryetar are hot and heavy there. Do not even think about going to Chicago. Stay far away."

"No problem." I shift gears. "Marci was surprised they moved forward with the arrest warrant so soon."

"We didn't come out of hiding and declare ourselves safe as they hoped we would after their first press conference," Christopher says.

"What planet were they living on to think we'd do

that?"

"It's a sign they're nervous about you." He lowers his voice. "Which means they'll probably act first and think second. Remember that, okay?"

"I still don't understand why Mother didn't take the money she stole and disappear to some beach or an ice castle in the Swiss Alps, out of prosecutorial reach," I muse out loud.

"None of us can figure it out either," he says.

Murphy clears his throat and points to his wrist.

"I need to go. I'll call again soon."

"Be safe," Christopher says.

"Tell Jonnie I'm doing this for us." I hang up and take a deep breath to build my confidence.

Looking at Murphy and Anna, I force a smile. "I have a plan."

Anna reaches for Murphy's hand, and their fingers intertwine. "Well, don't leave us in suspense," she says.

Chapter 30

Maggie

I look across the table at Anna and Murphy as they clasp hands and stare back at me. "Your mom is still employed by Reinhardt Corporation—"

"I don't want to put her in any danger," Murphy interrupts.

I nod. "I agree. I sympathize. I have a security company I've been working with, and I want her to have a protection detail. Some strange things are going on, and I don't trust anyone at Reinhardt right now."

"I can get on board with that." Murphy glances at Anna, who shrugs. "Convincing my mother she needs a detail may be another story."

"It really is important," I tell them. "If I can't convince

her, you'll need to talk to her. Tell her safety is paramount." They nod. "Do you think she'd meet with me?"

"You're not thinking of going into the lion's den, are you?" Murphy asks.

"No... I don't know exactly the best way to meet her. Maybe over a protected phone line? But I'd prefer for her to come here."

Murphy turns to Anna. "Do we tell her?"

"Tell me what?" My stomach is in knots. Have they already talked to Nancy and she wants me gone and away from them?

Anna smiles. "He means do we tell his mom I'm pregnant—with twins."

I wasn't expecting that at all. I jump up. "Twins? That's amazing!" I rush over to hug Anna and Murphy. "I'm going to be an aunt! Christopher and Bella are pregnant, too." My hand flies to my mouth, and I scramble to recover. "Although, that's their news. Oops. I probably shouldn't have shared that."

"That's great news," Anna says. "But of course we'll keep it to ourselves."

I take my place at the table again, and the gravity of the situation hits me. I can't stay here. I need to leave, and I need to leave tonight. "What if your mom can meet me, say...in Denver before coming here?"

"On one condition," Anna says. "You need your own protection detail."

She's right. I'm tired and I've only been on my own for a day. But I can't. I try to explain it so they'll understand. "I want everyone to be able to be honest if they're questioned by the police or, God forbid, the FBI. If they don't know where I am, they're not lying."

"You're important to all of us, which means your safety is important, too," Anna stresses.

I need to get this moving if I'm going to get out of here. "Okay, we need to make some calls."

Murphy steps out and returns with the phone, offering it to me. "This time you're calling from Prague."

"I'm a world traveler, I guess." I dial Jim.

"Jim Adelson," his deliberate and strong voice says in greeting.

"Hi, it's Maggie."

"You're in Eastern Europe?" he asks.

"No, but I'm safe."

I hear a frustrated sigh.

I start talking before he can ask the twenty questions I'm not going to answer. "Jim, I need a detail for my dad's old secretary, Nancy Newcastle."

"What do I need to know?" he asks.

"She's the mother of my half-brother," I offer.

"Does she know we're coming?"

"She will as soon as I hang up."

He's quiet for a moment.

"I need you to tell her to go to her son in Colorado."

"His grave?"

"Yes."

"What aren't you telling me?" he presses.

"She's in danger. If you can join her, you'll learn more. I better go. I need to let her know you're coming."

"The team can be there in twenty minutes."

I'm stunned by this. "Why do you have a team in Minneapolis? And that's probably sooner than she can be ready."

"Okay, let her know I'll pick her up with her detail in Minneapolis in...three hours." He doesn't answer my question, which makes me nervous, but I don't have time to press him. I suppose I'm not answering a lot of his questions either.

"Make sure your team accompanies her as she moves around," I tell him. "She's the key to this."

Nancy knows everything, I'm sure of it. It's time we all talk.

"Are you at your brother's grave?" he asks.

I'm not at his grave, but that's just semantics, right? "I am, but I won't be by the time you arrive."

"Maggie," Jim says. "I'm on your side in this."

"I know. I'd just rather you be able to be honest with the police if you're asked."

"I work for Marci," he reminds me. "If they ask, I'm covered by privilege. Everyone is worried about you. I'm bringing someone to stay with you. You shouldn't do this alone."

"We'll talk soon." I disconnect the phone and turn to Murphy. "We need to call your mom now."

He nods, dials his mother, and hands me the phone. I hope she picks up.

"Hello?" Relief floods through me at the sound of her voice.

"Nancy, it's me."

"I'm sorry, but I've already donated to the veterans fund."

I'm confused by this but realize she must not be alone.

"Nancy, I'm sending you a security detail. I'm with Anna. They're going to bring you here."

"That sounds like a great idea. Let's aim for a return call at four o'clock today. Would that work?" I hear the edge in her voice, and I know we need to act fast. It's less than a half-hour until four.

"Thanks, Nancy. His name is Jim Adelson."

"I'll watch for him then."

I hang up and turn to Murphy. "Something's not right. I need to call Jim back. Your mom's expecting a team sooner than we planned."

He nods, and I call Jim back. Before he can even acknowledge me, I blurt out, "Something is up. Nancy will be ready at four for your team."

"We'll be there. Please, can you stay put?"

"I have to make arrangements. I don't want to put

anybody in danger."

"Nancy's team should arrive in the next fifteen minutes."

"Thank you," I tell him, and I truly, truly mean it.

"I'll be there in a private plane at..." There's a short pause. "Seven o'clock to pick her and the team up. I need to file a flight plan, so I need to know where Murphy's grave is located."

I take a deep breath. "When you leave Minneapolis, land in Eagle, Colorado. I may meet you there, but for sure a friend of Nancy's will meet the plane."

Eagle is just outside Vail. It's an airport that mostly serves the rich and famous and their private jets.

"I have a client with a place near the airport. We can stay there, and you'll be safe and off the radar."

"I don't know, Jim." I was planning on heading to Denver tonight.

"Consider it."

"I will." I disconnect the phone and find Anna and Murphy staring at me.

"You're staying with Jim and not going underground on your own, right?" Murphy says.

"I don't know. Honestly, my plan is to stay away from anyone I care about." I'm fighting tears.

"I heard him say he has access to a place close by, which probably means Vail or Beavercreek. You could do that at least for a night or two. You need some rest before you rush into the hellfire," Murphy reasons.

All of a sudden, I'm exhausted. I can't even think straight to argue my point right now. "When do we need to leave for the airport?"

"If they're leaving Minneapolis at seven, they'll need time to drive to the airport, so they should land about nine. It will take us a little under an hour and a half, so we'll leave here about seven thirty."

I glance at the time. That's more than three hours away.

"Can I lie down? I drove all Saturday night and into this morning. I grabbed a hotel, but it was so loud, I didn't really sleep."

"Of course." Anna jumps up. "Follow me to the guest room. I'll wake you about seven. I'm making potato soup for dinner, and that will stick to your bones tonight."

"Sounds wonderful." I don't even undress and just crawl beneath the sheets. I feel safe, at least for the minute.

I must fall asleep quickly because it seems like I just laid down when Anna knocks at the door.

"Maggie?" she calls. "It's after seven."

I sit up and attempt to shake the fog from my brain. My feet feel like they're encased in concrete, but I move slowly to the kitchen. Murphy and Anna stop talking when I arrive. "I'm sorry."

"We were just discussing the plan," Anna says. "As tired as you are, we don't think it's safe for you to drive tonight."

"Unfortunately, I haven't grown wings yet, so flying isn't an option.

Anna pours me a dark cup of tea. "I think I should drive your car with you in the passenger seat, and Murphy will drive our car."

I feel like I should protest, but my body tells me it's a smart move. "Okay."

"You don't understand. The roads are dark, and we know them better," Murphy says. "If for some reason we need to go another direction, we'll be able to do that."

I cock my head, confused. "I agreed with Anna."

"Oh, I'm sorry." Murphy looks sheepish. "I expected a bigger fight."

"I know you think I'm being difficult, but I need to at least try to protect you. If these guys are coming after me, what will they do to someone who helps me? We can't fight this battle from twenty different angles."

He shakes his head. "You won't. You've got a team

behind you. You don't need to do this on your own."

I stand to give Murphy a hug, and my tears fall. "I'm so grateful you're my brother."

He returns the hug. "I'm glad you're my sister."

"You should eat." Anna thrusts a steaming cup of creamy goodness at me.

I swear, my eyes roll into the back of my head as I taste it. "This is amazing."

"I'll tell you my secret." Anna drops her voice as if we're in a busy room. "I use a dry soup starter and add ham and hard-boiled egg. It gives it more substance to stick to your bones."

After finishing a second serving of soup, I feel refreshed and ready to take on the world.

"Shall we go?" Murphy has an overnight bag. He looks down at it. "Just in case we have to stay in Vail with you while you meet with Mom."

"Good idea. I guess I'm as ready as I'll ever be."

"We're going to drive out the back way without the headlights. We'll go separately. I'm going to start south and you'll head north."

I'm not sure I understand what he's saying, but I attribute it to my lack of sleep. Anyway, I trust them. As we walk toward the barn in the dark, I pull my coat tight to keep out the chill. It's so dark, I can hardly see anything. "Will you be able to see where you're going?"

"Yes, we practiced this many times," Anna assures me.

As we drive, it's darker than I've ever seen before, yet Anna keeps the headlights off. "Why would you practice driving in the dark?"

"Murphy's really cautious about some of your family."

"I would've thought he was crazy until this all started."

I sit in silence so she can concentrate on the blackness. A few times we brush up against branches or hit a big bump, but she always rights the car. I'm holding the car door so tightly that the muscles in my hands begin to cramp, and my jaw hurts from clenching so tight.

I sit back in my seat, I close my eyes, and do a few Ujjayi breaths. Taking a deep breath, my lower belly fills. I imagine my yogi saying, *"Breathe and feel your lower chakras, one and two, fill. Let it fill your stomach up to your throat. Breathe in, holding a moment, and then breathe out slowly through your nose."* I do this a few times, and my anxiousness dissipates. I'm more relaxed and able to let go of the door.

We seem to drive forever, though, and after a while, my nerves return. We haven't been on any paved roads, and our time is running out. Then all of a sudden, we pull into the airport parking lot.

"Holy cow! We drove all the way here without getting on the highway."

"Our only risk was if we ran into someone else on the road, but this way keeps us difficult to follow in the dark."

I look across the parking lot and notice Murphy arriving from the highway.

I put the SIM card in my burner phone, and it almost immediately rings. "We're in final approach. Are you at the airport?" Jim asks.

"Yes."

"And how about your half-brother and his wife?"

"They're here with me, too," I tell him. "I guess Nancy has filled you in on a few things."

"She has," he confirms. "We'll land, pick you all up, and move elsewhere. Meet us as the private plane entrance."

"What's going on?" I ask.

"After talking to Nancy, I'm changing where we're headed."

"That sounds ominous." The hair on the back of my neck stands on end.

"Be ready." He disconnects just as I see a plane hit the runway.

I look at Murphy and Anna. "Your mom said something to the security team, and they're changing our destination. They're stopping to pick us up. I think we're going somewhere other than Vail."

I can tell Murphy's having second thoughts. He looks at his car and at Anna, then back at me.

"Talk to your mom if you're unsure," I tell him. "This change has something to do with what she said. And if you decide not to go, you can at least tell your mom your news."

The plane taxis up, and the side door opens. Jim unwraps himself enough to walk out of the small plane door and heads our way.

"Jim, this is my half-brother, Murphy Newcastle Reinhardt, and his wife Anna," I tell him as he approaches.

"Nice to meet you both." Jim extends his hand. "Your mom tells me she thinks they're closing in on you here in Colorado."

Murphy looks at Anna, and I can see panic in their eyes.

"We'd like you to join us, but we're changing our destination."

I can see the conflict in their faces, and Jim must, too. "Why don't you talk to your mom, and then you can make a decision."

"I'm sorry I put you in danger," I tell them. "This is my fault."

"You didn't. Things are just moving fast," Jim assures me.

Murphy and Anna climb the ladder to the plane, and I walk in behind them. Nancy wraps them a long embrace, and there are a lot of tears.

"They know you're alive," she cries. "You're not safe right now in your home. I'm so glad we're here together."

When Nancy sees me, she breaks away from them, and I brace for the verbal lashing I know I deserve for putting them in this danger.

"You saved them," she says, rushing to hug me. "I can't tell you how happy I was to get your call this afternoon.

Thank you for going to Murphy."

I'm not sure what she's talking about, but she seems to have convinced Murphy and Anna to keep moving—and me as well. We all take our seats on the plane, and we're quickly speeding down the runway again.

"We're going to Montana," Jim announces.

Chapter 31

Jonathan

The sun has set on Sunday, and I know I should be preparing for tonight's final round in the private poker tournament, but I can't motivate myself to leave the apartment. It's as if I think Maggie's suddenly going to come back if I just stay here.

There's a knock at the door, which I choose to ignore. But a few seconds later it comes again. *Who is knocking on my door and why won't they go away?*

The knocking persists. *Good grief!*

I'm in my boxers, and without looking through the peephole, I swing the door open wide. "What?"

Immediately I regret my choice of wardrobe and demeanor. I'm pretty much naked in front of Mason Sullivan and his girlfriend, Caroline Arnault—America's favorite lady. Her father snubbed his personal inheritance to start one of Silicon Valley's first technology companies with her mother. She and her twin brother were billionaires by eleven, and they've been tabloid fodder ever since.

"I'm sorry," I tell them. I know I'm blushing. "Come in. Let me get dressed."

"Christopher just called me," Mason says. "He told me what's going on."

I'm confused until I remember Mason is one of Christopher's business partners. I point them to the living room, trying to cover my junk. "Please have a seat." I point them to my bar. "Have a drink. There's some Mitchner's or other liquor there. You can help yourself, and I'll go throw some clothes on."

"Don't get dressed on my account," Caroline teases. She winks at Mason when he scowls at her, then leans in and kisses him on the cheek. My stomach tightens. They have what I want with Maggie—a great relationship.

I scurry off and search my bedroom for something to wear. For some reason, that seems hard. I'm not finding anything. "What did Christopher tell you?" I yell.

"Maggie was with me and the girls in Cecelia's room when she saw the press conference announcing that she and her brothers were missing. They're really pulling out all the stops," Caroline calls.

"It's all made up to force her to take over the company business, or work with the Albanian mob—or something like that," I respond.

"She was quite shaken," Caroline adds.

"You know the accusations are crap, right?" I ask.

"Of course. Christopher brought us up to speed," Mason informs me.

I've been so consumed by Maggie, I didn't think to ask. "Are Christopher and Bella okay?"

"They're probably much like Maggie was—feeling a

little trapped. Christopher also asked me to share with you that Jim has been in contact with her."

A huge wave of relief covers me. "Thank goodness. Where is she?"

"He didn't get an exact location, but he's trying to convince her to go back into hiding—or at the very least have a detail with her."

"Do we know where she's going?" I ask.

"Jim is talking to her on the phone and making arrangements to meet," Mason adds. "He's trying to get to the bottom of it all."

I finally pull on my jeans and throw a T-shirt over my head.

When I return to the living room, Mason hands me a tumbler of bourbon.

"We thought you might want to join us to watch the final night of the tournament," Caroline suggests.

"I don't know. I feel like I should stay here, close to my phone—where it's quiet, and I can hear her if she calls."

"Jim has her in his sights. He'll talk to her and help her get this figured out. There isn't much we can do. Why don't you join us and see who loses a small company and maybe a ranch or a plane today?"

"I have a plane. I can fly to her," I protest.

Caroline puts her hand on my arm. "Honey, she's worried about your safety if you're involved. That's why she left in the first place. Jim is a miracle worker. Let him do his job. You've got a lot going on right now. Let's focus on that."

I know they're right, but I hate feeling helpless. My plan was to ignore everything here at the hotel, wear a hole in the carpet from pacing, and wait for my phone to ring, but it doesn't seem like that's going to happen.

I nod and agree. "Let me change into something more appropriate to go downstairs."

"That's fine, but you only have a few minutes because Gillian tells me Queen Diva is due to stop by at seven, and I don't want to miss her," Caroline says.

I return to the bedroom and look through my dark suits. There's the one I want—my lucky suit, a dark gray Valentino made specifically for me. I wore it when I got the money to build the hotel.

I yell from the closet, "You do realize I can make that happen whenever you want."

"Sure, but this is her coming to a private group. It's small and intimate. Backstage there are dozens of people."

I roll my eyes. Caroline doesn't seem to realize who she is. I suppose that's part of what's charming about her. When things become halfway normal again, I should arrange dinner for them with Queen as an appreciation for their support.

I look at myself in the mirror and know this is as good as it's going to get tonight. If I can't be put together on the inside, at least I'll be put together on the outside.

I walk out. "Are we ready to go?"

"I'm going to be the envy of every woman in this hotel," Caroline singsongs. "I'm with two of the most handsome men around."

When we step out of the apartment, Caden and Kian are waiting with two people from Mason and Caroline's detail. I'm embarrassed to have so much muscle with us—until I witness the way Caroline is mobbed downstairs.

Women scream when they see her and rush up for autographs and photos. She's a trooper and signs them all and poses for some pictures. I chuckle as Mason takes the photos. Most people don't know he's a rock star in his own right. Because of him, they have social media pages to post their pictures on. He's the guy that financed the original social media companies, and he has the bank accounts to prove it.

When we finally walk into the private poker room, the crowd is larger than it was late last night. "So much for an intimate gathering," I tell Caroline. "But I promise I will arrange an audience for you and Queen Diva."

Caroline nods. "Only if she wants to. Don't make her

do anything she isn't interested in."

Gillian has set up spectator seating around the single remaining table. I smile, press the flesh, and make small talk. I miss Maggie like there's a hole in my soul, but I tell myself she'll be able to join me doing these kinds of events one day.

I progress into a little trash talking with the players still left, and Landon Walsh invites me to play—with the Shangri-la as a buy-in.

"I promise, you'd pay me to take it back," I tell him, shaking my head.

The room chuckles.

Travis arrives and whispers in my ear that Queen Diva is on her way.

I nod. That's my hint to start. "Ladies and gentlemen, thank you for coming out this evening. This group of players is unlike anything Gillian and I have ever witnessed. Last time we saw a chalet in Aspen, a ranch in Montana, and a small start-up all change hands. What tonight brings, no one knows. But here are the chip counts..."

I read through the list, which ranges from two million to twenty-five million. Everybody has plenty of money. "We'll play down to the last hand, and the winner takes all," I remind them. "Now, before we start, we have a special guest stopping by before she needs to be on stage tonight."

Travis opens the exterior door, and in steps Queen Diva.

"Ladies and gentlemen, may I present you the premiere act here at the Shangri-la, Queen Diva."

The room erupts in applause.

She waves to everyone, eating up the attention. "I wanted to stop by and say hello. I understand this is *the* game on the Strip."

"You're welcome to join us." Walker Clifton offers the seat next to him and grins like a Cheshire cat.

Queen Diva laughs. "I have a feeling all of you at this table far exceed my poker talents."

That gets a chuckle from the crowd. People approach her, and she signs autographs and takes photos. All the time she's smiling and seems incredibly happy. No one knows all the crap going on in her personal life. I definitely take note and know this is how I should also be behaving.

When she's done and ready to return to her dressing room, she gets a standing ovation. She wipes a tear. "You all are so wonderful. Thank you!"

I follow her out the door. "Thank you for doing that."

"I don't mind one bit. Those people keep our doors open, and it's the least I can do after all you've done for me." She gives me a hug.

"How are you doing?" I ask.

She shrugs. "Right now it's an hour-by-hour thing."

"I understand."

"Frankie was released on bond," she tells me. "Paid for by a friend of his—another woman."

That has to sting. I sigh. "I'm sorry."

She looks up and away, making sure the tears don't ruin her makeup.

"I'm happy to make sure he can't step foot in the hotel again."

She nods. "I like that idea, but not yet. His gravy train is over with me. I met with the lawyer today, and I'll serve him with divorce papers later this week. If he becomes a pain in my ass, I'll let you know. But once he gets the papers, the press will go crazy."

"Keep us posted. We'll make sure Travis's team is there to protect you. Should we set a detail for the kids?"

A cloud of anger crosses her face. "I swear to God, if the press goes after my kids, I'll go crazy."

"Travis and I will work on a plan and let you know. Now go break a leg with your show tonight."

She gives me one more hug. "You know the rumor mill is going crazy about you and that woman holed up in your apartment."

"There's no woman in my apartment." I can say that truthfully, unfortunately.

"Well, I hope she returns soon. You're a good man, and she's missing out if she doesn't see it."

"Thank you." I smile and squeeze her hand.

She disappears down the hall, and while I'm out of the poker room, I take the opportunity to call Jim. I'm not sure if anyone's tracing his calls, but as careful as both Maggie and Christopher have been, I don't want to assume Jim isn't on anybody's radar and his phone isn't being bugged. Still, I want to know what's going on.

After four rings, his voice mail picks up.

"Jim, it's Jonathan Best. We may have some needs regarding Queen Diva, and I'd love to catch up with you. Please call."

Chapter 32

Maggie

The push of the small jet speeding down the runway presses me into my seat. The darkness is punctuated by sprinkles of light, which grow smaller as we jettison into the clouds.

"Where in Montana are we headed?" Murphy asks as we become level.

"A client of ours has a ranch with a private landing strip, though our flight plan says we're heading to Canada. This will give us some time to formulate our plan."

Murphy reaches across the aisle for his mom's hand. "Are you okay?"

Nancy smiles. "I am now."

Seeing the love between Murphy, Anna, and Nancy is

surprising to me—not because they have such a strong bond, but because Nancy was so close to my dad, and that was not how we grew up in my house.

I sit back in my chair and wonder what it would have been like if my family had never had to take over Reinhardt Corporation. Maybe everyone would be happier.

"So, this is the plan," Jim begins. "We're arriving at a private airstrip, and we'll touch down only briefly. We'll need to exit the plane quickly as we want the flight to complete its flight plan to Banff, Canada, without interruption. Then it will remain there until we're ready to go."

My stomach clenches. I don't like how many people are involved with this. But Jim does seem perfectly in control, and he always has just the resources we need. As much as I hate this, I really do need him.

"We have a few cars picking us up, and they'll move us to the main house. Once we're there, I know it's late, but I'd like us to meet in the living room and start our discussions. Everyone will have their own room." Jim turns to stare at me. "No one will leave without a member of my team."

"What can you tell us now?" Murphy asks.

"When Maggie went on her trip to San Francisco, there was movement. People in New York began aligning things that appeared to put pressure on Maggie's mother and Herbert Walker in Minneapolis. When Maggie went dark, things escalated in Minneapolis, and we saw several people dispatched to San Francisco. With the first news conference, they were hoping to get the three of you kids to pop your heads out and assure everyone you were okay. If you had, we believe they were going to grab you."

"But that didn't happen," I say.

"No, it didn't. I don't think they expected you to be quite so resourceful." Jim smiles.

"I would agree with that," Nancy adds.

"They heard some rumors that Maggie might be in Las Vegas with an old friend, but they couldn't confirm it until you were caught on video buying a burner phone."

I sit back and close my eyes. "I outed myself."

"You did. But they didn't know where you were going. They dispatched teams to Salt Lake City, San Diego, and Denver," Jim says.

"How did they figure out Murphy?" I ask.

"Before I answer, Murphy, can you tell me why they thought you were dead?"

"I can tell you that," Nancy interjects. "But it's a rather long story. I worked for William Reinhardt, Maggie's father, for many years. I started as his legal secretary after my husband was killed, and I went with him to be his assistant when he took over at Reinhardt Corporation. After that transition, William went from being a kind and loving man to stressed all the time. His marriage to Catherine had led to the merger of two successful department stores, but William saw the writing on the wall and created Bullseye when he realized there was more room for competition at the lower end of the retail market. No one expected it to be such a big success, and that success created a significant rift between him and Catherine. She didn't want her family's department store legacy to be eroded by a discount chain."

"But Bullseye is the only reason Reinhardt Hudson's is still open," I say, shaking my head.

Nancy nods and looks down a moment. "It was an accident when William and I got together—too many late nights and too much work. But we fell in love, and from our love came Murphy, though we hadn't planned to have any children. I knew from the beginning William couldn't divorce Catherine. They had their own family, and his father's will was clear that they had to remain together. But he loved us as best he could until he died."

"Did my mother know about you?" I ask.

Nancy nods. "I think she encouraged it, really. She seemed to think if he was happy with me, he'd be more amenable to her demands."

This is news to me. "And was he?"

"Probably. And she was fine focusing on her volunteer commitments and her place in society." Nancy looks over at Murphy. "William launched a second mid-level department store, which he named Murphy's. That set Catherine off because it announced to the world that he'd had a child by another woman."

"I think I was ten when he launched Murphy's," I recall. "No one would have figured it out."

"Maybe not the general public, but most people in your mother's circle knew I had a son named Murphy." She shrugs. "As William's health declined, he revisited his will. He knew Christopher didn't want the business, and Stevie couldn't take it over."

My ears perk up. "Why not?"

Nancy shakes her head. "It's not my place to say."

"Please, it could be important," Jim insists.

"Stevie is a Walker, not a Reinhardt," Nancy mumbles.

I sit up straight in my seat. "What?"

She sighs. "Shortly after you were conceived, your mother shut your father out. It was fine by him, and he couldn't fault Catherine for her affair given he was having his own."

My world is rocked. "Does Stevie know?"

My father never treated him as anything other than his son. Knowing he was Herbert's son must have made their relationship difficult. Stevie and I live separate lives and always have, but I never suspected we didn't have the same father. *Does Alex know he has a half-brother?*

"I don't know if Stevie knows, but this meant that if Christopher wasn't going to take over the business, it should be Murphy. But Catherine wasn't having that."

I roll my eyes. "Good grief. Who cares?"

"Your mother did, and she set out to kill Murphy. But she spoke a little too freely about it, and your father found out. So we staged Murphy's death, moved him to Colorado, and put him in hiding from everyone—until your father was dying and told Maggie."

"How could my mother be so callous?" I don't like the image coming into focus of who my mother really is. "I knew something was up and Murphy was alive, because my dad shared it with me not long before he died. At first I thought he just wanted me to know how clever he was, but now I think he wanted me to make way for Murphy to take over the business. He knew the Foundation was my true focus." I look at Nancy and Murphy. "I'm sorry. I had no idea why you had to do what you did."

Nancy reaches over to squeeze my hand.

"Back to the original question, though," I add. "How did they figure out Murphy was alive?"

Jim looks at Nancy with raised eyebrows.

She shakes her head. "I'm not totally sure, but Catherine called me this morning and said my son in Colorado would never run Reinhardt Hudson. That's how I figured out they knew."

A bell rings from the cockpit. "We're preparing to land," Jim says. "Remember, I want the plane on the ground less than ten minutes so it can continue to Canada. We need to get off quickly."

The plane descends, and within moments of coming to a stop on the runway, we're exiting. Three cars are waiting, and the ten of us who exited the plane divide ourselves among them. Murphy, Anna, and Nancy go in one car, and I end up in another with Jim, Zack, and Thomas.

"Are you two my new best friends?" I ask them.

"You could say that," says Zack.

"I've missed you guys," I tease. "Travis's team couldn't keep up with me."

We ride up to the house—the centerpiece of a beautiful ranch owned by another of Jim's clients—and the cars drive away after dropping us off.

"Is there a chance they could find us here?" I ask.

"It would be difficult," Jim assures me.

When we enter the house, a round woman with blond curls and a wide smile stands with a man in a cowboy hat, boots, and plaid western shirt. "Welcome to Magnolia Homestead," she says. "We're the ranch managers, Molly and Frank Pierce."

"Nice to meet you," I mutter, as do the others.

"I understand you're meeting in the living room. I wasn't sure if anyone would be hungry, so I set up some food. Follow me."

We follow Molly to the living room and find a buffet big enough for an army. We swarm over the table of fruit, vegetables, and homemade pastries and breads.

"What sorts of drinks would you like?" Molly asks Jim.

"Whatever they want," he replies.

"I'd like a glass of scotch," Murphy says.

"We have a twenty-year blended scotch or a fifteen-year single malt," Frank reports.

"I'll take the blended."

"That's my favorite, too." I look at Murphy fondly. "May I have one of those as well?"

"Yes, ma'am."

After we've had a bite to eat, with drinks in hand, we get back to our conversation.

"So now we know why Murphy went into hiding." Jim turns and gazes at Nancy. "Do you know how the Kryetar got involved with Reinhardt Corporation?"

"I've heard a few things, but it's mostly speculation and conversations William and I had before his death," Nancy says.

"That's a good place to start. My team can chase down details and verify them," Jim says.

Nancy stares down at her skirt and picks an imaginary thread. "Back in the Hudson's days, Catherine's father worked hard to break into New York. There was a lot of competition from Macy's, Bergdorf's, Bloomingdale's, and

Gimbel's. To fight his way in, he worked with the Teamsters in the 1940s."

"But they weren't the Kryetar, right?"

"That's right. But over time, part of their organization was taken over by criminally minded Albanians, and those people eventually became the Kryetar." She takes a sip of her hot tea. "I don't know if Herbert Walker was also involved with the Kryetar or if it was Catherine who brought them over, but they now have their talons firmly in Elite Electronics, too."

"What do the Kryetar use these companies for?" Jim asks.

"Smuggling mostly."

He nods. "Drugs?"

"Yes, and anything else they want to have moved." Nancy looks away, not meeting anyone's gaze. "They have a complex logistics operation. For Bullseye, we produce under our own brand names, and more than seventy percent of our inventory comes from China. My understanding is we had a shipment last year that was fifty percent paper straws and fifty percent oxycodone, all manufactured in China."

"How did my parents allow this to happen?" I ask, incredulous.

Nancy looks at me. "That's a complicated answer."

Chapter 33

Maggie

I feel like I'm having an out-of-body experience. My parents allowed drugs to be transported around the country with their goods? The corruption would have to go all the way to the top of Reinhardt Corporation for this to happen.

I still don't understand. How could I have not known or figured it out?

Jim looks around the room. We're quite the rag-tag team—slouched over, yawning, and fighting sleep.

"You all look exhausted," he says. "Please, let's go to our rooms and get some rest. We can meet here tomorrow morning for breakfast at nine."

Molly and Frank lead us out, but Jim reaches for my arm. "Are you okay?"

I take a deep breath. "I don't know. This is a lot to take in. Today I confirmed my half-brother is not only alive but expecting twins, another brother has a different father than I do, and my parents are drug smugglers in bed with the Albanian mob. I mean, that's a normal day for most, isn't it?"

Jim's lips quirk. "It's a lot of information."

"I don't know what to think anymore." I sigh. "And I still don't understand how all of this involves me."

He nods. "I have some ideas, and my team will work on them tonight. Maggie, I understand this was tough to hear. Nancy was very worried about you on the flight in from Minneapolis. She didn't want to change your opinion of your father. I didn't comprehend what that meant until this evening. "

"I watched Murphy, Anna, and Nancy interacting on the plane here," I tell him. "There's so much love there. I was actually jealous. My mother doesn't have an ounce of that love for me. Maybe my father did, but he didn't show it the same way… " I'm determined not to cry. I pinch the skin between my forefinger and thumb. The pain distracts me from the pain my parents have caused me.

He studies me a moment. "You may feel alone, but I'll remind you that Christopher and Stevie are incredibly worried about you. And Murphy's love for his mother and wife spills over to you. He didn't hesitate to jump in, even knowing it would expose his secret. Also, I think there's a hotelier in Las Vegas who cares a great deal about you." He puts his arm around my shoulder and leads me to the base of the stairs. "You have more people who love you than you think. Your parents may be different than you thought they were, but you have a wonderful family despite them."

He's right. I do have a lot of people in my corner. "Thanks, Jim. I needed to hear that." I start up the stairs. "I'll see you in the morning."

Lying in bed a little while later, I stare up at the ceiling. The night is so dark here that I can barely make out the shape of the overhead light fixture. I lie on my side and take in the darkness of the land outside. There isn't another light anywhere on the horizon. It's black, cold, and almost eerie.

Insomnia haunts my night, just as fatigue rules my days right now. When I need to be lucid and clear, my brain begs for unconsciousness, for sleep at any price. But come the hours of darkness in the comfort of a bed, my mind lights up with new sources of disaster and danger.

I click through everything I learned today, and somehow some of it finally makes sense. It's as if I had a puzzle I didn't realize was missing so many pieces.

Stevie is my half-brother. While Christopher and I are blond-haired and blue-eyed, Stevie has brown hair—darker than my mother's, but the same color as Alex and his father's. But my father never treated him poorly, and for that I'm grateful.

Our logistics and supply chain will need a complete overhaul. That's going to take some work to figure out.

And why would my marrying Alex matter?

What does Alex know?

I want to let everything go, to count sheep and relax, but soon the sheep are telling me what might go wrong tomorrow because of some blunder I made today.

I watch the clock move past three, and I still can't sleep.

I want to talk to Jonnie.

I wish my brothers were here.

Finally, I realize I can either lie in my bed watching the color slowly seep back into the landscape outside, or I can get up.

I'm pondering my decision when there's a knock at my door. I roll over and blink back the sunlight. I fell asleep at some point. At first, I'm not sure where I am, and it takes a moment to get my bearings.

Then I remember. "Come in," I croak.

Molly peeks her head around the door. "The meeting is going to start shortly."

"I'm sorry. I'll be right down." I'm embarrassed I never set an alarm and had to have someone come looking for me.

She grins. "It's the fresh air—wipes people out. I'm waking a few of you."

"Thank you." I like Molly. She's warm, friendly, and makes me feel welcome at a time I really appreciate that. My head is pounding, but I can do this.

"Of course. Can I bring you a cup of coffee before you head down? I don't mind at all," she offers.

That sounds fantastic. "I guess—with a little cream and one sugar?" I'm going to need a lot of caffeine and energy today.

"Coming right up."

I pull the covers back, and the cold air bites at my skin. I want nothing more than to curl up and go back to sleep for the rest of the decade.

It's not like they need me for today's meetings. I mean, this is likely more of Nancy sharing what she knows about the company history and why we're in bed with the Kryetar...

But maybe Nancy has an idea of how I can escape this marriage.

I work my way to the shower, and the warm water gives me the energy to dress and go downstairs.

When I emerge from the bathroom, I find a carafe of coffee, a bagel with cream cheese, and a small bowl of mixed fruit. Back home, Hazel hasn't brought me breakfast in my room in years. I'll be spoiled by Molly if I stay here too long.

I'm the last to arrive downstairs, and Jim greets me. "How did you sleep last night?"

"It took me a while to fall asleep, but it seems I eventually did." I pop a grape into my mouth. "Today I'll need a lot of coffee."

"Me, too." He smiles and turns to the room. "Okay, everyone, we have a few people joining us this afternoon, so let's make the most of our morning so you can enjoy a bit of fresh air before they arrive."

"Who's joining us?" I ask.

"Christopher, Bella, and your attorney, Marci Peterson—"

My heart races. This is fantastic news. "What about Stevie and Genevieve?"

"They're coming from Florida and should be here at roughly the same time."

"Anyone else?" Part of me hopes Jonnie is coming, though I know that would be unwise—and probably impossible for his schedule.

"A few people from my team, but don't worry about them."

I survey the room. People are busily eating and drinking coffee or tea, and Nancy is sitting in a wing-backed chair, looking ready for the interviews to begin. I sit down next to her, and she reaches out to me.

"Thank you for all you've done for me and my family," she says.

I smile. "You're my family, too."

Jim comes over and puts his notepad on the table. "Good morning, ladies. Do you mind if we get right to it?"

When Nancy and I nod, he picks up approximately where we left off last night.

"We discussed yesterday some of the early history of Reinhardt Hudson's and what became the Albanian mafia. You indicated that William Reinhardt had told you the Kryetar were present in the company before he took charge. Is that correct?"

"Well, yes." Nancy stares down at her hand, and I notice a beautiful sapphire ring. I've never seen it before, but I'm sure my dad gave it to her. "They weren't always as bold as they are these days, though. That has definitely gotten worse over time. As William diversified the company, their demands to be involved with Bullseye and Murphy's made his life miserable."

"How so?" Jim asks.

"Well, I remember our logistics manager left one day, and a new guy started. William was extremely upset and angry about this. I still remember him telling me about it over dinner." Nancy looks out at the white snow. "He didn't go into it, but it seemed the Kryetar were pushing to expand their presence and wanting more leverage. With the help of the logistics manager, William had been resisting their most overt efforts, but then we later learned they'd killed the logistics manager and replaced him with a Kryetar member."

"Ah…okay," Jim says as he makes a few notes. "Nancy, what do you know about the impending merger between Elite Electronics and Reinhardt Corporation?"

"Catherine is driving that, though I don't know if she's following orders from someone else. But she's been involved with Herbert since around the time Christopher emancipated."

"Were you aware my mother was embezzling funds from the Foundation?" I ask.

She nods. "Your father suspected it and confronted her." She dabs her eyes. "I'm convinced she killed him."

"What?" I nearly shriek.

"He was so vibrant, and all of a sudden he wasn't. He started pulling away from me. He told me I needed to move on." She grasps my hands. "Your father and I didn't mean to fall in love, but we did. He assured me his will provided for me and for Murphy. Then after he was gone, the lawyer told me there wasn't anything for us."

"What? Wait? You were told the will didn't give you anything?"

She nods.

"When that same lawyer, Patrick Moreau, read *us* the

will, we were told you, Christopher, Stevie, and I were each getting a quarter of the company. I was pretty sure Murphy was alive, and your quarter was meant to be passed to him. My *mother* didn't get anything. I have a copy of the will. Hold on just a minute." I jump up and run upstairs to get it.

When I return, I hand it to her. "As you can see, it does have a provision for you."

She sits back and shakes her head. "I can't believe this."

"We'll have Marci work through this and make some recommendations when she arrives," Jim says.

He then shifts gears to ask a few more follow-up questions, further solidifying Nancy's statements from last night.

After a little while, Molly removes the breakfast food and begins to replace it with snacks. Then Frank enters the room and nods at Jim.

"Perfect timing," he says. "We've got a plane on approach."

My stomach knots with anticipation. "Do we know who's on this flight?"

"This is Stevie and Genevieve." Frank glances at his watch and adds, "And Christopher and Bella have just touched down."

Suddenly I'm nervous. "May I go out to the runway with you, Frank?"

"Sure, the planes aren't on the ground long. They're taking off and heading to Canada to throw things off."

I follow him to the foyer, grab my coat, and in minutes we're in the van driving out to meet the planes.

As both planes taxi in, my heart beats quickly. I'm anxious to see my brothers. I'll feel better when we're all together.

Christopher and Bella deplane first, followed by Marci, and before Stevie's plane even comes to a stop, their plane has taken off again. As quickly as the other plane was on the ground, Stevie's plane is soon also on its way.

Shortly thereafter, I'm enveloped in a massive Reinhardt hug.

"We're so glad you're safe," Stevie says.

"What were you thinking, leaving without anyone knowing where you were?" Bella demands.

"If you try that again, I will hunt you down myself," Christopher warns.

"Is there heat somewhere?" Genevieve asks.

"I'm so glad you're all here." I jump up and down.

"I'm pretty glad to see you too," Marci giggles.

"Let's get you all back to the house and warmed up," Frank suggests.

We pile into the van and Frank heads back to the ranch.

"You sure do have a surprising way of taking over the company," Stevie says.

"Trust me, this was not the plan. Have you been updated on what's happening?" I ask.

"I think so. I still don't understand why Alex would go along with this," Stevie says.

"I have a few ideas, but it ultimately doesn't matter. I'll be fine if I never speak to him again."

When we return to the house, Molly has put out a huge spread for lunch. Christopher and Stevie spot Murphy across the room and freeze in place for a moment. Christopher looks at me with wide eyes, and I just nod, telling him he's correct.

He turns and bolts across the room. "Holy shit, man! I thought you were dead." He opens his arms.

"I can't believe you're here," Stevie adds, right behind him. "How is this even possible?"

"It's a long story." I sigh.

"How did you know Murphy was alive?" Christopher asks me. "How did you know where to find him?"

I shrug. "Dad mentioned it in code, just before he died."

"In code?" Christopher asks.

"He used to talk about Murphy and the accident. In

particular, he was all over the place one day while we walked around the lake. He gave me the address of a house outside of Aspen and said I should visit one day. Then when the will was read, it all came together."

"We have a lot of catching up to do," Christopher says. He puts Murphy in a friendly headlock.

If they're going to wrestle or something, that's my cue to leave. I look around the room and spot Marci talking to Nancy.

"We're so glad you're safe," Marci tells her.

I excuse myself from my brothers, pick up a copy of the will, and walk over to join them. "Marci, Nancy told us that when she received information about my father's will, it excluded her."

Marci flips through the pages. "Hmmm... We should get a copy of the will that was filed with the state. Let me call someone at the firm in Chicago to inquire about that." She steps away.

Nancy pats my arm. "It's so wonderful to have all you together. That's what your father and I always wanted."

"I'm truly sorry about my dad's death, Nancy. You were always his greatest love."

She smiles. "No, you were his greatest love. I didn't mind following you, though."

My eyes begin to water. "I miss him every day."

"Me, too." Nancy bites her lip.

"What has you two so upset?" Murphy asks, and suddenly we're surrounded by everyone.

"We were just reminiscing about Dad," I tell him.

"If everyone has had a chance to get something to eat, I'd like to continue our interviews," Jim announces.

The afternoon progresses as we listen to Nancy share about the Kryetar and how over the last two decades, they've become more embedded within the Reinhardt Corporation.

When Nancy has told us everything she can think of, Jim turns to Marci. "What do you think?"

"The Foundation is incorporated in California, isn't it?" Marci asks me.

"That's correct. Why?"

"What good news." Marci turns back to Jim. "We need to talk to Walker Clifton in the San Francisco US Attorney's office."

"I can fly him in tonight, if he's up for it," Jim says.

"I'll call him and find out." Marci walks out of the room with Jim close behind.

While we wait for her to return, Molly comes to show my brothers where they're staying. "We put all you kids on the same floor in the west wing of the ranch," she says. "Frank has put your luggage in the rooms. Hopefully, we got everyone put in the right rooms together."

"Don't want to end up with strange bedfellows." I snicker.

"I know," Molly exclaims.

The remainder of the day is a blur. We have dinner a little while later, and as we're finishing up, Walker Clifton and two members of the San Francisco FBI arrive.

I can tell my nerves are shot because part of me remains convinced they're here to arrest me.

"Let's all adjourn to the living room," Jim suggests.

The entire group gets up and changes rooms. Genevieve and Stevie sit on the love seat, and I can tell Genevieve is getting tired. Then I notice so are Anna and Bella. It hits me again that I'm going to be an aunt four times over. Despite everything, I have to smile.

No matter what happens, the next generation of Reinhardts is going to be better than the one before.

Chapter 34

Jonathan

"Jonathan? Have you heard anything I've said?" Gillian asks.

"What?"

It's Monday morning. We're recovering after last night's colossal game, and we're all a bit tired. But I was also thinking about Maggie, wondering where she is. Did she get on a plane? She could be anywhere in the world. Does she have a car? She could be in Los Angeles, or maybe she's driving back to San Francisco. I have so many questions and no answers. Why would she not talk to me and tell me she was leaving?

Okay, I would have tried to talk her out of it. But what is she going to do without someone to protect her? I've failed.

This is tearing me up.

I sigh, focusing my attention on Gillian. It's amazing I managed to drag my sorry butt over to my office this morning. "I'm sorry. Can you repeat what you said?"

"Cecelia Lancaster is missing."

"What do you mean she's missing?"

How is that possible? Where could she have gone? She has her own security team. Why aren't they with her?

"She was last seen with Maggie Reinhardt. We now know Maggie left the hotel through the back stairs by your apartment, and we have Cecelia a little later on video leaving the resort out to the Strip through The Boardwalk. But there's no indication they were planning to meet up elsewhere."

Could she and Maggie have planned this? "What do you mean through The Boardwalk?"

"She walked through the casino into The Boardwalk and went out the west entrance. She circled the property and disappeared."

No! This can't be happening. I cover my face with my hand and try to get myself under control. "Where's Nate?"

"He's in his suite. He's a wreck. Can you go see him?" Gillian asks.

It suddenly sinks in. Maggie left, and Cecelia left. *Both* are missing.

I nod. "Of course. I'm on my way."

I walk through the hotel with four of our security guards. I tell them to not let anyone approach, as I need to get to the Paradise Suite immediately.

I knock on the door and Nate's body man, Kevin, answers.

"Will he see me?" I ask.

He nods and lets me step inside the door. "Can you wait here a moment?"

"Of course."

This is one of our best suites—three bedrooms, a grand sitting room, and a table that seats twelve, all overlooking the fountains and Strip below. Truly a beautiful room.

Nate walks out, and he's a skeleton of a man. His eyes are sunken, with deep, dark circles.

"Jonathan, do you know anything?" he asks.

"I just heard. Maggie disappeared at the same time, and I don't know where she is either. What is the FBI telling you? Do you think they're together?"

His eyes grow wide, and he stands up straight. "I don't know, and I don't know why she would have left the hotel without her bodyguard. Have you told the FBI Maggie is missing?"

"They know." I pat him on the back and guide him to the couch. "Tell me what you know."

"Cecelia went for a walk outside the hotel, and they lost her on the cameras at the southeast corner." He is visibly upset. "What am I going to do? Where did she go?"

"Have we asked the neighboring hotel for their footage?"

"Yes, but I guess there's a blind spot, and she disappeared there. I wish I knew where she went—or at least why. We had a good marriage. We had rough times, but we've never strayed and always made our way back to each other."

I thought Maggie's situation was killing me. This is worse. "Does she have any friends who live here in Vegas?"

"Not that I know of," he says.

We sit watching the afternoon sky for a while.

"What am I going to tell my kids?" Nate cries out suddenly.

I don't have an answer to that, and my heart aches for him. At least I know where Maggie is.

I take off my jacket, walk over to the drink cart, and pour us both a glass of his favorite scotch. Then we sit on the couch and wait. Neither of us drinks, and we don't talk. The sun moves through the sky, and we sit.

"We met in middle school," he finally says. "She had

this long, beautiful black hair, and every day she had a big braid to keep it out of her face. I couldn't help myself, I would pull it. It was my excuse to touch her." He shrugs. "What can I say? I was thirteen and such a nerd." He begins to weep.

I wish I could tell him something—anything—that might give him some comfort.

"What am I going to do without her?" he cries.

We watch the sun set. My cell phone pings.

Christopher: Maggie is in Montana. She's safe.

Me: Is she alone?

Christopher: Don't worry, I don't think she picked up any strange men.

Me: Cecelia Lancaster is missing, and Maggie was the last to see her.

Christopher: Shit.

How do I respond to that? He doesn't say anything else.

Me: Can you ask?

He's quiet, and I don't see any rotating bubbles. I say a silent prayer that they're together.

Christopher: I checked with Jim. No sign of Cecelia with Maggie.

My heart sinks. That would have been too convenient.

Me: Thanks. We've got nothing, then.

I show Nate my phone and the texts. "Christopher says she isn't with Maggie."

He shakes his head. "She really liked Maggie," he murmurs.

Time passes and the sun sinks below the horizon. After we've watched the fountains play through their sequence numerous times, there's a knock at the door. After a moment, Kevin comes in to report. "Emily Nicols and David Carson with the FBI are here to see Mr. Lancaster."

Nate nods, and we stand, anxious to hear what they have to say.

The agents walk in behind Kevin and shake our hands. They run through a series of questions about where we both were when Cecelia disappeared. They exchange a look when they learn she was last seen with Maggie.

"Were you harboring a fugitive?" they ask me.

"No. She left shortly before Cecelia disappeared when she learned there was a warrant out for her arrest. My understanding is she was heading to see her lawyers in San Francisco." That's not the truth, but it's what I want them to believe, and at least that drives them to Maggie's attorney.

"Driving?"

"Yes." I decide I should leave it at that.

Agent Carson nods. "Well, one thing at a time. We honestly don't have much right now on Cecelia. She was last seen at a corner where your cameras lose her—"

"We could be in violation of federal laws if we go too far into our neighbors' property and their security," I explain. "But we have a good relationship with all of them, if you'd like me to make any introductions."

Agent Nicols holds up her hand. "No need. We're already reviewing what they have. Unfortunately, some of their cameras seem to have been shut off at the time she went missing."

Nate crumples to the floor. "Where is Cecelia?"

I don't know what to do.

Chapter 35

Maggie

The next few days are a whirlwind of interviews. I meet with the US Attorneys for the District of Northern California and the Central District of Minnesota. I meet with multiple FBI agents. I've been asked and answered the same questions over fifty times in fifty ways. By the time I'm done, I feel like they've done a body cavity search. It's overwhelming and exhausting. But slowly but surely, with Jim's help, they shore up their case and come to understand the truth.

Apart from that, it's great having all of my siblings here. I can't remember ever being this happy as a family. There's only one person missing, and it pains me constantly that I can't call him or talk to him. The attorney has recommended that—for everyone's safety—I keep a low profile, which means I don't contact my mother, Alex, or Jonnie. No big sacrifice on the first two, but I miss Jonnie terribly. The time we had together—even though I was in hiding—was truly wonderful. I've never had friendship or companionship or support or anything like that. I need to apologize to him for leaving without explaining my plan. I know now that's not what people who trust each other do. And I do trust him. I fall asleep thinking about Jonnie, and when I wake up, he's right there again. I wonder what he's doing. Did he figure out who was stealing from Queen Diva? Does he miss me?

In my free time—which I actually do have a bit of once the initial onslaught slows—I go horseback riding. And one afternoon I have a spa day with my sisters in law. As I'm getting a pedicure, I finally drop the bomb. "Okay, ladies. When are your due dates?"

The girls look at me like a bunch of gophers peeking out of the ground.

"You all have certain things in common," I tell them. "You're exhausted, and no one is drinking except me. 'Fess up!"

Anna laughs. "I'm pregnant with twin boys, but you already knew that." She elbows me. "We're due in the spring."

I look over at Bella, and she's grinning. "We're also due in the spring, but we don't know the sex yet. I'm thinking we may wait."

"It's a surprise no matter when you find out, but I'm thrilled," I tell her.

We all look over at Genevieve. "I can't believe you figured it out!" she says. "We didn't want to overshadow or stress anyone out. But we're also due in the late spring."

I do a happy dance, but the nail tech isn't very happy because I get nail polish all over my foot. I shrug. "Sorry. Anyway, I'll be a great aunt, and I promise to be a good babysitter—that is, if I'm not in jail."

After a few more days of planning with our attorneys and preparing what we'll bring to our PR firm so they can help Reinhardt handle the shitstorm we're about to be facing, I realize we've been holed up here for two weeks, and we leave in the morning to go back to real life—Minneapolis.

I'm nervous. But the FBI is preparing for several arrests, including my mother and Herbert Walker, and things are falling into place. Thankfully, it looks like arrest is no longer a risk for me since they've figured out my signature was a forgery, and I had nothing to do with Alex's finances.

∞

Bright and early Monday morning, my three brothers and I board a private plane with Marci, our Chicago attorney, both the Northern California and Minnesota US Attorneys, and a swath of FBI agents. Today is the day I face the music and break free from my mother's talons, but I hope we're not jumping into the fire. Just in case, we're leaving the pregnant ladies behind for now.

Once settled in my seat, I put my head back, shut my eyes, and roll my head from side to side, trying to relieve some of the tension in my neck. This is the big day. We're coming out of the shadows.

When we land at the Minneapolis airport, there's a podium set up, and the press is easily six people deep. How are six *people* even interested in this, let alone the papers these people represent? I stand between Christopher and Murphy. The humidity and the heat do nothing to stop the sweat from pooling between my shoulder blades.

"Stop biting your lip," Murphy tells me. He squeezes my hand. "This is the easy part."

"Says you. I hate this."

"At least you look beautiful doing it," Christopher says.

I turn to him and grin. Bella has trained him well.

A woman approaches the podium, and the press calms down. "Ladies and gentlemen, Walker Clifton, the United States Attorney for the Northern District of California; Diane Carlson, the United States Attorney for the Central District of Minnesota; William Sweeney, Assistant Director-in-Charge of the Minneapolis Office of the Federal Bureau of Investigation; and Carl E. Dubois, Sheriff of Hennepin County, today announce the arrest of Catherine Hudson Reinhardt and Herbert Michael Walker, along with forty-seven others in eight jurisdictions, in connection with a multimillion-dollar scheme of selling, importing/exporting, and trafficking illegal controlled substances across state boundaries and national borders. Additional federal Racketeer Influenced and Corrupt Organizations Act—RICO—charges have also been levied. The defendants are scheduled to appear before a U.S. Magistrate in federal court later today in Minneapolis."

Diane Carlson, the U.S. Attorney in Minnesota, walks up to the microphone. "The defendants have allegedly engaged in a brazen scheme to unlawfully transport and conceal millions of dollars of controlled substances believed to be derived from illegal activity. They allegedly did so for personal profit and with the aim of avoiding law enforcement detection. My office is committed to rooting out such criminal activity."

FBI Assistant Director William Sweeney then takes the microphone. "Transporting illegal goods across state lines is criminal in and of itself, but operating an unlicensed money-remitting business, especially from outside of the United States, will almost certainly result in additional federal criminal charges. The FBI is committed to working with our law enforcement partners to ensure this type of behavior ceases to exist."

Sheriff Carl E. Dubois approaches next. "We continue to work closely with the FBI and our other federal partners, and the success of this long-term investigation is proof of the benefits in these relationships. Illegal importation of drugs poses a great risk to our residents. Law enforcement must continue to work together to deter criminals from operating and engaging with organizations that allow them to break the law."

Finally, Marci approaches the podium. "It's been widely reported that my clients—Margaret, Christopher, Steven, and Murphy Reinhardt—had absconded with millions of dollars and gone into hiding. I'm pleased to announce that the Reinhardt children are all here and accounted for. They were, in fact, instrumental in taking down the crime ring, which has put both their company and their personal safety at great risk. We want to thank the San Francisco and Minneapolis US Attorney's offices, the FBI, and the Minneapolis Sheriff's Department for their help."

Reporters wave their arms and begin yelling questions, most of which aren't focused on the arrests but on us and our involvement. Marci patiently answers those that address what she's agreed to speak about, and she deflects the rest.

A publicist steps in and stops the questions after an hour, and our security team moves us out. A fleet of Suburbans transports us to the Four Seasons, where we're ushered into a ballroom with coffee and snacks while the official paperwork is filed.

"I notice the press didn't seem to catch on to the RICO portion of the announcement," I note.

"They didn't, did they?" US Attorney Walker smiles. "That's good news for Nancy, for the time being. Maybe she won't be quite so high on the Kryetar target list."

"They aren't dumb. They have to figure she'll rat them out," I say.

Walker stirs his coffee. "Nancy will have a dedicated protection detail, so she'll be okay."

The Kryetar arrests are more complicated and will take some additional legwork. Some have gone underground, but others are expected to be rooted out after the arrests of my mom and Herbert. In the meantime, we all have our own protection, thanks to Jim and Clear Security. I hate it, but until things settle down, I know it's the smart thing to do.

"I'm not sure I want to know, but what happened with Patrick Moreau and Alex Walker?" I ask Marci.

"Mr. Moreau was also arrested for his part in the embezzlement from the Foundation. He's singing like a bird on a beautiful day." She winks at me.

"Marci, thank you for pulling the will filed with the state," I tell her. "I'm glad to know I had the correct version." I look to the heavens and thank my dad for helping me out. I'm sure he's guiding me through this.

"I'm glad too." Murphy puts his arm over my shoulders and pulls me in for a side hug.

That's great for Murphy and his mother, but not so great for me because I'll still need to marry to take charge of the business. I may have escaped Alex and the Kryetar, but my personal life remains in shambles. We need to talk to the executor of the estate. Marci has indicated that he could be firm and follow the will to the letter, but we won't know until my siblings and I sit down with him.

As usual, any time my thoughts drift to my personal life, I think of Jonnie. After leaving literally in the middle of the night, and not being able to contact him since, I'm not sure what he's going to think about my stability as a partner. Honestly, I'm not sure either. The time I spent with him made me realize I've never had a real relationship, and Christopher said he was worried out of his mind when I left.

But now that we're out in the open again, the restrictions are off, and I have to at least try reaching out to him. I take a moment to text.

Me: I'm so sorry about everything. This is the first time they've allowed me to reach out to you. I miss you. (This is Maggie BTW)

It's crazy with people around me. I see the bubbles

rotate, but I don't see a message pop up. I must check my phone every two minutes. But nothing. Maybe it's technical difficulties? Or maybe not... I can't blame him.

The conversation around me is focused on my mother and Herbert and the Kryetar. I realize I'm not hearing anything about Alex.

"What about Alex?" I ask no one in particular.

"He was being blackmailed as well, but he will be arrested and probably go to jail for the theft of funds from his inheritance. The trustee is his mother, and she was very angry. She's anxious to press charges against her husband, Moreau, and Alex," the Sheriff says.

"Is there any way he'll get out of it?" I ask.

"Depends on his plan to replace the funds," Marci says.

That makes me sad. I still can't believe Alex betrayed our friendship, but I know the reason he took the money was loneliness, not greed. He has a bad picker when it comes to men. I hope he gets his life figured out.

"Thank you for letting me know," I tell them.

I walk over and join my brothers, who've huddled in a corner. They're talking excitedly, but their conversation tapers off when I approach.

"What's going on?" I ask.

"We're just talking about getting together more often," Christopher assures me. "Let's be involved in each other's lives. You know, now that we're a whole family again."

We all laugh.

"Actually, I was wondering—do you *want* to run the company?" Murphy asks me.

"I suppose," I tell him with a shrug. "I mean, it doesn't seem like any of my brothers are interested." I give Christopher and Stevie the evil eye. "Murphy, your life is in Colorado, so that leaves me. Dad prepared me, and I'll be okay. I know you're all just a phone call away. But honestly, my ability to do it could change once the court-appointed executor reviews the will. If he confirms that I have to be married, I'm currently out of luck. So we'll have to wait and see."

"Well, perhaps I can help you out," Murphy says. "My future is looking a little different than it was just a few weeks ago, and I'm wondering if you'd like some help? Now that I'm not dead, and with the twins on the way, Anna and I would like to be closer to my mom, so my life might not be in Colorado anymore."

I look at him. "Really?"

He nods. "We'll still have the person you hired managing the day-to-day—and I did go to business school despite being dead. I know enough to run the board, with all of your help. And then you can keep managing the Foundation and you can be married or not married—whatever you want."

I almost can't believe what he's saying. That would be perfect. "What do you guys think?" I ask Christopher and Stevie. My heart races. This would solve everything. I can manage my own love life—and make sure it includes *love*—and I won't have to be messing with the stores. I can focus on my passion.

"I love it," they say in unison.

I jump into Murphy's arms. "Thank you, thank you, thank you." I give him a kiss on the cheek and look at him. "I can't tell you how much it would mean to me if you would do this job."

"You'd be free to come out to California any time—" Bella tells me.

"Or fly down to Florida," Genevieve interjects.

"And you'll have your family home in Minneapolis, too," Anna says.

"That's too much house for me." I look at Christopher and Stevie, and they nod. "You know, Hazel and Richard would love to have children in the house again. I'd recommend at least a night nanny, but there would be room for your mom, too. It's the family home, and if you're going to be chairman of Reinhardt Corporation board, it's where you need to be. Plus, I've always wanted to live in a cool downtown loft."

He looks unsure. "I'll talk to my mom and Anna about it. I'll have to think it over."

I nod. "Murphy, it's the right thing to do."

Richard appears. Always dependable, he's ready to bring us home.

We rush over to greet him, and Christopher engulfs him in a hug.

"How did you know we'd be here?" I ask.

"I have my sources. Plus, they arrested your mother this morning at five, and we were told there'd be a press conference later today. Hazel has been cooking up a storm. I hope everyone is coming for lunch."

"I wouldn't miss it for anything," I tell him and give him a huge hug of my own.

My brothers and I pile into the car and fight for shotgun like we're teenagers again.

"So, Richard," I ask as he pulls away from the curb. "What would you and Hazel say to a few little kids at the house?"

"I think we'd love it." He smiles, his eyes never leaving the road.

Chapter 36

Jonathan

"Hey, man," Christopher says as he answers my call.

"Hey, I saw the news yesterday," I tell him. I lean back in my chair and cross my legs at the ankle on my desk.

"You mean the fact that Minnesota is blanketed with snow in early September and we here out west are sitting pretty?"

"Yeah, that. The whole quarter of an inch of snow." I roll my eyes. He knows I'm talking about his mother's case. She was sentenced yesterday. "How are Stevie and Maggie doing?"

He blows out a big breath of air. "We're all doing okay. The news that my mother is looking at fifty years is a little difficult to swallow—not that we don't think she deserves that and more after what she did—but she is still our mother. They were going to keep her in the minimum-security prison in Minnesota, but instead, it looks like now they're moving her to a medium-security place in Pennsylvania, given current developments."

"What happened that makes her a risk?"

"She tried to bribe a guard to take out Maggie and Murphy."

"What? Take out? What do you mean?" I'm stunned by this. It didn't make the news, and I've been watching the case carefully. "Why?"

"She hates Murphy because he doesn't have any Hudson blood, and he's inheriting a quarter of the company and will be chairman of the board. And she's angry that Maggie helped put her in jail—not to mention, she's always been jealous of the relationship Maggie had with my dad."

"How did this not make the news?" I ask.

"We only learned about her shenanigans at the sentencing yesterday."

"Were you there?"

"All four of us were. We thought we'd show her our support, and when the prosecutor's office told us they were petitioning to move her out of state, we didn't understand why. Once they told us, we asked if it could be in the sealed record for the sake of privacy."

"I hate to ask, but was she upset about the change?"

"Only someone who knows her would ask that." Christopher chuckles. "Remember the time we were in the basement, smoking pot with those two girls we were hoping to screw?"

I draw a sharp intake of breath and cover my junk at the memory. "She was that upset?"

"Times at least one hundred." Christopher snickers.

"Wow. That's pretty pissed."

"During the sentencing, the judge asked Maggie and Murphy if they wanted an apology."

"That must have been fun. What did she say?"

"She wouldn't apologize." Christopher snorts. "The judge was dumbfounded. But Maggie was awesome. She stood up and addressed the court and explained that obviously Mother's actions were misguided and misaligned with the values she'd tried to instill in us growing up."

"Good for Maggie!" I say.

"It gets better. Maggie never faltered or stumbled. She didn't look at Mother, but she wished her the best as she navigates her prison sentence. She stressed that no apology could ever wipe away the bribery, embezzlement, trafficking, and extortion—nor would it ever be genuine—so it wasn't of any value."

I sit back hard in my seat. "Wow. Maggie is going to be a total rock star as chairman."

"Actually, Murphy is going to take over running Reinhardt. He and Anna want to live closer to his mom, so he's going to move into Reinhardt House. Maggie will continue running the Foundation for us, and she's considering moving out to San Francisco. Right now, though, she's fully consumed with managing the PR campaign to keep the company afloat. She's doing a lot of work to put the scandal behind the brand, but I hope she can get past it herself, too."

He clears his throat, and I know what he's getting at, but for some reason I panic.

"My mom wants to make a meal for you guys," I tell him. "She's beside herself that Catherine would do this to her children."

He sighs. "Your mom is awesome, but tell her that while we really appreciate it, right now the only thing keeping Hazel going is cooking. Well, that and preparing for four babies."

"Four babies? Who's pregnant?"

"Who isn't." Christopher quips.

My heart skips a few beats. "Maggie's pregnant?"

He laughs. "I bet you're panicked. No, Murphy's

having twins, and Stevie and I are both expecting."

Surprisingly, I wouldn't be panicked—as long as I was the father, of course. It would move things along for Maggie and me. "Well, that's fantastic news for all of you. Congratulations, man."

"Thanks," Christopher says.

Then he's silent, and I know I have to talk to him about this.

"I miss her," I tell him.

"Have you called her?" Christopher asks.

"I did. She sent me a text after the press conference, and I called her back, but I spoke with some yahoo who would only take a message." My heart hurts. "Then I got paranoid that it still wasn't safe to be calling her. But I miss her, man. I keep hoping she'll reach out to me."

"I know it's not unsafe for you to contact her at this point, and I know she misses you, too. It's funny, she's finally free to do what she wants to with her personal life, but I don't think she's had time to do much of anything. She may not be running the company, but she's burning the candle at both ends to make sure we still *have* a company, and she's still dealing with all the lawyers. She's been bouncing between Minneapolis, Colorado, New York for the PR company, and San Francisco. She's a trooper, though. Don't give up on her."

I need to change the subject. I didn't realize that talking to Christopher would only make me miss her more. And I really need to find a way to talk to her about that, not him.

"So, Murphy, Stevie, and you are all pregnant?" I laugh. "That'll make the tabloids for sure: 'Reinhardt Men Pregnant.'"

"Okay, you're right, *we* are not expecting. However, our wives are. Well, Genevieve is refusing to marry Stevie right now, but I think they're common law."

I suppress a snort. "When is everyone due?"

"All in the spring and early summer."

"And you guys didn't even plan this."

"Total coincidence," he assures me.

"What's the plan for baby showers?" I ask.

"I don't keep up with that shit," he scoffs. "I just go where I'm told. No messin' around, no arguing. Just show up and shut up is my *modus operandi* these days."

"Sounds like a good plan. You know I'd love to host you here at the hotel," I offer.

"I like that idea. It might give the guys something fun to do. Check with Maggie—she's organizing it."

Maggie. There's my reason to reach out again, and perhaps a way to get to see her too. I just need to figure out how to get her to agree.

"Thanks, man, I will," I say. "And, please, let me know if there's anything I can do to help or just be a sounding board—although I'm not sure I can offer anything better than your show-up-and-shut-up plan."

"Trust me. With all these pregnancy hormones, it's my best bet."

"I'm taking notes," I promise.

We talk for a few minutes longer about how the Vikings will win it all this year—at least in our fantasies—and my mind starts trying to figure out how to plan my next move with Maggie.

When we hang up, I take a deep breath and text her.

Me: Hey. I just spoke with Christopher and he said you have the monster task of organizing three baby showers. Have you ever considered the Shangri-la?

It takes her some time to respond, and each agonizing second seems like hours.

Maggie: I didn't know how to ask, but that would be perfect. Would you have room for two hundred-plus guests in early January?

I have no earthly clue, but I would bump someone for this. I quickly call Gillian. Once I explain what I'm looking for, she asks, "What day?"

I'm acting like such an amateur. I should know better.

Me: What day?

Maggie: How about the weekend after New Year's? We'll celebrate a new year and a new family.

Me: I'm checking.

"Just after the New Year," I report to Gillian.

I hear a few clicks on the computer. "We'll see the tech high rollers on this, right?"

"Yes, I assume most of them will be invited."

"Then we want the Paradise Room with views of the fountains. I can make that work. Have someone call me, and I'll work on getting it taken care of."

Excitement zings through me. That's still a few weeks away, though. Now that I know there's no danger, I have to see her.

"Thanks, Gillian. I'll let her know."

Me: The first weekend after New Year's works. You need to come out and meet with Gillian. She can help you party plan and get blocks of rooms reserved, and we can have dinner.

I reread what I sent, and it doesn't say anything I want it to.

Maggie: Outstanding. Thanks. I hope you'll be able to at least stop by.

I plan to be attached to her arm that night. Why is she

so distant?

Me: I miss you. Come spend the holidays with me. Please?

She doesn't respond. I want so much to be with her and help her through everything she's dealing with, but she has to at least talk to me first. I'm not even sure where she is right now.

I rest my head against the back of my chair and close my eyes a moment. I'm not sure if I feel better or worse than I did before I spoke to Christopher. The idea that Maggie's mother tried to put a hit out on her blows my mind. I feel like I grew up with her family, yet I'm realizing once again that her parents are *so* different from mine. It must be really difficult for Maggie to trust people and to make room for things in her life besides work. I think that makes what we had together all the more special. I just have to get her to see that.

I try to go back to work, but it's really hard to concentrate.

Chapter 37

Maggie

The weeks have flown by since I made the arrangements with the Shangri-la for the baby showers, and we're now in the crunch period for the Foundation's work with Operation Happy Holiday. I'm finding a new normal — living part-time in San Francisco and part-time in Minneapolis, spending time with my brothers, visiting the PR agency in New York, running back and forth all over the place to meet with lawyers as we try to resolve the rest of this scandal and get Reinhardt Corporation back on solid footing, and then immersing myself in the Foundation.

Once we're out of the woods, I can tell Murphy won't need me for much more than to attend quarterly company meetings. He has called a few times asking for my advice, but his instincts are spot on, so I'm not too worried about him. In fact, I've found a place to live in San Francisco full time. I want to be out of my brother's guest house before the baby comes, and I need my own space. In a lot of ways I feel like my own person for the first time in my life. Alex has reached out to me from jail, but I've ignored his calls. Maybe one day I'll be able to forgive him, but not right now.

All that's truly missing is Jonnie. His text message about spending the holidays with him is tempting, but this is the first time my siblings and I will all be together as a family. I'm torn. I want to be in both places. Maybe he'd come to me?

I spend my entire flight from New York to San Francisco thinking about Jonnie. Now that I'm free from Alex and the constraints of the will, I can see a possible future for us. That is, if I can apologize. I need to just try. I need to get it out there. If I can't spend the holidays with him, maybe he can come celebrate with us, or maybe I can go out early before the shower, and spend some time with him, and see where this goes — see if what we had works when I'm not hiding in his apartment. But I need to stop avoiding the hard conversation.

I'm going to call him from the car on my way into San Francisco.

The driver is waiting for me and Brian, my current security guard, when we arrive. I hand off my luggage, slip into the back seat, and pull out my phone. Jonnie's line rings four times, and I'm disappointed. My mind scrambles. *Do I leave a message? What do I say?* I need to be honest.

When the voice mail beeps, I just start talking. "Jonnie, it's me. I have so much to say to you. First of all, I'm really sorry for just cutting out in the middle of the night. I really thought staying any longer would put you in danger, and I had a plan. Turns out it wasn't a perfect plan, but thankfully Jim and his team were there to help, and we got the job done. I know you were worried about me, and I'm sorry I put you through that. Thank you for caring. Things are starting to be somewhat normal again, and we're celebrating Christmas together as a family for the first time in Minnie. You're welcome to join us. I'd love it if you could. Will you please call me back?"

I disconnect the call and breathe a moment. The ball is in his court.

It's time to focus on my next meeting.

Lately I've been working with Kate to finalize this season's partnership with Brighter Future for Operation Happy Holiday. We were going to run with sixty inner-city school launches for the coming holiday season, but her team got ambitious and reached out to sixty inner-city school *districts,* which now means we're active at over two hundred schools. But her business plan is solid, and the request for mentors is going out later this week with a press junket. With the Bullseye name behind it and the PR company helping with our image, we should be fine.

We hope.

Anyway, right now I'm excited to be living in San Francisco—a new city and my own apartment, though I'm having some work done on it, so I'm not quite living there yet. But this will be the first time I'm standing on my own. I walk down the sidewalk with my wool coat wide open. It isn't anywhere near the sixteen degrees it was at home in Minneapolis when I left. And it's still November.

I wave as I enter the restaurant and sit down at the table across from Kate. "Sorry, I'm late. The traffic from the airport was worse today."

"You just flew in?"

I pull my arms out of my coat and try to center and calm myself before I get so caught up in the rush of things that I get our meeting off on the wrong foot. "I did. I left this morning from New York."

"We didn't have to meet so early. I'm sorry."

"Don't even worry about it. I'm here all week, and we'll probably need to meet a few times. You've been so ambitious with your plans. I hear things are going super well."

"I think so. The kids are working hard. Our reports show a significant uptick in kids going to school consistently."

"That's fantastic!" I beam. "You should be so proud of this."

"Well, it's a group effort." She leans in. "And thank you for keeping Jim so busy. He didn't notice I wasn't around much."

I smile. "I'm sorry about that. He's so proud of you. That man is over the moon whenever I bring up your work."

She blushes. There's a glow about her I just love. It's a draw for everyone around her.

"How many mentors are we aiming for?" I ask.

"We need more than thirty thousand," she says without skipping a beat. "Right now most of the stores are reaching out to people, so we're already making progress and the number is much smaller than that, really."

"Are the bag inserts helping?" We put flyers in each bag and educated the cashiers on how to pitch the program in specific stores—mostly higher-income neighborhoods.

"Yes," she says. "Those are working great. My team has also reached out to various professional sports teams, and in several cities we have some local celebrities on board."

"Sounds like you've got this under control," I tell her.

"You know, the first time we did this, I was short forty mentors so one of our board members put us in touch with Jim. Now look at me a year later! I'm weeks away from getting married."

"Jim is a great guy."

A question has been in the back of my mind, and I can't help but ask. "I'm not sure if you know anything, but does he have any news about Cecelia Lancaster?"

Kate shakes her head. "That's been really tough. They thought they'd have a request for ransom a long time ago, but there's been nothing. The trail is completely cold."

I nod, my stomach sinking. "This is awful. She was so kind to me when everything started to shake out with my recent family troubles."

Kate nods. "Nate and Jim are best friends. Cecelia was amazing to me—always kind, open, and welcoming. Her poor family."

"I've been told I was the last person who saw her before she left the hotel." I sigh and look out the window of the restaurant. A guy is playing the guitar on the corner for donations. Where could she be? She talked about her kids all the time.

"I didn't realize that," Kate says. "I just knew she left the hotel on foot, and the cameras lost her when she left the grounds."

"She left without her security detail?" I've been so caught up in my own crap, I haven't thought much about it. I should reach out to Nate or at least send him a note conveying my support. I'll do anything I can to help.

"Yep. It was strange."

After a moment, we get ourselves back on track and spend the remainder of the morning going through the updates on this season, as well as plans for future phases of our partnership. We decide I'll stand with her as we do a national call-out in the final push for mentors.

"We've set up a phone bank to take calls and send questionnaires and do some background checks," she says.

"It doesn't sound like you need much from me."

"Just wait until the press conference on Thursday morning."

"I'll be there," I promise.

We begin stacking the piles of papers we've spread all over the table, and I send a message to let the car service know I'm ready for my ride.

She smiles at me. "I know Jim is in your employ, but would you like to join us for dinner one night while you're here? We'd love to have you over to the loft, but I don't want you to feel like you're doing too much with your employees."

"I don't think of Jim like an employee. He's a trusted

friend who has my best interests at heart. I would love to join you for dinner," I tell her. "You let me know which night and what I can bring."

"How about tomorrow night and bring a bottle of your favorite wine," she says. "My specialty is linguine and clams. Are you okay with that? I can make something else if you can't eat shellfish or don't like clams."

"Nope, that sounds amazing. What time should I be there?" I ask.

"How about seven?"

"Sounds great. See you then."

On the ride back to Christopher's, I listen to my messages. None of them are from Jonnie. I'm beyond disappointed.

Chapter 38

Jonathan

Walking up to the sign-in table, I smooth out my khaki pants, take a deep breath, and put a smile on my face. I'm at the East Las Vegas Bullseye. They did a call for volunteers to help with the Reinhardt Foundation/Bullseye and Brighter Future's Operation Happy Holiday. I know this is Maggie's baby, and there's no way I could have said no—regardless of whatever is, or isn't, going on between us. Plus, what a great way to make an impact. I recruited my entire management team and a few others from the Shangri-la to join me. I don't see them anywhere, but there are two Bullseyes in town hosting shoppers today. The two hundred dollars I spend will help a child from a disadvantaged school have a Christmas.

I spot the sign-in table and walk over.

"Welcome to the Operation Happy Holiday Shopping Day at Bullseye. What is your name?" the woman at the table asks.

"Jonathan Best," I say in a low voice, hoping it doesn't cause a ruckus. I spot Queen Diva dressed in jeans and a T-shirt. She told me she was volunteering under her given name. I'm also starting to see several other entertainers and the GM of the The Gates Resort and Casino.

The woman smiles, checks my name off a list, and hands me a packet, which includes a gift card. "Welcome, Mr. Best. You should have received a bio for your match, Arnold."

I nod. He's a bright kid who's doing well in school.

"Jennifer here will take you over and introduce you."

I follow Jennifer while she searches for Arnold.

"Do you live here in Las Vegas?" I ask.

"Yes, I do." I'm quickly realizing Jennifer doesn't recognize me. It's very refreshing. "What do you do for a living?" she politely asks.

I shrug. "Like everyone else, I work down on the Strip."

She spots Arnold. "Oh, here we go. Mr. Jonathan Best, this is Arnold Miller."

He doesn't look me in the eye, but I extend my hand. "Hey, Arnold—or should I call you Arnie?"

He tentatively shakes with me. "Arnie is fine."

"Do you have a list?" I ask.

"I do." He shows me a half-sheet of paper that has several names with lists of requests and sizes and departments next to them. He seems to have mapped out his plan. I like a planner.

There's a woman up front dressed in white jeans and a white T-shirt, accented with a red handkerchief headband and red chucks.

"Ladies and gentlemen," she calls over the crowd.

It takes a few moments for everyone to quiet down.

"Thank you all so much for joining us this bright and

early morning. For some of you, I know mornings just aren't your thing, and we can't tell you how much it means that you made it anyway. Your contribution, just by being here, is so appreciated. My name is Nora Reynolds, and I'm the store manager for Bullseye East Las Vegas. When we learned we were a host store for Operation Happy Holiday's first foray into Las Vegas, we were beyond thrilled. We are even more excited to see so many winners. Congratulations. Your mentor has two hundred dollars for you to spend. And that fancy green bracelet we attached to your arm entitles you to a fifty-percent discount on your purchases, including sale and clearance items."

The kids are so excited; they just doubled their money.

"And, if you look in your packet, you'll see a gift card. That's an additional two hundred dollars from the Reinhardt Foundation. Students, you've all worked hard, so spend it well."

The crowd goes crazy.

"I hope you have eight hundred dollars of things on your list," I tease Arnie.

"They did the same thing last year out in San Francisco. We heard rumors they might do it again," Arnie says smugly.

"That's awesome. Where should we start?"

We go inside, and I follow Arnie around the store for two hours. He came armed with his parents' and three younger siblings' clothing sizes, and he's smart. He buys things off the sale racks first and makes careful decisions. When we check out, he fills four tubs, and they're labeled with his name. A volunteer explains that he'll get the gifts on Christmas Eve when Santa brings them to a party.

"This is going to be quite the Christmas at the Miller home," I say with a smile.

He nods. "I can't wait." He looks around and in a low voice adds, "I'm not supposed to tell you, but my mom works for you. If you can make sure she doesn't have to work and can come to the party on Christmas Eve, I'll happily give you the money you gave me back."

I'm shocked by his sacrifice. "Arnie, your secret is safe with me. What is your mom's name? I'll make sure she has Christmas Eve off for the party."

"Thank you," he says. "Her name is Sue Miller. I can't wait for her to see the necklace I got her."

"I'm sure she'll love it."

He smiles and finally looks at me. "My brother and sister don't know Santa doesn't exist, so hopefully no one will let it out of the bag that I did this."

"Excellent point. I'll pass the word. Do you need a ride home?"

"Nope. My buddy Josh and I are taking the bus—with a detour by the arcade."

"Sounds like a fun afternoon. Here's my contact information, if you need anything." I pass him my card, which has my personal cell phone number on it. "I promise to make sure your mom has Christmas Eve off for the party."

"Thanks." I watch as he disappears into a crowd.

"Makes you feel good, doesn't it?" I look over and see Queen Diva standing next to me. Without her makeup and wigs, she seems tiny and years younger.

"Yes, it does. I grew up with the Reinhardt kids—Christopher is my best friend. Nothing would have stopped me from participating today. Thank you for coming. I appreciate it."

"I keep saying this, but you're too good for this town." She grins up at me.

"Says the woman who's here despite her life being splashed across the tabloids," I snark.

"He's getting what he deserves."

"Agreed." We high five and hug goodbye.

Chapter 39

Maggie

I'm still living in my brother's guest house while they renovate my new apartment, but at least I've set the Foundation up with a San Francisco office. I'm at my desk, in the bright, cheery space with a fantastic view when I open up an email from Kate on Wednesday afternoon. She's sent a link to a private gallery on the Brighter Future website that features pictures taken across the country on Operation Happy Holidays shopping day. There are hundreds for every location. I attended the event here in San Francisco, and it was fantastic to be with so many of my new friends. Caroline and Emerson have included me in so many of their activities that I've met quite a few people I really like. Amazingly, they also seem to like me — and that has nothing to do with my mother or my family name. I have to remind myself of that sometimes.

Scrolling through the pictures, everyone has a smile and a glint in their eye. We had so much fun this past Saturday. My student was Alicia, and she was a rock star. She's a senior, so this was her final year. She's won all three years and was so excited. We walked the store for over four hours, and I'm pretty sure she talked the entire time. She was a complete delight, but I was exhausted by the end. She promised she'd bring her father to the Christmas event. Her mother is away, nursing a sick parent in El Salvador. Their family may not have much, but they sure have a lot of love.

I spot pictures of Christopher, and he and his mentee are having a Nerf gun war in the aisles. It's so him. Then I see one of Caroline looking at nail polish with her mentee. It really is great to see so many people having fun together.

After looking through the photos of San Francisco, I click into a store in St Paul and see a few people I recognize there. And in Florida, I spot Stevie looking at baby goods with his mentee. I wonder if he's buying for himself or his mentee is buying. And then I can't help but look through the Las Vegas photos. I find Jonnie—who I didn't even know had volunteered—in a picture with a young boy and a cart that's overflowing. Obviously, that student maximized his money.

Jonnie looks good, and my heart aches when I think of him. I reach out to touch the screen and feel tears fill my eyes. I miss him so much. He's so handsome in a pair of khakis and a blue striped button-down shirt with the sleeves rolled up.

There is another of him standing with his mentee, and they both smile wide for the camera. The other photos highlight some of the local celebrities who volunteered.

I go through the pictures slowly a second time to look more closely. I spot Jonnie in the background of another picture talking to Queen Diva, though you'd hardly know it was her. The tabloids have been taking her to town over her divorce.

In another shot, I catch Jonnie laughing with a pretty blonde, and my stomach clenches. Seeing him with someone else physically hurts me.

I groan and try to shake it off. He hasn't reached out since I left my message. I don't know what that means—I guess that he's not interested in getting together over the holidays anymore? I'm so bad at this. My lack of experience in relationships really makes sorting out this sort of stuff difficult. I was just hoping he'd at least call me back—even if it was to tell me it wouldn't work. I tried putting myself out there, and I don't now what more I can do.

Either way, I'll be in Vegas in a few weeks, and I'm sure I'll see him at the hotel. Hopefully, by that time, I'll be able to smile and be nice to him, regardless of how he's feeling about me. I did so many things wrong with him. It's easy to see that now.

Still, I can't help myself; I pick one of the pictures of him with his mentee and send him a text.

Me: Thanks for supporting Operation Happy Holiday. I saw this photo and thought you'd enjoy a copy.

The little dots immediately begin rotating, and I anxiously await his response.

Jonnie: Thanks. It was a lot of fun.

That's anticlimactic.

Me: Great to hear. I hope you can stop by during the baby shower.

Jonnie: Planning on it.

He doesn't respond after that. I wait and keep checking my phone all day, but there's nothing. At the end of the day, I turn my computer off and head home. This heartache is the type where the sun doesn't shine and the world is gray. I resolve that my experience with Jonnie will be my teacher and the reason to keep seeking real love.

Chapter 40

Jonathan

"What do you mean, she doesn't have a reservation here?" I demand.

Connie, my most accomplished concierge, is starting to look nervous. She works her way through the reservations for the Reinhardt combo baby shower again. Guests are arriving for the event, and I've been looking forward to this for weeks. Maggie may not respond to my messages, but she can't avoid me in person. She's not getting out of here before we have a real conversation. I thought she would have been here by now.

"Does she have a room in a neighboring hotel?"

"I couldn't say, Mr. Best."

I'm upset, but not with Connie. I pick up my phone and

dial Gillian. "Do you know where Maggie Reinhardt is staying?"

"I don't. She just said she didn't need a reservation," Gillian reports.

Well, maybe that means she's staying with me? My heart leaps. "When does she arrive?"

"She's been here all week," Gillian informs me.

"All week?" I pinch the bridge of my nose. *What the hell?* Connie is staring at me, waiting for direction. "Can you please call all the hotels on the Strip and find out if anyone has a reservation for a Margaret or Maggie Reinhardt?"

"Of course, sir. I'll text you once I find her," she says, doing her best to smile.

I see Christopher and Bella crossing the lobby.

"Jonnie!" Bella calls.

I hug them both. Bella looks stunning. She's glowing and all belly.

"Pregnancy suits you," I tell her. "You're positively beautiful."

She grins. "Thank you. I feel huge."

"You don't look it." I turn to Christopher. "Where are Stevie and Maggie? I need to meet Murphy, too."

"Did I just hear my name?" a voice says behind me.

I turn and spot Stevie with his beautiful girlfriend, Genevieve. I greet them both and tell Genevieve, "You're glowing."

"Beware, I think this man has a pregnant-woman fetish," Bella warns.

Everyone laughs.

"I can't help it." I point at Christopher and Stevie. "I remember both of these dweebs when they couldn't get a girl to look at them twice, and now not only do they have stunning women in their lives, they even knocked them up."

Christopher puffs out his chest. "We're studs."

Another couple arrives, and right away I notice the Reinhardt resemblance. The women hug and Christopher makes the introductions. "Murphy, Anna, this is Jonathan Best. He is my best friend, the owner of this fine resort, and our host this weekend."

"So nice to meet you both," I tell them. "I'm so glad you all decided to have your shower here. You're pregnant with twins?" I ask Anna.

She nods and sighs. "And they're very active today." She holds her belly and grimaces.

"Unbelievable. You make carrying twins look easy."

She smiles and winks at me. "Aren't you the sweet talker."

"We've determined he has a pregnant-woman fetish," Bella notes.

I grin and shrug.

The conversation quickly deteriorates.

"We're all having dinner tonight together at the Grill," I announce, hoping to regain some control. "Where's Maggie? She's the only one missing." I silently hope someone will tell me where she is.

"She said she'd join us for dinner," Anna says.

"I haven't seen her yet. I'd love to catch up with her," I tell them.

We stand around and talk for a few minutes, but I can tell the women are ready to take a break. "I can offer you wonderful non-alcoholic drinks in the VIP lounge if you'd like to sit down and put your feet up?"

"Sounds great. I'm in the mood for a virgin mojito," Genevieve announces.

"Ohhh, that sounds fabulous," Bella agrees.

I walk everyone over to the VIP bar and get them settled. My phone rings, and I see it's Connie.

"Yes?"

"Mr. Best? This is Connie at the concierge desk."

"What did you learn?"

"I don't have good news, I'm afraid. There are no reservations for a Margaret or Maggie Reinhardt anywhere on the Strip, downtown or off-Strip."

"Thank you, Connie. I appreciate you looking."

"Of course." She hangs up, and I'm truly stumped about what she's up to.

Christopher looks up from his phone. "Maggie is on her way over. We'll be complete."

Sure enough, a few minutes later she arrives, and my heart jumps to my throat. She looks amazing. I hadn't realized my memories of her had begun to fade, or maybe now that she's not hiding in my apartment, she has her typical glow about her again. She gives everyone hugs and kisses, and when she gets to me, she offers a forced smile.

"Jonathan, so nice to see you again."

Jonathan? I've been Jonnie since we were in elementary school. WTF?

"When did you arrive in town?" I ask.

"A week ago."

Bella and Anna begin peppering her with questions, and she essentially ignores me. Talk about a blow to my ego.

"Well, I need to get a few things done before I meet you all for dinner. I'll see you in an hour," I say.

They wave goodbye, and I go to my office. On the way I see Gillian.

"Hey," she says.

"Hi. Are we ready for the group tomorrow?"

"Yep. And it looks like they're doing another game tomorrow night after the shower."

"Good. The event starts at three and ends with dinner?"

"Yes, but the bouncy castle and the ice cream sundae buffet will remain in place all night for anyone who wants them. We're not kicking anyone out. The weather is a bit cold to swim, but with the heating lamps, all the attendees will be fine to hang out as long as they need or want to."

I nod. Rather than going to my office, I walk over to The Grill. We have a private room reserved.

"Mario, the women in this group are drinking a lot of virgin mojitos. They may change their minds, but let's make sure we have plenty of limes and are ready for that."

"Of course, Mr. Best."

A little while later, I hear them before I see them. I turn around and spot the motley crew. This is my family. I adore them all.

Anna insists we alternate men and women around the table, so I sit between Bella and, fortunately, Maggie. I smell her soft floral perfume and it alone makes my pants a bit tighter. She looks stunning in capri pants and a blouse that accentuates all of her assets. I daydream a moment and wonder how beautiful she'll look when she gets pregnant.

"Why didn't you tell me when you were arriving?" I ask.

"You didn't seem interested. I left you a message after you asked me to come for the holidays and invited you to our Christmas in Minnie, but I never heard a thing from you."

I'm at a loss, and I can feel my heart beating against my ribs. "I promise I didn't get any messages from you. I would have called you back, and I would have come. I swear!"

"I saw the picture of you and the GM of The Gates. You looked very cozy," she says feigning indifference.

"There's a picture of us?" I'm completely confused.

"Yes, it's in *Las Vegas Living*."

"Ahh, I remember that. Jennifer is happily married to her partner, Rachel, and they snapped that picture as we were talking about Cecelia Lancaster's disappearance. We lost track of her in a blind spot between our camera coverages."

"I didn't know that," she murmurs.

"Why didn't you tell me when you were coming?" I ask.

"I did, just before Christmas."

"But I asked you to give me your dates, and I asked you to stay with me."

"No, you didn't."

I'm positive I did.

I pull out my cell phone to show her. Then I see an error next to two messages that were never sent. I turn the phone toward her. "When you sent the picture of me and Alex from the Operation Happy Holiday shopping day, we were dealing with Frankie. He'd violated the restraining order, and LVPD and Shangri-la security were arresting him. I don't understand why they didn't go through, and I'm sorry I didn't realize it until now. I also don't know why I never got your message. But you have to know, I've missed you so much."

She reviews the text messages. "And you're not dating anyone?"

I look up at the table. "Can you all excuse us a moment?"

They hardly pay attention as I grab Maggie's hand and walk her out to the casino. I take both her hands in mine and look her in the eye.

"I'm not dating anyone. I'm in love with you, Maggie. I have been since I was fifteen. Like I told you, I built this place for you, and the time we had together here was fantastic. I was devastated when you left, and I've watched every ounce of news coverage I could find to keep track of how you're doing. I will do whatever it takes to have you in my life, and if you don't want to be here in Las Vegas, I will sell the hotel and move to Minneapolis or San Francisco or Timbuktu for you. I still have the software business, and I can run that from anywhere. Just tell me what you want."

"You'd sell the Shangri-la for me?" She's wide eyed, and her mouth is open.

"Yes. I only want it if you want it."

She turns away from me and crosses her arms. When she turns back, she rubs her hands over her face. "I don't know what I want."

I grab her hand and lead her toward my apartment. We need privacy to hash this out. "Maggie, you mean everything to me," I say as we walk. "I wish I was better at telling you this, but I want to have you in my life."

She shuts her eyes, and tears cascade down her cheeks.

"Why are you crying? Are you okay?"

"I missed you so much, and thought you'd changed your mind about me."

We step in the elevator, and once the doors close, I push her up against the wall. "I didn't change my mind. You're the only woman in the world for me." I lean down, and our kiss is electric. When the elevator opens at my floor, I go to the wall safe in my apartment and take out the Cartier box.

I open it and get on one knee. "Maggie, I bought this for you the day after Christopher's wedding. I've known my whole life we were made for each other. You're everything to me. When I'm with you, the world is in color. Please make me the happiest man alive and marry me?"

Maggie begins to tear up. "I'm so sorry for everything I put you through. I was so worried about you, and then my life has been crazy, and I realize over and over that I don't know how to do any of this because of my mother."

"Your mother is a flat-out bitch. I love you. Please, you're doing fine, and you mean the world to me."

She's crying now, and I can't be sure those are tears of joy.

Then, leaning down, she takes my face with both of her hands and kisses me. "Jonnie, I love you so much. Yes. Yes, I'll marry you."

My heart beats fast, and I pump my arm in the air. I slip the ring on her finger, and our lips meet and tongues explore. I pick her up and swing her around. "You make me so happy."

"Don't sell the Shangri-la. I can live anywhere. Murphy's running the company, and I'm doing what I love with the Foundation."

My cell phone pings.

Christopher: Where are you? Dinner is on the table

and we're waiting.

Me: We're on our way. Start without us.

"We need to get back. Can we tell them?"

"I'd love to keep this secret between us for a while, but you'll never get them all together again." She smiles, and her eyes sparkle. "Now, I can't guarantee they won't beat the crap out of you, but if you're ready, let's do it."

In the elevator, I move in close. "I don't care where you've been staying, but tonight, you're staying with me and we're going to celebrate."

"I'm staying in Queen Diva's guest house."

"She knew and I didn't that you were coming to town?" I ask incredulously.

"I sent her a picture of her shopping with her Operation Happy Holiday student, and when I told her I was coming, she insisted."

"I'm going to fire that woman," I mutter.

"Why?" Maggie frowns.

"She didn't tell me," I say.

"I asked her not to. But I will tell you, she's quite a fan of yours."

"Well, the feeling is mutual."

When we walk back into the private dining room, everyone is almost done with their dinners.

"It's about time," Stevie announces. "What was so important that you had to run off?"

I hold up Maggie's hand. "I needed to propose."

"What?" The girls are squealing, and we're surrounded by everyone.

"Congratulations!" Murphy announces.

"Finally!" Christopher says.

Once things settle down, we sit and begin to eat.

"You know, I'd warn anyone looking to join our family about how crazy things are, but you know better than anyone," Christopher says. "I've always called you my brother, and this will make it official."

Champagne and sparkling cider appear, and we toast and celebrate. As happy as I am, I'm anxious to get Maggie back to my apartment alone, and I'm grateful when the pregnant ladies want to end the night early.

"I've not seen much of your hotel. I'd love a tour," Murphy says.

"I'm happy to provide that tomorrow. When do you think you'd be available?" I ask.

"Don't you want to go out with us?" Stevie asks.

"Nope." I want to celebrate naked with Maggie.

"Okay, we can just hang out at your place and watch the game," Christopher says

I look him up and down. "If you think I'm going to let you guys cockblock me, you have another thing coming."

He grins at me. "She's my sister. It's our job to cockblock you."

Maggie puts her hands on her hips. "Go away. Go somewhere else. You will not ruin this night for us."

They hang their heads and snicker as they leave.

"You know, I really like it when you're bossy," I tell her.

She smiles. "I can be as bossy as you want as long as you punish me when I need it."

I stalk her like the prey she is. "Oh, I'll punish you, all right."

She giggles as we rush into the elevator, and we barely make it to my apartment. Tearing each other's clothes off, we're naked before the door closes behind us.

"I've missed you so much," Maggie moans as I bury my face between her glorious tits.

"I promise to show you many times tonight how much I missed you."

I run my finger down her slit. Maggie curves her back so her hips push up into me. Her eyes stay on mine, her mouth open, eager. I glide my finger across her pussy, so wet and pink and mine—mine to play with, mine to please. I dip my finger inside her, and she lets out a moan. I pump inside her before slipping my finger out and giving her clit some attention. Her face flashes with passion, and I know she's going to start begging me soon for more. I love that she always needs more.

She reaches down between our bodies and takes me in her hand. God, her hand—so small but so assured on my dick. I slip my finger back inside her pussy, and she pumps me at the same tempo I do her—matching me, showing me she can take it if I can.

I'm not actually sure my body can take it. I fall to the bed beside her, fingers and hands still in place. Face to face, we work each other, our breath mingling in the small space between us.

We belong together. Now and forever. We've weathered a big storm and come out even stronger. Nothing is going to stop us now.

Epilogue

Jonathan

"Detective Kincaid is here to see you," Travis says over the phone.

I'm watching my favorite group of high-rolling poker players entranced by their latest private game. They were here for the baby shower earlier today, so we figured, why not? It's early, but they're already getting the big guns out. They've gotten used to playing together now, so the gloves are off.

"I'm all in, plus I'm adding my fifty-acre ranch on Maui that overlooks the North Shore. It's worth twenty-one million," Viviana Prentis announces.

Three players fold, and Jackson Graham studies her. "I'll see your bet and add my Lear jet that seats twenty-two people and is *also* worth twenty-one million."

Viviana turns over four Jacks and an Ace high. "Can you beat this?"

There's a collective intake of breath before he puts his cards down.

"I believe my straight flush does beat four aces."

The room erupts. It's only the first night, and we're at complete pandemonium.

I walk out, chuckling to myself. These guys have too much money. I spot Detective Kincaid just down the hallway and extend my hand. "Good to see you, Detective."

"I understand all the players are back this weekend?"

"Yes, they're playing poker right now. In fact, you just missed one of the players losing a fifty-acre ranch on Maui."

"Definitely too rich for my blood." He looks at me. "There's been a development in the Cecelia Lancaster case."

"Nate's not playing tonight."

He was at the baby shower earlier, but he didn't feel like gambling.

"We've already spoken to him, but I'd like to update the rest of the group."

I nod. I assume we're all suspects, but he isn't willing to tell us that outright. "Come with me."

He joins me as we re-enter the room.

"This is quite the view," he says, looking out at the fountains.

The group is on a break, but it seems all of them are still here. "Everyone, there's been a development in the Cecelia Lancaster case."

The room immediately quiets down and everyone stares at us.

"Hello to all of you," the detective says. "I'm Detective Kincaid with the Las Vegas Police. I need to let you know we've found Cecelia Lancaster."

"Why don't you look happy about that?" Christopher asks.

Detective Kincaid sighs. "She's in the morgue. We'll

have an autopsy done, but it appears she was murdered."

Note from Ainsley

Hello Reader,

Thank you so much for reading *House of Cards*. It means the world to me. I really loved creating this book and developing the start of what I hope you find is an intriguing series. It's beyond fun!

As a special gift to my VIP mail subscribers, I've written a bonus novella, *Gifted* to share with you about Jim and his love, Kate. Just a small disclaimer-it's pretty racy and a fun story. If you want to join Ainsley's Naughty Readers use this link https://dl.bookfunnel.com/zi378x4ybx. This novella is only free to my subscribers!

If you're interested you can sign up here. VIP mailing list. If you were already a subscriber and look for the release email of the book that there will be a link attached for the ebook!

Keep on reading for a short excerpt of Royally Flushed Jackson Graham and Corrine Woods, my next Tech Billionaires book. And excerpts from Forbidden Love, the first book that started it all with the Venture Capitalist.

Thanks again for reading my book. I could not do this without you!
XOXO,
Ainsley

Sneak Peak

Royally Flushed

Book 2 Tech Billionaire

A Preview

by
Ainsley St Claire

Chapter 1

Corrine

"What do you mean, he broke up with you on the news?" my best friend, Gabby, screeches.

Heads turn all along the bar to see what she's so worked up about, and I can feel my face turning red.

She's been dating her boyfriend for a little over a year and they're planning a wedding.

I look down and feel tears forming in my eyes. "I got home late last night from work. I was watching a rerun of *NCIS* and eating popcorn for dinner. A news teaser about him came on, so I stayed up to watch it. The segment was at the end of the news, so it was almost eleven when it played. The interviewer stuck a microphone in his face and said, 'I heard there's a new lady in your life. Are you allowed to date a cheerleader?' His response was that it was nobody's business but his own if he chose to date a cheerleader."

"But, I thought you two were serious," she implores.

I look at her as if she's grown horns and developed a forked tongue. "So did I, but apparently he's moved on without telling me."

"Have you heard from him?"

I shake my head.

"Have you tried to call him?" she pushes.

I shake my head. "He never liked that I gave so much to my job, so I knew one day this was coming. I just thought he'd have the balls to tell me—not announce it on the news to the world."

"Bartender?" Gabby waves to the man. "Another cosmo for my friend." She turns to me and reaches for my arm. "I'm sorry he was such a shit."

"I fucking hate this city. Commitment phobia must come from something in the water, and the rest of the guys don't have the social skills to date. I'm almost thirty years old, and I have a roommate. If my dad didn't pay towards my rent, I'd be homeless—and I make a decent living."

My drink arrives, and it goes down quickly. I'm going to be feeling this tomorrow.

"It's his loss," Gabby stresses. "Jeez, you're beautiful, smart, and you're the whole package."

"You're my best friend. You're required to say that."

She giggles. "I wouldn't say that if I didn't mean it."

I look up at the bottles surrounding the bar and push the tears away. "What am I going to do?"

"You are going to get up and not let this dickhead affect you. You can't let him take a minute more of your energy. I bet there are at least a dozen hot guys you could take home to fuck their brains out tonight. Forget all about 'Bobby Sanders, Quarterback for the San Francisco Goldminers.'" She air-quotes and rolls her eyes.

I shake my head. "You're too much. You're right on so many levels, but I'm not going home with anyone tonight." Something flashes in my periphery, and I see him staring at me. "Oh, shit."

"What?" Gabby looks around frantically.

"It's my boss and his current Barbie," I say through clenched teeth.

"Barbie? Where?" She looks around again.

Not so subtle, that one.

"Stop! He's over there with the woman you could use as a flotation device." I point with my eyes. "Shit, he just saw me. Crap. Do I need to go over and say something? Knowing my luck, he'll just ask me to get them drinks."

"She's very pretty, in an artificial way," Gabby notes.

"She definitely looks good, but the elevator doesn't go to the top on that one. It seems to get stuck at her chin."

Gabby snort-laughs.

"Try not to draw any attention to us," I plead.

"He's looking over," she says under her breath.

"Fuck! Try to ignore him."

I made reservations for him elsewhere. Why is he here? I just want a break from work. Plus, I've had plenty to drink. I'm probably a little *too* honest for my boss right now.

The bartender appears with two drinks. "These are from the couple over there." He hooks his thumb toward my boss.

My heart drops to the floor. He's seen me, and I'm a blubbering mess. I glance across the bar, paste a plastic smile on my face, and raise my glass. "Oh my goodness, it's my boss, Jackson." I lift my glass and mouth at him, "Thank you."

He smiles and nods.

"What a smug asshole," Gabby says under her breath.

Through clenched teeth, I say, "Just be thankful for the drink and that he's keeping his distance."

"Oh no he's not. He's coming over with two of his friends."

"Fuck. Those aren't his friends. They're his bodyguards."

"Corrine, nice to see you here." Jackson Graham is a girl's version of a wet dream. He's a Chris Hemsworth lookalike with Daniel Craig's piercing blue eyes. He's also founder of an alternative energy company that has made him a billionaire. I'm his assistant, and I must get two dozen calls a day from women asking him out.

"Nice to see you, too. I didn't know you'd be here tonight. I thought I made a reservation for you at Bix?" I only make the point of asking because with his entourage, they reserve three tables in prime locations. If he stands them up, I'll have a problem the next time he wants to go there.

"You did, but Valerie is getting bored with Bix. I called and canceled."

He can make his own calls? That's new. "Oh, I think I called her Jennifer today. Sorry about that."

He looks back at her with his brows furrowed. "She didn't mention you calling her the wrong name. Enjoy your drinks." He smiles and walks back to his table.

Every woman's eyes in the packed bar are glued to him.

Gabby leans in with a bit of a drunken slur. "Your boss is positively hot."

I shake my head. "That might be true, but he likes the surgically enhanced and he can't stand brains."

Her phone pings with a text, and she gets this funny look on her face. *Love.* I know exactly who she's talking to: her boyfriend Damien.

I haven't had my phone on all day. While Gabby sexts with her boyfriend, I reluctantly turn mine on. I've got to do it at some point, and it might as well be while I'm partially drunk. It lights up and buzzes with multiple texts. My stomach ties in knots as I stare at the messages rolling over on the locked screen.

What happened with Bobby?

When I find out, Elly, my supposed best friend from high school, I might let you know.

I knew it would never last.

Thanks, Mom. In her mind, to get a man, you need to give up everything. I'd take her advice if she hadn't been married five times.

I thought you had some great summer plans with Bobby?

Angela, you're such a nice roommate. We had plans with other players and their wives to go to a lake in Wisconsin. I'm probably off that invite list. So much for any summer vacations. I can't afford to do anything.

How does any man compare after dating an NFL quarterback?

John, you broke up with me and only wanted me back when you found out I was dating him. Bobby wasn't perfect. But I liked that he made twenty million a year and was four years younger than me.

I put my phone on mute and toss it in my purse. I can respond later. It suddenly occurs to me that none of the other players' wives or girlfriends sent me texts. We were all planning for the game on Sunday. I guess in the back of my mind, I thought a few of them would stand by me, but apparently not. That might hurt more than the breakup.

Gabby is ready to go find Damien, so we say our goodbyes. As I walk out of the bar, I look over at Jackson and his date and wave. She scowls at me. Whatever.

I take a rideshare across town to my meager apartment in Presidio Heights. It's a fancy way of saying I live behind the old Army base, the Presidio, and in the Avenues. The beautiful people look down on those of us who live in the Avenues, but it's considered affordable. I don't consider it affordable. I share a three-bedroom apartment—my bedroom used to be a closet—with two others and pay an entire half of my monthly salary toward my portion of the rent. And that's *with* the thousand dollars my father contributes each month. I hate San Francisco.

I let myself in and crawl into bed—still wearing my dress and without washing my face or brushing my teeth. That's very unlike me, and I cry myself to sleep. *He broke up with me on the news.*

∞

My alarm sounds, and my eyes are crusted shut from my tears. My mouth feels like a cat strolled by while I was asleep and took a crap. I roll over and look up at the stained ceiling. I'm not going to let Bobby Sanders get to me. I take a big breath and sit up. *Oh, I can't move that quickly.*

I go slowly into the bathroom and wash my face, determined to make today a better day. I can't let this keep me down. I'm better than this.

As I do each day, I stop at Starbucks and pick up Jackson's and my coffee order. He likes a double espresso with steamed milk, and I treat myself to a mocha cappuccino. No one's going to see me naked for a while anyway, I reason. Who cares about the extra calories?

Jackson typically beats me to the office, as he works nonstop. Placing the cup on his desk, I remain standing and prepare for our brief morning meeting. "Here's your double espresso."

He nods without looking at me.

"Thanks again for the drinks last night."

"Glad you enjoyed them," he says without looking up from the spreadsheet he's studying.

He doesn't elaborate, so I begin to walk through his calendar for the day. "You're all set for your Tuesday meeting with your team. You have lunch with Mason Sullivan at noon at Quince regarding your business plan. If you don't have any changes, I'll get that bound and ready. Your afternoon is full, and I've marked you busy from two thirty to four to return phone calls."

"Thank you, Miss Woods."

He still hasn't looked up, so I turn to leave. He's in a bad mood today—like most days. As I open the door, I hear, "Oh, I almost forgot." I turn, and he's pointing to a box by the door. "That was delivered to you this morning."

"Okay, thanks." I pick up the lightweight box and carry it out to my desk. Before I tackle it, I take a big swig of my mocha. "Ahh."

"I saw the piece about your boyfriend," my officemate, Heather, says. "I guess he moved on."

"They always do," I say. Heather is the executive assistant to Jackson's chief financial officer—the fourth one since I've been here. We get along okay and will occasionally grab lunch together. I made the mistake of telling her about Bobby, and she shared it with the entire building. Lesson learned. If you don't want anyone to know your business, don't say anything.

Pulling the scissors from my top drawer of my desk, I cut the seal on the box, and immediately the wretched smell hits me. Before I can even discern what's inside, I slam the box shut. The overwhelming stench fills the office.

"What the hell is that?" Heather asks. Her face is scrunched up, and we're both breathing through our mouths.

"I have no idea."

I carefully pick up the box, walk it to the elevators, and ride it to the lobby. The smell is still escaping, and it's just awful. I want to vomit.

As the doors open, I see our security guard. "Tommy, can you call maintenance? We got a package that I think is full of dog poop. Can you have them fumigate the executive level and the elevator?"

"Dog poop?" He cocks his head to the side.

"Yes, someone sent me a package. I'm going to open it outside."

"Don't! That could be a bomb! Put it down and back

away."

I'm already mostly outside, so I set it on the sidewalk and look at him, confused. *Why would anyone send me a poop bomb?*

When I walk back into the lobby, Tommy is on the phone to 9-1-1. He gives them our address, and I watch him pull the fire alarm. It's barely eight and people are still arriving. It's quickly chaos.

He stands with me as we look at the box. "The police are on their way."

After that he moves right into leadership mode and keeps repeating, "This is not a drill. Please leave the building."

I look at him in panic. "This may have been a threat to Mr. Graham."

As the crowd grows outside, I watch Mr. Graham exit the elevator.

People are piling out of the building. Some seem thrilled to have a free morning, while others are clearly perturbed.

Mr. Graham walks up to me. "What the hell?" he says. "First our office smells like shit, and now this?"

"The box you gave me was filled with something disgusting. Tommy thinks it might be a bomb."

"Sir," Tommy interjects. "The box was filled with manure, and it can be used in bombs."

A uniformed officer pushes us away from the doors. "Please step back."

Mr. Graham looks at me. "Why would anyone want to send you a bomb?"

I shake my head as the police come racing up in a van that says *Bomb Squad.*

People give them a wide berth, and an officer approaches the three of us.

"Tell us what you know," he says.

I walk them through what happened. Mr. Graham's security team arrives, and they usher him away. Great. At least he'll be safe. Don't worry, I'll be fine in the superhero costume hiding under my clothes.

The bomb team pushes us farther away from the door. "Don't leave," one of them tells me.

I nod and shiver against the cold. I left my coat upstairs.

The news vans have arrived and are setting up. This is not the kind of publicity Mr. Graham is looking for. If I have a job after this is over, it'll be a miracle.

I watch the bomb team examine the box from afar. They seem to agree on something, but I'm not sure what it is, until I see a robot wheeling out to the sidewalk.

The crowd begins to grow. The police have cleared out the entire city block.

An officer returns to drill me with questions. "Has Mr. Graham received any threatening letters or other mail?"

The head of Mr. Graham's security, Jim Adelson, materializes next to me. He drapes a coat over my shoulders.

"Thanks, Jim."

"We've received a few small threats in recent months, but we've passed them along to Detective Lenning."

"Tell me more about how you got the package."

"It was delivered to Mr. Graham's office, addressed to me, and he pointed it out to me when I arrived."

"Why didn't you call the police immediately?" the officer presses.

"It never occurred to me that it could be anything other than a stinky box."

"A stinky box?"

"The stench was strong, so I just shut the box and held it as tightly as I could while I took it down in the elevator."

"How do you know the threats you've received are insignificant?"

I shrug. "I figured it was an environmental group unhappy with the company."

They've evacuated the neighboring buildings now, and

people are fleeing quickly. I can't blame them.

We watch through a camera as the robot approaches the package behind a piece of glass that I'm told will withstand a blast. I spot the television crews zooming in, and everyone can see what's going on.

An arm extends from the robot. It carefully opens the first flap. I'm holding my breath. The robot opens the second flap. I'm freezing, yet sweat is running down my back. A camera extends and zooms in on the box, focusing on a note that is partially covered in what looks like feces.

Once I read what it says, I want the Earth to open up and swallow me whole. *Keep your hands off my man.*

The robot carefully removes the note, and a man or woman dressed in a Pillsbury Dough Boy suit takes it away. The robot then reaches into the box. The officer explains that the camera is looking for signs of electronics, but nothing is sending off any signals. After a moment, the bomb squad seems visibly relieved.

I watch in horror as the robot clasps an article of clothing and pulls it out. It's a Goldminers jersey— number eighteen with Sanders in block lettering across the shoulders. It's covered in feces.

This is not a threat for Mr. Graham. It's for me.

Every single one of the twenty-five hundred employees that have been spilled onto the sidewalks are going to be pissed at me. Jackson will be beyond pissed because he's lost an entire day of productivity because someone wants me to disappear from the asshole's life.

I can feel eyes on me, and I fight back tears. The news crews are watching every moment.

As the police pack up and people file back into the building, I take the stairs to the forty-second floor. I can't stand around and listen to the snark. If Heather hadn't spread it around the building that Bobby and I were dating, I could play dumb. Bobby didn't name me specifically when he broke up with me on the news, but thank you, Heather, for making sure everyone can fill in the gaps.

By the tenth floor, I'm asking myself why I chose to walk up. I stop to catch my breath and overhear a conversation in the hallway beyond the stairwell.

"I bet *she* did it for attention."

"Why would Bobby Sanders date her? She's not that pretty."

"Did you see her smile when Jackson Graham walked up to her? He was pissed."

"We should start a pool to see how long she has her job."

"I'd bet on that..." They move down the hallway, and I don't hear the rest.

I keep climbing. I hear others, but I don't want to stop to listen. It only makes me feel worse.

I finally make it to the forty-second floor, and I won't have to go to the gym today — or maybe even all week.

There are three women standing with Heather when I return to my desk, and all of them look me up and down with complete disdain. I sit down hard in my chair. Jim walks out of Jackson's office with a police officer.

He smiles at me. "Come on in."

I nod. "I'll be right there." I click a few buttons on my computer, print a document, and open a few files. I'm ready to be fired. This is it.

He points me to the couch. It's just him and the officer in the room.

"This is Officer Parker," he tells me. "Jackson was clear that a messenger sent over the package?"

I nod. "He said it arrived early this morning."

"Did you break up with your boyfriend?" he asks.

"I believe so," I say.

"You don't know?" Officer Parker asks.

"Well, he didn't call and tell me to my face," I explain.

"Is he ghosting you?" Jim asks.

"No." I take a big breath. "He announced it in response

to a question at a press conference."

"Press conference?" Officer Parker asks.

"I was dating Bobby Sanders, from the San Francisco Goldminers."

"Tell us about the news conference," Jim says gently.

I walk them through what happened. I add that I was out with a friend last night and ran into Mr. Graham.

"Have you called him?" Officer Parker asks.

"No. He made his decision abundantly clear during the press conference."

"When did you call his girlfriend?" he asks.

"Never. I haven't reached out to either of them. The last time Bobby and I talked was Sunday after the game. It was a tough loss, and he wanted to be alone."

Jackson walks in with his team. I stand.

"I need to speak to Mr. Graham," the officer informs me.

I nod silently, wondering if this embarrassment could possibly get any worse. I guess I'm going to find out.

As I return to my desk, my cell phone begins to ring. Eight missed calls. It's Gabby.

"Hi."

"Oh my God, you made the news wire."

"What?" *This can't be happening.*

"There are at least six news agencies now talking about whether or not you sent it to yourself. Through his agent, Bobby's saying he and his new girlfriend, Colette, had nothing to do with it, and you're mentally unstable."

"Are you kidding?"

"I wish I was. I'll send you some links. The coverage is split. The real news stations say you called the police because it was a suspicious package."

"It was Bobby's jersey, and it was covered in shit."

"What kind of shit? Paint?"

"No. I mean actual shit."

"Why?"

"It had a note that said *Keep your hands off my man*," I whisper into the phone. "I'm so embarrassed. The police are talking to Mr. Graham now. The whole block knows, and it's all over the news."

"How about drinks after work?"

"If I still have a job—we lost the morning, so I don't know how late I'll be."

"Call me if you're up for it," Gabby insists.

I hear muffled voices approaching the door. "I've got to go. I hear him coming."

"Thank you for your time," Officer Parker tells Mr. Graham.

"Anytime," Jackson says. He gives me a nod.

Officer Parker stops at my desk. "None of your fingerprints were on the inside of the box. We'll continue to investigate. What's the name of your ex-boyfriend's new girlfriend?"

"I'm not sure. Someone called her Colette, but I don't know if that's correct or what her last name is. I know she's a cheerleader, though."

I watch him leave. Heather is ignoring me, so at least that's a positive.

Finally Jim steps out of Mr. Graham's office. "Corrine, can you please come in here a moment?"

I nod. This is it.

PreOrder *Royally Flushed* on Amazon.

Also by Ainsley St Claire

The Venture Capitalist Series

Forbidden Love (Venture Capitalist Book 1) **Available on Amazon**
(Emerson and Dillon's story) He's an eligible billionaire. She's off limits. Is a relationship worth the risk?

Promise (Venture Capitalist Book 2) **Available on Amazon**
(Sara and Trey's story) She's reclaiming her past. He's a billionaire dodging the spotlight. Can a romance of high achievers succeed in a world hungry for scandal?

Desire (Venture Capitalist Book 3) **Available on Amazon**
(Cameron and Hadlee's story) She used to be in the 1%. He's a self-made billionaire. Will one hot night fuel love's startup?

Temptation (Venture Capitalist Book 4) **Available on Amazon**
(Greer and Andy's story) She helps her clients become millionaires and billionaires. He transforms grapes into wine. Can they find more than love at the bottom of a glass?

Obsession (Venture Capitalist Book 5) **Available on Amazon**
(Cynthia and Todd's story) With hitmen hot on their heels, can Cynthia and Todd keep their love alive before the mob bankrupts their future?

Flawless (Venture Capitalist Book 6) **Available on Amazon**
(Constance and Parker's story) A woman with a secret. A tech wizard on the trail of hackers. A tycoon's dying revelation threatens everything.

Longing (Venture Capitalist Book 7) **Available on Amazon**

(Bella and Christopher's story) She's a biotech researcher in race with time for a cure. If she pauses to have a life, will she lose the race? He needs a deal to keep his job. Can they find a path to love?

Enchanted (Venture Capitalist Book 8) **Available on Amazon**
(Quinn and William's story) Women don't hold his interest past a week, until she accidentally leaves me a voice mail so hot it melts his phone. I need a fake fiancée for one week. What can a week hurt?

Fascination (Venture Capitalist Book 9) **Available on Amazon**
(CeCe and Mason's story) It started when my boyfriend was caught in public with a girls lips on his you know what. People think my life is easy - they couldn't be more wrong. As my life falls apart, can we make the transition from friends to more?

Clear Security Holiday Heartbreakers
Gifted **Available on Amazon**
(Kate and Jim's story) Forty kids are not going have a Christmas and I don't know how to fix it. I send out a call for help and my prince appears and that's when the wheels really fall off this wagon. Can he help me or am I doomed to fail all these deserving kids?

Tech Billionaires
House of Cards (Tech Billionaires Book 1) **Available on Amazon**
(Maggie & Jonnie) Would you agree to a marriage to avoid going to jail? Maggie is the heiress to the Reinhardt Department Store fortune. Her father died and the board of the company expect Alex to run the company but they've never had a nonfamily member run the company. The board

has a simple solution—she needs to put the family first and marry Alex. Forget the fact that she isn't his type and she loves someone else.

Stand-alone Women's Fiction
In a Perfect World **Available on Amazon**
Soulmates and true love. They believed in it once... back when they were twenty. As college students, Kat Moore and Pete Wilder meet and unknowingly change their lives forever. Despite living on opposite sides of the country, they develop a love for one another that never seems to work out. (Women's fiction)

Coming Soon

April 2020
Royally Flushed (Tech Billionaires Book 2) **Available for PreOrder on Amazon**
(Corrine & Jackson) Staying with him will be dangerous...They call him Billionaire, Environmentalist, and Playboy. I call him Boss. I try to keep it professional, I want to resist him, but the pull is too strong. A bomb threat, a ransacked apartment, mysterious warnings, all telling me to leave him alone. Yes, staying will be dangerous, but leaving him will destroy me.

Follow Ainsley

Don't miss out on New Releases, Exclusive Giveaways and much more!

www.ainsleystclaire.com

Join Ainsley's **newsletter**
And get a FREE copy of GIFTED!

Follow me on **Bookbub**

Like Ainsley St Claire on **Facebook**

Follow me on **Instagram**

Follow Ainsley St Claire on **Twitter**

Follow Ainsley St Claire on **Goodreads**

Visit Ainsley's website for her **current booklist**

I love to hear from you directly, too. Please feel free to email me at ainsley@ainsleystclaire.com or check out my website www.ainsleystclaire.com for updates.

Are you wondering where it all started?
Read Emerson & Dillon's steamy story.

Forbidden Love
Billionaire Venture Capitalists book 1

A Preview

by:
Ainsley St Claire

CHAPTER ONE

Emerson

I wasn't supposed to fall in love with him. I wasn't supposed to need him. I wasn't supposed to want him. But I did fall in love with him, I do need him, and I most certainly want him.

In the beginning....

I can't believe that today of all days I'm running late. I'm usually never late. I live the mantra that late is if you aren't at your destination fifteen minutes before scheduled time. Ugh!

Running into the new office in downtown San Francisco, I am greeted by a well put-together receptionist at Sullivan Healy Newhouse, often referred to as SHN. We're the preeminent venture capital firm in the Bay Area. As of last Friday afternoon, they purchased my company, Clear Professional Services, and I'm now joining the firm as a partner to manage the professional services of all their investment start-ups. It's a way to have a steady paycheck and work with some of the brightest people in San Francisco and the Bay Area.

The offices are bright and open with sparkling clear glass walls, leather office chairs in bright colors, white shellacked desks and tables, and bamboo wooden floors helping to give the space a clean and sharp look. Exiting the elevators, I introduce myself to the receptionist. "Hi. My name is Emerson Winthrop. I'm supposed to meet Sara White."

Smiling, she stands from behind her desk in a soft blue skirt suit that meets just above her knees, a black patterned silk blouse and a soft blue matching jacket. Her highlighted blonde hair is up in a tight chignon, and her jewelry is tasteful yet expensive. Reaching out, she shakes my hand and says, "Welcome, Emerson. I'm Annabelle Ryan. We're happy to have you here at SHN. I'll let Sara know you're here." She makes the call and alerts Sara of my arrival, then tells her she's going to bring me back to her office with a detour by the company break room. "Emerson, follow me. We'll grab coffee and breakfast, and I'll walk you back to Sara's office."

I saw the break room during the process of SHN buying my company; it was impressive then and even more so now. Located in the center of the office, it hosts coffee machines that make coffees, teas, different cocoas, and ciders, an espresso machine where you can make your own, and also a Nespresso machine. Lined atop white Caesarstone counters, there doesn't seem to be any escape from caffeine should anyone desire it. Next to the sink is a glass-fronted Sub-Zero refrigerator stuffed with sodas, juices, waters, fresh fruit and vegetables. Open shelving on the walls gives the kitchen a giant pantry feel with each floor-to-ceiling shelf containing unending rows of almost every snack you can imagine.

In the center, an island which stores all the various plates, silverware, chopsticks, napkins and a food buffet. This morning's breakfast food selection includes various fruit salad selections, bagels, pastries, a cheese plate and a warming plate with eggs and bacon. I'm awestruck. "Is this the spread every day?"

"Unfortunately for my waistline, yes. The guys can eat like crazy, though most of us girls here don't have the metabolism to eat like this. I usually bring in my own coffee so I'm not tempted. Lunch is catered every day and arrives about noon. There is a menu on the fridge so you'll know if you want to bring something in from home. And for those working late, there's a light dinner brought in most evenings." She reminds me of Vanna White as she points out the various amenities. "In the fridge is an assortment of sodas and beers. If we don't carry your favorite, let me know and we'll stock it."

I fill my cup with pure black coffee and an artificial sweetener and follow Annabelle to meet with Sara. She's the corporate counsel and currently runs all the operations at SHN. I'll be taking all the human resources and talent pieces off her plate. She's my peer and the only other female partner. During the purchase, we bonded, part of the reason I chose to sell to SHN.

Sara stands and approaches me with open arms. "Emerson! I'm so thrilled you're here." We make polite chitchat, and then she hands me a calendar for the day. It tells me I'll spend the morning with her going through paperwork, have lunch with the partners, and then I'll be with one of the partners in the afternoon—Dillon Healy.

Before I know it, the morning is gone, even though the

real part of my onboarding paperwork was taken care of last week in the lawyer's offices when I sold my company for three times its value. All ten of my employees are transitioning this morning, too, but they all work remotely. Honestly, my business was small potatoes compared to the deals SHN works, but it was a lot to me.

Over the past five years, I grew Clear Professional Services into a dominating provider of all the back-office things small- and mid-sized businesses need, but may not want to do here in Silicon Valley and beyond. We handle billing and accounts receivable, accounts payable, manage the HR function which includes recruitment, and our goal is to never say no when a client asks for something for their business.

Sara and I walk over to lunch to stretch our legs and enjoy a bit of the rare sunshine. "I love this area, but I sure do miss the sunshine," Sara admits.

"It's getting hot out in the desert. It'll bring the fog in, and summer will be gone. Tell me how things are going with your new boyfriend... Henry, was it?"

Blushing, she shares, "He's great. It's still new, but it was unprofessional of me to tell you about him. Please don't let the guys know I said anything. They are very particular that our personal lives should remain personal."

"I understand. It will be our secret. But tell me about Henry. I have no social life, so I need to live vicariously through you."

"He's positively wonderful. I've never been able to be so free and open with anyone like I am with him. He works for a start-up down in Palo Alto."

"Sara! I don't want his stats, I want his *stats*! Is he a good kisser? Does he make you feel all gooey inside?"

Sara blushes a deep shade of pink, which turns even her ears. "He does. He has this way of making me feel good about myself but also seems to want to hear my opinions and ideas. We're moving fast, but we both agree this is pretty great."

I squeeze her arm. "That sounds amazing. I'll admit, I am a bit jealous, but it gives me some hope that there are still some decent guys out there."

We arrive at the trendy waterfront restaurant and are shown to a private room, where the three other partners are waiting for us.

CHAPTER TWO

Dillon

Sara and Emerson walk into the meeting, the girls both look amazing. I played with Sara before she joined the firm, but she wanted more from me than that. It had been a mistake, and thankfully only Mason, one of the other partners, figured it out; however, we almost lost Sara and her partnership because of it, which would have been devastating. Though looking at the two women now, I can't help but briefly fantasize about the three of us together.

Emerson is beautiful. She's tall and also wears a significant heel, which puts her over six feet. I love her blonde hair cascading down her back below her shoulder blades. The slit in her black pencil skirt is demure enough, work appropriate, but at the same time it makes me want to peek underneath to see what she's wearing. Her silk cream blouse with a black velvet trim is sexy in a librarian way.

"Ladies, welcome. Please have a seat." We put Emerson at the head of the table and order a bottle of 1992 Screaming Eagle Cabernet Sauvignon. It's expensive, but we're excited to have Emerson as part of our team. We toast to her joining us.

It wasn't an easy sell at the beginning. Emerson had put together an interesting concept, and she didn't need us. Her company would do all the business management for various hot start-ups across the bay area and a few other tech hubs across the country—pay bills, recruit, stock option management, manage building issues and anything else that keeps the start-up from doing what they're supposed to be doing.

Before meeting Emerson, I remember someone talking at a party about the business management concept, and I didn't understand the value. Now I know that all those things are part of running a business, and it's certainly beneficial for someone else to deal with it.

In the last three years, we became the most sought-after venture capital firm in the Bay Area. Mason has an MBA from Harvard with an uncanny ability to understand the business side and positioning for sale or going public, Cameron brings a strong technology background to the table, and I bring the knowledge of the numbers. All three of us met at Stanford as undergrads. We were recruited by various start-ups out of school, and we lucked out with all three going huge, making us extremely wealthy very young.

We began our funding of start-ups together as a hobby and a way to share some of our luck, giving seed money to projects we liked as a side gig to our jobs. When four of our investments were bought for millions of dollars each, we were addicted to the gamble and the high of identifying a winner when investing in an exciting idea. Don't get me wrong, not everything we invested in has been successful, but our hit rate has been pretty high, and we like to get in early.

Sara was our company attorney at a law firm we used. We hung our shingle as Sullivan Healy Newhouse, or SHN, about three years ago and hired Sara out of the law firm, offering her partnership. Now we have close to fifty employees helping with the various start-ups and investigating up-and-coming trends. However, we knew something was missing, though we couldn't figure out what it was.

Then we watched a few of our start-ups not make it because they seemed to get bogged down in the operations side of the business and were no longer doing what they were supposed to be doing. It was then that I understood why a professional services company appeared to be a solution.

We're regulars at the Venture Capital Silicon Valley Summit. It offers concepts and start-ups an opportunity to present their ideas and business plans to venture capital firms and individuals. Each is looking at various kinds of funding and are hoping some will invest in their ideas and help make them realities—and the owners very wealthy.

During the conference, we usually sat in private rooms and met with potential investments. I'd never paid attention to nor attended any of the breakout sessions. Randomly, Emerson's talk on "How to Do What You Do Best Without Complications" caught my eye. It seemed to call to me, so I decided to hear what she had to say. I arrived a few minutes late and sat in the back with no expectations.

She was not only a knockout in her conservative black suit with a soft pink blouse and high-heeled black pumps, but she was smart. And not just smart—she was brilliant. Emerson gave an insightful presentation and answered question after question. She could speak to managing accounts receivable and multiple human resources issues, and her pet saying, "How to see the forest for the trees," hit home for me. I knew she was someone I could work with, so I collected all the marketing materials she had and brought them back to the team. They could hear my enthusiasm for what she could bring to our investments to make them stronger and better.

We put our research team on her and her company, and it seemed to be a no-brainer. At least for us.

I reached out to her with a request for coffee, and she politely brushed me off. She ducked my calls and emails for two months. I felt like a dog in heat when she finally agreed to meet me. Apparently, she had four other VC firms looking at her. I knew it was going to be tricky, mostly because she had no interest in selling. It took constant calls before she finally agreed to talk over the phone. My team shared our feelings that we would all benefit by working together. Sure, we could create it, but she had already worked out the kinks, and she was magnetic and would be a great asset to our team.

We went into full buy-mode with her. We invited her to the offices, and again she put us off. We sent her flowers and still no response. Before we could give up, our marketing team suggested we send a crate of oranges to her office with a note written by Mason, as the managing partner, asking "Can you squeeze us in?" She sent back a photo of her and a few members of her team drinking orange juice with a time and their address. The meeting was finally going to happen.

She impressed us all with her negotiation skills. When we got a look at her profit and loss statements, we were pleasantly surprised. She was extremely profitable and would be bringing a significant amount of business as well as ten employees across the Bay Area, plus one in San Antonio. She wasn't negotiating for herself, but we liked that she wanted to look out for her team. It took six months, but finally she and her team joined SHN.

Conversation during today's lunch was fun. We all

laughed as Cameron shared a story about his weekend, getting stranded in a biker bar in Sacramento and being hit on by one of the biker's girlfriends. Apparently it was a mess, but he now has new fans in Sac.

We talked about a partner retreat, some business issues, and what we have pending. The two-and-a-half-hour lunch was an excellent start to our working relationship.

San Francisco is my favorite city. The City, as it's referred to by the locals, is simply urban. Tall concrete buildings in an exact grid pattern, the grass saved for parks and the occasional backyard. Ever-present skyscrapers are smudged by the haze-filled sky, offering no direct sunlight and few birds. Cars race between red traffic lights, stubbornly flickering in their gray surroundings.

Sara decides she can't walk the eight blocks again in ˙hoes and chooses to ride back with Cameron and Mason office, who extend the offer to Emerson. Peering the buildings at the cloudless skies and taking a deep says, "It's such a beautiful day. Dillon, we don't ˙her half hour. I think I'd like to walk back. Do ˙eet you back at the office?"

˙t her passing up a ride, I tell her, "I would ˙ith you."

˙e-inch heels, she's confident in herself. I ˙ stride, the way she holds her head up

˙ke idle chitchat. "Where are you

˙kets, I walk and turn to her at ˙t. What about you?"
˙ miss the sun so much. We ˙ Diego."
˙ hot desert valley brings ˙ow long have you lived

"I moved to Palo Alto for undergrad and then went east to law school. After graduating almost eight years ago, I came back. And you?"

"I moved here when I was eighteen—which was a long time ago—to attend Stanford and never left."

There were people everywhere. Panhandlers, business suits, the workout-clad and tons of tourist with cameras. We dodged them all like salmon running upstream.

"Do you have any brothers or sisters?" she asks.

"I have a younger sister. How about you?"

"I have four brothers. I'm the baby."

"Four? Wow! That must have been crazy growing up."

"Any guy who looked at me would get the evil eye, and if he talked to me, they might take him out. Made me undesirable to boys while growing up."

"Are they all still in Denver?"

"Yes. All married with at least three kids. What about your sister?"

"She lives in Texas and is married but no kids yet. I'm expecting a call anytime now. She's a teacher, and my brother-in-law works for a big insurance company. They live to focu on their family."

"I suppose that's the way it should be."

We enter the building and I hold the door to the eleva "You're probably right. Meet you in my office in fi minutes?"

To purchase or borrow from KU, please g Amazon